Praise for
The Troublemaker Next Door

A *Publishers Weekly* Top 10 Romance for Spring 2014

"Filled with strong-willed characters and a reluctant love affair. The love scenes…will make readers sweat. Readers will get caught up in this story and feel like they have a front-row seat to all the antics."

—*RT Rook Reviews*, 4.5 stars,
Top Pick! Gold

"The first in Harte's McCauley Brothers series… [is] a winner. The story is fast-paced, with countless spicy scenes that will make readers hungry for the next installment."

—*Booklist*

"Ms. Harte kicks off a new series, Nora Roberts style except with a lot more erotic heat. Ms. Harte is hands down one of the best erotic sex scene writers I've ever read."

—*La Crimson Femme*

"*The Troublemaker Next Door* is definitely a character-driven romance. There is humor, laughter, emotional connections, and a hero and heroine who strike delightful sparks off of the other. It's a fast, easy read with a lot to enjoy."

—*Long and Short Reviews*

"Ms. Harte has a writing style that rivals Nora Roberts, yet includes the steam that many readers like to read. Fun to read and wickedly hot."

—*Romantic Romp*

What readers are saying about Marie Harte's McCauley Brothers series

"*The Troublemaker Next Door* was a great, easy, panty-dropping sexy read. I can't wait to read the other books in this series."

—Nancy

"Here come Seattle's finest: the McCauleys! Hunky, Alphas, down-to-earth, and so totally male they'd wake the woman in my dear ol' granny."

—Lydia P.

"If I could give this book 6 stars I would! Absolutely LOVED the McCauley brothers, who are the most realistic men I've ever read. The romance was poignant and so very special. I wholeheartedly recommend this book to anyone who loves a spicier version of Jennifer Crusie. I must read them all. Sooooo hooked."

—Karen D.

"This book really blew away every expectation I had and I can't wait to read about the rest of the McCauley Brothers."

—Carrie S.

"I adored…the humorous interactions and conversations amongst all the characters. I'm really looking forward to *How to Handle a Heartbreaker*. I have a special fondness for Abby and can't wait to find out how Brody draws her out of her shell."

—Chrissy D.

Ruining Mr. Perfect

MARIE HARTE

sourcebooks
casablanca

Published by Sourcebooks Casablanca, an imprint of Sourcebooks, Inc.
P.O. Box 4410, Naperville, Illinois 60567-4410
(630) 961-3900
Fax: (630) 961-2168
www.sourcebooks.com

Printed and bound in Canada.
WC 10 9 8 7 6 5 4 3 2 1

Mom, this one's for you.

Chapter 1

"HELLO?" CAM KNOCKED AS HE OPENED THE DOOR. "Yo, Mike, you here?" He entered the house and closed the door behind him. A study in brown, his brother's living room might not be stylish, but it provided comfort and the perfect place to indulge in family Friday night poker.

But on this particular Friday afternoon, the house seemed dead.

A door opened and slammed shut, and a whirlwind of energy burst through the kitchen into the living room and stopped.

Cam noticed two things. Colin McCauley looked as if he'd been playing with Mike's grease gun again, and he heard the shower running.

"Hey, dude."

Colin didn't smile, didn't blink, and gave him the snake eye.

Cam sighed. For a six-year-old, his nephew could hold a mean grudge. "Still mad I told your dad about your prank on Abby?"

Used to be the place was full of nothing but men. Mike's wife had died giving birth to Colin, and none of the McCauleys seemed to be able to hold on to a woman like their dad had. Then again, Beth McCauley was special.

Now they had a houseful of hot women living next door. Flynn and Brody had already claimed two of them, leaving the best for Cam. That's if he could get the stubborn woman to stop arguing long enough to ask her out.

Colin continued to glare at him. The spitting image of Mike with those bright blue eyes and short black hair. They even shared the same dimple.

"Colin," Cam tried again. "You know dumping water on someone in the shower is a no-no. And especially Ubie's new girlfriend." Ubie was short for Uncle Brody—Brody Singer, the blond "adopted" McCauley who had grown up as part of the family.

"But he told me to do it."

Cam blinked. "He did? Well, you should never—"

"Dad thought it was kind of funny after he yelled at me." Colin gave him a sharp nod, then added with a smirk, "Dad said he used to do that to you, and that you cried like a *girrrl*." Considering Colin's anti-girl phase, that was a high insult.

"Is that right?" Cam frowned, remembering being the butt of too many jokes while growing up. "Mike has no idea what he's dealing with. You think your dad's tough? Watch Uncle Cam." Knowing he shouldn't encourage the mischief in his nephew's eyes but unable to stop himself from the unspoken dare, Cam hurried to the kitchen, found a large glass and filled it with ice-cold water. Considering the freezing January wind outside, Mike would be basking in a hot shower to warm up. Cam grinned, looking forward to his brother's howl of misery.

Colin trailed him like a puppy. "Oh wow, Uncle Cam. Are you going to get Dad?" He clapped.

"Shh."

"Oh, sorry." Colin's big grin showed a missing front tooth.

Cam walked down more ugly brown carpet that looked as if it had been vacuumed to death—Mike and his obsession with cleanliness—and tiptoed into the big guy's room. He made sure he had a clear exit. If his goliath big brother caught him, he'd be toast. Fortunately, he could move like a gazelle.

Gliding into the master bathroom, he readied himself. One, two...*three*. He yanked open the curtain and tossed the cold water at...*Vanessa Campbell*?

He stared in shock at the sexiest woman he'd seen in a long, long time. Naked, her creamy skin glistened with water as she gaped at him in horror. Which quickly turned to anger.

"Cameron McCauley!"

"Oh, wow." He couldn't look away. Even as manners dictated he close the shower curtain and give her privacy, he couldn't stop staring at her slender belly, legs toned from years of running, and those beautiful breasts tipped with rosy pink nipples. God, he'd imagined what she might look like, but reality far surpassed his fantasies.

She yelled a string of obscenities as she whipped the curtain closed.

While Cam tried to catch his breath, he heard muffled laughter behind him and turned to see Colin with his hand over his mouth. His nephew's eyes widened and he took off.

Cam caught him easily, though the kid had made it to the kitchen before being snagged. As he took Colin by the collar, Mike strolled into the kitchen from the attached garage.

"Colin, I said get me the paper towels five minutes

ago." Mike glowered at Cam holding his son. "What's up, little brother?"

Gritting his teeth, because he hated always being reminded that he was the baby of the family, Cam shook Colin like a rag doll.

Colin, of course, laughed and asked him to do it again.

"Your son played a nasty prank."

"Yeah?" Mike's lips quirked. "What did he do?"

"He convinced me to throw cold water at you. In the shower."

Mike frowned. "But I'm… Shi—oot." Mike looked from Colin to him and tried to hide a grin. "So, um, how is Vanessa?"

"Why is she in your shower?" He'd called dibs. Secretly, but still.

"Wouldn't you like to know." Mike's wide grin wasn't helping. "So you froze her thinking it was me, eh? Poor, poor Cam. You never learn. I am the master of the prank."

"And me," Colin added proudly. "Shake me again, Uncle Cam. It's fun."

"Gah." Cam dropped Colin, tickled him soundly, then gave him a light swat on the behind. "You owe Vanessa an apology."

"Oh?" Mike crossed his mammoth arms over his chest. "Seems to me you're the one who threw cold water on my unsuspecting neighbor. Or are you trying to tell me that my six-year-old forced you to mess with her?"

Cam glared. "You're just encouraging him."

"Now, now. Take responsibility for your actions. Act like the twenty-seven-year-old you should be."

"I'm twenty-nine, moron. Just because you're older doesn't mean you can boss me around like you *tried to* when we were kids."

Mike just raised a brow. Then Colin did it. The similarity made it hard not to laugh.

"For God's sake. Fine. I'll apologize." He turned.

"Might want to wait until she's dressed. Then again, if what I saw at Christmas is true, maybe not." Mike chuckled at the look Cam shot him and yanked his son with him back into the garage.

"What, Dad? What did you see?" Colin pestered as Mike shut the door.

There hadn't been that much *to* see. After Cam and Vanessa had eavesdropped on Cam's parents, they'd hidden in Colin's room, so as not to be discovered. Then, well, then Cam had kissed her. To keep their cover when his parents found them. Yet honesty compelled him to admit he'd been dying to kiss her for months. Ever since Vanessa had moved next to Mike nearly a year ago, he'd been fascinated by her.

Drawn to her beauty, her brains, and that waspish tongue that never stopped moving. But holy hell, when she'd used that tongue during their kiss, she'd hooked him but good.

He waited in the living room, wondering how to take the next step with her. She was going to be livid after getting spied on in the shower. And on a normal day, Vanessa wasn't a typical woman to be wooed with charm and wit. She saw through games. A lot like him. Unfortunately, he had a feeling the truth would freak her the hell out.

I think we'd be good together. Let's date, see where

*it takes us. Then we'll get married, have kids, double the
size of our mutual portfolio...*

Fifteen minutes later, Vanessa stalked down the hallway holding her bag. She must have brought a hair dryer
with her, because her golden blond hair gleamed down
her back. Her blue eyes were lighter than his, bright and
full of a cold anger.

How screwed up was he that her rages turned him on?
She was so different from other women he'd dated. She
didn't try to cozen up to him or flatter him with true but
tired compliments.

"So, Cameron. What do you have to say for yourself?"

"I apologize for dousing you with cold water." He
couldn't hide his grin, especially when her arctic eyes
narrowed on him in displeasure. "I was aiming for Mike,
but Colin steered me wrong."

"Hmm. Colin. I can see where that might happen. I'll
have a talk with him."

Poor kid.

"But that doesn't excuse *you*."

"I said I'm sorry."

"Yeah? Well that didn't stop you from getting a nice
long look, now did it? I don't think you blinked once."

He hid another satisfied grin, knowing that would
only irritate her more. "I was in shock, not expecting
to see *you* there. You don't look a thing like Mike."
He cleared his throat and added innocently, "I'm really
sorry if I interrupted anything between you guys. I just
never expected to find you with him—"

She interrupted, "Give me a break. Mike and I are
not together, in any way. Abby's taking her sweet
time in the bathroom at home and I have a work thing

to get to. Your brother was nice enough to lend me his shower."

"Because Mike is all about being neighborly to attractive women."

She smirked and seemed to relax. He hoped she'd forgiven him.

"Where are you going? You look nice." Nice? She looked like a model wearing a pair of wool gray trousers and a silky top that clung to her beautiful breasts.

She sighed. "You're no longer seeing me with clothes on, are you?"

To his delight, she wore a blush. "No, Vanessa. Sadly, I'm not." He gave her another thorough once-over. "I just have to say, you are toned all over. Just, wow."

She flashed him a surprising grin. "Good. I aim for *wow* but always worry I'll fall short of an *oh boy*."

He chuckled and thrust his hands in his pants pockets, to keep from reaching for her. "So you have a work thing?"

"Yes. My boss apparently doesn't believe in giving us minions time off. But it's okay. A corporate anniversary party for a job well done." She paused. "I think when McNulty leaves, Peterman's going to offer me the partnership."

Cam smiled. "That's awesome. Congratulations." The woman couldn't be more than thirty, if that. And a full partner? "So instead of McNulty, Peterman Accounting, it'll be—"

"Peterman, Campbell Accounting, hopefully. McNulty is retiring." She shrugged. "I'm pretty sure I'll take it."

"Why 'pretty sure'? Aren't you the firm's top

accountant?" It was something he'd heard her say often enough.

She snorted. "My skills are not in question."

Translation: her skills *were never* and *would never* be in question. "Then what?"

"I don't know. Maddie and Abby working on their own makes me question why I continue to work for someone else when I'm more than capable of handling my own business. But I like my job."

"So stay."

"You work for yourself."

"Yeah, but I'm me."

She crossed her arms and raised a brow at him. "Meaning?"

He swallowed a sigh. In that position, her breasts plumped up, giving a tantalizing view of cleavage where her shirt parted. "Meaning I graduated high school early, college early, and am pretty much a genius in the world of finance. Not bragging."

"I know."

That she seemed to accept his words as truth warmed him. "Yeah, well, two years spent interning with an investment bank taught me a lot. I prefer working with high-net-worth clients and small tech companies on the cusp of sharing new ideas that influence society. I'm snooty like that."

She nodded. "I can see the appeal."

"Yeah. Most of my clients know what I'm talking about when I mention investment strategies and hedging risk." He flushed. "And on that note, I'll stop before I get carried away."

Vanessa looked interested. "I like the way your mind

works, Cameron. It's just other parts of you I find less than thrilling."

"Not my body." He smirked at her. "Because if I recall, that kiss in Colin's bedroom had you practically begging me for another go. I'm more than happy to oblige."

A smile darted over her lips, then disappeared. "It's a good thing for you that you're handsome, because charm is not in your vocabulary."

"Actually, it is. I was spelling bee champ all through middle school. Gave it up in high school because it was no longer a challenge."

"Are you through bragging? If you want my opinion…" She studied him from top to bottom and shook her head. "Meh. Not bad. Average, I'd say. Now I really must go."

He gaped at her. "Average?"

"But you have nice eyes. I'm partial to blue." She gripped her bag tight. "Tell Mike thanks for me, would you? And let Colin know I plan to get even. That should make the little cretin sweat." She gave him a sly smile. "Later, Cameron."

It took him a few minutes to compose himself. After he'd borrowed the tool he'd initially swung by the house to get, he drove himself back to his condo and let himself inside. Then, like the rest of the McCauleys taught to handle tools from birth, he fixed the leaky faucet in his bathroom sink.

"*Average?*" He pulled too hard on the wrench and water sprayed. As he cursed and hurried to fix the problem, he thought about how next to deal with the blond making his days, and his nights, a sexual hell.

—~~~—

Vanessa spent the evening with her coworkers trying to enjoy herself, but she couldn't for the life of her stop thinking about her encounter with Cameron. He'd seen her naked…and he seemed to like what he'd seen. She felt overly warm.

"Enjoying yourself, Vanessa?" Bill Peterman, her boss, asked. He took a sip of what smelled like Scotch and nodded to the full lounge they'd rented for the evening. A swanky celebration for the firm's twenty-fifth anniversary. Not bad, especially having made it through the economy's bumps the past few years.

"I am. Thanks, Bill." She smiled. She genuinely enjoyed Bill's company. The older man was devoted to his family, ran a tight ship, and expected the same kind of results Vanessa lived to perform.

"No date tonight?" he asked.

She thought about Cameron. It had been on the tip of her tongue to ask him to join her, but he might have taken the invitation as a weakening on her part. Vanessa didn't do weak. "No. But I'm sure I'll have someone on hand for our annual Halloween bash. Last year's was terrific."

He nodded with pride. "We do our part with the community. Pitching in is great PR, and it honestly builds stronger friendships in town."

She agreed. "So what are you and Anna doing for your anniversary? In another week, right?" She knew because Bill had made it a point to announce to one and all that he and Anna would be celebrating their thirtieth anniversary on Valentine's Day.

How wonderful to be so in love with your spouse. She envied their close affection, wondering if she'd ever find the same. She sure as hell couldn't look to her parents for inspiration. Connubial bliss? She didn't think her parents had ever felt anything resembling bliss in the whole of their lives.

Bill prattled on about his plans to surprise his wife with a cruise. Vanessa eventually mingled with the others, seeing a few friends and wishing she were back at home, hanging with her roommates. For all that she, Abby, and Maddie were different, they were family. She didn't have to pretend to be super nice or super friendly with them. They accepted her, bitchy, funny, snarly, and all.

One of the interns took a good look at her and walked in the other direction. She sighed then smiled, trying not to scare anyone else by looking too stern.

"Uh, Vanessa?"

She turned to see Joshua Taggert, Peterman's nephew. He was their newest intern, a fresh college graduate. She'd made the kid cry a few months back when he'd been on the verge of losing their clients *a lot* of money.

"Josh. How's it going?"

He grimaced. "Not great. I, uh... I wanted to thank you for setting me straight."

She blinked. He'd steered clear of her since the incident. "Oh?"

"Yeah. I really screwed up."

"Yes, you did." She appreciated his honesty.

"I just wanted to show Uncle Bill I can do the job. I hate that I'm thought of as the boss's nephew. It's so demeaning." Yet true.

"Well, it'll take time to understand—"

"Yeah, see, that's what I wanted to ask you. Would you be willing to give me help? Like, tutor me in the job so I learn what not to do?"

She hadn't anticipated that. Flattered but not sure what to say, she collected her thoughts.

"I'm not trying to kiss your butt or anything." He flushed and glanced at her rear, then hastily blinked at her. "I just meant you're the go-to person at the office. We all know it. I want to be that person someday. I know I have a lot of failings, but if given the chance, I could do better."

"You know, that's not a bad idea. Not about me," she said to stop his effusive thanks. "But getting you with a mentor would help you a lot. It would also help the staff to get to know you."

He nodded and grinned. "Thanks. That's great. I'd really appreciate it. I mean, I'd rather you helped me. But I know how busy you are."

"Sure, Josh. And, uh, I'm sorry I upset you. Before."

He paused.

Awkward, bringing up his crying jag, Vanessa.

"I was such a wuss. I'm sorry. I was trying so hard to impress you and my uncle."

"Me?"

"I meant my uncle. He's a stickler, you know," he said in a rush. "They were tears of frustration, because I wanted to get it right. Please forget I cried like a baby. So embarrassing."

He looked so sweet just then. "No problem. Go mingle. Enjoy. Did you bring your girlfriend?"

"No. Not tonight. Honestly? She's too needy. I think we need to break up."

TMI. But she understood. Most of her dates turned out to be needy and annoying too. "Good luck. The clingy types are hard to shake."

He laughed and smiled at her, his gaze approving and not at all wary, as she might have expected for making him cry.

After he walked away, Francie joined her with Jeanine, another friend. "So what's with you and the junior hottie?"

"Really, Francie? Didn't we graduate high school, like, ten years ago?" she said in her best cheerleader voice.

Jeanine snickered. "Yeah, Francie. He's an attractive young man. Not a hottie."

"And not someone to be drooling over, you old bags."

"Please, Vanessa." Francie frowned. "I'm in the prime of my youth. I'm twenty-eight. Hell, you're twenty-eight. So why do you always seem so much older?"

"Maybe because I'm not drooling over the boss's nephew."

Jeanine smirked. "Hmm. Seems to me he's drooling over you."

"Shut up, you ho. Now tell us about your last date. Did Brian rate a sleepover or did you boot him out of bed after round one?" Vanessa wanted to know, since she kept landing dud after dud. The last guy she'd met at the gym, so she'd had hopes they'd have something in common. But no one could love John as much as he loved himself. She'd chalked him to her *loser* column, with all the others.

Not one man she'd met had held a candle to Cameron McCauley, and she knew it. But what to do about that fact? With both her roommates in love with his brothers, exploring their attraction might make things sticky. Especially since he seemed to be the family type—great mom and dad, deep relationship with his siblings and cousins. So unlike Vanessa and the way she handled her emotionally distant relations. She worried that if she involved herself with Cameron, even sexually, he'd demand more. And that she'd try to give him what she didn't have in her to give.

Chapter 2

SUNDAY AFTERNOON AT THE GYM, VANESSA WORKED up a sweat on the elliptical she'd been eyeing the last time she'd visited. Sundays normally weren't as crowded as work days, and she enjoyed exercising without so much chatter around her. That…and *he* normally arrived about now. She eyed the clock on the wall.

"Well, hey there." Cameron smiled at her from the machine to her immediate right.

Relieved to see him but refusing to act like she'd been looking for him, she refrained from increasing the speed on the machine. It was difficult, because she didn't want him to think she'd been slacking off her normal regimen. *And I should care what he thinks…why?*

"Cameron."

He gave her a subtle once-over, and she had a bad feeling he was mentally comparing her clothed to unclothed.

"Take a picture. It'll last longer," she snapped.

He smirked. "You're in fine form today. For the record, I was checking out your shoes. I've been thinking about getting a new pair, and I hear those insoles are incredible. They new?"

"Oh." She blushed. "I, um, my old ones were pretty worn."

He nodded and started his workout. "How's the arch support?"

She answered and tried not to look at his elliptical

console, but she couldn't help noticing he'd started at a workout level higher than her own. She continued to study him out of the corner of her eye, wondering when she should increase her speed without looking foolishly competitive.

After a few moments spent chatting about her shoes, he said, "Good to know, thanks. I think I'll get myself a pair." The bastard wasn't even breathing hard. "So tell me, because I'm dying to know. How was the office party?"

Man, he had nice legs, as well as broad shoulders, trim hips, and an ass she'd do anything to bite, just once. He normally dressed in tailored clothing that flattered his coloring and rangy frame. But here in the gym she was treated to nylon shorts, a cotton T-shirt, and exposed muscle that showed off his lean runner's build. *Yum*.

"The party?" he asked again.

She blinked. "Oh, ah, the party. Good as far as office functions go. I did my best not to scare off any more interns."

"Oh?"

She filled him in on her altercation with Taggert a few months ago, and he laughed.

"He'll remember that ass-chewing. Hell, I still remember my first one."

Pleased he didn't view her as the ogre her coworkers had not-so-quietly compared her to, she asked, "What happened?"

"I told you I interned at an international bank. Well, I thought I was hot stuff, so one day, after I'd been there a few months, I took the liberty of intercepting the secretary to assist one of the bank's larger clients. She'd come in a few times a month, knew everyone in the upper echelons, and had a big wallet. I wanted to meet her too, to show I was part of the team."

"And maybe strut around a little."

"Yeah, I wanted to strut. Did I tell you I was the youngest intern they ever hired?"

"No, but thanks so much for that detail."

He grinned. "Anyway, I did nothing more than get her—"

"Her? The client was a *her*? Oh, now I see."

"She was a fifty-year-old grandma. Gimme a break. Anyway, I just went to get her coffee and chat her up a little. She smiled and seemed to appreciate my charm. And yes, I can be charming when I try."

"That has to be seen to be believed."

He laughed.

"So what happened with the client?"

"After we chatted a while, she let me help her to her feet, kissed my cheek, then went in to see my boss. No mess, no fuss. I'd done my part to ease the client. An hour later, my boss took me into a private office down the hall, shut the door, and went ballistic."

"Really? Just because you were being polite?"

"Apparently the older lady thought I was offering my services and wanted to take me up on them."

She frowned. "Is that what you were doing? Because that's serious stuff. Even I know stealing a client is bad etiquette, Cameron."

"I wasn't trying to steal her. And she didn't want me for my financial skills. She wanted a different kind of service."

"I don't get it."

"She'd met her last boyfriend at the bank. She thought

I was into older women, that I was hitting on her. She wanted me—and not to invest her money for her."

Vanessa gaped. "Really?"

He grimaced. "Really. It made things awkward when the partners had to talk her down and try to manage the embarrassing situation. Totally not my fault, but it wouldn't have happened if I hadn't been acting like I knew what the hell I was doing. There's a reason only certain people attend the big rollers. Lots of egos and money mixing it up can turn volatile in a heartbeat. Fortunately she had a good sense of humor and we didn't lose her as a client."

"So what happened to you?"

"I served time in the mail room for two weeks before I was allowed anywhere near my boss's office again." He chuckled. "Yeah, good old Gloria Mannett."

She blinked. "*The* Gloria Mannett? The billionaire hotelier? You almost lost *her* account?" Like Trump, the woman was a household name.

"Yep. Me and my pretty blue eyes nearly stole her away." He sighed.

She stared at him. "You're making that up."

"Am I?" He batted his eyelashes and blew her a few kisses. "Thinking about moving your money around now, Vanessa? Do you have a sudden urge to check out my...*annuities*?"

"Idiot." She snickered and shook her head. "Wow. Gloria Mannett."

"I saw her years later and we laughed about it. She's actually a very nice woman and currently married to a man thirty years her junior. He's husband number four, I think."

"Man. I don't ever remember getting in trouble for working hard. Or for flirting when I shouldn't have."

"All work and no play, eh?"

"You know it." She continued to step, and feeling a sudden burst of energy, gradually increased the tension on her machine, so that it bypassed Cam's level.

Of course he noticed. He raised a brow. "You want to race?"

"I'm just working out like I always do."

She waited.

He didn't disappoint. The natural competitor increased his workout, and soon they battled each other to see who could sweat the most without falling off their machines.

Not more than ten minutes later, they both called it quits and headed to the smoothie bar in the back.

"It's on me," Cameron said as he ordered himself a fruit drink. "Put them on my tab," he said to the girl behind the counter and slid her his member card.

"I'll have what he's having," Vanessa ordered.

Cameron nodded and accepted his card back. "So."

"Yes?"

"Our contest. On the elliptical."

"What about it?"

"I won. Just saying."

She frowned. "In what universe? I was exercising before you even got here."

"Yeah, for maybe ten minutes. I saw you stretching while *I* was finishing up five miles on the treadmill. By the way, two guys nearly killed each other with dumb-bells while watching your shirt ride up. Nice abs."

She tried to think of a comeback just as the girl

handed them their drinks. "Was that the loud noise I heard earlier?"

He grinned. "Yep. Two muscleheads nearly killed themselves by the free weights while the oblivious hot blond everyone always talks about did her warm-up." He sighed. "I love when you warm up."

"Shut up." Her cheeks felt hot and grew hotter when he laughed. "You're the one with the nice legs."

He preened. "I am handsome, aren't I?"

"For God's sake." Before his ego got the better of him, she took him down a peg. He returned the favor, and they had a wonderfully invigorating argument about who had nicer calves and hamstrings that carried them through the gym to their cars.

"Same time next Sunday?" Cam asked before he got in his sporty coupe.

She nodded and entered her car, then started it and rolled down the window. "And for the record, I won." She burned rubber and tore out of the garage, then reduced her speed like the responsible, careful driver she actually was.

Her hands remained at ten and two as she smiled the whole way home.

—⁓—

"Why do I always have to be partnered with Mike? We never win," Cam complained five days later. The four McCauleys sat in Mike's kitchen, the only part of the house Cam liked, and enjoyed Friday night cards.

Mike glared at him and gave a hard look at the table, where he'd just played a heart.

"Seriously, Mike. You suck at table talk." Brody

laughed and took the next hand. They'd all opted for spades instead of poker. With Colin hanging out with Abby and Maddie next door, they felt free to let the curses fly.

"Yeah?" Mike growled. "Well sorry, blondie. We weren't all born with the ability to cheat at cards. It's like you had a full deck in the fucking womb."

"Full deck? Brody? Not from where I'm sitting," Cam muttered. Brody could be so annoying, especially since it was impossible to catch him cheating, even if you knew the guy had three aces up his sleeve.

"True. My boy's glands are probably overheating again." Flynn gave Brody a commiserate nod. "It's been what? At least twenty-four hours since you got laid?"

"Hey, moron, that's my future wife you're talking about." Brody smacked Flynn in the back of the head. "It was more like eight hours. I had a nooner for lunch."

Mike and Cam exchanged a grimace while Flynn high-fived his immature partner.

"It's like you two have regressed decades. You're not eighteen any more, fellas," Cam said with disgust.

Mike agreed. "Yeah. I expect Flynn to be that obnoxious, but not you, Brody."

"Hey. I'm the good one." Flynn took the next trick and the following two. "It's not my fault you two are in denial. Sexual denial."

"It ain't just a river," Brody intoned, "but a sad state of life for some."

He and Flynn smirked at them. To Cam's relief, they didn't just pick on him, but Mike too. So nice to finally not have to defend himself against *all three* of them.

"Look, you two fuckheads, just because Cam and I

actually work for a living—not shoving our hands down people's toilets—doesn't mean we don't like women." Mike ignored the finger Flynn shot him. "I'm too busy to play nice with the ladies right now. And genius boy has been working his ass off to move everything from his East Coast office back here."

Cam hadn't realized anyone had noticed. "Yeah. What Mike said."

"Suck-up." Brody made a face at him.

"Hey, say what you want. But when I go after a woman, it's with a lot more maturity. And dignity"— he paused, giving them both a look—"than what you two showed. Christ, guys. Maddie and Abby are wonderful women. And you both nearly managed to screw up your relationships." He turned to Mike. "It's like they're, well…"

"Idiots?" Mike helpfully supplied.

Cam snapped his fingers. "That's the word. *Idiots*."

"Morons, dickheads, nad-nozzles?" Mike continued.

"Nad-nozzles?"

Mike shrugged. "One of the neighbor kids called his brother that. I immediately thought of those two."

Brody grinned widely at the score sheet. "That's just sour grapes because we're kicking your asses. Yeah. Next dinner out is on you losers."

Mike scowled.

Cam sighed. He couldn't refute numbers. "Hell. Anyone want another beer?"

He got two yeses and a request for a Coke. After fetching them more drinks, he turned to put them on the table and saw something outside streaking toward the window. Fast.

"Mike?" Cam nodded to the back door. "I think you're about to get company."

Before they could blink, Colin rushed through the back door wearing his pajamas and rubber boots.

"Colin?"

Vanessa, Maddie, and Abby soon joined him.

Colin pointed a finger at Vanessa and scowled. "She's mean."

"Tell us something we don't know," Abby muttered.

For all that Abby resembled Lea, Mike's deceased wife, she was truly her own person. A petite beauty with long black hair, brown eyes, and a smile that lit up when she spotted Brody.

Like her roommate, Maddie gave her man Flynn a special grin. With her redheaded temper and eyes normally golden with a furious fire, she totally gave his brother a run for his money. The rock on her finger gleamed, and Cam had to hand it to Flynn for buying his fiancée something to be proud of.

But it was Vanessa who always stood out to him. She rolled her eyes and dragged Colin back by his collar, not at all put off by Mike's mother-hen glower. "What the alien is upset about is the fact that I told him he couldn't have my sesame candy. I also told him I'd ask you first, to see if he could have his own. He didn't want to wait. I caught him red-handed, crunching down honey and sesame seeds."

"Dude. You got caught?" Brody shook his head.

"Brody, shut up," Mike snapped. To Colin, he crooked a finger. "Come here, boy."

Colin looked visibly upset. No longer funning. "B-but Dad. I didn't—I mean, I was gonna ask—" He burst into tears and covered his eyes. Then he ruined it by peeking through his fingers at the crowd.

"Colin," Mike growled. He turned to Brody. "He only does this because *you* taught him to cry on command."

Everyone tried to muffle laughter, except for Vanessa. "Hey, Mike? He took *my* candy at *my* house. I can handle this, if that's okay."

Mike seemed torn.

"She's got it," Cam prodded. "Let's get back to the game. You know, so we can make up for getting beaten by Thing One and Thing Two?"

"Shut up, loser." Flynn snickered.

"Vanessa, I don't know…" Mike, such a pushover with that kid.

"I had something in mind for the little faker." Vanessa narrowed her eyes at the boy.

Cam asked her, "You going to beat him?"

"Not where it will show."

"There. Come on, he'll be fine." He turned to the table and started dealing, knowing Colin deserved and even needed the discipline. Not that Mike didn't do a good job, but in Cam's opinion, he could be too easy with the boy. "Okay, new game. Brody no longer deals. And winners get not one, but *two* dinners from the losers."

Mike grudgingly turned around. "No bruises I have to explain," he said over his shoulder.

"Dad!" Colin cried as Vanessa dragged him outside.

"No problem." Abby sounded way too perky. She leaned closer to Mike. "She's going to put him in the corner. Kids hate that."

"Good luck." Mike snorted. "I've been trying that for years. Doesn't work."

"It does when Vanessa's in charge. Trust me." Maddie shivered. "She's going to make him explain, in detail, why he thought stealing was a bad idea. Then she'll argue him down with logic until he begs for her to stop."

"Yeah, he'll truly suffer." Abby sighed.

Maddie agreed. "Been there, done that. But that's what you get when you try to take what's Vanessa's."

"Ouch." Cam grinned. He *really* needed to figure out how to get that first date.

———※———

Vanessa took the subdued boy back to the house and nudged him into the corner of Abby's study. She waited a few moments for him to stop squirming. "Well?"

"Huh?"

"No, no. Keep your nose in that corner, young man." The only thing she could favorably say about her parents—they'd taught her the benefits of discipline and firmness. "Tell me what you did and why it was wrong."

"I was just teasing."

"No. You took my candy and you tried to be sneaky about it. Own up. Tell the truth." Her personal mantra. It made her feel good that Cameron had displayed no objection to her taking care of this. Mike had worried, but Cameron showed trust.

"I'm sorry." Colin started crying—in earnest this time—just as Abby and Maddie returned.

"Oh, Vanessa. Can't you—"

"Maddie, out." Her cousin, the soft touch.

"Fine. I'll be waiting in the kitchen with *my* candy." Maddie left, stomping down the hallway.

"I'm just here to observe," Abby said softly. Since

dating Brody, she'd become a much more settled person. She'd always smiled a lot, but now she looked happier, prettier even.

Vanessa nodded. "Well, Colin?"

"I took y-your food and d-didn't ask."

"And that's bad, why?"

"Because it wasn't m-mine." He wiped his nose and Abby handed her a tissue to give him.

Vanessa thought he looked pretty miserable. Check. "Why is taking what's not yours bad?"

She moved close enough to see him frown into the corner. "Because it's bad."

She turned him to face her and used another tissue to wipe his nose. God, he was so adorable. He made her think about someday having her own children. With no prospects on the horizon and a deathly fear of turning into her mother if she ever did procreate, she knew better than to even spell motherhood.

"Stealing is wrong because what you did hurt me," she corrected in a quiet voice. "Not because you took my candy, but by ignoring what I told you, you hurt my feelings. I thought we were friends. And you shouldn't hurt your friend's feelings."

"Oh." He sounded miserable.

"That and the candy was mine. How would you like it if I took something of yours without asking? Always treat other people the way you want to be treated."

He nodded. "That's what Dad tells me too."

"Your dad's a smart man," Abby piped in.

Vanessa glared at her, and Abby rolled her eyes but closed her mouth.

"He is. Now, you messed up with the candy, but

maybe if you call him and *ask* if you can have cookies, because *I* said it's okay, you could have a few. It's good to take responsibility for your actions."

He looked so hopeful, she prayed Mike would say yes.

"Okay. I'm really sorry, Vanessa. I won't do it again." He crossed his heart and held out his hand.

She took the grubby fingers in her own and shook. "Let's call the old man."

Ten minutes later, Colin sat fat and happy with her and the girls as they watched an old Godzilla movie. It was as if the corner had never happened. Man, to be that young and innocent. But innocent was a relative term. Vanessa had once been six, but she'd never been so carefree. She'd never eaten cookies with her parents or watched television with them. Not unless the program could be classified as educational.

"So who's our green lizard fighting?" Maddie asked as she munched on processed popcorn. "Mega-somebody?"

"Not Mothra, I don't think." Abby frowned. "Megaguirus, maybe?"

Vanessa cringed. "That you even know which monsters he fights is a bit frightening."

"You're so smart, Abby." Colin continued to consume sugar at a frightening rate. But since Vanessa would soon be returning him to Mike, and the kid had owned up to his issues, she figured he deserved it.

"Yeah, smart at B-movies and how to handle blonds—myself excluded." Vanessa smirked.

Abby stuck up her hand and peeled down all her fingers but the middle one, then put her hand back before Colin observed the profane gesture.

"Crude but effective. On that note, I'm getting something to eat. How you guys can shovel that crap in your mouths is beyond me."

"Everything is 'beyond you,'" Maddie muttered. "Including fun."

"I heard that."

Colin laughed with the others.

Vanessa laughed with them as she walked away, but deep down she had to wonder if Maddie was right. So many people saw her as this robotic, cold woman. Just because she enjoyed something as dry as accounting and didn't take shit from losers, she was labeled the un-fun roommate. Well, numbers didn't lie. Numbers delivered the same thing to everyone. No playing favorites, no changing rules. Once you had a formula, it stuck and made sense.

She'd spent enough time with her cousins to know that her parents had borderline personality disorders. Neither of them could tell her they loved her, if they felt it at all. She'd never hurt for food or a roof over her head, but their affection they doled only on their studies. Geniuses in their respective fields of mathematics and physics, yet complete dumbasses when it came to celebrating a birthday, holiday, or kissing a boo-boo.

Fortunately, Vanessa had grandparents and cousins, and good old Aunt Michelle—Maddie's mom—who loved to hug and kiss and play the doting aunt. Still, life with her parents had taken its toll. While Vanessa knew why she at times behaved too rationally or emotionlessly, she was helpless to stop being herself.

A flaw.

More truth. Sometimes she hated her overwhelming need to be honest with everyone.

As she rummaged in the cabinet for her organically grown corn kernels and oil for popping, the back door rattled. She turned to see Cameron's face in the window, and her heart raced.

Exhaling a long breath, she forced herself to be calm and crossed to unlock the door. "Yes?"

It was either move back or be walked over, so she stepped back while he entered and shut the door behind him.

"Just checking on the little guy," Cam said in a low voice. "Mike can be such a hoverer—"

"Where's the boy?" Mike asked from behind him.

She pointed to the hallway. "Living room."

Mike left, and she and Cameron stared after him. Mike returned moments later, gave Vanessa a nod and a grunt—of approval?—and left.

"Told you he's mental about the kid," Cam reiterated.

She frowned. "Did he really need to check on me? What? He thought I might beat Colin for taking my candy?"

"Nah. I kind of hinted he might want to see what you guys were up to so I could come with him. To see you." Cameron smiled at her.

How she'd ever called him average with a straight face, she didn't know. The man was her every fantasy made flesh. A great body, handsome face, and amazing mind. And God, he could *kiss*. As much as she wished she didn't continually replay their embrace, she hadn't forgotten that kiss at Christmas.

"Oh?" Damn, she sounded out of breath.

Cameron stalked her until she realized he'd backed her into a corner of the kitchen, away from the view from the hallway.

"Cameron?"

He planted his hands on either side of her on the counter. What the hell?

"The guys are on break while we order pizza. The crap kind from a chain." He sighed. "What can you do?" He glanced at her popcorn and grinned. "Oh, that's my favorite. Just a bit of oil and it pops up a storm." He looked back at her mouth. "Great taste." Pause. "I just came over to say what a good job you did being firm with Colin."

"Ah, okay."

He moved in closer.

"Cameron?" she squeaked on a whisper, for some odd reason not wanting the others to know he was here with her.

"Your lips are so red. So pretty. Do you wear lipstick?" He leaned in and kissed her before she could answer or even think to refuse.

Vanessa stood still, letting him control the kiss, his lips soft yet firm, his tongue sipping then penetrating slowly. No rush, but a leisurely exploration that turned her knees to jelly.

He moaned low in his throat and deepened the kiss. Not enough to overpower her, but enough that she felt a raging lust to wrap her legs around him and hold on until the storm passed.

Instead she remained frozen, her hands gravitating to his waist, her mouth under his.

He eased back. His blue eyes looked cloudy, his lips slick from their kiss. He smiled, and the curl of that grin shook her foundation, made her want with a passion that shocked her.

"No lipstick." He wiped a thumb across her lower lip. "See?"

"Yeah." She unconsciously gripped his hips, and he shifted, putting his hard body flush against hers.

"I need to get back," he said to her mouth.

"Yeah."

"They'll be waiting on me."

She heard Colin's laughter and Maddie's creature-roar from the living room, and once again answered, "Yeah."

Cameron kissed her again, and when he let go, she felt light-headed. Her panties would need a good washing, and that impressive steel in his pants told her she wasn't the only one affected. The only thing keeping her from feeling like a complete idiot for saying nothing but "Yeah" for the past minute.

"See you soon, Vanessa." Cameron took a deep breath, then stepped away from her. He turned and left the house as stealthily as he'd arrived.

"You're missing it, Vanessa," Colin yelled. "The big monster bugs are getting the people."

"C-coming." She cleared her throat, then went to the refrigerator and opened it. After shoving her head inside to clear her thoughts, she pulled back and quickly popped herself some corn.

Returning to the television and pretending all was well took effort, but she pulled it off. Two hours later, while she lay in her bed, she tried to understand what had happened. Cameron McCauley, the most devious of the bunch, had kissed her senseless. She, Vanessa Campbell, had allowed a man to make her lose her mind. And he'd done it so effortlessly. A brush of his rock-hard body, a kiss that tasted like beer and man and sex, all wrapped up in a McCauley.

God, she'd underestimated his appeal. Oh sure, she'd been attracted. But that kiss had taken her from normalcy to extreme lust between one breath and the next. To her mortification, if he hadn't pulled back, she'd have mounted him then and there *in the kitchen*.

The jerk.

With any luck, he'd suffer one acute case of blue balls to torture him into tomorrow. How the hell was she supposed to sleep now? To dream or fantasize without throwing his smirking face on top of any man she imagined having sex with?

It had been tough enough before, *without* knowing how he could kiss. She'd tried so hard to forget Christmas, to chalk it up as a one-time wonder. Now she had another reference point. Carnal knowledge of the man's mouth, which made her wonder what else he excelled in besides kissing.

If he can perform like that without a bed, imagine what he'll be like on top of a mattress, plunging deep with more than that tongue?

She fanned herself and tried to sleep, but each glance at the clock showed the hour growing later. With no other recourse but to handle things, she sought Mr. Frisky from her bottom drawer and eased herself into a nice long sleep. One that unfortunately resulted in dreams of Cameron McCauley at the gym wearing nothing at all…but Vanessa.

Cam spent the evening trying to keep up with his brothers when every instinct he possessed told him to go back to Vanessa's, pull her upstairs, and fuck her until neither one of them could move. Talk about chemistry. The woman had been lethal *before* that second kiss. But now he could think of no one but her.

She wore nothing better than that look of confusion and vulnerability, showing him the real woman underneath all her bluster and arrogance. Granted, he liked that side of her, but he absolutely loved the sensitive soul hiding under the brash woman.

The rest of the weekend passed without fuss. He did errands and cleaning on Saturday, keeping his already spotless condo unit clean. Like Mike, he believed in organization and a clutter-free space. Unlike Mike, he'd been that way his entire life. His older brother had only started with the clean crap after Colin's birth.

Vanessa suited him in that respect as well. Bright, organized, smart, sexy. Hell, could the woman not see they were made for each other? He needed to lure her close, let her think she'd taken charge. *Then* pounce.

Pleased with his reasoning, he joined the family for dinner on Sunday, knowing he'd see Vanessa and her roommates again. Though Brody and Flynn had only snagged two of the girls, his mother and father had always invited Vanessa as well.

They used to have family dinners more often than they did now. About once a month everyone would congregate at his parents' house and eat one of his mother's amazing meals. Of course, with his parents not seeming to get along lately, he had to wonder how much longer these happy gatherings would continue.

He sat at the table after helping his mother set out a few dishes. When he caught Vanessa's gaze, he winked.

She blushed before looking away. Vanessa, shy? Then he noticed Mike's absence.

"Where's Big Foot?"

Maddie and Abby glanced at Vanessa.

She glared back at *him*. "Not funny, Cameron."

He frowned. "I meant Mike."

Flynn and Brody laughed as Vanessa scowled at her roommates.

"He's not coming," his father said. "We asked him not to."

The laughter around the table faded.

Their mother joined their father, not touching, not standing too close.

Cam had a sick feeling in the pit of his stomach. "Dad?"

Their father continued. "We were going to wait until after dinner, but… Your mother and I are working through some things. We're going to be living apart for a while."

"*What?* Mom?" Flynn looked to their mother.

She had tears in her eyes, but none fell as she answered, "Your father thinks it best we live apart."

"Beth," James growled.

"And I agree. He's moving out."

Everyone sat in silence.

"Where will you go?" Brody asked, then nodded. "You can always stay with me."

His father shook his head. "No, son. You're busy, and Flynn, I know you and Maddie spend as much time at your place as you do at hers." He cleared his throat but didn't look at their mother.

What the hell was going on? How had his parents' perfect marriage degenerated to this?

"I plan to continue to see my grandson," Beth said with a firm bitterness completely alien to the woman who'd busted her ass baking cookies and chaperoning all his childhood field trips with a perpetual grin on her face. "I won't be made to feel awkward because you need a place to stay."

James blew out a breath. "Fine. I'll stay with Cam."

Everyone turned to him. He had no idea how to respond, so he said the only thing he could. "Sure, Dad. I've got plenty of room."

Chapter 3

"I MUST BE OUT OF MY FUCKING MIND." CAM STARED AT Mike the next morning at an impromptu emergency meeting. Flynn and Brody sat with him at Mike's table. With Colin at school, they had the place to themselves. "Mike, did you know about Mom and Dad splitting up?"

Mike sighed. "Mom told me yesterday afternoon. She came over and filled me in because she didn't want to make the announcement with Colin there. So we stayed home."

"Wish I would have stayed home." Cam groaned. "Dad moved his clothes in last night. What am I going to do with him?"

"Um, I don't know. Deal?" Flynn snorted.

"It's not funny," Cam snapped. "Dad and I get along like oil and water. He thinks I'm a 'Nancy,' and yes, I know he still calls me that."

"Not all the time," Mike said kindly as Brody smirked.

"Mike. Please. Dad gets along best with you and the knuckle draggers." He nodded to Brody and Flynn.

"Fuck you." Flynn frowned.

"Yeah? Well fuck you too. This situation sucks." He gritted his teeth. "I'm not just talking about Dad moving in. What's going on? What did Mom say?"

They all looked to Mike, who sighed. "Not much. Just that she and Dad have been having problems for a while. She wouldn't go into it, and I didn't want her to cry, so I left it at that." His gaze narrowed on Cam. "You need to talk to her. She confides stuff to you."

"Yeah, fine. I'll talk to her later today. I have to get to work soon."

"Us too," Brody said. "I just wish I knew how to fix this. I mean, we all noticed they hadn't been as affectionate as they used to be."

Flynn nodded. They'd had this conversation before. "Not in years. But it's never been like this. Like Mom and Dad don't *like* each other."

"Do you think it's another woman?" Cam asked.

Three sets of angry eyes turned to him.

"Hey, I'm not saying he's cheating, but can you imagine any other scenario that would have Mom so angry with him they'd break up? Because yesterday she made it sound like it was all his idea."

Flynn sighed. "I heard that too. I don't know. I hate to think that, but they're hardly together. And he doesn't seem to mind while Mom's made cracks about his absence."

"I've seen that too," Brody admitted. "I'm wondering if Pop did something to Bitsy." What Brody called their father and mother. "I don't know, but I see sadness in Bitsy's eyes. In his, I just see him tired or angry."

"That's how he always expressed his feelings," Cam said, and not without a little hostility. Unlike his brothers, he and his father hadn't been tight while growing up. Too much a *momma's boy*—his father had called him. Jokingly, but Cam heard a ring of truth. No matter how much he wanted to be like his father, they just didn't share the same interests.

And they'd be sharing the same house for the foreseeable future.

"What the hell have I gotten myself into?"

Mike patted him on the back. "Sorry, man. Hey, if he gets to be too much, I'll break you."

Cam stared.

"Not break, as in half." Mike flushed. "I meant I'll give you a break. We'll trade. You get Mom off my ass and I'll get Dad off yours."

"She still on you about finding a good woman?" Brody asked.

Mike rolled his eyes. "Yeah. And now I see why. Maddie was right, Flynn. I think Mom's transferring her loneliness to smothering Colin with hugs and kisses. It's a grandkid thing."

"Bummer for you." Flynn looked relieved. "So glad I found Maddie. No need for Mom to fix *me* up."

"Found?" Cam barked a laugh. "You lucked into that. Don't question it."

"Trust me, I don't." Flynn's amusement faded. "I want to patch this thing with Mom and Dad. But I don't know if we should butt in."

"Please." Brody snorted. "Bitsy and Pop have done their share of butting in. Time to turn the tables and fix *them* for a change." No doubt he recalled just a short month ago when he'd been in a funk and the family had descended on him en masse to cheer him up.

"Yeah, it worked with you." Cam ignored Brody's frown. "So Mike, you deal with Dad today. Try to feel him out at work. I'll swing by tonight and take Mom to dinner. I'll talk to her then."

"Good." Mike nodded. "We do this together. None of us going off on our own or siccing our girlfriends on Mom to mess things up."

"Hey." Flynn looked offended.

"Seriously. Abby's nice." Brody huffed. "Lay off the ladies. Not our fault you can't get laid. Don't hate, Mike. Go get your own girl."

Mike jeered, "I had one, numbnuts. I got the kid to prove it."

"You sure he's yours?" Flynn taunted.

When Mike just looked at him, Flynn sighed. "I know. Lame joke. Kid's like your little clone."

"Damn straight." Mike puffed with pride. "I'm saying we need to be subtle. Except for me and Cam, I'm not thinking you two know the meaning of the word."

"I know I can't spell it. That's why I have Abby." Brody grinned, always proud of his girlfriend, the writer.

"Hell. Fine." Flynn stood and glanced at his cell phone. "Come on, Brody. We have to get to work."

"Me too." Cam stood as well. Before he could follow the guys out, Mike stopped him. "What's up?"

"You okay with Dad crashing at your place? I know he can be a real hammer sometimes."

Cam shrugged. "It's been a whole night. He hasn't complained." Yet. "Good thing I left the guest room the way it was."

"Using that third room as your office?"

"Yep. It was going to be a temporary space while I tried to wrangle a better deal on my lease downtown, which fell through, by the way. My assistant has been working out of his condo, since he has a huge loft. But it seems like I need to find a new office, pronto. I can't imagine working at home next to Dad twenty-four-seven." Consolidating his East and West Coast businesses, he'd been planning the move for months. Something close to the condo, he hoped.

At his current rates and progress, he could well afford it.

"I feel for you, Cam." Mike rubbed the bridge of his nose. "I just… I can't wrap my mind around Mom and Dad not being Mom *and* Dad, you know?"

"Yeah." He blew out a breath. "Mike, I don't get it. I mean, if they can't make it work, how the hell can any of us?"

Mike paused. "You have someone in mind?"

He didn't know whether to say or not.

"Someone tall, blond, and cool? Someone hot but mean? Your type?"

Cam huffed. "Obvious, huh?"

"Uh-huh. Like at Christmas when you two were all flushed and close in Colin's bedroom? That look of 'I just sucked face'? Yeah, I saw that."

"Oh. That." Cam scrambled for some excuse and came up with nothing.

"Hey, if anyone can tame that woman, it's you. I believe in you, bro." Mike grinned. "Is that why you're always working out at the gym when you have your own fitness place in the condo?"

"Not a word."

Mike held up his hands. "Not from me. But she's not stupid. The first time you take her home, you… Oh hell. You can't take her home. Not with Dad in the next room." For the first time that morning, Mike laughed with real amusement. "You're fucked."

"I know." Glum and realizing his love life—that he didn't even have yet—was already suffering, Cam swore and made his way to his real estate agent, now desperate for an office away from his father.

———

Hard at work on Wednesday afternoon, Vanessa found her thoughts wandering to Cameron and his new roommate. What must that be like, living as an adult with one's father?

She shivered to think of her own and focused on her clients' audits. As a senior accountant, she had a number of people working under her. Which meant the potential for a lot of mistakes. After looking over Francie's impeccable—as always—work, she picked up her ringing phone. "Vanessa Campbell."

"Vanessa? Can you come to my office?"

"Sure, Bill. Be right there." She saved her work and headed down the hall. McNulty, Peterman employed two hundred and fifty people and was considered one of the top accounting firms in the city. She was proud to be a part of a company she respected, as well as working for a boss she not only trusted but also liked.

After hearing how Maddie's boss had sexually harassed her and the many dozens of stories told by her other friends, she treasured Bill Peterman. He saw her value, of course, but he would also never ask anyone to do what he himself wasn't prepared to do.

She knocked. When he told her to come in, she entered and halted. Dear God. Not this guy again.

John Willington, the man she'd dated a few weeks ago, the same one who'd gone on and on about how great he was, stood smiling. "Hello, Vanessa. We meet again."

She turned to Bill with confusion. "Ah, Bill?"

Bill smiled, though the expression didn't reach his eyes. Not good. "Vanessa, you already know John

Willington, I gather. John's representing our newest client, Bellemy Tech. He specifically requested that you work with them."

Not one to pull punches, Vanessa flat-out rejected the idea. "I'm flattered, but as John and I previously dated, I don't feel it would be right to blur professional lines with personal ones."

John surprised her by smiling. "That's why I asked for you. That driven, professional reputation you have precedes you."

Bill started to relax. Vanessa, not so much. She had a funny feeling. "Oh?"

"Yes. A few of your clients, specifically friends of mine at Drey Dining and Anna Lee's, all recommended you as an honest accountant who won't steer me wrong. Our personal history aside, I'd like to hire your company to work with us."

"What happened to your previous accountants?" Bellemy Tech had a large number of employees, and their current revenue had made the *Forbes* top twenty list of technological companies on the rise.

"I'm in charge of the accounts department, but we outsource the more detailed work with taxes. Our last cooperative didn't work out. The breaks we'd assumed we'd get ended up putting us in some hot water with the IRS."

"Ouch." She nodded to her boss. "It's up to Bill, of course. But I'm sure he's explained how we work. If he doesn't think our strategies will hold up with Uncle Sam, we won't do it. We tend to be shy of aggressive but more than middle of the road."

"Perfect."

Damn. She still didn't trust his wide smile, but the

references he'd mentioned were legit, and really? Would a company as large as Bellemy use a lame excuse like needing an accountant to get John a second date?

Feeling foolish for her arrogance, she held out a hand and shook John's, ignoring her discomfort when he gripped it a little too long. Bill didn't seem to notice, all smiles.

"Well, I have to get back to work." She subtly slid her hand away.

John nodded. "Great. I'll set up a time for us to get started with Bill, and I'll see you soon."

Not him specifically. One of his people, no doubt. Well, perhaps the initial meeting would involve John, but after that, she'd work with his underlings. That she preferred.

She returned to her office, where she found Josh hovering outside. God, just what she didn't need— another aggravating man standing around, sucking up her oxygen.

"Hey, Josh." She'd been working on being nicer, though it went against the grain. "What can I do for you?"

He frowned. "Can we talk in your office?"

"Sure." She swallowed a sigh and preceded him inside. "Vanessa…"

"Josh, spit it out. I have work to do." So much for her attempt at nice. She couldn't even go a whole three days. She'd start again next week. Just like she had last week.

"I—I think one of the women might be, ah, harassing me. Man, this is more embarrassing than the last time I was in here."

She blinked. Was there some kind of weird vibe in the air or what? "Say that again?"

"Forget it. I feel stupid." He made to stand when she stopped him.

"No. Tell me."

His cheeks had turned a blazing red. Not making this up, then.

"It's just…sometimes when I go in to ask the others for help, a few of the ladies make comments that make me uncomfortable. I've tried to joke it off, and I feel like a moron for saying anything, but if I go to HR, they'll make a big deal of it. Everyone here respects you, and if you happened to say something, they'd stop." He paused. "You know pretty much everyone is afraid of you."

She did sigh then. "Fine. Tell me."

He spilled the details, and she grew furious on his behalf. The kid was barely out of school, working his tail off studying for his CPA exam, and trying to fit in with the corporate world, away from academia. He didn't need the attitude from some of their older employees. And especially not from divorced-four-times and perpetually horny Dana Lawrence.

"Dana, Trish, and don't tell me, Gina too, right?"

He shrugged.

"Josh?"

"Yes, all of them."

She stared at him.

"You believe me? I'm not making this up."

After a moment, she said, "Josh, let me ask you something unrelated·to this mess."

"Uh, okay."

"How serious are you about working here?"

"Very." He sounded earnest.

"You've been with the company for four months. We'll expect you to take your CPA exam and get your license after two years. Are you content to be with us that long?"

"Yes. Uncle Bill explained all this. I'd also like to be certified as a fraud examiner and cash manager, like you did."

She nodded. "Good for you." He'd done his homework. "I've been working for this company for seven years. And I've worked my ass off to get where I am now." She gave him a hard look. "I don't let anyone or anything stand in my way. I don't mean to say I'm a backstabber. I'm honest and I do my job, but I don't tolerate bullshit. Not from the men or women in this place, not from my boss, and not from you."

"I swear. I'm not bullshitting you."

"Fine. I'll go talk to the women downstairs. But know you're going to be occasionally teased simply because you're related to the boss." She shook her head. "It would have helped you a ton if Bill hadn't introduced you as his favorite nephew. But if you want that stigma to go away, work on it. Stop calling him Uncle Bill and start calling him Mr. Peterman or boss. Talk to him about it, would you? Don't worry about the harassment. I'll deal with them." She paused. Dana had a thing for younger men. "Before I talk to them, tell me something. You didn't have sex with any of them, did you? Because that might make this more complicated."

"*Hell no*. I mean, no." He tried to hide his disgust, and she couldn't stifle her grin.

"Good. Be smart, and don't screw around at the office. This place is too small for that."

"I know."

She glanced down at her calendar and, seeing no impending calls she'd forgotten, decided to deal with this nonsense straight away. When she looked up, she saw him focused on her blouse. "Josh?"

He blinked. "Sorry. I was zoning. It's been a tough day. Nothing like what you've done, I'm sure. But for a newbie, it's a lot to take in."

She nodded. "Jeff helping you?" The guy was an idiot as a human being, but a decent accountant.

"Yeah. He's great." He cleared his throat. "Told me to steer clear of you. That you eat men for breakfast, lunch, and dinner."

She grinned. "Yeah, I do. Listen to Jeff. Now get out of here and get back to work. I'll handle the hens clucking around you."

He chuckled and stood. "Thanks, Vanessa. I owe you."

"Do your job, and we'll call it even."

He nodded and left, closing the door softly behind him.

She rubbed her temples, not needing to deal with this on top of everything else today. "Gotta love the first quarter crunch." Corporate taxes gave her such a headache. Her phone rang, and she picked it up. "Vanessa Campbell."

"Hey, Vanessa. It's Bill. I had Irene check your appointments. She booked you and John for the fifth, which is next Friday. That's the soonest he can fit you in. In the meantime, he's sending a courier with some business vitals we need to familiarize ourselves with, in addition to the e-file I'm forwarding to you. I'm putting you on as account manager." He paused. "Are you okay with that?"

"It's a huge client. Yes, I'm fine." More than fine. If she took good care of them, she'd make partner for sure, no question.

"Good." He let out a breath. "I was worried for a minute. John seemed pretty taken with you."

"It was one date and all he did was talk about himself. I hadn't thought I'd ever see him again, honestly. But I'm good at my job. Don't worry that I'll muck it up by sleeping with the client. Trust me. That's *never* going to happen."

He laughed long and hard. "And that's why we love you, Vanessa. You call 'em like you see 'em."

"I do indeed, Bill." Then saying to hell with it, she gently laid into him for mollycoddling his nephew. He realized his error immediately and promised to do better. After she hung up, she rose and cracked her knuckles. "Your turn, Dana."

—◦◦◦—

She spent the next few days working until she grew bleary-eyed, trying to take care of their current clients while familiarizing herself with the Bellemy account. She'd done her stint as a staff and senior accountant, had bypassed manager straight to senior manager. Though she'd been honest with Cam about thinking Bill might promote her to partner when McNulty retired, the thought still boggled the mind, because it normally took a lot longer than seven years to get to partner. Like maybe ten to fifteen.

She glanced around and saw no one but herself and the cleaning crew in the office. Sunday afternoon and she had nothing better to do than work, despite Bill ordering everyone to take the weekend off. Yeah, fast tracking had its share of sacrifice. Stretching and deciding she'd had enough for the day, she left in her workout gear and headed for the gym.

So busy the past week she'd skipped her workouts, she now felt an urge to run and not stop. As usual, when she took her nose from her computer, her thoughts streamed to Cameron and what he must be doing. She hadn't spoken much with her roommates, so she had no idea how Beth and James's separation was going. Part of her missed the camaraderie she used to have with Abby and Maddie. But with them having solid men in their lives and her burdened with work, she hadn't had time to feel lonely.

At the gym, she quickly worked up a sweat. She'd just finished her crunches and leaned back for a good stretch when John Willington loomed over her.

"Hey, Vanessa. Haven't seen you here in a while."

She nodded. "John. Been catching up on my new client." She spared him a grin. "Bellemy Tech is impressive."

He sat next to her and lay back, linking his hands behind his head. He seemed to be there to exercise, not flirt with her, and she relaxed. "Yeah. Great company." He paused. "My dad started it."

Somehow they hadn't gotten to that during their one and only night out. He'd mentioned his million-dollar house in Green Lake, his cabin in Tahoe and his beach house in St. Croix, his job as a tech specialist, and then a rundown of the things that interested *him*. Nothing about the name of his company or that Daddy owned it.

"Nice." What else did one say to a statement like that? Congratulations?

"Yeah. My sisters and I all work there. Company's been doing great with new processor chips."

"I read that in the press release you gave us. Don't worry. We'll keep you in compliance."

"I have no doubt." *Okay. There.* She noted the direction of his gaze, on her legs, and showed him she'd witnessed his study with a raised brow.

He grinned, unrepentant. "Hey, what can I say? You're beautiful."

"Thank you." *I know.* "I'll see you on Friday." With that, she rose and walked away, not willing to waste her precious free time on John. She'd been immersed in his company for days. She'd see him on Friday and be done. For all that he hadn't made a pass, something about him unnerved her. She didn't trust that happy-go-lucky grace he'd shown with her unspoken rejection.

As she made her way toward the juice bar in the back, lingering with no desire to go home to an empty house, she ordered a vitamin smoothie and sat at the bar.

"Hey, Vanessa. What's shakin'?" Cameron sat next to her, his T-shirt damp and his dark hair plastered to his forehead. One of the few men she knew who didn't smell overly ripe after working out. Oddly enough, evidence of his hard work made him sexier.

She immediately relaxed. "Well, stranger. How are you doing?"

"Not nearly as good as I should be." He groaned and sipped his drink, what smelled like coffee. "My father is driving me nuts."

She drank her vitamins, thirsty for more than juice— for more of Cameron McCauley. When she said nothing, just sat listening, he poured it out.

"God, Vanessa. For the first few days we didn't talk much. A good thing. He's been working hard, and I've been hustling to find myself a new office."

"Did you find anything?"

"Just signed the papers yesterday." He told her the area and she nodded. As suspected, Cameron had money to afford looking at that primo section downtown.

"So now I can escape to work," he continued. "Well, next week I can escape to work. I'm currently having the office decorated."

"Using Maddie?" Her interior designer roommate.

"Of course." He frowned. "Flynn keeps telling her to charge me full price."

"If you're leasing that office space, you can afford it."

He shrugged. "Yeah, but doesn't mean I have to." He sighed.

She felt for him, knowing his grief had nothing to do with Maddie's prices and everything to do with his parents. "Is life with your dad that bad? You look stressed."

"I am." He looked at her, and she saw his exhaustion. "When I pulled everything on the East Coast to consolidate out here, it was with the intention of making this my home base. Which I still intend to do. But if my father continues to make his stupid comments and gripe about what I eat, wear, buy, and do, I might lose it. Seriously."

"Cameron?" She put her hand on his shoulder, concerned.

"I'm thinking I get twenty-five to life for manslaughter. It would be a slaughter, I promise you. He's big, but I'm quick."

She pulled her hand away and grinned. "Idiot."

He snorted. "It's either laugh or cry, and let me tell you, James McCauley can really make you cry."

They both paused to drink. Then she asked the question she'd wanted to know. "Any idea on why they separated?"

"I have a vague idea. Dad won't talk to me except to grunt or complain. Mike's handling him. Poor bastard. When I talked to Mom, I caught the gist."

"And?"

"Nosy, aren't you?"

"Oh, come on. I live through your family. The Flynn and Brody drama. Who's setting Mike up with which woman, and now your parents. I know, I'm terrible." Again, truth. "But considering my life consists of financial controls and investments for decreased tax liability on a much lower level than yours, and that I haven't run in nearly five days, you can see I'm standing on my own ledge."

"Yeah?" His gaze narrowed. "You okay? I saw you talking to your buddy earlier."

She grimaced. "He's not my 'buddy.' We went to dinner once." She lowered her voice and leaned in, conscious John might have friends close by. "He's now a client. Bellemy Tech."

Cameron whistled. "Nice."

"Yeah. He wants me to head the account, which my boss agreed to. I'm supposed to meet him Friday to discuss specifics." She hadn't mentioned her feelings to anyone at work, not even her friends, not wanting to sound paranoid. But for some odd reason, she knew she could talk to Cameron. He wouldn't judge her, not for this. "I get a weird vibe from him."

He straightened. "Weird how?"

"I don't know. It's just... It would be totally stupid to think he came to our accounting firm just to be with me. We're the best in town. Companies as big as Bellemy don't hire people to get their staff dates. But John specifically wanted me to head the account. Again, I am the best, but it would make more sense for either of my bosses to head things. I'm a senior manager, but they're big money."

"Hmm."

"Yeah. He and I are supposed to meet for dinner to discuss work. I preferred my office, even his, but he said he only has time in the evening." She looked into Cameron's deep blue eyes, feeling foolish. "I'm being overly sensitive because of one lousy date, aren't I?"

"What does your gut tell you?" he asked softly.

Cameron's intensity soothed her, because in all the time she'd known him, he'd never shrugged her off or acted as if she were having a "Van-zilla moment," as her roommates were fond of saying. He took her seriously.

"It tells me to watch him."

"Then listen to it. You're a smart woman, Vanessa. Trust your gut." He finished his coffee. "Now how about I walk you to your car?" He leaned in to bring her to her feet.

When his face neared hers, she whispered, "What are you doing?" Cameron had pulled a fast one with that kiss in her kitchen, in private. Like her, he had never seemed big on public displays of affection.

"He's looking over here," he murmured. "Why don't you kiss me and show him you're not available?"

"Oh." *Hell.* She sounded disappointed. When he blinked and gave her a slow smile, she knew he'd heard and discerned her feelings. "Shut up."

She kissed him quickly, but the lingering warmth remained. Stupid libido.

"Great. Come on." He walked out of the gym with his hand at the small of her back. They passed John, and she nodded at him.

He nodded back, a frown on his face.

At her car, Cameron waited while she unlocked it and got in. Then he leaned down as she powered down the window. He had to be freezing in the cold garage, especially in those silky nylon shorts. The shorts that outlined his every muscle and bulge. *Oh wow*. She felt hot.

"Yeah?" she growled, needing to leave before she did something stupid, like pet him.

"Yeah?"

She cleared her throat. "I meant, thanks for walking me down."

"So your dinner on Friday. Where are you meeting?"

"At the Four Seasons."

"What time?"

"Seven. Why?"

"Well, I thought I'd give myself a nice break from Dad. Maybe I'll get a room there Friday night. I'll have dinner around seven or eight, so before you leave, you might bump into me."

She flushed. "You don't have to do that."

"I'll meet a client for drinks and write it off. How's that?"

She chuckled. "Drinks, huh? Glad I'm not your accountant."

He grinned. "I'll make it all official, don't worry. But a luxury hotel room overlooking the water, what's not to like?" He straightened, waved good-bye, and walked back toward the stairwell.

As she drove away, she sighed to herself. *Cameron McCauley—what's not to like?*

Chapter 4

CAM SPENT THE NEXT FEW DAYS WORKING ON HIS PLAN to woo Vanessa. The coming week would make the perfect stage to slowly seduce her. He'd be there for her, showing support. Maybe tempt her into a drink or two. Then move on to a real date. That's if he didn't truly go to jail for killing his father first.

"Boy, you got anything that tastes like real meat?"

With the refrigerator door open, he could only see half of his father's torso, waist, and legs. If only his father's invisible head would mute the man as well.

"How about the bacon, made from *real* pork?"

"Yeah, but it's apple smoked and has pepper all over it. I think those are peppercorns. *Peppercorns.*" James snorted. He was a big man with a hearty laugh and a giving heart that had room for anyone needing him—except his youngest son.

From birth, it seemed Cam could do no right by the man. He'd heard the story of how he'd cried when his father had first held him. How he'd peed on the man, tried to hit him with a wiffle ball bat many times as a toddler, and how he never gave his father the time of day while growing up. In *elementary school*, but God forbid his father let the stories die.

Cam had been intimidated. His father always seemed so overwhelming. For all that his boys took after him, James had handed down his personality to Mike, Flynn, and even Brody, but not Cam. Cam took after his mother. More cerebral in his pursuits, quieter, deeper.

He had that McCauley competitive edge though. And the temper, though his was slow to boil. Case in point, almost two weeks of living with his father and he hadn't brained the man.

His father closed the fridge with an unnecessary slam, then foraged for snacks in the pantry. He found pretzels and some cheese chips he'd bought himself—because Cam wouldn't touch the death traps filled with excess sodium and things he couldn't pronounce—and sat next to Cam on the couch.

They sat in silence while the Lakers played on TV.

"So." James finished chewing and spoke again. "You and I haven't talked much about the situation with your mom."

Much? Try at all. "No."

"You okay with it?"

Cam turned to regard his father with incredulity. "You're kidding, right?" Rage boiled to the surface, an anger he hadn't known had been brewing. "How the fuck can I be okay with you and Mom splitting up? What did you do?"

His father's brows drew close. "Me? Why do you think I'm at fault?"

Something in his father's expression cautioned Cam not to push, that he wouldn't like what he found if he continued his quest for answers. He ignored the warning. "I know Mom. That woman loves you like crazy. She's torn up about this. Really hurt. So I know this is you." His brothers might be too in awe of their father, suffering from longtime hero worship, but Cam had always seen his dad as human. A loving and caring man, but a gruff person with his share of issues.

"You know, I'm not taking our separation that easily either," James answered in a low growl.

"Yeah, right." Cam snorted. "You're still working with Mike, laughing it up with your beer buddies, and shoving your face full of whatever crap you want now that Mom's not here to tell you no."

"You mean not here to nag me." James glared. "Yeah, I work with Mike. We have a fucking business to run. What? I'm supposed to sit and cry my eyes out like a pussy because your mother can't—" His father broke off and swore.

"Can't what?"

"I'm *trying*."

"To what? Have a heart attack before you hit sixty-one?" He looked at the bad carbs around his father, still not sure how James maintained such a trim form. "Is it another woman?"

"No."

But his father's cheeks colored.

"*Oh my God*. You're cheating on Mom?" Cam stood, horrified to be right.

"Boy, it's not like that. Damn it." James stood as well and dumped half a bag of chips on the couch. Making a mess, as he apparently did wherever he went.

"I can't believe you. Mom has always been faithful to you."

"Shut your mouth for two seconds and listen. I'm not cheating on your mother."

Relieved, Cam nodded.

"Not exactly."

"*What?*"

"I've been faithful to that woman for thirty-six years. Never once stepped out on her, and trust me, I had opportunity." His dad's eyes glowed with anger. "For over three decades I did whatever that woman wanted. I left the Corps, took up with my own father in the construction business when I'd really wanted to go to school. Yeah, I wanted to study. Scary shit, huh?"

Cam just stared.

"I did for my family, because that's what a real man does. We settled here near your mother's people. Not mine. My folks are in Wisconsin, but you know that. Everything I've done has been for your mother in one way or the other, and I'm tired of it."

"That's crap, Dad." Cam didn't like his father's tone. His dad's…resentment. "You're telling me you've been unhappy for so long and none of us knew? This is insane. A midlife crisis, right? Or is it about you getting a piece of ass? Something on the side?" He wanted to vomit. "I looked up to you."

"Bullshit. Credit me with some intelligence. You never looked twice at me for anything. Not like your brothers."

"Why? Because I refuse to swing a hammer or a wrench for a living?"

"There's nothing fucking wrong with that!"

"I didn't say there was!" What the hell? "Let's stick to topic, shall we? Who is this other woman?"

"There is no other woman. Shit. I never should have talked to you in the first place. Knew you wouldn't understand."

"Why? Because I'm a *Nancy*? A momma's boy?"

"Yeah, that's right." James snorted. "Jesus, Cam.

You're still pissed off about shit I said when I was teasing? And you wonder why we never 'talk,'" he ended in air quotes. "I can't say boo without you crying about hurt feelings."

Cam couldn't believe his father could be this dense. So wrong about everything. No matter what his father thought, Cam did look up to him. He reined in his temper and said in a calm, controlled voice, "Dad, despite what you think, I do respect you. You taught me how to be a man. How to treat a woman. To go for what I want in life. I see—*saw*—your marriage to Mom as something to emulate. That I might one day aspire to have that kind of loving relationship. You're really going to throw that all away on someone else?"

His father stared at him, big bad James McCauley clenching his fists and breathing hard, a spark of fury in his berserker blue eyes. Looking like a meaner, older version of Mike. But instead of answering, he turned on his heel, stormed to the closet to grab his coat, and slammed out of the condo.

Cam stared at the mess on the couch left in his father's wake. "*Fuck*."

—⁂—

James McCauley hadn't been so mad in…well, probably since the last real argument he'd had with Beth. She and Cam were so much alike. The boy and he butted heads, no two ways about it. Mike, James understood. Hell, looking at Mike was like looking at himself as a younger man. And Flynn and Brody, two better, more capable men he'd yet to meet. But Cam. The little prick.

Part of him wanted to take his son over his knee and

spank the shit out of him for such disrespect, twenty-nine or no. But a bigger part of him felt so proud that he'd raised such a refined, together young man. A financially successful, physically and emotionally secure adult. One who thought his father could actually cheat on his mother.

Steaming, angry because it felt better to feel rage than hurt, he walked through the snow-cleared sidewalks to a coffee shop on the corner and stopped in for a cup of joe. As he waited, he realized he hadn't stopped in to his favorite place in a while. The coffee shop on the corner in Queen Anne, where the barista, Amelia, always met him with a smile and a cup of his regular. She had a pretty grin and a spark in her eyes for him, a man a good fifteen years her senior.

No, James wasn't cheating, but not for lack of wanting. At the thought, he tucked his hands in his pockets and mumbled his order, not making eye contact with the young thing behind the counter.

After paying for his coffee—black, not fancied up—James sat in the back, away from the other patrons.

What had seemed like some harmless flirtation months ago had turned him on his ear. A good-looking woman seemed genuinely interested. He'd been told by many women that he looked good for his age, that if he weren't married, they'd have made a play. But it had been so long since he'd felt like a real man. Someone attractive, sexual.

Amelia always had a welcoming smile and an extra something she'd give him in the mornings that he never had to pay for. At home, Beth would have nothing for him but criticism. She'd meet with her retired friends, those hoity-toity jerks from the English department of that stupid college where she used to work. They'd always looked down on him.

Through the years spent attending functions with her, he'd suffered in silence, putting on a big smile. Beth would gently prod him about returning to school to get his degree. More work on top of the hellacious construction hours he put in daily. To make ends meet and support his family, he'd worked overtime, holidays, and taken on the odd project. All to make his beautiful wife happy. And for what? So that she could continually try to make him *better*? Into something he could never be, a grown-ass Cameron?

She'd succeeded with that one. The boy had never liked his old man. James had tried. He'd teased and cajoled to toughen the boy, not wanting Cam to be bullied the way he'd been when younger. He'd included all his boys in family games and outings, finding common ground with Flynn and Brody, Mike, and even young Colin, the apple of his eye.

But Cam remained distantly out of reach. Like his untouchable mother.

Sex with Beth had never been a problem. Until she'd started holding back. The past few years she'd withdrawn, slowly. Until the last few months when they barely touched. A peck on the cheek, a graze of her hand against his. What the hell did a man have to do to get his wife naked nowadays?

He sighed and felt his age creeping close all over again when an attractive young woman looked right past him as she headed toward the back. He grimaced at his coffee, at a loss.

What was a man to do when he'd spent his life trying to make his wife love and respect him, only to find it all for nothing?

—⁓—

Vanessa had dreaded Friday's approach. Though Cam had said he'd be at the hotel on business, she didn't like the thought he'd come for her, because then she'd owe him for the help. Better for both of them *when*—not *if*—they eventually came together, that they entered the playing field on equal footing. And then there was John to consider.

He'd called once to confirm their meeting in the hotel's dining room. Where candlelight and views of Elliot Bay set such a professional atmosphere. She snorted. *Yeah, right.*

Dressed in a black business suit with an A-line skirt that hit her at the knee and a stylish jacket over an ivory silk blouse and smoky hose, she thought she gave the right impression. She wore her hair pulled back in a severe bun, her heels high but not hooker-high, and walked smartly into the dining room of the hotel. After giving her name to the maître d', she clutched her leather briefcase and called on her inner strength to take charge of the meeting.

The head waiter took her to the table where John already sat. John stood and waited until she sat before seating himself once more. To her annoyed dismay, she hadn't passed Cameron or seen him in the dining area. Not that she needed him there. Not to do her job.

She pasted on a smile. "Hello."

She had to admit John wore a suit well. He had

intelligence and an appealing aesthetic, if one were into pretty boys. Vanessa had never been into surface attraction, which made her fascination with Cameron all the more perplexing. Yet underneath that handsome veneer, she knew he had actual substance.

But as she scanned the room, she noted he hadn't seen fit to keep his word. He was nowhere in sight.

Ignoring her inner whine, she made small talk with John and got right down to business. After a lovely meal, a glass of wine, and the rudiments of what she could do for Bellemy Tech, she sat back to see him staring at her.

When he continued to say nothing, she bluntly asked, "What?"

He smiled. "Such charm, Vanessa."

She chuckled. "I'm sorry. We've eaten, we've signed contracts. I thought we had your business."

"Pending gross negligence, you'll be fine."

"Gee, thanks."

He grinned. "So what are your plans for the evening?"

Talk about jumping in with both feet. "I was so busy concentrating on this meeting, after we conclude our business, I'm going home to get a good night's rest."

"So I've been on your mind so much I've exhausted you? I'm flattered."

"Don't be." He appeared taken aback. "I meant that I give this kind of attention to all our clients. No one suffers for holidays or sick leave. We work weekends, holidays, whatever it takes to make the client happy."

He relaxed and toyed with the stem of his glass. "Whatever it takes?"

Ugh. The sticky situation she'd known was coming. She wanted to be free to be herself and tell him point-blank, *"No way in hell, Slick."* But this would be her first big client on her path to a partnership. Bill was counting on her.

"Whatever it takes *within reason*, of course," she smoothly added.

"Let me be blunt, Vanessa."

Thank God. "Please do."

"I want you. You're beautiful, smart, and I thought we had chemistry the last time we went out." He paused. "Obviously something went wrong, because you never returned my calls."

"Not true. I messaged you back after that first text."

"You said *Thank you for a nice night.* Nothing else," he said wryly.

"Yes. Nothing else."

"Why?"

Could the man be kidding? "Seriously?"

"Yes. Why? I've got money, I'm handsome, and I'm good in bed."

She studied him, wondering if he could be that dense. "You talked about yourself all evening. You didn't once ask me what I thought or felt about anything." He'd asked for honesty. "I found you narcissistic."

"Oh?" He smirked at her and leaned closer. In a low voice, he answered, "I find you beautiful but cold. It intrigues me to think I might be able to thaw you out. As for why I never asked you anything, I don't care. I didn't ask for a date because I wanted to talk."

She sat in stunned silence while the waiter arrived to clear their plates. Once he left, she gathered her composure. "I'm really glad we never had more than one date, in that case. Imagine how awkward this dinner could have been," she said drily. *What an egotistical ass*.

"I'm just being honest. I thought you liked that?"

"You know, I was impressed by your candor. Part of me still is, while the other part is grossly offended."

He huffed. "This isn't because of that guy at the gym, is it? I know you're single. I asked around."

"Whether I am or not is irrelevant." She relied on her ability to detach herself from the situation and answered with *cold* logic. "The fact of the matter is we had one date and didn't suit. Not money, appearance, or the size of a man's cock is a factor in who I decide to fuck. Honest enough for you?"

He nodded, his eyes wide.

"We're going to be working together. I'm not arrogant enough to assume you asked for my company's services because you're hard up for a woman. However, if this situation makes it awkward for us to do business, you're of course free to opt out of the contract for our agreed fee and go elsewhere for assistance. Or you could assign someone else as your liaison when dealing with me. It's up to you."

He shook his head and smiled. "You really are one cold bitch, aren't you?"

She blinked. "Do you really want to ruin your company because you managed to mess with the wrong woman? I don't mix business and pleasure. Ever. We don't do that at McNulty, Peterman. Which is one of the reasons why we're the number one firm in the city."

He stared at her in silence, and she wondered if he could hear her heart racing as she did her best to appear calm and not at all frazzled by the fuckhead she wanted to kick really, really hard.

"This has been educational." His lips twisted in a half smile.

Educational. The story of her cold, emotionally unfulfilling life. "I'm glad."

He laughed. "You're something else, Vanessa Campbell. If you ever change your mind…"

"I won't."

"Even if I were to think about pulling my business and taking my assets elsewhere?"

"Do what you need to. I won't change my mind."

He sighed. "Fine. I think it best for all involved if you deal with my assistant Henry from now on. But I want you to know there's no one I'd rather have working for us than your company, and you specifically. I trust you, and I can see why your references are so amazing." He stood, and she stood as well. She was more than ready to leave.

"One more thing."

"Yes?" she asked, gripping her briefcase tight. If this asshole expected her to pay the tab, she'd tell him to stick that bill up his—

"I like Jameson's Gym. Can I assume it won't be awkward running into you there?"

"Not if you don't mind that you couldn't buy your way up my skirt." She couldn't help at least one zinger.

He snorted. "I'll survive. See you around." He walked away.

Not planning to stick around for another agonizing round of *educational*, *cold*, or *frigid* adjectives in case he came back, she sought the lounge around the corner. After making sure John hadn't decided to do the same, she ordered a drink and sat at a table, alone, facing the bay.

She wanted to cry. God, what was wrong with her? She'd handled that jerk with aplomb. He'd tried to buy her, like she was a whore. There were thousands more Johns where he'd come from. Dicks who thought they could snap their fingers and get whatever they wanted because they had money or looks or fame. But the references to her being nothing more than a body for him to use to slake his lust hurt. He'd seen her around and wanted a date. But not to talk. Not to get to know her. A lot like the many other men she'd dated in her life. They'd been drawn to her beauty then complained of her coldness. She either moved too fast or not fast enough. After the sex, she never satisfied anyone.

Least of all herself.

"Hey there." Cameron sat next to her, dressed in a black suit and a white shirt unbuttoned at the throat. Like John, he had looks and money. And the warmth so many women appeared to be looking for in a relationship.

"Hey." She drank, finishing her glass.

"Need another?"

"Sure."

He signaled to a waitress. "Another…"

"Diva in Pink."

"Diva in Pink and a Scotch." He turned to her. "What's in that?"

She shrugged. "The bartender said it's like a cosmopolitan on steroids."

Cameron nodded. He looked so handsome, so…together. Why the hell was he sitting with her?

"I caught your conversation with the jackass." The ice in his eyes froze her to the spot.

She stilled.

"Nicely handled, by the way. Personally, I'd have gone for his throat. That or his tiny, tiny dick. Yeah, saw him in the steam room once. You didn't miss anything there."

She snorted with amusement.

"But you handled it with class. I was proud of you. Don't know that I could have done that."

A ball of something heavy sat over her chest. She rubbed it and blinked hard.

"Vanessa?"

The waitress brought their drinks, but Vanessa stared past hers at the ocean, watching the waves roll. A rhythm of swells coming and going. But never staying.

"Cameron? Can I ask you something?"

"Sure," he answered softly.

"Do you like talking to me?" She didn't want to see his expression when he answered, didn't want to know what he really thought. For all that he could get on her nerves, Cameron was a kind man. He would tell her what she wanted to hear.

He didn't speak. She heard him take a sip and then he said, "Look at me."

She forced herself not to feel and turned. "What?"

His tender expression confused her, because she wanted to hold on to it as much as she wanted to look away. "I love talking to you. I think the first thing about you that attracted me, aside from those long, long legs, was your mind."

She sighed. "Right."

"No, really." He smiled warmly. "I live with people who think I'm both a nerd and a moron, which shouldn't actually be possible. My family treats me like a girl half the time—no offense. And my job sounds interesting to women until they ask me about it, and I tell them. They don't want to hear me. They just want to look at these fine features and get a crack at my stellar skills in bed." He leaned closer. "You would understand if you'd *really* tangled with my tongue."

She found herself smiling when moments ago she'd wanted to cry.

"I know what it's like to be misunderstood. Trust me, I've been living with my personal demon for almost two weeks now. And I've never felt more alone or useless in my life."

"I'm sorry." She knew how hard family could be. "My own parents and I never talk. They don't do birth-days or holidays or... Hell, they don't do fun. Never have. If it wasn't for Aunt Michelle—Maddie's mom—I'd probably be a sociopath. Or so Maddie likes to say."

He laughed. "Maddie's so dramatic. She's cute, but if I had to put up with that roller coaster of emotions all the time, I'd shoot myself."

"I *know*." She sipped her drink and watched Cameron's throat as he swallowed his. Why she found that sexy she couldn't say.

"Vanessa..." He paused. "This isn't going to sound right. But I'd like to continue our conversation in private. Would you like to come up to my room?" Before she could answer, he hurried to say, "I have a suite. We'll sit in the living area. Clothes on. Straight up—this isn't a pass."

Even if I want it to be?

"I could use someone to talk to, and I think you could too. What do you say?"

Chapter 5

CAM WAS NERVOUS. NORMALLY WITH A DATE, HE experienced sexual desire, a flutter of eager anticipation, not uncomfortable anxiety. Vanessa was different.

When he'd overheard that dipshit talking to her as if she were nothing more than a toy to service him, he'd wanted to pound the guy until he lost those bright white teeth. Cam's table along the wall had been close enough to overhear but discreet enough not to be seen in case dickwad had remembered him from the gym.

Dickwad's comment, "I know you're single"—that had really bothered him. Cam didn't want men thinking Vanessa was available. He wanted her off the market, clearly labeled as *his*.

He hated the vulnerability in her eyes as she stared out his balcony windows at the ocean. He'd turned on the light in the far corner of the room, enough to give the room some illumination without being overpowering. But he could still see the hurt she tried to hide.

"Nice view," she murmured.

"Yeah. The clients like it."

She turned to him and raised a brow.

"You made me feel guilty about writing off this suite for pleasure, which of course I'd never, ever do." When she snorted, he laughed. "So I arranged for three of my newer clients to meet me here in the suite to talk strategy. It was worthwhile, trust me. Since I don't yet have a working office, I'm keeping this for the week-end. My getaway from the old man." He raised his glass and took a sip, aware her glass remained nearly full. "Not thirsty?"

"Not in the mood to get drunk. Alcohol is a depressant, and I don't need the help."

"He really got to you, didn't he? Want me to go smash his face in?"

She blew out a breath. "Yes and no. I wanted to be the one to kick his balls through the roof of his mouth. But he's not worth it."

"You got that right." He sat down next to her. "Talk to me. What's really going on?"

"No. Tell me about your dad. Let me get back to you on my psychoses."

He shrugged. "Sure. In a nutshell, my father has bitched about every goddamn thing in my condo he could. My food is gross, my décor something that makes him more than uncomfortable, and I don't get the requisite sports channels Mike does."

"So why the hell doesn't he move in with Mike?"

"Trust me. I wanted to tell him to leave, but Mom wants to be able to see Colin without running into Dad."

"Ah."

"Yeah." He swallowed more Scotch, wishing for a heady buzz and only feeling the mellow release of whis-key. "We had a huge blowup yesterday and haven't talked since." He sighed. "I think he's cheating on Mom."

"*What?*"

"Yeah. He didn't come out and admit it. Made a lot of bullshit excuses about all he's sacrificed in his lifetime, how everything's been for Mom. Then he went off on me like I don't respect his work. When did I ever say I hated his job?" He was baffled as to the man's thought processes. "I would have thought he was just deflecting except I swear he seemed really hurt."

"Well, you've said you and he don't have that much in common. Maybe you aren't the only one bothered by that."

"I guess." He nursed the thought. "I just don't see why he and Mom can't work things out, talk to each other."

"Have they tried marriage counseling?"

He snorted. "My father? You have met James McCauley, haven't you? The man who knows everything about everything?" Was it his imagination, or did she flinch a little? "What? If you were in a relationship, say married, and you were having problems, wouldn't you seek professional help?"

"I would hope so. That seems like a rational and logical recourse. But then, I don't know that I'd want to share my personal problems with a stranger."

"Not even to make your marriage work?" He set down his glass and caught some stray blond hair that had escaped from her bun. He had no idea if she did it on purpose or not, but that hairstyle dared a man to muss it up and take it all down. To run his fingers through it and drag her face closer for a kiss.

She swallowed hard. "I, ah, I can't say. Never been married."

He scooted closer, until their thighs touched, and she turned to better face him. "You ever think you'll marry?" he asked.

"Maybe." She looked glum. "My problem is I have

high standards, and I refuse to lower them just to have a baby or marry because I'm getting old."

He let her hair go and frowned. "Old? How old are you?"

"Twenty-eight."

He snorted. "Yeah, you're ancient. Hell, Vanessa. I'm twenty-nine. What's the rush on marriage and kids? More people are waiting to commit until they're older anyway. Financially it makes sense. Kids are expensive."

"I've heard."

He settled his hand on the back of the couch, near her shoulder. "You want to take off your jacket and relax?" He held up his hands, lest she get the wrong idea. "Or not. I swear I'm not making a move or anything. But I'm kind of hot." He shrugged out of his jacket. "Though I'm thinking it's the Scotch."

She shook her head. "Lightweight."

"Oh?"

"Hey, I'm driving home tonight. I need to stay sober. Besides, takes more than a few Diva in Pinks to sink me."

"Good. I respect a woman who can hold her liquor." He grinned. "I'm the same. Personally, getting falling-down drunk lost its appeal in college. And then only once or twice. I had priorities back then. Grades."

She nodded. "A job, scholarships, dean's list."

"Exactly. The guys used to make fun of me for being a dweeb, but I didn't pay a cent for school. Not to toot my own horn or anything."

"Toot away. You're among friends."

"I'm pretty financially set thanks to those grades and my continued effort to succeed."

"Good for you." She reached for her glass and

clinked it against his. They both sipped from their drinks before she said, "It's funny how your brothers tease you, when the four of you, five if you count your dad, are so much alike."

"How's that?"

"All of you are wildly successful in difficult careers. Plumbing? Construction? Finance? You're all your own bosses. Even Mike and James are partners, not employees."

"True. Hardheads. Mostly that's from my dad."

"Or your mom. I've spent enough time with Beth to know she's no one's pushover." Vanessa paused. "You think she knows about your dad and some 'maybe' other woman?"

"Yeah. I think so." He leaned his head back on the couch and closed his eyes. "What a mess. After that fight with Dad, I just felt worse. Like I'd kicked a puppy. A feral, mongrel, freakishly large dog, but a wounded one nonetheless."

"Man. Tough position to be in."

"Yeah." He sighed.

She sighed.

They sat together like that, so near they could have been cuddling. But they weren't. Two friends sharing tough times, and damn, but Cam felt closer to her than he'd ever felt to a woman not his mother. And he definitely had no maternal thoughts toward Vanessa. At all.

When he blinked his eyes open again, he saw that outside had turned dark and hours had passed. The clouds obscured the moon, so that only faint moonlight trickled over the water. Stars teased behind wisps of cottony indigo, while a bright blond head rested on his chest.

He ached from his uncomfortable position. He half-sat, half-slumped on the couch under Vanessa.

He didn't know whether to wake her, then thought she might get pissed if he didn't.

"Vanessa?" he whispered.

"Cam?"

The first time she'd shortened his name. In her husky voice, it sounded like a sexual request, and his body woke up as if he were on fire. She shifted against him, and his cock sprang to life.

"You awake?" he asked softly.

"Yeah. You nodded off, and I just felt so comfortable. I must have dozed a little, but I was debating whether to leave when you woke."

He stretched out under her on the couch and pulled her fully on top of him.

"Wow. You're pretty strong. I'm not that light."

He chuckled. "I like that about you. A strong wind won't blow all that muscle away." He rested his hand on her hip. Not a good idea, because he started rubbing her side, taken with the strong yet supple flesh of her waist.

"Cameron?"

"Yeah?"

She leaned up on her hands to look down at him, and to his satisfaction her bun had loosened, strands of hair caressing her face and making him think of a fallen angel out to seduce him into sin.

"Would you mind if I kissed you?"

He groaned. "I think I'll explode if you don't."

She lowered her mouth, and he grasped her hips to keep her right there, grinding against his groin while she feathered her breath over his lips. He arched up, prolonging the contact, before she pulled away.

"I don't think you understood me," she rasped. "*I* kiss *you*."

"Oh. Sure." He forced himself to lie back and take what she gave him, and it was so incredibly hard not to roll them over and consume her.

The kiss, when it came, started out tentative. Soft lips met his. Her tongue tunneled into his mouth and swept through like a whisper of heat, branding him with carnal need.

He rubbed her hips, unconsciously urging her against him as he rocked up, seeking her warmth. Her kiss deepened, and she slanted her mouth over his until he couldn't think past the need to sink inside her.

She tore her mouth away and trailed kisses to his ear. "You taste so good. Like Scotch and sex."

"Vanessa," he hissed as she tongued his ear and nipped his earlobe. He bucked, his cock harder than it had ever been in his life. "Take your shirt off. Let me see you. Let me feel you."

She leaned up, fitting her warm core directly against his erection. She had to inch her skirt up to spread her legs wider, and he nearly choked when he saw garters holding up her stockings.

"Tell me you're still wearing your heels," he demanded, hoarse.

She winked at him and nodded at her left foot since the other was hidden by the couch cushions.

"Fuck me," he swore.

"I intend to."

He whipped his gaze back to hers and watched as she

slowly discarded her jacket. Then her buttons, one by one, until her silk shirt hung open, showcasing a lacy white bra.

He wanted to devour her, but he didn't. *She'd* kissed *him*. This was her show. "You tell me what to do, and I'll do it." He nodded. "Anything you want. It's yours."

"Hmm. Where to start." She inched her shirt off until it pooled around her elbows. "Touch my breasts."

The desire in her eyes set him aflame. She wanted this, as much if not more than he did. She squirmed over him, and her nipples stood stiffly under her bra. He raised his hands to cup her and moaned with her, the feel of her under his palms exquisite.

"Vanessa, you're so beautiful." He thumbed her nipples, and she arched back, thrusting her chest out.

"Take it off," she rasped. "The bra."

He had it unfastened in seconds.

"Hmm. Someone has had practice." She smiled and slowly unbuttoned his shirt, spreading it so she could touch his chest.

He pushed her shirt off so he could get rid of the bra. And then he stared at the most perfect breasts in existence. Full, high, and tipped with small rosy nipples. "I want to suck your breasts. Suck them and bite them. Such pretty little nipples." He didn't recognize his own voice.

"Yes," she breathed and lowered herself to him.

When he took her nipple in his mouth, she cried out and ground against him. He licked and teased, feasting until she pulled back to give him the other. While he sucked one, he cupped and stroked her other breast to fullness.

"I want you in me," she whispered. "God, I need you inside me."

"Yeah," he mouthed around her nipple. "Up in you."

"Just you and me. No condom."

He froze and took his mouth away from her breast, his heart pounding with excitement. "You sure?"

"You clean?"

"Hell yeah. I always use a condom." But he didn't want to with her.

"Me too. But tonight, I don't know. I just… I want you inside me." She drew a breath and let it out in a rush. "I'm on the Pill. And I'm so wet. I want you now."

He groaned. "I'm going to come too soon."

She stilled. "Should I slow down?"

The uncertainty on her face pulled at him. "No. You're in charge. Whatever you want this time. But next time, I set the pace."

She relaxed and smiled. "Okay." She scooted back to move from the couch, then removed her skirt and panties, leaving her in just the garters, stockings, and heels.

"You look like a pinup. No, leave the hair. So fucking sexy."

She flushed, and damn but he fell hard. He'd known this Vanessa existed, but he hadn't thought to see her so soon. The sweet, shy woman buried under the take-charge honey who was hungry for what she wanted. She knelt by him and took off his shoes and socks, pushed off his shirt, then unbuttoned his slacks.

Instead of taking them off, she slid her hand inside his boxer briefs and closed her fingers around him. "You're so big."

"Yes. Oh shit. Vanessa," he groaned.

"And hard. And hot." She rubbed her thumb over his slit, and his eyes crossed. "And wet."

"And about to come if you don't put that sexy pussy over me."

"Not my mouth?"

He swore softly. "I'm only human. And I really, really need to fill you up before I come in your mouth. Trust me. Right now, if you were to blow me, you'd drown in me."

She chuckled. "It's so nice to know you care."

"You witch. Come on. I'm dying here."

She pulled his pants and underwear down and he kicked them off. Then she straddled him on the couch and lowered that hot, wet heaven over him.

They both moaned as they joined, her sheath clutching him tightly as she settled over him.

"*Vanessa*. Don't move."

"No?" She shifted.

"I'm gonna come. I want to wait."

"No. Come in me. Give it to me, Cam." She rose and fell hard, then rode him until he couldn't think.

He gripped her hips, palmed her breasts, and stared up at her while she watched him losing control.

"That's it. Come, baby. Inside me." When she twisted her hips and slammed particularly hard, he lost it. He reached between them to rub her clit as he came inside her, dimly aware of her grabbing his fingers and pushing harder against her flesh, of her body squeezing him tight.

"Cam, yes, *yes*."

He felt like one huge nerve, exposed and raw and quivering as he spent inside her. The perfect woman. His Vanessa.

She slumped over him, breathing fast. She raised her head and stared at him with wide eyes. "Holy fuck."

He grinned at her, then started laughing. She joined him, and they laughed so hard he had trouble breathing.

"Holy fuck," he repeated when he'd caught his breath. "So romantic. Yet so appropriate."

She smiled, a real grin that touched him deep inside. "Who knew you had it in you? And no, this is not where you make some juvenile remark about it still being in me."

"Damn. You take all the fun out of immaturity."

She snickered. "Jesus, Cam. I wish I would have known I was missing that. I would have let you have me much sooner."

"So it was all about proving myself, huh?" He stretched under her, pleased that they remained joined even though he'd started to soften. "How do you know that wasn't just a lucky orgasm?"

She blinked. "Lucky orgasm?"

"Yeah. Women can have those. You know, a guy gets lucky the first time. I should definitely prove I'm good for at least another round. Or two."

She pretended to consider him, tapping her chin. "You make a sound argument."

"The probability that it's not a fluke goes up the more we have sex. Make love. Fuck. Call it what you will, but I really think we need to continue this in the shower."

"Oh. Shower sex. I can do that."

"Honey, you can do anything. That's why I like you. You're so positive."

"Dork." She lifted herself off him and ran to the bathroom. "Ack. You made a mess!"

As long as that's all I made. He trusted Vanessa implicitly. She wasn't the kind of woman to take chances with her body or her future. He doubted she planned to conceive without a detailed list of how to go about it. Spontaneous sex with Cameron McCauley, sadly enough, would probably not appear on the list.

Yet some small part of him wondered *what if*. What would their child be like? What would Vanessa look like carrying a piece of him inside her?

"Well? Come on, Methuselah. I'm not getting any younger," she called out and started the shower. "Oh man. This is like a spa!"

He grinned. "Coming, dear."

"Ass."

He joined her in the shower and decided to show her how a real man pleasured a woman. After he got her nice and clean. With soap and water. And his tongue.

———

Vanessa couldn't believe she'd actually had mind-blowing sex with Cameron McCauley in the Four Seasons Hotel. Nothing seedy or deviant about their coupling. She hadn't expected anything raunchy—like Abby's sexy books. But she also hadn't expected he'd be so good at pleasing her. Her orgasm had satisfied, for sure. And his orgasm... Watching him come had been right up there with her all-time favorite images. A sunset over the ocean. A rainbow on a sunny day. The tigers at the zoo. Cameron in climax.

"Come on, lazy. Let me wash you." He pulled her closer and proceeded to shampoo her with a decadent scalp massage.

"Oh, wow. You should do this for a living." She moaned.

"But my happy endings are strictly for you."

She laughed and tried not to swallow too much water.

"Easy now. See? That's what it would have been like if I'd let you go down on me. Drowning."

"Yeah, right. You made a mess, but it wasn't a rainfall."

"Hey. Stop trying to unman me. I came hard."

"You busted a nut, all right."

He took his hands away and stared at her. "Quite the vernacular."

She laughed at him, amazed to be having so much fun after sex. Normally she didn't climax, or she did and just wanted her partner gone.

"Now your body." He held the soap up. "Arms up. I promise not to tickle."

He washed her with gentle hands, spending a large time between her legs and on her breasts.

"Um, Cam? You washed my left breast five times already. I think I'm clean."

"No. You're a very dirty girl." He sighed and continued to fondle her, enough that he aroused her again. "Have I told you how much I love your body? Your breasts fit in my hands. Not too big, not too small. Juuuusst right."

"Okay, Goldilocks."

He snorted with laughter, and she looked into his impossibly blue eyes and felt something deep give inside her.

"Now, Vanessa, I did say I'd get my turn."

She looked down and saw him half hard. "I don't think you're ready yet."

"You are. Now hold still." He angled her so that the shower hit her back and shoulders. Then he put down the soap and knelt between her feet.

"Wh-what are you doing?"

"What I want. It's my show now, sexy. Buckle up and hold tight."

Chapter 6

VANESSA STARED DOWN AT CAMERON IN SHOCK. HER breath caught as his mouth drew closer. He kissed her. There. In that place where few men had ever done more than waste her time. Yet a hint of his breath and she felt ready to go off like a rocket.

"So sweet," he murmured in that throaty voice that immediately put her in mind of hot, steamy sex.

The water rained over her back while Cameron licked her into another swell of arousal. The first man who made her experience more than tepid sensation, but full-out, tantalizing desire.

"Oh God, that's so *good*." She stroked his hair and placed a hand on his head, the other on his shoulder as he brought her to new heights. The notion that she stood there, unmoving, while he had his way with her body dumbfounded her. She couldn't remember the last time a man had taken charge in the bedroom—and she'd let him.

"Yeah, let go, baby. All over me." He groaned and gripped her hips as he licked deeper, penetrating with his tongue.

Not sure if she wanted that much intimacy, she squirmed and tried to ease back. "Cam, I…"

He pulled his head back and stared up at her, his blue eyes brilliant with lust and a touch of amusement that surprised her. "Uh-uh. You just stand there while *I* call the shots. Trust me. Do what I tell you and you'll come so hard you'll be crying my name."

She snorted, unable to help herself. "Yeah, right."

"Oh, challenge on." He smirked and focused back between her legs. He petted her, and her breath hitched when his fingers slid between her folds.

He leaned closer and licked her clit, and she shot up on her toes.

He nudged her legs wider. Then he fingered her folds apart and clamped his mouth over her clit. He sucked hard, tonguing the ripe bud and inserting a finger inside her, which he quickly withdrew, only to penetrate her again. The slow rhythm built as he sucked and nipped, his earthy moans and skilled mouth shoving her into a climax she hadn't expected, not after that first earth-shattering ride on the couch.

She cried out as she came, gripping his shoulders as he continued to lick her into spasms of delighted release.

He kissed his way up her body, and she couldn't miss the return of his erection. His lips found hers, and she wrapped her arms around his taut shoulders and thanked him without words for his generosity.

"Turn around," he whispered against her lips.

Knowing she'd aroused him boosted her already healthy ego. Healthy—thanks to Cameron. How could any woman not find herself desirable when touched with such urgency, such care? She turned to face the wall.

"You're so sexy. So hot." He ground his erection against her ass. "I need you again."

Need, not *want*. Semantics, but Vanessa liked to think he used the word as more than a coincidence. She loved the idea of being needed for herself, that she might have something to offer that was more than work-related. He'd made her come twice. In one night. And she hadn't once had to touch herself to get off. She more than wanted to repay him.

He pulled her hips back, and then he was there, thrusting into her wet heat.

"Fuck. So good," he crooned as he slammed the rest of himself inside her. The hard push rocked her forward, but his subsequent strokes, his breathless groans and muttered swears increased her ardor, leaving her less exhausted from her previous orgasm than she would have thought.

"Fuck me harder," she whispered. "Give it to me." Normally men liked her to talk sexy, but these words were for her. "I need it."

He obeyed, rutting with a fervent desire neither could miss. "Yes, yes, Vanessa. Baby, so good." He gripped her hips and ground into her. "I'm coming, *so hard…*" He shouted and shuddered inside her.

As if she hadn't been stupid once with unprotected sex, she'd gone for twice in one night.

And she couldn't have been happier.

Vanessa took birth control, a daily pill she never forgot. She'd never had sex without a condom before, with the exception of her first time with a fellow virgin.

But Cameron… A man who looked like a dream, who unselfishly saw to her pleasure first, had touched her in all the right places.

He continued to move inside her, a slow pull and push, until he finally withdrew.

"Left another mess," he said in a guttural voice, then cleared his throat. "But you know, I'm thinking it's probably safe now for me to come in your mouth."

"Always looking ahead." She laughed.

"Yep. Always looking for head."

She rolled her eyes. "There's that immaturity again."

"I'm due. Come on. You came hard." He turned her around and leaned against her, pushing her back against the cold wall tile. "All over my mouth. So sexy." He grinned and kissed her.

"Yeah." She sighed and wrapped her arms around his neck, returning the affectionate embrace. "So I guess that wasn't a lucky orgasm after all." To her chagrin, she felt fluttery. Like those idiot women who looked gooey-eyed at their partners in all those rom-com movies—like Maddie and Abby stared at their men. She wondered if Cameron saw her softening.

"No tensing up," he warned, apparently sensing her anxiety. "You earned some feel-good time after dealing with Mr. Smallest Dick of the Year."

She snickered.

"There. That's the mean little laugh I love to hear." He kissed her again, then nuzzled her cheek, and the affection went straight to her head. "Now before the water turns cold, let's dry off, order up some food, and make the rules you know you're dying to put in place."

Considering she'd been wondering how to go from tonight to tomorrow, his words made complete and utter sense. Yet she wasn't sure if she liked him knowing her that well. "Not sure what you mean." She cleaned herself once more, taking care to wash Cameron's mess away and feeling weird that she missed him being a part of her.

"Uh-huh." He turned off the water and left to get them two towels. He returned to the large glass stall and tossed one to her, then dried himself off. "Dry off before I'm tempted to go down on you again."

She flushed and watched him work the towel over himself, fascinated with his body. Such corded strength in his compact frame. Those legs, that ass, that... Even flaccid he seemed large to her. When he caught her ogling him and raised a brow, she quickly finished drying herself off and stepped out with him.

He handed her a plush hotel robe, and she gratefully put it on, suddenly feeling shy, which made little sense. Vanessa didn't do shy. Or embarrassed, or sensitive. Yet right now with Cameron, she felt all three. As she turned away to towel-dry her hair, he grabbed a matching robe from the small closet and put it on. Then he hung up his towel.

She nodded and hung hers next to his, her hair no longer sopping wet, but damp. He gestured for her to precede him into the living area. "Hungry?"

"Famished." Surprisingly. She noted the darkness outside. "But it's..." She glanced at the bedside clock. "Four a.m.?"

"So? They have twenty-four-seven room service."

"Oh." How decadent, to dine in this late. "Sure." She'd probably have to sell a kidney to afford a coffee, but the sumptuous idea of a late-night snack with Cameron after that incredible sex went straight to her head.

She sat next to him on the couch, hip to hip, and pored over the menu. They decided on two fruit and cheese plates and a bottle of wine to go with it.

"You have good taste," she said as he idly toyed with a strand of her wet hair.

"Yes, I do." He smiled at her and wiggled his brows when his gaze moved down to her chest.

She fought a huge grin and tried to look stern. "Cameron…"

"You need all three names. Say it like this." He infused his name with a deep bellow of authority. "*Cameron Thomas McCauley*."

"Nice."

"Yeah. Been hearing that my whole life." He shrugged. "And I was the good McCauley. Not like the other slobs I used to live with."

She smiled.

"How about you? Any brothers or sisters?"

"Nope. Just me."

"Wow. I can't imagine what that must have been like. I grew up waiting for the bathroom, wearing hand-me-downs, and fighting with my older brothers over just about everything. Even when I was trying to be good, one of them would suck me into a brawl. Usually Brody or Flynn."

"Very different from my childhood. It was mostly quiet. My parents always had their noses buried in a book, a thesis, or work. They're college professors."

"Oh?"

"Yeah. At a big university where they're allowed to work on their theories and proofs. I grew up surrounded by math and physics. Fun, fun, fun." She made a face.

He shrugged. "Hey, they could have been lit professors. Be thankful for small favors."

She laughed. "True." They fell into an easy silence. Cameron held her hair, studying it in the dim light, while she ran her fingers over his free hand, marveling at how much larger his palm was than hers, how graceful his fingers. For all that they stood close in height, he had much more muscle. And she'd never been more grateful for the differences between genders.

"This is nice," he said and looked into her eyes. "Being with you."

"Um, yes." She felt her cheeks heat. Stupid. "It is."

His slow smile warmed her all over again. "So you want to tell me the rules now?"

"Rules?"

"Please. After you finished screaming my name—"

"I don't recall screaming your name."

"—and after I had my wicked way with you, reason returned. We're a lot alike, you know. Rational, intelligent, concerned about tomorrow. Always looking ahead."

That flattering comparison she could live with. "And?"

"And you're no doubt wondering what tonight meant in terms of our relationship."

His cool detachment irked her. "Oh?"

"See? I even know that frosty tone. I somehow offended you without intending to." Far from looking abashed, Cameron grinned. It should be illegal to be so charming, handsome, and assured of his appeal. "Vanessa, I really like you. For more than the sex, though the sex is… The sex is something we need to do *a lot*. To get really, really good at it."

She smirked. "Uh-huh."

"I think we should try a few dates and see what happens."

"As in, we're dating."

"Isn't that what I just said?"

"Just you and me."

"Well, I sure the hell don't want to double with Flynn

or Brody anytime soon." He grimaced. "I love the guys, but they can be such jackasses."

"True." She worried her lower lip, then immediately stopped when she realized Abby did the same thing all the time when nervous. God forbid she take on her roommate's neuroses. "We enjoy each other's company, like the same foods, love to exercise, and we're far more intelligent than the people we live with."

"Exactly."

"Intelligence is important to me." She sounded like a babbling idiot, and the captivated look on his face made her feel even more moronic.

"Me too."

"So what if things don't work out? Not that I'm leaning toward anything long-term, but when Brody and Abby hit the wall, we didn't get along. You and I."

"Actually, we got along fine. You were the one with the bug up your ass. You were also in the wrong; you just refused to admit it."

"Excuse me—"

"But I forgive you."

"Forgive this." She shot him the finger.

Instead of volleying back an insult, he laughed, dragged her into his lap, and kissed her. "God, you make me so hard when you get mad."

"Cam."

He groaned. "And that. You always call me Cameron. But when I was inside you, you called me Cam. Like it's a pet name or something."

"You'd rather I called you something else?" She hadn't realized she'd been doing that.

"Knowing you, it would be *dickhead* or *Mr. Tiny*. I

don't need disparaging remarks about my cock, thank you very much."

She chuckled. "Why? Performance issues?"

"No. I just don't want you confusing me with your new client."

Her laughter deepened. "No worries there. You know, I still can't believe he had the nerve to talk to me like that."

"See? Now you're thinking about him again. Think about me." He kissed her, and the kiss turned from teasing to carnal in seconds. He broke away, breathing hard. "Damn. You really get to me."

"Yeah." She sighed, especially when his hand found its way into her robe and cupped her breast.

"So? We dating now or what? I mean, exclusively dating." He pinched her nipple.

She sucked in a breath and let it out with a shaky moan. "Do I get more of this if I say yes?"

He smiled. "Maybe. I'm thinking you get a gym partner, a running buddy, a sympathetic ear when your roommates get on your nerves, and more orgasms. Along with the golden opportunity to please me at my beck and call." At her look, he amended, "Or whenever our schedules mesh."

"Better." She leaned into his warmth, loving that he had no problem keeping eye contact while caressing her breast. Cameron always paid attention to her. Not just her body, but to Vanessa, the woman with a brain. "If I have another business function, can I take you?"

"Yeah." He shifted under her. "And when we have uncomfortable family gatherings at my parents' house, you have to buffer me from the hordes."

"I can do that. I'm good at putting people in their places."

"You are." He kissed her, but this time with a lingering softness. "You put me in my place right off. I respect that."

"Oh good. I'd hate for you to not respect me. Especially after tonight."

A knock sounded at the door.

"Why don't you get that while I try to hide my hard-on?"

She laughed and left him on the couch.

"Charge it to the room. I mean it," he growled.

"Like I'm going to argue that?" she said over her shoulder as she opened the door.

The waiter wheeled in a cart carrying the tray, and after depositing it on the table, he handed her the bill. She signed it and added a nice gratuity, to which the waiter nodded and left with a smile.

Vanessa turned and brought the tray to Cameron, setting it on the nearby table "So we eat this, then what?" She had to know.

Cameron didn't sigh, roll his eyes, or demand she relax. "Then we take another nap. You'll have to go home to change, and then we'll spend the day together. First, a workout at the gym. Then we'll go sightseeing."

She just looked at him.

"Or not. What would you like to do?"

"Well, after we work out, there's a string of foreign films playing downtown."

"Subtitles?"

"Yes."

"Not arty flicks?"

"No, a few new kung fu movies I've been dying to see."

"*Oh*. Count me in."

They smiled at each other.

Cam continued. "So we eat, we nap, you fellate me, and then I take you home so you can change."

"Fellate?" She raised a brow at his hopeful grin. "I'll *blow* you, Mr. Dictionary. On one condition."

"My first child? Done."

She snorted. "No. That you prove you aren't all about two lucky orgasms. I'm thinking they might have been flukes."

"Now Vanessa. No need to get mean. All you had to do was ask. Or beg. I like when you beg."

She frowned. "I don't beg. I might ask. Maybe." She gave him a mulish frown. "But I won't say please."

"Fine by me. Now pass the fruit. And the wine."

As they dined together, Vanessa knew she'd never had a better date—that wasn't exactly a date—in her life.

Vanessa spent what remained of her weekend playing. *Playing*. She hadn't been so carefree and smiling in… well, in forever. After Vanessa's time with Cameron ended, she spent Monday catching up and introducing herself to Henry, her new contact at Bellemy. Monday night, after working out alone since Cameron had work to do, she returned home to find Maddie and Abby gossiping at the kitchen table.

"Well, well. Van-zilla's back." Maddie grinned at her. "The smiling scourge of Seattle has returned."

Vanessa glanced at Abby, who shrugged and apologized. "Sorry. We've been trying to come up with better names for you. Maddie prefers Van-zilla, but I liked Scourge of Seattle. I like the alliteration. Adds some zing."

"Whatever." Vanessa headed for a bag of blue corn chips and sat down with her friends. "So what's new with you two? Pregnant yet?"

Abby choked on her water. "No."

"Not yet. We're waiting until after the wedding to start," Maddie said calmly. "How about you?"

Vanessa ate some chips, then answered, "Nope. I've always used birth control. We Campbells are all about safe sex."

"So you're having it then."

Abby and Maddie stared at her, as if mesmerized.

"Do we really need to have a kiss-and-tell moment?"

"Yes," Abby and Maddie said together.

"Fine. Cameron and I are dating."

Her roommates high-fived each other. "Hot damn." Abby punched Vanessa on the arm. "You sly dog. When did this start?"

"If you must know, this weekend," she said, feeling smug. "Right after I dealt with John It's-All-About-Me Willington." She told them about their conversation, gratified when her friends immediately took to anger on her behalf.

"What a dick," Maddie fumed. "Such a loser."

Vanessa laughed. "Cam said I was lucky. He saw John in the steam room. Said it wasn't a pretty sight."

"Good." Abby grinned. "So you missed the small fry, but landed a..."

"Great catch. A really, really big fish." Vanessa ate more chips, suddenly super hungry.

"Wow. It's like the McCauleys don't make duds. At least, not in bed. I wonder what Mike's like?" Abby mused. They stared at her, and she blushed. "Oh stop it. Not for me, you goofballs. I love Brody. I just wondered what he must be like… Forget it. No matter how I try to explain this, it's coming out all wrong."

Vanessa raised a brow. "Um, yeah it is."

"I'm just glad you can laugh when we talk about men. You were a little scary in your man-hater phase," Maddie said.

"Men are stupid." Vanessa shrugged.

"Is *Cam* stupid?" Maddie asked in that smarmy voice that always drove Vanessa nuts. Even as a kid, her cousin would get that smug tone in her voice and use it with unerring precision, landing on Vanessa's last nerve.

"He's a man, therefore he's flawed. However, he's not as idiotic as Brody or Flynn, and that's something to be proud of." She gave Maddie an overly wide grin.

"Witch." Maddie stuck her tongue out.

"Oh. That hurts. Not the tongue." Vanessa laughed at her. "You know, I still think you should have majored in theater in college, not interior design."

"Thanks so much for your unasked-for opinion."

Abby sighed. "Ding ding. Okay. Back to your corners." She ran a hand through her hair. "And to think I missed our girlie chats."

Vanessa smirked. "You missed me, you mean."

"The ego. It never quits." But Maddie smiled as she said it.

"So tell us about *Cameron*." Abby drew out his name. "Come on. You have to give us something."

Vanessa thought about his smiling eyes, his deep laugh, the hands that sent her soaring. And the keen intelligence and dry wit. She glanced up to catch a look between her roommates. "What?"

"Oh, nothing." Abby cut off whatever Maddie had been about to say. "So the Four Seasons, huh? I bet the room was nice."

"Oh yeah. A suite overlooking the water. Really classy."

Maddie perked up. "Hmm. Maybe I should have Flynn take me there for Valentine's Day."

"Speaking of that," Abby segued, "Brody and I have been talking about Bitsy. I mean, Beth." Only Brody called Beth McCauley by the cute nickname, the same name he'd been calling her since she'd pseudo-adopted him so many years ago. "This is her first Valentine's Day in over thirty years where she'll be alone. We were thinking of spending it with her."

After a pause, Vanessa said, "You know, you two probably have plans. Mike will be with Colin, I'm sure. Why don't I spend the night with her?"

"But what about you and Cam?" Abby asked.

She shrugged. "We're pretty new. Besides, we're keeping this casual. Low key. So I'll spend the night with her, and Cameron too, if he's not busy, and you guys go out like you were planning to."

"You sure?" Maddie asked.

"Yeah." Besides, this way she wouldn't be so nervous about her relationship progressing too quickly.

"Okay, then. If you're sure," Abby agreed. "You've got Beth. One other thing I wanted to remind you guys. The book club is meeting here on Thursday night. Don't forget. And Vanessa, don't even *think* of wriggling out of it." She turned a pretty pink. "We're reading my book."

Maddie grinned. "Oh. Which one?"

"*Paradise Between My Legs*? Or *The Perfect Pussy*, Volume Two?" Vanessa asked with a straight face.

Abby scowled. "You're horrible. The book is *Fielder's Folly*. My second *Policemen Do It Better* romance."

"Oh, that one. Well, it's got dominant heroes, suspense, and sex, so I guess I'll read it." Actually, she'd read it when the book had first released. Abby had a real gift with words, and she could write a sex scene like nobody's business.

"Gee, Vanessa. Don't do me any favors."

"I'm not. Well, I am. But I said I'd come, so I will."

Abby shook her head. Maddie muffled a laugh and said, "I'll be there, Abs. Robin and Kim too, even though Kim says she's not that into the male sex parts."

"See? Another friend taking one for the team." Vanessa chuckled at Abby's growl. Then the three of them took bets on what Mike might really be doing for Valentine's Day, especially if Beth kept throwing eligible women at him.

Vanessa continued the conversation, her mood light. Yet a part of her wondered how Cameron would react to her taking charge of Valentine's Day plans. Would he be angry she hadn't consulted him first? Only time would tell, and she waited on pins and needles to see the real Cameron McCauley stand up.

Chapter 7

CAM PUT DOWN THE PHONE AND STARED AT IT. VANESSA had decided to spend Valentine's Day with his mother? "Is she serious?" he asked aloud.

Wednesday morning in his new office, and he couldn't concentrate on the handsome but comfortable leather furniture Maddie had selected. Or the slate gray walls with accents of dark blue and brown around the room. His modern desk, with its sleek design in a dark composite, was a true work of art. But since spending an ideal weekend with sexy Vanessa, he'd had a difficult time focusing on his job.

Now to find out the woman he thought of as his had plans to avoid him on what could have been their first holiday together? *Hell no.*

He thought about it, needing to handle this first test. He knew Vanessa, as much as she might not want him to. This avoidance and how he reacted would show the stubborn woman exactly how much of him she could manipulate. That he'd *let her* manipulate.

A woman like Vanessa had her own mind. He respected that about her. But he refused to be constantly maneuvered in this relationship. They would be equals. Not one dominant over the other, even if the woman had a reputation for running right over anyone who opposed her fascist sense of right. She needed a man she could trust, one who wouldn't bow to her every whim. She needed him.

With that in mind, he called the one person he knew would help him, no questions asked.

She picked up on the third ring. "Hello?"

"Abby, it's Cam."

"Oh, hi, Cam. Don't you sound all grown up on the phone."

He laughed. "Thanks. I think."

"What can I do for you? Just name it."

Her desire to help pleased him. "I need help. Vanessa has volunteered herself to spend Valentine's Day with my mother, but I had plans for our first holiday together."

"Oh. Hmm." She paused. "You know, Mike talked to Brody and Flynn about this just this morning. I'm sure he'll be calling you soon. He was planning to surprise your mom. An evening out, just the two of them at dinner. I told him Vanessa would watch Colin, since she'd volunteered to help in the first place."

"That won't work." Not if he planned to have her to himself for the better part of the night.

"No. I see that. Hold on." She muffled the phone and told Brody something before she came back. "Cam?"

"Yeah?" He grinned, wondering why she sounded so breathless all of a sudden.

"Stop that." She cleared her throat. "Sorry, not you. The plumber is distracting me."

He heard Brody say something he couldn't make out, but it made Abby laugh.

New love. He envied them. "Tell him to shut up so you can help me."

"I did. Brody, sit."

He wondered if she realized she used that exact same tone on Hyde—the dog.

"So we need to get another babysitter," she was saying. "No problem. I have just the person."

"Someone trustworthy, I take it?"

"Cam, you wound me. Truly. Look. Kim and Robin are perfect to watch Colin. If they won't work, between me and Maddie, we have a ton of other friends who can successfully keep Colin out of danger—and jail—while you romance Vanessa."

Brody's laugh came over the phone loud and clear. "*Vanessa*? You're a real risk taker, Cam. My hero."

Cam pinched the bridge of his nose. "Tell the pipe jockey to mind his own business. And thanks, Abby. Do me a favor and keep this between us? Muffle the blond idiot too, okay?"

"No problem. Trust me, if he doesn't want to sleep alone, he'll be quiet." In the background, Brody groaned. "Bye, Cam. And good luck."

He disconnected, feeling better about things.

Until his father walked into his office.

They hadn't spoken much since their blowup on Friday. Cam had spent the weekend with Vanessa, barely at home. With his office now functional, he'd decided to bury himself in work until he figured out how best to interact with his old man.

"Cam. Nice place."

Surprised his father didn't insult him for his posh office, Cam accepted the compliment. "Thanks."

They stared at each other in silence. Cam behind his desk, while his father stood with a growing frown, dressed in his work clothes. Spattered jeans, a hooded sweatshirt under a stained flannel overcoat, and work boots.

After a moment of silence, they said at the same time, "I'm sorry."

His father sighed. "Go ahead."

Figured James would allow Cam to apologize first. What a guy. Cam swallowed his annoyance and did the mature thing. Vanessa would be proud. "I'm sorry for Friday. I didn't want to argue with you. But it seems like that's what we do best."

His father nodded, and a smile worked its way over his firm mouth. "No shit. You sure are an ornery kid."

"Gee. Who do I get that from?"

"Your mother."

Cam grinned, not taking offense at the intended humor. "So we're good?" *Even though we still haven't really talked about anything bothering us? Easier to shout and pretend it's better than to deal with our issues, eh, Dad?*

"We're good." James glanced around him before sitting down across from Cam. "Pretty nice spread you got here."

"It's perfect."

"Did you get this because of me? Because I'm staying at your place?"

"No. I'd planned to find a space when my last landlord raised the rent. I happened on this place sooner than planned, actually. You might have spurred my decision to look, but I'm glad I'm here. The rent is pretty decent, considering the location." Only a few blocks from his condo. He could walk the distance to work in less than ten minutes, as he had that morning.

His father looked back at him. "This reminds me of your primo bachelor pad. Every time I walk into that lobby, I swear those people are deciding whether or not to frisk me before letting me into the elevators."

Cam tried not to grin.

"Hell, you know it's true."

Cam silently compared his suit with his father's stained clothing. "Well, it's not like you can dress in Armani while tearing down cabinets and putting up drywall."

"You got that right." His father blew out a breath. "So, the other reason I'm here. Valentine's Day is coming up. Should I go somewhere so you can bring the girl home?"

Cam blinked. "What's that?"

"Come on, boy. Everyone's talking about you and Vanessa. Do you need me to clear out? Yes or no?"

Cam wanted to ask his father about his own plans but found he didn't want to know the answer. "Well, if you don't mind, that would be nice. Maybe I can show her what a great cook I am. Entice her to see me again. I'm taking it slow, though. Can't move too fast with a woman like Vanessa. I need to keep her on her toes."

"Good plan." His father nodded. "Woman that sharp will have you by the balls if you're not careful." He grinned. "Your mother..." His smile left him and he cleared his throat. "Just thought I'd see if you needed the space. I'll stay with your aunt and uncle. Guess I'll get to work then." James stood to leave.

Cam stood and rounded the desk to join his father. The blow to his back didn't completely fell him. He righted himself quickly, not sure why his father considered the gesture one of affection and not abuse. Personally, Cam preferred a hug or a handshake.

"Boy." His father nodded. "You're getting stronger. Looking good." His dad winked. "Must be the blond making the difference."

"Yeah, Dad. I'm buff for Vanessa," Cam said drily. "Because she's *so* into appearances."

His father guffawed. "Good luck with that one. Then again, if anyone can woo her, it's you."

A compliment? Cam chose to view it that way. "So I'll be home tonight for dinner if you want to eat together." An olive branch, since his father had shockingly initiated the truce.

"Sounds good. I like that chicken you make."

"Perfect. Lemon chicken and salad—"

"But no leaf. How about chicken and potatoes? Maybe some vegetable smothered in cheese sauce? Something meaty."

"Meaty vegetables?"

"Don't get smart," his dad grumbled. "*I'll* bring the beer. The kind you like, God help me."

His father nodded and left Cam staring after him. Wow. Girlie beer—as his siblings and father called his fine taste in select microbrewery offerings. His father really was trying to make amends.

The phone distracted him, and he rounded the desk to get his cell. *Speak of the devil…* "Hello?"

"Yo. It's Mike."

"I saw that, and yet I still picked up. You're welcome."

"Dick." Mike chuckled. "So I'm calling because—"

"On Valentine's Day, you're taking Mom out. You need someone to watch Colin. I got it."

"You—oh."

"I talked to Abby."

"Right." Mike paused. "So you and Vanessa are hot and heavy, eh?"

"Who told you? And why did you blab it to Dad?" Because if anyone had filled James McCauley's ear, it had been his oldest son, the man practically his twin.

"Sorry, *little* buddy."

Cam gritted his teeth.

"I heard it from Brody and Flynn, and of course I'm gonna tell Dad. It's a big lover's day coming up. You know women love that shit. Even Vanessa no doubt gets all wobbly at the knee about hearts and flowers."

Would she? Cam didn't know. But he intended to find out.

"I thought Dad should know to clear out to give you space. You and he talking again yet?"

"Yeah. He just came by my office to apologize. I thought I was seeing things at first."

"Yep. That's Dad." Mike chuckled. "Always full of surprises." The gentle teasing told of Mike's closeness to their father, a relationship Cam had always envied.

"Is he doing okay?"

"Not really. He pretends and jokes and stuff, but I can tell he's missing her. He mentioned some woman he kind of liked, but I get the feeling she's a stand-in. Like, he's not into her as much as he wants to be."

Cam frowned. "What?"

"Hell. I don't know. The sensitive crap is your bag. All I'm saying is that Dad misses Mom but he won't talk to her. And whenever I try to bring Dad up when I'm talking to Mom, she goes all stone-faced and silent on me. It all gives me a headache, you want the truth. I just want them happy. Period."

Wanting to change the subject, Cam sought a topic Mike had been avoiding. "Okay. Enough about Mom and Dad. Let's talk about something else. Like your investment strategies. I was thinking—"

"*No.* Not before a cup of coffee and having to deal with a cranky father. Make whatever changes you think I need."

"Not without talking to you first."

Mike swore. "I… Oh hell. We'll talk next week, okay?"

"Fine. But don't think of weaseling out of our meeting like you did last time. I'm not kidding."

"Yeah, yeah. Go crunch some numbers, poindexter." Mike disconnected the call before Cam could tell him to go screw himself.

"Yet another stimulating conversation with Michael McCauley," he muttered.

Someone knocked at his door, and he glanced up to see his cousin. More family, but this one he genuinely liked.

"Hey, Hope. Come in."

As one of the Donnigans who didn't irritate him just by breathing, Hope always made him smile. He'd planned to tempt her into some side work for him, since his lone associate already had so much to handle. "So I piqued your interest?"

Petite, blond, and a knockout, Hope Donnigan wore a shy smile that reminded him of his Aunt Linda. The only girl in a family with three brothers, and she was a middle child. He truly felt her pain, because being the youngest irritated him. She had to deal with not just two, but *three* brothers who thought they knew best about everything. Even Theo, who'd just graduated high school.

Hope gave him a kiss on the cheek before sitting across from him at his desk. "Are you talking about the email telling me I'd make millions if I said yes? I admit, I'm intrigued. Especially because I didn't know secretaries made that kind of money."

He pointed to his seat. "Not secretaries. Assistants. And they do when they work for me. Of course, that's a twenty-five-year plan if you invest wisely. But my knowledge is your knowledge if we come to acceptable terms. Here's what I was thinking…"

Mike hummed under his breath along with tunes from the classic rock station he and the guys preferred. On the job, the chatter didn't fill the empty space between buzz saws, nail guns, and swearing so much as the radio did. As he nailed another piece of drywall into place with Rod, he waited for his father to join him.

He'd beaten the old man into work this morning, which would no doubt stir up his father, who'd been on edge since his blowout with Cam. Tired of the family feuding, Mike had practically ordered James to meet with Cam and clear the air. While his father dealt with the youngest, Mike worked hard to wrap up this renovation in Tacoma to get back to his next project in Queen Anne. He didn't like being far in case Colin needed him. Considering his kid was normally the one who smashed a finger or bruised his skull, he kept his cell phone tucked into his back pocket. At thoughts of Colin and accidents, Mike knocked on wood and thanked God his kid had a hard head.

"Mike, I'm taking a quick breather. Back in five."

Mike nodded at Rod and continued to work. Moments later, he heard footsteps.

"What the hell?" a deep voice boomed from behind him. "Where did everyone go?"

Aaannnd his father had returned.

"Hey, Dad. I'm finishing here, then you want to help me with the last window?" They were installing energy-efficient windows in the living room and had one left. They'd already waterproofed the opening, now they just needed to set it. After he finished the drywall, he joined his father outside the house. They held up the window and fit the sill into the bottom before lining up the window's nailing fins against the wall. How many times had he done this? Fifty? Sixty?

"Let's get this shit done. I'm freezing." Twenty degrees out, and being Seattle, it was a wet cold that made him want to hide under his comforter until summer.

"Yeah, yeah." His father snorted. "Take it easy, Nancy."

They worked together well, as they always had, making sure of the window's level, eliminating any gaps, adjusting the frame a few times, and again leveling off the window until the jam was plumb. The radio played as Mike seated the nails, and he and his father settled into a familiar rhythm. As they worked, Mike watched his breath expel in clouds around his face. *Fuck*, it was cold. But far be it from his father to complain, because for damn sure Mike would fire the old "Nancy" insult right back at him.

Nancy—as in, you're such a *girl*. A common jibe Mike had always ignored, especially because he knew his dad meant nothing by it. They'd had their share of female employees who kicked ass. The Nancy comment was old-school machismo at its best, especially because it irked Cam. Even Colin turned a deaf ear to it, and his six-year-old had entered an anti-girl phase, so *Nancy* really meant something to him. But to hear Cam tell it, their father had only ever used the "nasty insult" on him. Friggin' overly sensitive number cruncher. Mike appreciated a good row. Hell, he and his father argued every damn day. And their *discussions* only made them closer.

At the thought, he decided to give his dad a ration of shit. Screw playing nice. "Please. You're just jealous because you're only good for flooring and tile work. And let's face it, when it comes down to you or Sal on tile, it's a toss up as to who's better."

"Smart-ass." His father double-checked that the windows were square before he grunted his assent and sealed the perimeter. Rote actions from doing the job forever. "Spoke to your brother."

"Which one?" Mike flexed his fingers to restore feeling to them. He wore fingerless gloves while his father went bare knuckle. Tough bastard.

"The *little* one." His dad grinned. "Pisses him the hell off when you all call him that."

"I know." Mike laughed and waited for his father to continue the conversation.

His father grunted but said nothing, and Mike let him work out whatever seemed to be on his mind while James finished with the outside caulking, flashing, and fitting in the sash. Then they both walked into the house together to do the rest.

Once Mike finished sealing the inside, he had a good hour to wait before adding more foam. So he started going through the house, double-checking the work in progress. As usual, he had no fault with his crew. It had taken McCauley Co. Construction a good ten years to find a decent group of guys who stuck. He'd been working for his father for fifteen years, the last five as a partner in their small but valued company.

So much blood and sweat poured into the job that now seemed to run like clockwork. Hell, they had people lined up to get their attention, and he no longer worried about being able to afford to send his son to college. *If* he sent him. Because according to Cam, at the rate Colin listened to Brody, Mike might very well have to save for future bail money. As if Mike would let that happen. Cam, such a worrier.

Mike returned to the downstairs kitchen area, which was mostly intact since his father had taken over the room's construction. The cherry wood cabinets gleamed and the granite counters looked amazing. Between Gardner's—Maddie's design firm—McCauley Co. Construction, and McSons Plumbing, this house would be a showcase and one of their best remodels yet.

"Nice work," he said to his dad.

Another grunt.

"Well?"

"Well what?"

Mike swallowed a swear. "You said"—he paused and lowered his voice to imitate his dad—"'Spoke to your brother.' And…?"

"Oh. We patched things up."

"I still don't get why you think Cam hates what we do. He never said as much to me. I think he likes knowing he's got an in with a reputable construction company."

Mike grinned, but his father shrugged. "What did he say when you asked him?"

"Nothing."

"Cam said nothing? I doubt that." The guy liked to talk things to death. Kind of like Brody, but instead of sparring with taunting words, Cam went deep. Like, emotionally messy deep.

"Hell. We made up. Were we supposed to kiss and cry?" his father sneered.

Mike sighed. "Whatever. So you're getting along. About fucking time. So are you going to *not* talk to Mom too and make up?"

"Not funny, Mike."

"No, it's not." Mike stared at his father over the counter, seeing so much of himself in the man. "Come on, Dad. Can't you just talk to her?"

"I've tried for months. Woman closed down on me." His father ran a large hand through his hair, which needed a cut. "You don't need to be hearing this. This is between me and your mother."

"Not when it affects all of us. We love you guys. You and Mom both." He hated to ask, but it needed to be said. "Have you two gone to couples therapy?"

"No."

"I hate to butt in—"

"Then don't."

"—but it seems to me you're both too close to the problem. You don't feel comfortable telling me about you and Mom, but you've shared that you're into some other woman." Which hurt like hell, but Mike tried to be impartial. Wanting to beat common sense into his father wouldn't help.

"It's not like that."

"Right." *Could have fooled me. Don't judge, Mike. Don't judge.* "Whatever. Point is, you won't talk to Mom. You won't talk to me or the guys. Won't talk to Uncle Van, and I know because I asked him." His father's brother-in-law, Aunt Linda's husband. "Why not talk to someone impartial? Someone who doesn't know you or Mom and won't take sides?"

His father looked uncomfortable but didn't disagree.

"Dad, think of it like this. How would you feel if you knew Mom had a thing for some other guy?"

His father just stared at him.

"What? She *does*?"

"Hadn't realized your voice could get that high," his father said in a droll voice.

"No way. Uh-uh."

"Yep. It's exactly like that. Hard for me to compete with those college types."

"Dad, you're wrong." Mike knew for a fact his mother loved his father. Beth McCauley wasn't the type to be unfaithful. Then again, he'd never thought his father would look at another woman either. "Look, see someone. Why don't you—"

"Son, I know you want to help, but again. This is between me and your mother. Keep the fuck out of it."

Feeling like he was losing the battle, Mike tried one last time. "You know, Lea and I had our share of problems." He and his deceased wife had loved each other like crazy, every damn day they'd had together. Through the fights and the make-ups, the ups and downs. "But we got through them. Until it was too late. You never know how much time you have left," he said, wishing he didn't sound so gruff. But even now, after all these years, it hurt to think about her.

His father softened. "I know, boy. But that's the point. Time is too short to deal with mistakes and the knowledge you can't change who you are inside." James rounded the kitchen island and put his hand on Mike's shoulder. "Some things just are. You know better than most how true that is."

Mike nodded and turned away, not wanting his father to see the shine in his eyes. He hadn't cried for Lea in six long years, and he refused to now. But the thought of his parents no longer together touched him deep down inside. Made him feel the pain of separation all over again. "I'll be in the living room."

"Mike…"

He left his father behind, praying Cam had more luck with their mother. Because he sure as shit had no idea what to do with the obstinate man.

Chapter 8

VANESSA HURRIED HOME THURSDAY NIGHT, HOPING TO get in a run before Abby's book club. Sure, she'd liked the book. She didn't need to talk about it. She needed to *run*.

Between work and the last four days of celibacy since Cameron, she felt ready to jump out of her skin. She hadn't realized how sexualized he'd made her, but since their time together, she couldn't seem to turn off her libido—for Cameron.

After shutting the front door behind her and stepping out of her heels, she ran upstairs only to hear Abby yelling at her to hurry and join the others. So much for a run.

Changing into a comfortable pair of yoga pants and a thick sweatshirt, Vanessa took a deep breath and let it out, preparing for a long night of boring talk. Once they passed the sex parts of Abby's book, Vanessa would zone out, not caring to discuss the emotional angst she'd skimmed through. Deep feeling wasn't her thing, especially not after a hellacious workday.

She joined the others and looked around at a few people she didn't know, and one she hadn't realized would be coming.

"Del?"

Del nodded and rolled her eyes when Abby turned away. The ash-blond mechanic had fit into their small group surprisingly well the last time they'd all gone bowling.

Vanessa couldn't see Del's fascinating sleeves of tattoos, as the woman wore a dark sweater to combat the weather. She wore a diamond stud in her nose and a small hoop in her brow that somehow made her look tough and sexy, as opposed to metal-grunge. She also wore her hair in a loose French braid, which should have softened her appearance but didn't. The woman's hard gray eyes and angular features screamed *don't screw with me or I'll end you*. Vanessa had automatically liked her.

"So you got roped into this too?" Del murmured in a husky voice when Vanessa sat next to her on a kitchen chair someone had dragged into the living room.

Before she could answer, Maddie entered with a tray of goodies. She wore her hair up. Her favorite emerald earrings—which Flynn had bought her—danced brightly against her delicate lobes, and her fully made-up face and fancy dress had her resembling a model from a magazine.

"Oh, good," the redhead said with syrupy sweetness. "Nessie's home."

Another childhood nickname she'd thought her cousin had permanently buried. Then again, it sounded better than Van-zilla.

"Madison." Vanessa nodded. "Nice to see you breathing on your own again."

Their good friends Kim and Robin, sitting together on the couch, frowned. "She's having trouble breathing?" Kim asked. Fair where her partner was dark, and feminine with frills, she had a mind as sharp as a tack and ran a successful interior design firm with her life and business partner, Robin.

"Yeah." Vanessa sighed, pretending grief. "Poor

Maddie's been lip-locked to Flynn so often I worried she'd forgotten how to breathe on her own."

Robin and Kim laughed. Abby chuckled. Maddie scowled, and the three women Vanessa didn't know looked from her to Maddie with wide eyes.

"So is this going to get physical? Because I gave up watching a killer MMA fight to be here." Del sounded bored.

"Did you read *Fielder's Folly*?" one of the women asked. She looked to be in her mid-forties. Attractive, plump, and by Vanessa's guess, a true Abigail D. Chatterly fan. Abby's pen name had actually garnered her more than her fair share of hero worship the past few times she'd gone into the local bookstores. A fact that confirmed what Vanessa had known from day one—her friend had skill, and finally the confidence to stop hiding behind her pen name and be proud of her books.

"I did," Del answered without flinching.

"And who are you?" Vanessa cut in, since Abby hadn't seen fit to introduce anyone.

"Vanessa." Maddie glared.

"I'm sorry." Abby's pink cheeks amused Vanessa—and Del, by the quirk of her lips. "Essie, May, and April, my roommate Vanessa. Vanessa, you already know everyone else."

"May and April?" May was the attractive fan, and April looked enough like her to be her sister.

April sighed. "We have another sister. Don't ask. I'll just tell you. Her name is June."

Vanessa cracked up. "Wow. Your parents really went all out on your names, hmm?"

"Jesus, Vanessa." Maddie let out a loud sigh. "I apologize for my cousin in advance."

"Don't. She's right." May groaned on a laugh. "My mother's name is Muriel, named after her mother. But in order to save us from a lifetime of living as Gertrude and Ethel—our great-aunts—we got May and April. I'm okay with it. It's only when we do mass introductions that life gets weird."

"Okay, everyone." Maddie whistled to grab their attention. "Drinks are in the kitchen, along with a few other snacks, so help yourself. But now, it's time to talk about the book. Abby, why don't you start us off?"

Vanessa took some lactose-heavy cheese and a gluten-full cracker and nibbled. It was going to be a long night.

Or so she thought. Two hours later, she was surprised to find she'd enjoyed herself. Essie, May, and April loved Abby's books, which made Abby sparkle. That in turn pleased Vanessa to no end. Giving her roomies crap amused her, but there was nothing quite like a friend's success to give her the warm fuzzies.

As the night wound down and the new girls escaped with hasty good-byes and promises to return next month—*God help me*—Abby pulled Del aside and said something in a low voice.

Vanessa frowned, because Del looked right at her and nodded.

"What?" she asked.

Del waved her away. Had Vanessa not been a fitness nut, she might have been intimidated by the woman's muscular form not quite hidden by her bulky clothes. She'd seen Del handle a bowling ball like it weighed nothing. From what Abby had described, the woman could turn a wrench and fix a heavy tire in no time at all. Vanessa respected strength, especially the discipline it took to exercise regularly. That and Del had a pissy attitude she more than appreciated.

"Fine. I'll do it. But you owe me." Del looked resigned.

Abby squealed and hugged her, and Del started before awkwardly returning the embrace.

"Aw, isn't that cute?" Robin teased, standing next to Vanessa while holding Kim's hand. "She's got that scared-of-a-friend look you often wear."

"Who, me?" Vanessa turned to see Robin smirking at her. "Hey, I'm not the one scared of making friends. Or of making a commitment." Big fat lie. "It took you— what—four *years* to propose to *your* friend? Slow as molasses pot calling kettle black. Hello."

Kim laughed. "She's got you there."

Robin frowned at her partner. "Hey, I was building up to marriage. I just wanted to make sure you were worthy of my fine affection."

Kim just looked at her.

Robin flushed. "Or maybe I was building my courage. You're a scary woman. Probably why you and Vanzilla get along."

Vanessa turned to Maddie, who grinned. "Great. Now you've got them calling me that, too?"

Kim patted her on the cheek. "Don't worry, honey. I prefer Va-Nessie. Like Old Nessie? That Loch Ness Monster? The one with the big feet?"

"Nessie's a water serpent. No feet, just a big-ass tail." Del shook her head. Then she glanced at Vanessa's socks and whistled. "But wow. Vanessa does have some big dogs, huh?"

"*Et tu*, Del?" Vanessa scowled at her.

Del held up her hands. "I surrender. Don't kick me. You might dent my spine." She snickered. "Later, guys. I have to get home. Business to run early in the morning, you know."

Vanessa watched her leave. "Charming she is not. And yet, for some odd reason, I find I like Suzie Tattoo."

She turned to see Maddie and Abby eyeing her with speculation. "What?" She looked at her cousin. "Why do you keep giving me that weird look?"

Maddie shrugged prettily. "Gee, Vanessa. I don't know what you mean." The wattage of her smile warned Vanessa to be wary.

"I'm watching both of you." She pointed two fingers at her eyes, then at them and back again. "Like a hawk." Unfortunately, a yawn took the sting out of her threat.

"I'm bushed." Abby yawned too and stretched. "Thanks for coming, guys. That was a lot of fun."

"It was," Vanessa agreed. "I'm beat. See you guys in the morning."

She trudged upstairs. After settling into bed, her thoughts immediately turned to Cameron.

They'd talked only briefly this week, both of them slammed with more work than they'd anticipated. Perhaps they'd run together again this weekend. She hoped. What with Valentine's Day on Sunday, they could at least spend the day together before watching Colin. That might be fun. And maybe, just maybe, she could seduce him again. Because God knew she needed the respite from the images of naked Cameron running through her mind every five seconds.

As predicted, she dreamed about him without

meaning to. But her fantasy turned into a nightmare
when he bent down on one knee to propose, and she
said *yes*.

———∿∿———

Sunday evening, Beth McCauley waited anxiously for
her oldest son to finish sprucing himself up for his big
Valentine's Day date with Sheila somebody. Not one of
the women she'd picked for him from her network of
friends, but if Mike had decided to stop playing around
and start dating again, she was all for it.

"Where's he going, Grandma?" Colin asked, jumping
around the living room. The boy had no off switch to
speak of and only stilled when asleep. At three months,
he'd started crawling. He hadn't slowed down since.

She smiled and stroked his cowlick, having no success in smoothing it down. "Your daddy's going out on
a date tonight."

Colin scowled. "With a girl?"

When he made that face, he looked like a carbon
copy of his father. Such a funny little sweetheart. Mike
had been just as fervent in his desire never to kiss a girl
at six years of age. And then he'd met Lea and hadn't
been the same since.

"Yes, dear. With a girl. Someday you might find
love as well." Girl, boy, vegetable... If her grandson
opened his heart and gave all of himself, she couldn't
care less about his chosen partner. So long as the boy
didn't take after his arrogant, hurtful grandfather.

Just thinking about James made her sad—mad.
I'm past the hurt. Or so she kept reminding herself.
Their problems had been growing for years, and she

automatically grew angry when she thought about all she'd sacrificed in her life to make that man happy. Thirty-six flipping years, and for what? So that he could ignore their issues and make eyes at some trollop in the neighborhood coffee shop?

It didn't help that said trollop had to be a good ten or more years younger than Beth.

She wanted to punch him. Hard. In the head. Many, many times. Ring his bell and get him to stop such non-sensical thoughts.

"Okay, I'm ready," she heard Mike say as he left his bedroom and walked down the hall to join them.

"Wow, Dad. You look fancy. You smell good, too." Colin's eyes narrowed. "For a girl?"

Mike nodded. "For a very special girl. My favorite girl in the world." He wore a black suit—complete with bow tie—that highlighted his powerful build and brought out the bright blue in his eyes—eyes that smiled at her.

My special, special son. So handsome. Just waiting for the right woman to… Favorite girl? "What?"

Mike gave her a hug. He lifted her off her feet and chuckled, ignoring Colin's laughter and her breathless pleas to be put down.

He finally set her on her feet. "Okay, Mom. Time for us to go."

"Go? But I'm watching Colin while you go on your date."

The back door opened, and in moments Vanessa entered the living room with Cam trailing behind her. Both of them smiled at her. Such a handsome couple. If things went as she hoped, she might just get a marriage to balance her inevitable separation. She took a quick grip on her emotions and forced herself not to cry.

Yes, Cameron and Vanessa. A new beginning. Then she'd just have her oldest boy to handle. The most difficult of them all.

"Here are our sitters." Mike nodded. "Thanks, guys."

"No problem." Cam grinned.

"No," Colin moaned. "Not him." He pointed at Cam and made shooting sounds. "He's no fun. And she's a girl."

"Thanks, Captain Obvious," Vanessa said drily. She turned to Beth. "Have fun on your date."

"What date?"

When Cam handed Mike a bouquet of flowers he'd apparently been hiding behind his back, she didn't know what to think. Because Mike suddenly held them out to *her*.

"Mom?" Mike said in a deep voice, sounding so much like his father it hurt. "I need a date tonight. As embarrassing as it is to be a thirty-three-year-old single man on a date with his mom, it *is* Valentine's Day. And you're pretty available."

Vanessa chuckled. "Oh, smooth, Mike. Like but-tah."

Cam snickered.

Mike glared at them. "Hey, I'm talking. Shut it, you two." He cleared his throat and turned back to Beth. "Well? We have plans. Time to get you home and into that pretty blue dress you and Maddie bought together on Monday. Come on, woman. We have a dinner reservation at seven."

Beth couldn't help it. She teared up. "You're so thoughtful. All of you." She smiled and wiped her eyes, feeling so loved despite her circumstances. The man who should have been here wasn't. But the boys she'd raised to be fine men had stepped in for their mother. "Oh my goodness. I'll have to take a shower. I need to get home and dressed. I have to do my hair!"

Mike raised his gaze to the ceiling, as if asking for divine providence. "Ma, that's what I'm saying. *Come on.* We have plans." He nodded to Cam. "You have my number if you need me."

Cam waved him on. "Yeah, yeah." Moving to Beth, her youngest smiled and gave her a big hug and a kiss. He smelled like expensive cologne and wore nice jeans and a sweater. Casual yet dressed up…for Vanessa.

She hid a smile. "Happy Valentine's Day, sweetie." She kissed him back, then hugged Vanessa and gave Colin a peck on the cheek.

The little scamp wore a smile too wide for his little face. No doubt prodded to be nice by Mike when she hadn't been looking.

"Happy Valentine's Day to you *too*, Grandma." Then in a less pretentious tone he added, "I love you."

She leaned down and whispered in a loud voice, "There's a box of chocolates waiting for you on your bed. You didn't think I'd forget to find a treat for my favorite sweetheart, did you?"

He hugged her and gave her a sloppy kiss before hooting and tearing down the hallway.

Mike frowned. "What—"

"I'm betting you don't want to know." Vanessa cut Mike off before he could get started on the importance of not buying his son more sugar. "We got the kid. Go have fun."

Mike sighed and crooked his elbow. "Mom? Shall we?"

"I think we shall." Beth took his arm and walked off with her son, her hurt lessening at the idea of not spending Valentine's Day with that sorry husband of hers, and realizing that life did indeed go on without James McCauley by her side.

———

Cam had been trying not to look at his watch while his brother took his damn time getting their mother out of the house and into his truck. They drove away just as a black '69 GTO pulled into Mike's drive.

Behind him in the living room, Vanessa chattered with Colin about his newly found chocolates. She showed him how to press the bottom of each chocolate to determine its flavor, thus hiding obvious smush marks when Colin found the ones he didn't want so he could give them away. Clever girl.

The doorbell chimed, and Cam answered with undue haste.

"Hel-lo?" Del stood with her hand raised to ring the bell again.

"Hey."

"Del!" Colin dashed past Cam and hugged his hero fiercely. Ever since she'd fixed a tire when Colin and Abby had been on the way to soccer practice a few months ago, Del could do no wrong in Colin's adoring eyes. This despite her obvious gender and his dislike of girls. Problem was, Mike could be fussy about who he let hang with his kid. And, Cam personally thought, big brother had a thing about Del's fine ass. Because he sure had paid attention to it when the woman bent over to bowl not so long ago.

"Hey, kiddo. How's tricks?"

"Tricks?" Colin pulled away. "I have tricks. Lots of 'em. Ubie showed me a bunch. Got a quarter?"

Vanessa snorted. She advised Del, "Only give him the money you won't mind never seeing again. Kid's a con man. He's good though."

"I always say you should put a hundred and ten percent into everything you do." Del nodded. Tonight she wore punk-looking braids that still managed to make her look attractive. Cam could see why Mike had fixated on her.

"So kid, you got plans for tonight?" she asked Colin. "'Cause I'm thinking some cards or cartoons would be fun. Or maybe a monster movie?"

Colin looked from her to Cam and Vanessa.

"Wait. Why are you here?" Vanessa asked.

"Del, you have my number," Cam said, realizing he sounded just like Mike. "Call if you have problems. We'll be downtown at my place. Near Eighth and Olive. Food and drinks are in the kitchen with pizza on the way."

"Yes." Colin pumped his arms in celebration. Sad that the boy was more excited to see a woman than his own uncle, but hey. At least Colin seemed happy about the change in sitters.

"I really appreciate this," Cam thanked her again.

She shrugged. "Sure. Why not? Not like I had anything better to do." She glanced at Colin and smirked. "Valentine's Day is so gross. All that kissing. And boys. Blech."

"Yeah, so gross." Colin bobbed his head, and Cam had the notion the kid would agree to anything she said.

"Wait." Vanessa tugged his arm. "So we're dumping the scam artist with Muscles McGee?"

Del raised a brow at the nickname.

"Ah, yes." Cam took Vanessa by the arm and gently pulled her to the back door before she could offend Del into leaving. "Time to go. I have an evening planned."

Vanessa blinked but said nothing, nor did she protest his lead.

Over his shoulder, he saw Del give him a thumbs-up, which Colin promptly imitated with a wide, toothy grin.

"Game on," he murmured as they walked to his car and got in.

"What's that?" Vanessa buckled up and stared at him, her blue eyes narrowed in thought, and no doubt in challenge.

"Happy Valentine's Day, Vanessa." He leaned over to kiss her, then fastened his seatbelt and started the car. Fingers, toes, and every other vital body part hypothetically crossed that he'd make a memory tonight neither would soon forget.

Chapter 9

VANESSA DIDN'T KNOW HOW HE'D DONE IT, BUT Cameron had managed to outflank her into a genuine Valentine's Day date. Granted, she could have said no at any time, but he'd stoked her curiosity. He'd arranged for a sitter so that they could be together. Half of her secretly hoped they'd get to that mind-blowing sex again. The other half wondered if he'd screw things up between them. Men tended to do that with her. A lot.

So she sat back and let his competency at the wheel lull her into a dreamy lassitude, her head full of what she hoped tonight might entail. The building he took her to turned out to be a surprise.

"We're eating here?" The Hyatt downtown was a snazzy place.

"Kind of." He parked inside the garage and led her to an elevator. They rode several flights up to his floor, then exited. "I live here."

"Not too shabby, McCauley." Okay, color her impressed. She'd known Cameron made a nice living. But this...*wow*. She'd once priced these condos in an attempt to dream big, once the money in her investments reached its cap. These units above the Hyatt had a nice price tag attached to the many amenities and views of the city. Amenities... She frowned. "Hey, don't you have an exercise room here?"

He shrugged. "It's normally too crowded. Not that

convenient to have it on hand and never get to use any equipment."

"I guess." She followed him down the hall.

"Here we are." He unlocked his door and ushered her inside.

She walked in and looked around, nodding. "Yep. This is you." Urban, tasteful furnishings. He apparently favored a Scandinavian style, with lighter woods and a modern feel to the place. Though neutral in tone, the space had a comforting, homey vibe. Not a chrome-and-glass kind of guy, Cameron had a sense of style, apparent in his day-to-day wear. "I have to ask. Are you sure you weren't adopted? Because I've seen your brothers' homes."

He laughed and drew her along for a tour. They moved through the open dining and living space to one side of the condo. There they found a den and bedroom—where his father's clothes lay haphazardly all over the place.

She felt for him as he shook his head and closed the door to contain the chaos inside.

"Your dad isn't here?"

"Nope. He's spending the night elsewhere."

"Oh." *Elsewhere?* "Awkward."

Cameron shook his head. "With my aunt and uncle, not his new mistress. Apparently, his relationship, and I quote, 'is not like that.'"

"Then what is it like?" She could almost hear her roommates telling her to drop the painful subject, but curiosity won out over polite convention.

"Who the hell knows?" He snorted. "The good news is that we're getting along now. Of course, we never talked about why we *weren't* getting along before, but that's the James McCauley way."

"Typical. No offense, but most men are idiots when it comes to emotions."

"You got that right."

They grinned at each other, and she wondered that she could feel so at ease yet stimulated by a man.

He continued through the roomy unit to the other side and showed her an amazing media room, as well as his bedroom. "If you're good, I might let you study my ceiling. From flat on your back on the bed." He wiggled his brows and ushered her to the kitchen.

She loved his sense of humor. "Dream on."

"Oh, I do. A lot." He leered at her. "Mostly of you naked and on your knees. Sometimes doing my taxes, other times…not."

She chuckled. "*Ooh*. Naughty work fantasies. Love it."

"Now sit and prepare to be amazed." He handed her a glass of wine. She sat—out of the way at the large counter over the sink which served as a dinette—and watched him take things out of his refrigerator and put them into the oven he'd turned on.

"Small space, but the flow is terrific."

"Yeah," he agreed. "All stainless-steel appliances, state-of-the-art electronics, hardwoods, you name it. I'm never leaving this place. I figure they can bury me in the media room." He chuckled.

"What about kids?" As soon as she asked it, she inwardly cringed. Talk about personal. He might get the wrong idea, like maybe she wanted to make said kids with him.

"What about them? I have a spare bedroom and a den, which could always work as a nursery if needed. At some point in my life, I figure I'll have kids. Just not yet."

She let out a quiet sigh of relief that he hadn't read anything unintended in her words.

"What about you?" he asked and puttered with the makings for a salad. "Oh, and before you ask, yes. Everything is organic or grass fed—the steaks—and completely gluten free. This isn't my first rodeo."

She lifted her wine in a toast. "Amen to that. Do you know how refreshing it is not to have to defend my choice to eat healthy? Jesus, it gets old."

"Trust me. You've met my family. You know my pain."

She nodded.

"So, kids?"

No dodging the question, apparently. "I don't know. My childhood was less than stellar. My parents weren't abusive, but not loving in any normal kind of way. I think my dad thought if I understood science, he'd done his job as a parent."

"Your mom?"

"She was just as bad, but with math. The theoretical stuff I didn't care for, but I admit to loving statistics and probabilities. Must be genetic." She shrugged and finished her glass.

Cam, on the spot, poured her another.

"Thanks. This is good."

"It's a nice blend. A friend of mine recommended it. He's always cluing me in to new stuff."

"I'll make a note." She stared at her glass. "I guess I never thought much about kids until we moved next door to Mike." A surprise she'd just admitted to them both. "Colin's so cute. Mike's doing such a great job with the delinquent."

Cam snorted a laugh and dumped salad ingredients

into a bowl. Plain white dishware. No frills, classy yet practical. Just like the man himself.

"Maddie's mother had her way too young," Vanessa continued. "My mother used to prodigiously warn me to keep my legs closed throughout high school and college."

"Touching."

She raised her gaze to him and grinned. "Yeah, but it worked. Seeing my Aunt Michelle struggle to raise Maddie opened my eyes. I lost my virginity in college, mainly because I was curious."

"Was it any good?"

"Hell no."

He frowned. "Sadly, it never seems to be for the girl. My first time I nearly lost my mind. So incredible. Totally not the same as your own hand."

"I'm sure." She felt overheated, and by the sly look on his face, he knew it. "So anyway," she said, preferring a discussion about children over the thought of him pleasuring himself. Because if she jumped him right now, she'd prove she had no self-control. "I like sex. I'm responsible, financially solvent, and yes, the thought of making another little Vanessa speaks to my biological imperative to add to the human race. But now? I'm not ready yet."

"I see."

She frowned. "Are you laughing at me?"

"I don't know that I've ever heard a woman refer to getting pregnant as speaking to her *biological imperative*. We're not the Borg, you know. Affection can enter into it."

"How would you know? Maybe this is all a virtual dream, and your robotic self has been programmed to make you think you're human."

"Hmm. Interesting."

They delved into a lively discussion about science fiction versus fantasy, perception and reality. Before Vanessa knew it, she was seated at the dining table and she'd finished a second glass of wine.

He'd put out candles and flowers while they talked, and she had to admit he'd really set the mood for Valentine's Day.

"You did a great job." She nodded at the plate of angus filet with arugula salad and a baked squash casserole that he placed in front of her.

He grabbed himself a full plate as well and sat across from her. "Thank you. I hope the candles and flowers are okay. They frame you with a romantic light." He winked. "Of course, when Flynn saw me in the store buying them, he called me an idiot. Said that you wouldn't appreciate the roses. Cliché, I know. But I like the smell."

"Flynn's a moron. I love them." She wanted to kick him for teasing Cameron, who'd gone out of his way to be nice. "Besides, I happen to know he bought Maddie a full bouquet of them, *and* gave her a stupid little card with some schmaltzy, cutesy poetry on it. Embarrassing."

Cameron laughed. "Yeah. They all give *me* crap for being the sensitive one, but who do you think they go to when they strike out with their girlfriends? Cam, that's who."

She smiled. "Well, I might not be the go-to girl for romantic advice, but trust me, when my roomies need a way to figure out tough problems, I'm the answer-man. So to speak."

"See? Competence kills."

They shook their heads and commiserated over being so efficient. It was so nice to talk to someone who understood her. Even appreciated her. She watched Cameron eat and even liked the way he cut his food. *Oh boy*. Her appreciation for the man had grown from a stupid crush to like to deepening affection. She felt it taking hold but had no idea what to do about it. Then she figured, what the hell? It was Valentine's Day. No need to worry about feeling lovey-dovey. The season brought it on. But surely to reward him, she might have to make that fantasy of his come true later. The one where she didn't do his taxes for him…on her knees.

Cam had guessed correctly on the flowers and candles but resolved to not show her the card he'd bought for her. The chocolates… He still had no idea what to do about them.

They finished their dinner agreeably arguing about the merits of *Star Trek* versus *Star Wars*, and she cleared the dishes with him. He didn't ask. She didn't offer. They just worked together.

Man, he had it bad. Hearing her mention she'd lost her virginity out of curiosity hadn't turned him off. Instead, he'd felt an insane jealousy for the boy who'd first had her. And he wanted to go visit her parents and give them a stern lecture about how to properly love a child. Then he'd kick their asses. His rational sense seemed to have deserted him as he stared at the play of candlelight over her features, her laughing blue eyes, her full lips parted in a smile. God, she was so sexy. He kept remembering how amazing it had felt when he'd taken her in the shower.

Shit. If he kept thinking like this, he'd have to hide in his seat under the table until his erection went away.

Wiping down the table and then drying it off, Vanessa had her attention on cleaning. While he tried to calm himself down, he decided to go for broke and left for his bedroom. He returned moments later to find her fiddling with his stereo.

"Turn to preset three," he offered.

She did, and low, smooth jazz filled the room. "Hmm. Nice mood music. A great meal. You hoping to get lucky, Cameron?"

Not hoping. Praying. "Vanessa." He tsked. "As if I'd ever think to manipulate you into something you might not want."

"Yeah, you have that whole snake oil salesman vibe down to a science." She smirked at him. "Come on. The wine? The nice meal? Why don't you just ask me for sex? No need to pretty it up."

"Yet you seemed to like the flowers and candlelight," he said softly. "And chocolates? Do you have a preference?" He held out two red heart-shaped boxes to her. One held light chocolate, the other dark.

She licked her lips. "Okay. I admit. I liked the flowers. And the candles. And yes, I have a thing for chocolate. The dark. Milk chocolate is too sweet."

"Hmm. *Bitter* chocolates. You make it only too easy to tease you."

"I know. But I'd hoped that a man with a mind as nimble as yours would go for something harder. More complex."

"Harder. I can do that."

She laughed. "Oh shut up and bring me the candy."

He put the milk chocolates aside.

Vanessa sat on the couch and tapped the spot next to her. "Come, boy. Feed your mistress."

He quirked a brow, and she winked. He loved her like this, so playful, at ease. And hungry for him, if he had his way.

Cam sat and found himself under her kiss before he could blink. He let her take control for a few seconds before easing her back. The woman liked to dominate, and if led by his cock, he'd have happily let her do whatever the hell she wanted. She got him hard in a heartbeat. She knew she could make him come without effort. But not tonight. He wanted to play.

"If you insist." He set her back gently and reached for a chocolate on the table. He took one and bit into it.

"Hey." She gave him a mock frown. "That's mine."

"Nah. It's coconut cream. You'd hate that. Not bitter enough."

"Bitter, my ass. I love coconut cream." She frowned and he shoved the rest of it into her mouth before she could argue with him.

She tried to garble something, so he put a finger over her lips. "Don't talk with your mouth full. It's not polite."

She opened her mouth wide to show him the masticated chocolate, and he grinned.

"Hmm, let's try another one and see if that sweetens your disposition." He picked another chocolate at random and offered it to her. "No, don't grab it. I'm feeding you, my mistress."

She'd been the one to call herself that, so he figured she wouldn't mind the game.

After she swallowed her candy, she shrugged. "Fine

by me. *Slave*." She stuck her tongue out at him before accepting the candy he placed in her mouth.

This time while she chewed—with her mouth closed—he scooted closer and teased the bottom of her sweater before sliding his hand under it. She tensed, then let out a soft breath when he ran his hand over the bare skin of her tight stomach.

"Yep. Sweet. Not bitter at all."

She finished chewing and swallowed. "Sneak."

"Mmm hmm." He pulled her into his arms, having her straddle his lap so he could look directly at her. Then he slowly drew her mouth down to his and savored her. After a kiss that made them both breathless, he murmured, "Maple. I love the maple candies. Let's see what else you have in there."

He reached around her and blindly grabbed another. But this time, as he fed it to her, she grabbed his hand and nipped his fingers. She held his hand by her mouth and finished the candy. Then she sucked his index finger, and his dick immediately responded.

"You had some chocolate there," she said with a throaty chuckle. "Oh wait, there's more."

She squirmed over his lap, putting more pressure on his obvious arousal while she sucked his finger with a skill that demanded to be proven. Maybe they'd get to a blow job this time.

When she let his finger go, he leaned his head back on the couch and tried to calm down. Not easy with her still riding him. After a few deep breaths, he removed her sweater and bra without waiting to ask. He cupped her breasts and sighed. "Good try, mistress. But I'm not ready to come yet."

"Too bad." She pouted, then smiled at him. "Because you feel more than ready."

"Yeah? That's true. But I know what will help slow me down." He brought her forward, engulfing one nipple in his mouth. As she whispered his name and clutched his head, he tormented her nipple with hard suction that made it difficult to think. Each draw on the tight bud had her rocking over his dick, and he was perilously close to forgetting himself and fucking her.

He pulled back and watched her as he unsnapped her jeans. He slid the zipper down, and she helped by kneeling up to give him better access. He slid his fingers inside her panties to the wet heat between her folds. Then he sucked her other nipple and stroked her, loving her keening for more.

He looked up to watch her riding him, lost in the beauty of her pleasure. Her eyes were half-closed, her mouth slick from his kisses, her lips parted on breathy moans. Her loose hair flowed like spun gold over her shoulders.

"I love your breasts," he murmured and licked her nipple again. "So full, just perfect for my mouth." He nipped one, then the other, while she surged against his hand. He felt a burst of moisture against the inside of his jeans and knew he neared his own end, but only perseverance and the need to see her come first kept him from exploding.

"Cam, yes. Oh yeah. So good," she moaned, clutching his head while she ground against him. He put another finger inside her and rubbed hard against her clit.

He wanted to suck her, to lick that sweet cream between her legs. Like an aphrodisiac, her scent and taste went straight to his head. But to leave her breasts meant denying her this pleasure. Next time... Because no way in hell would he let her leave without coming inside her at least once. Where they both belonged. *Together*.

"I'm coming, Cam. So close, oh God."

He let go of her breast and she kissed him with a ferocity that satisfied on so many levels. Then she tightened around his fingers and moaned into his mouth, clenching him as her climax rushed through her.

He ended the kiss to watch her face flush and her nipples swell. Her breath washed over him, the sweet scent of chocolate and sex making him hungry for more. For everything she'd give him.

Through it all, his cock ached, his balls needing the release only she could provide. He wanted to feel her surround him, as intimate as two lovers could be.

After a few moments, she calmed, and he kissed her again, this time gentling her.

But she would have none of it. "No." She nipped his lower lip, and he couldn't help himself from surging up against her. "You're so sexy. I love when you're hard, so thick against me."

She lifted herself from his lap and stripped down to nothing.

"You are so beautiful." He was panting like a freaking dog, but he couldn't look away. That flushed creamy skin, high breasts, and her face. He never wanted tonight to end.

"Take off your shirt."

He'd never unbuttoned his clothing so fast before. He tossed it aside, and the white T-shirt he'd worn under it too. When he went for the button of his jeans, she stopped him.

"No. That's my job."

His heart raced so hard he feared stroking out. Then Vanessa was there, kneeling between his legs. Naked, wet, and wearing a devious grin.

"Oh shit. You're going to torture me, aren't you?" He couldn't wait. Vanessa seemed to drop all her barriers. He saw her open, honest, and not afraid to take what pleased her.

"But of course." She unbuttoned his fly one excruciatingly slow button at a time. When she had his jeans parted, *finally*, she reached in and found him commando. "Oh, Cam. Now this I really like. You're thick, aren't you?"

He groaned and dropped his head back again, feeling her fingers dragging him free of his parted jeans.

"Scoot up some."

He did and let her tug his denim down to his upper thighs, baring his cock and balls for her pleasure.

"Yes, this I *really* like." She lowered her head, breathed over his tip, and licked him.

"*Fuck me*. Vanessa," he groaned. "I want to, but I won't last. It's been too long." He swore when she licked him from root to tip. "Shit. I'm really full. Sit on me."

"Nope. Not this time." She smiled up at him, and his heart broke wide open. "Happy Valentine's Day, Cam." Then she lowered her head and enveloped him.

All of him, to the back of her throat.

Chapter 10

VANESSA HAD NEVER FELT SO DESIRABLE OR WICKED IN her entire life. Cam's moans and gasps empowered her, and she took joy in giving him such pleasure. Normally the intimacy of such an act, her lips and a man's cock, put her off. Very few men had earned such trust. But Cameron? She wanted to give him back everything he'd given her.

"Vanessa. Oh please." He arched, surging deeper into her mouth.

She'd never had any complaints before, but her skills with oral sex hadn't been practiced all that much. Vanessa was a firm believer in working hard to achieve the preferred results.

Though from Cam's reactions, she'd aced this particular exam.

Smiling around his shaft, she bobbed up and down, slowly, drawing out his enjoyment—or torture, as Cam liked to call it. He made the most amazing sounds during sex. Unlike the few adult videos she'd watched, which had never done much to arouse her lust, Cam's sensual delight carried through to her, hitting her right between her legs.

She'd just come, but she wanted to feel him there again. After this, a gift he'd more than earned. Despite his teasing last week, they hadn't quite progressed to her "fellating him."

"Gonna come. So hard," he moaned and put a hand to the back of her head. Not shoving her down to gag on him, but holding her while he jerked his hips. "Suck me, baby. Yeah, wrap those lips so tight. *Fuck*."

When he swore, she knew he'd lost his control. Such a turn-on, to get a man with such discipline lost to all but Vanessa's will. She put a hand between his legs to rub his balls and sucked harder, and he cried her name as he poured into her.

Cam tasted like soap and man. Clean and musky. Nothing about him turned her off. And his orgasm revved her to get him going again, just as soon as he could.

He kept his hand on her head and shuddered, then pleaded with her to suck him dry.

After a few moments, he shivered and she eased back, licking her lips as she rose to see him watching her.

His half-lidded eyes and flushed cheeks made him look like a well-pleasured god. All that glowing muscle... Not a spare roll or flap of skin anywhere. Taut, solid, strong. And all hers.

She liked knowing he belonged to her. Maybe a little too much. Because that growing affection she'd felt started to blossom into something more. Especially when he smiled at her, his gaze approving, warm, and much desired.

"Mmm. Come here." He patted his thigh, and she straddled him again, accepting his hugs and kisses. "God, Vanessa. You make me lose my mind. I swear, at this moment, I wish I smoked. I think I could really go for a cigarette."

"Me too." She kissed his cheeks, his nose, his chin. "I think this might be my favorite Valentine's Day ever."

"Oh yeah. For sure." He stroked her back, and she pulled away enough to see him watching her.

"What?"

He looked somewhat tense. "So was it as good for you as it was for me?"

"I doubt it. You pretty much screamed so loud they heard you in Canada."

He chuckled and relaxed. "Yeah, but your sigh was so heartfelt and deep. Heaven shook at the rush of pleasure *I* delivered."

"Poetic. Not bad. You might give Abby a run for her money…with that purple prose." She sneered at him and laughed when he frowned.

"You know, that's mean. I don't know if you deserve round two or not."

She straightened and stopped laughing. "Round two?"

"Nope." Cam's eyes laughed as he tried to hide his smile. "I don't think you look sincere enough. And just think. I was saving my next big, thick erection for your sweet little pussy."

"Cam." She flushed. For all that they engaged in sex, the dirty words made her tingly and felt weird. Because she really liked them.

"Aha! A vulnerability." He laughed. "Perfect. Something I can use to weaken your resistance. Dirty talk."

"Oh, was I resisting earlier? Before or *after* the blow job?"

"Silence, woman." He slapped her ass, not hard, but enough to get her attention. "Now, when you're properly repentant, I'll let you witness my glorious ceiling from the confines of my bed."

"Joy." She snorted, trying hard not to laugh at his antics.

"Sure, it sounds like some boring missionary work, but I'm sure I can work the kinks out of the tedium sure to set in."

Two hours later and working on her third orgasm of the night, Vanessa moaned his name and wrapped her ankles tighter around his waist as Cameron pounded into her. He kept hitting that spot deep inside her that sent her synapses firing up her pleasure center without cease.

She cried out, lost to any sense of circumspection, while he groaned and grunted, muttering things that would have turned her scarlet had he said them anywhere but in bed. Instead, he turned her into a writhing woman desperate and greedy for another orgasm.

"Yes, yes," she screamed and came as he ground against her, his cock so hard she felt him all the way to her womb.

He rode her through her orgasm and into his own, stopping only to shout her name and spend inside her.

When she'd finally stopped seeing stars, he withdrew and left. He returned to clean her up, because, as he liked to say, he'd left a fine mess inside her.

"Oh yeah. You look good like that, your legs spread wide," Cameron teased as he finished wiping between her legs, the gesture curiously intimate considering he'd just been joined inside her right there. Then he did the strangest thing. He leaned down and kissed her, a soft peck right between her legs. He straightened and did the same to her cheek. "I hate to add to your already healthy-sized ego, but you are one gorgeous woman."

He left her again, missing her blush. Men told her she

was pretty all the time. But Cameron complimenting her made her feel the pretty all the way to her toes.

She dragged the covers over her body so that when he returned, he found her bundled under the comforter.

"Move over, slick." He joined her, his feet cold. Then the bozo had the nerve to put his feet on her legs.

"Cut it out. Oh!"

He chuckled and pulled her against him, so they lay on their sides, chest to chest.

She tucked her face into the curve of his neck and smiled against him. "Bully."

"Takes one to know one," he said in a laughing voice. "God, Vanessa. You make me feel so good. Thank you."

The simple thanks touched her deeply. "You're welcome."

He chuckled. "Now you're supposed to thank me for having such skills. I mean, come on. My tongue is golden."

"Hmm. True. But you're a bit cocky for my taste. We'll have to work that out of you…next time."

"Yes, mistress," he said, as if trying to sound meekly obedient.

"Goof." She tugged his chest hair, and he winced. "How about this? Thank you, Cameron, for making this a wonderful Valentine's Day. I'm normally not a big fan of Cupid, in any form."

"Yeah." He sighed and hugged her tight. "This might not come out right. I should be more romantic and less competitive, but somehow I can't help thinking that our Valentine's Day seriously kicked my brothers' collective asses. I mean, you and me? Dinner, wine, chocolates? And the sex wasn't half bad."

They laughed softly together, kissing and cuddling.

Vanessa Ann Campbell willingly cuddled with a man, lingering in the intimacy after sex.

God, she was really losing it. Worse, she couldn't seem to make herself care.

———

Mike finished a terrific meal with his mother, having enjoyed himself more than he'd expected he would. His mother looked beautiful, and despite the sadness he'd occasionally glimpsed in her eyes, she seemed to be having a great time. They talked about Colin, his brothers, and even the newly developing relationship Cam seemed to have going on with Vanessa. Best of all, she didn't mention him dating once. Thank God.

After they left the restaurant and took in an overly sentimental chick flick together—only for his mother—he drove them back to her house. "You sure you don't want to stay with us tonight?"

She laughed. "I'm not sick. I'm not scared. And I'm not lonely. You have work and Colin has school tomorrow. I'll be fine here. Without your father messing up the house, it's actually quite nice to have my evenings to myself."

Having a six-year-old constantly underfoot, he understood the need for one's own space.

"Your call." He shrugged. "But thanks for going with me tonight, Mom. It was fun." He meant it.

"Did you really like the movie?" she asked.

"I hadn't thought I'd like it, but I was pleasantly surprised."

She laughed at him as they exited the truck and

walked to the door. "The look on your face was price-less when you let me decide on the picture. What a good son you are to take poor old Mom to a movie about rival doctors in love." She smiled. "I wasn't looking forward to tonight. I…" she drifted off as they approached the porch. A single white rose and a box of candy lay before the door.

Mike stifled a smile. His father was acting like an ass, but he hadn't forgotten today's significance. *Good one, Dad.*

His mother didn't say anything when she stooped to pick up her presents.

"Nice." Mike waited, but still she said nothing. So he wasn't prepared for her to toss the flower at him.

"Give that to Vanessa from me when you get home. But screw him. I'm keeping the candy." Then she gave him a peck on the cheek, unlocked the door, and slammed it shut behind her.

He left, knowing his parents had a lot of work to do before things got back to normal. If they ever did. Mulling over failed love on the way home, he frowned to see an unfamiliar car sitting in his driveway. He parked next to it and got out, locking the truck before walking to the porch. Tugging at his stupid bow tie, he opened the front door to see Colin sleeping snugly next to…Delilah Webster? Glancing around for Cam and Vanessa, he was nonplussed when the woman held a finger to her lips to shush him. In his own house.

He frowned at her as he crossed to the couch and bent to lift Colin in his arms. He carried the boy off to bed, tucking him in with a kiss. Eleven o'clock and the tiny tyrant had been sleeping in his pajamas on the couch next to a virtual stranger. Well, sure, Mike had bowled with the woman. Didn't mean he knew anything more about her than that she'd once changed Abby's tire and had thrown a decent game.

He returned to see Del turning off the TV and straightening up. He couldn't have said why, but something about her put his back up. She looked mean, sexy. Disturbing. The tats and piercings didn't put him off, though they should have. She wasn't his type at all. Mike liked soft, rounded women. Not muscular types who wore steel-toed boots and looked as if they could kick his ass. Yet her pale gray eyes, in contrast with that yellow hair in various shades and streaked with brown, mesmerized him. The one time he'd seen her, she'd seemed to wear a fuck-you attitude while daring him to get closer.

"What are you doing here?" he asked, uncomfortably aware of how ungrateful he sounded. He cleared his throat and tried again. "I mean, I left Colin with Cam and Vanessa."

"Yeah, well, Romeo needed to romance his lady away from the kid." She shrugged. "Abby asked me to fill in, and since I'm a sucker for a happy ending, I said yes."

"Abby?" What the hell did she have to do with this?

"You know, the short one who looks shy but then won't shut up once she starts talking? The one with the book club I'm now forced to attend?" She grinned, giving lie to the idea she did anything she didn't want to.

He started to respond when he saw a multitude of candy wrappers on the couch, cans of soda and chocolate Kisses scattered across the coffee table, and a large pizza box on the dining room table. "What the hell is all that?"

"My people call it food. What do yours call it?"

"Well, *smart-ass*, I call it unnecessary sugar that my kid shouldn't have and a mess." He stepped closer, feeling the need to take her down a peg. Not that he'd do anything to scare her. She had watched Colin, after all. But her aggressive approach needed a definite adjustment.

Except Delilah Webster didn't back away. The fool woman stepped closer and poked him in the chest. "Look, 007, me and the kid had a great time tonight. He didn't give me any shit, and he didn't pull any stunts. So credit me with some intelligence. I know how to handle a six-year-old."

"Oh? Have a lot of them working at the garage with you, do you?" *007, my ass*. He hated that fucking bow tie. Only for his mother had he put the thing on. "Look. I get that you somehow think I owe you for watching him, but—"

"You don't owe me shit. I did a favor for Abby. Plain and simple."

"—*the fact is*," he continued, "I'm the boy's father. If I say he should eat green food, get to bed *on time*, and brush his teeth, then that's my prerogative, isn't it?"

"Too bad about the stick up your ass. Doesn't go too well with the penguin suit." She poked him again.

He noticed the ring of darker gray around her ice-gray irises. Wolf eyes. She sure the hell seemed like she wanted to gobble him up and spit him out.

Unable to stop himself, he leaned close enough to feel her soft breath over his lips and growled, "Well, now, princess. You don't like what I'm saying, feel free to let the door hit you on the ass on your way out." *On your fine ass*, he thought but didn't say. He hated himself for even thinking about her like that when she was so annoyingly attractive—*annoying. Just annoying.*

Her glance wavered from his eyes to his mouth, and the small moment lingered in his brain and went straight to his cock. For half a heartbeat he thought she might bridge the distance between them and kiss him.

"Whatever." She stepped back and crossed her arms over her chest. "So I watched your kid. You're welcome, by the way. Dickhead."

Aroused, frustrated, and angry about all of it, he removed his wallet from his back pocket. "What do I owe you for the babysitting?"

She narrowed her eyes on his wallet before glaring *through* him. "How about you kiss my ass and we'll call it a night?" She sneered and gave him a baleful once-over before stalking out of the house. To her credit, she didn't slam the door. He heard the purr of an engine as she backed out of the drive, then she gunned it down the street.

Mike ripped the bow tie off his neck and flung it to the floor. "Well, fuck."

———

Vanessa couldn't stop smiling for an entire week. The people at work, all but Josh, gave her a wide berth, scared of her good mood. Her roommates continued to tease her about what getting laid could do for a girl's disposition. Yet they were both much worse than Vanessa. Maddie still sang Flynn's praises while

Abby thought the sun rose and fell on Brody and his messy dog.

She'd confided to Cameron that she liked Hyde now, but she refused to let the others know she'd come to appreciate the mongrel Abby sometimes brought to the house. And by mongrel, she meant the dog, not Brody.

Grinning at her private joke, she checked her calendar and realized she had a date with Cameron at his mother's the following night. Beth had taken to spending time with her sons and their fiancées individually. Cameron's turn would be tomorrow, and she'd invited *his girlfriend*—Vanessa—as well.

Still giddy about being Cameron's girlfriend and not minding at all, she finished her run around the neighborhood, since Seattle had a dry evening for once, and returned to the house. Inside, Brody and Flynn sat arguing in the kitchen, loud enough to wake the neighbor.

Of Maddie and Abby, she saw no sign.

Enjoying her well-earned sweat from a hellacious five-mile run, she tugged her ponytail tighter and joined the testosterone in the kitchen.

As soon as she entered, both men glanced up at her and grew quiet.

"Seems to me like I only saw one pair of shoes by the front door," she commented mildly.

To her satisfaction, Brody's face darkened but he hastened by her to take off his shoes.

Flynn chuckled. "You're good, no question. I can see how you have my little brother wrapped around your finger."

It annoyed her that they never seemed to give Cameron the credit he deserved. "Oh? Because if I'm not mistaken, you dance to Maddie's tune awfully easily. Didn't she tie you up and shove a ball gag in your mouth not so long ago?" He turned a lovely red.

Brody entered in time to overhear and laughed long and loud. "Jesus. She's got you pegged."

"Please." Flynn scowled. "You're one to talk. Maddie told me it's embarrassing. Abby says *jump* and you beg to know how high. Pussy."

"*I'm* a pussy? Yeah right. Didn't you serenade your redhead for V-Day?" Brody scoffed.

Flynn responded with another taunt.

Pleased they'd turned on each other so easily, Vanessa hummed as she finished her water and then fixed herself a nice salad. After a moment of silence, she glanced up to see both men studying her. "What?"

"You sure seem happy." Brody smiled, all innocence. "Nice to see you not so, ah…"

"Tense," Flynn supplied.

"Yeah, tense. Abby told me they're working you ragged at the office."

"It's tax season, but I like my job. And speaking of jobs… It's kind of a chore to entertain you two after the long day I've had. Where are my roommates? Or did they finally annoy you into burying their bodies out back? I'm only asking because if you're not careful, Hyde will dig them up and walk around with leg bones in that black hole of a mouth, outing you to the police before you can say boo."

They just stared at her, wide-eyed.

She sat across from them at the kitchen table and munched on her salad. She'd gotten to like both men very much, appreciating their honesty and love for her extended family—Abby and Maddie. Roommates, sisters in heart, and despite Maddie's overly dramatic aptitude for dealing with life, sadly, a genetic relation.

"You really are one scary woman," Brody said.

She smiled. "Thanks. That means a lot coming from a man like you."

He frowned, but before she could add something else obnoxious, the front door opened to admit the chatter of excitable women.

"Oh my gosh." Maddie entered the kitchen, breathing hard. "Flynn, you are never going to believe this."

Vanessa frowned. "What happened?"

Maddie and Abby glanced at each other before sitting down at the table with them. They placed a paper bag and a carton of coffee in the center.

"Honey, what's wrong?" Flynn asked. His voice turned gentle when he spoke with Maddie. The love was no act.

Brody grabbed Abby's hand and kissed the back of it. "Yeah. Spill. What's up?"

Abby cleared her throat. "We went to get coffee at your parents' favorite place." A pause. "We saw your dad there."

Vanessa studied her, and then she just knew. "Uh-oh."

Flynn frowned. "What?"

"Flynn," Maddie said softly. "Your dad was smiling and, well, *flirting* with Amelia. The woman behind the counter?"

"She's a barista..." Abby trailed off as Flynn swore, Brody sighed, and the guys seemed to deflate right in front of her.

Vanessa decided she needed to lighten the mood in

the kitchen. Because if her friends tried to interfere, she had no doubt they'd screw everything up. "Come on, guys. Would your dad really flirt, in public, in a place he knows his sons and future daughters-in-law frequent?"

Flynn perked up. "Probably not."

"Unless he's thinking with his dick," Brody muttered. Abby socked him in the arm, and he rubbed it. "Ow. Sorry, but men can be assholes. You all know it."

"Yes," Vanessa agreed. "But James is an intelligent man, correct? Maybe he was just being nice." She gave her cousin the eye.

It took her a minute, but Maddie nodded. "Oh. Right. You know, Abby, we might have misread the situation. If you think about it, he smiled at us too. He didn't look guilty or anything. I think he would have if we'd caught him being overly friendly."

Abby frowned. "Really? Because—"

Vanessa kicked her under the table and frowned.

Abby glared at her but must have realized it best to keep quiet about the truth.

"Now don't you two feel *better*?" Vanessa emphasized to Flynn and Brody.

Abby sighed. "Oh hell. I didn't mean to stir gossip, guys. Forget I said anything. Now I'm not sure what I saw. I just miss him with your mom. I'm not used to seeing him around other women without Beth there beside him."

Brody pulled her into his lap. Vanessa hated herself for noticing, but damn, they really did look good together. Why the hell did she continue to discern these things? Now she was seeing hearts and romance all over the place.

Had to be Cameron's influence. Understanding this, the old Vanessa would have cut short their relationship and gotten some distance. But the new her liked the closeness of this group, and in particular, her association with Cameron. She missed his presence, even though she knew he'd had to cancel plans with her tonight due to a meeting with a new client *she'd* recommended to him.

Determined to stop mooning over Cameron and help the man and his brothers, she changed the subject. "Now that that's settled—"

"It is?" Abby asked.

"Why don't you guys tell me what you had planned for tonight's double date?"

Flynn gave her an odd look, then shrugged. "Not much." With a sly wink her way, he added, "Too bad genius boy is working or all six of us could have gone out together."

"Oh, what fun," Brody drawled. "Gee, what could we have done? A wine tasting? Maybe an art show? I know. A poetry reading."

He and Flynn snickered, and she let them tease about Cameron's taste in entertainment. She smiled to herself, knowing how she'd have spent the evening. Wrapped around her studly financier.

"Excuse me." Abby frowned. "How is a poetry reading a bad thing?"

Maddie glanced at her own fingers. "I don't know about you guys, but I wouldn't mind going to get my nails done. We have some time before that movie you wanted to see later."

"Oh hell." Flynn groaned. "Maddie, you don't take your fiancé with you to paint your nails."

"That's too bad." She made a sad face. "Because there's this lingerie place a few doors down, and I thought we could swing by after and pick out a few—"

"I'm in. Let's go." Brody stood with Abby in his arms and darted down the hallway.

Abby laughed and ordered him to put her down.

"So easy," Maddie snickered, and Flynn grinned with her.

"Isn't he?"

"I meant you." She rolled her eyes and said to Vanessa, "It's like once you divert the blood flow from the big head to the little head, they can't focus."

"Nothing little about my heads, Maddie." Flynn leered.

"Ew. Get out of here, you sexed-up pervs." Vanessa shooed them out of the kitchen, mentally congratulating herself for lightening the mood.

Then she resolved to get down and dirty and figure out once and for all why Beth and James were on the outs. It was the least she could do for Cameron, a man she was coming to appreciate more than was healthy... for them both.

Chapter 11

SITTING NEXT TO HER *BOYFRIEND*, VANESSA WIPED HER mouth with the cloth napkin Beth had laid out. Like Cameron, his mother had set the table with candles and a bouquet of flowers. But the feel at her dinner was less about romance and more about class. Vanessa could see where Cameron had inherited his fine taste and ability to act with dignity and decorum.

"Beth, this chicken is wonderful." She smiled.

Beth beamed. "It's one of my favorite recipes. You should have Cam cook it for you sometime."

"He's quite the chef," she agreed. "I, sadly, can barely boil water."

"No kidding," Cam muttered. At her glare, he smiled widely. "Yet your presence is all I need to sweeten the meal."

"Gimme a break."

Beth laughed. "That was bad, Cam. Just a bit over the top."

"Hey, Mom. Cut me some slack. I'm trying." He winked at Vanessa. His openness about their relationship in front of his mother made her feel special. They'd been in each other's pockets all week long, and she had yet to be tired of him.

She kept waiting for him to annoy her, or for her to freeze him out. But the sex continued to get hotter, and their time together more exciting and enjoyable. It baffled her. She'd never lasted this long with any man before. To top that off, technically, she'd known Cam for an entire year. Still, they remained friends.

"Let me get started on the dishes," Beth said with a smile and left the table with a few plates.

Cam's cell phone rang. He frowned and took it from his pocket, then sighed. "Sorry. I need to take this. It's Hope."

Vanessa nodded. She liked that he wanted to bring his cousin into the business. "I'll help your mom in the kitchen."

He answered, "Hey, Hope." Then he kissed Vanessa on the cheek and left the dining room to go into the living area, where she heard him ask, "So what's this about the lock?"

Vanessa joined Beth in the kitchen. "You are one heck of a cook." She put a hand on Beth's shoulder.

The woman's hands lay buried in the soapy water. "Thank you, Vanessa. I'm glad you enjoyed it."

"I like you, Beth. So I'm just going to ask. What the hell happened with you and your husband?"

Beth blinked. "I, uh, what's that?"

"Everyone's dancing around it. There's a rumor James has a thing for some chick at the coffee shop." Bluntness was Vanessa's most effective tool. "And you act like either a whipped puppy or a mute statue whenever anyone brings up his name. So what's up?"

"Whipped puppy?"

"Hey, I call 'em like I see 'em. If he screwed around on you, why are you taking it lying down? Go get a makeover, get a date, and live a little."

"I..." The rage left her between one blink and the next. "Makeover? What's wrong with the way I look?"

"Nothing if you want to be Grandma for the rest of your life." Vanessa, Maddie, and Abby had discussed Beth in detail. Maddie's expertise with clothing and design notwithstanding, even Vanessa had seen that Beth needed a wake-up call. "Beth, you're beautiful."

"I'm fifty-six years old."

"Congratulations. Abby is twenty-six and still thinks clogs are fashionable. Age is not an excuse to dress dowdy."

"*Dowdy?*" Good. The woman looked riled.

"I'm just saying that with some highlights to accent the silver in your dark hair, and some fitted clothing, like that dress you and Maddie bought—yeah, she showed it to me—you'd be a stunner. If James is out trying to score a chick and can't see the hot one in front of his face, his loss. Get out there and live a little. If anything, make him so jealous he can't see straight. I can tell you from personal experience that revenge can be very, very satisfying."

Beth straightened and started to smile. "Hmm. I hadn't thought about that." Her smile faded. "The woman he likes. I think she's a lot younger."

"And stupid if she thinks she can compare to you. I just don't get it. All I've heard from the guys is how great you and James are together. How did it go wrong?"

Beth frowned. "I don't know. We used to do everything together. Then I retired from my job as a secretary. Twenty years working for the college and suddenly I was just another homemaker."

"And mother of four stubborn men. Don't forget that."

Beth snorted. "As if I could. I guess…maybe I lost some of my identity when I finished my job. I don't know. James never acted like he appreciated my work anyway. I thought he'd be happier when I stayed home. Instead of being together, he put in more hours at work. I got lonely. Then I started going out with my friends from the college. Lunches, sometimes dinners. I tried to get him to go with me, but he didn't want to."

"So you pulled away. He pulled away. Then this?"

She looked baffled. "It's the oddest thing. It's like we went from full in love to blah to nothing in seconds. I can't put my finger on it, but we just weren't *there* anymore. You know?"

Vanessa nodded, though she'd always been able to pinpoint when a relationship went sour.

Beth continued. It was as if once she'd started talking, she couldn't stop. "James didn't want to walk with me, go out with me, spend time with me. Anytime I tried to get him to eat healthier or take care of him, he'd snipe at me."

"Doesn't sound fair."

"No. It isn't." Beth glared. "When I begged him to talk about it or go to therapy, he shut down. So I did too." She glanced over her shoulder, then whispered, "We stopped having sex months ago. That's when our relationship really went downhill."

McCauleys had sex in their fifties and sixties. Check. "That's got to hurt. That lack of intimacy." Or so the talk shows always said.

"Yes." Beth looked sad again. "I had no passion for him, this stranger I lived with. Then to know he'd been with that younger woman…"

"They had sex?" Vanessa asked bluntly.

Beth frowned. "I don't know. He said they didn't but that he had *feelings*." She sneered. "What about *my* damn feelings? What about all the time I spent caring for him, for this family? I wanted to work longer, you know. I quit to make him happy."

"Oh."

"And then he treats me like dirt. Without any reason! I never deserved that."

"No."

"That man." She punched the soapy water, and bubbles went flying.

Cameron walked into the kitchen with a smile on his face that disappeared as he looked at them. "Hey…Mom?"

Beth snorted. "I'm done being a victim. Thank you, dear." She leaned close and kissed Vanessa on the cheek. "I'm going to think about what you said. A lot." She beamed at Cameron, and he looked puzzled. "Now let's have dessert."

An hour later, after they returned to her house, Cameron asked her, "What the hell did you say to my mother?"

Vanessa shrugged. "Only that she needs to update her look. I mean, your mom is very pretty, but she's dressing like she's eighty."

"You think?" He frowned.

"I like Beth. If she feels better about herself, her confidence will have a positive effect on her and everyone around her, right?"

"I guess." He didn't seem sure, and she didn't think it wise to tell him that Beth had plans to knock James on his ass. Cameron probably wouldn't thank her for her much-needed advice.

"Now what did you have in mind? You sleeping over? Or do you have to ask your mom for permission first?"

"Funny." He drew her in for a kiss. "As much as I'd love to stay, I have an early appointment in the morning. Apparently the key jammed in the lock so Hope couldn't get in tonight. I'm meeting a locksmith early tomorrow."

"Too bad."

He kissed her again. And again. "But I'm sure I could be persuaded to stick around for a little longer."

Vanessa's heart raced. They hadn't spent much time at her place. Normally at his condo or out about town, they'd seen movies, had dinner, played cards. Had sex. But here, in her sanctuary, she wanted him to stay. Despite the potential of her roommates returning at any moment, she wanted to have Cameron in her bed, surrounded by her things. Before, his presence might have felt like an invasion. She believed in keeping her private life private. But now, with her new *boyfriend*...

"You want to come upstairs?" She swallowed hard and tried to make light of what should have been no big deal. "See my etchings?"

He stared into her eyes and brushed her hair aside. "I'd love to. I'd also love to spend the night, but I do need to get back."

She nodded, secretly relieved he would be going afterward. Their closeness at times worried her. Because she was letting him into her life in a way she'd never let anyone else. He felt like a stable, almost permanent fixture. And now, having him in her room? Around her things? Making memories of Cameron in her bed?

"Lead on, sexy." He kissed her once more, then nudged her to the stairway.

She told herself to stop acting like a drama queen and

walked purposefully to her room. She locked the door behind them, then slammed him up against the wall and kissed the breath out of him.

He groaned and started to fight back when she pinned his wrists to the wall. "Oh shit. Go ahead. Your turn."

He was always saying things like that, as if he had a mental tally of who got to be on top. But so close, feeling so much as she always did around him, she let it go and devoured him.

Between kissing and touching, she removed her clothes while he ripped off his shirt and lowered his pants and underwear. He'd gotten them down to his upper thighs before she knelt in front of him and took him deeply to the back of her throat.

"Christ, Vanessa. You're way too good at this." He gripped her by the hair and pumped into her mouth, his expression one of awe and desire. "I want to come inside you. With you squeezing me tight."

She sucked him harder, wanting to see him lose control. Needing to know she owned this moment to give order to the chaos of emotion shattering her.

"*No*. Not without you," he uttered through a clenched jaw. He tugged her hair and pulled away, then lifted her in his arms and pinned her against the wall. In seconds, he had her legs wrapped around his waist as he slammed inside her. "Oh yeah. God, come around me."

She moaned and gripped his powerful shoulders as he slammed into her. Punishing strokes that showed his urgency and increased her desire. Cameron without his careful limits turned her on and made her feel special, powerful. *She* caused him to lose himself in her. And she reveled in it. Especially because he brought her pleasure, made her forget herself as she climbed to orgasm.

"You're so hard," she moaned.

"For you. God, I'm going to fill you up. So much." He jerked his hips and ground against her clit.

She cried out and came, clenching him tightly as her world exploded.

"Yes, oh yeah." He thrust hard and stilled, shaking as he poured into her.

From downstairs the door opened, and she heard her roommates talking with each other. But she didn't care if they knew Cameron was with her. In fact, she wanted them to know. To put her claim on the man coming to mean so much to her.

"You make me crazy." Cameron kissed her gently. "If I had the strength, I'd do it all over again."

"Yeah," she sighed and kissed him back, running her fingers through his hair. "You're not bad at this sex thing."

He grinned, his blue eyes deep and dark. "I try. But it's good we keep me in practice."

She chuckled and caressed his neck, enjoying his shiver. "Ticklish?"

"Not there. It just feels so good." He squeezed her ass, and she realized he still held her in place. "You feel good."

"You're a lot stronger than you look. I can't believe you're holding me up."

"Thanks," he said drily. "But the wall has most of your gargantuan weight."

She smacked him on the arm. "You're not supposed to tell a woman she weighs a lot."

"Hey, truth is truth. Besides, muscle weighs more than fat."

"Technically, that's not true. Because—"

"The only softness you have settled in all the right places," he said over her and rubbed his chest against her breasts. "You know, if I hang around long enough, I'm sure we could go again."

She licked her lips. "I'm game. But Maddie and Abby are downstairs. Do we really want them to hear you moaning my name?"

"Please. You're the one always crying, 'Cam. God, Cam. In me, *yes*,'" he ended in falsetto.

She slapped a hand over his mouth, suddenly not wanting anyone to intrude on their time together. "Shush."

His wicked grin amused her. "Embarrassed? Is my Amazon shy?"

Whenever he referred to her as his, she got a funny feeling in the pit of her stomach. A deeper sense of belonging she wanted desperately to be true.

"Oh shut up, studly. Now put your... Well, I'd say put your clothes back on, but you only managed to lower your pants and underwear. How decadent."

"Only you would use a word like *decadent* after sex. And yeah, my dick is the only thing hanging out of my pants and still buried inside you. Decadent applies. So does heaven on earth."

They grinned at each other, then he withdrew and grabbed a T-shirt from the floor to stem the mess between her legs.

He nodded, his eyes dreamy. "Have I told you how much I love coming inside you?"

"Just about every day."

"Good. Because it's true." He looked as if he wanted to say more, then footsteps sounded on the stairs. "I guess I should head back. We're on for a run tomorrow evening? Say, seven?"

"You know it." She quickly threw on a bra and a pair of sweats and walked him downstairs. They didn't pass her roommates, who must have gone into their rooms. "Thanks for tonight. I had a great time."

He ran his hand over her hair again and cupped her cheek. "Me too." He gave her a brief kiss. "See you tomorrow. Oh, and don't think I bought that explanation of what you said to my mom. The woman looked ready to kill the dishes. I'll get the rest out of you."

"Dream on."

"I intend to." He chucked her chin, then left whistling.

She smiled and closed the door, so totally smitten and enjoying the moment before reason returned and she thought about where this future might lead her. Letting herself ease back into the real world, she turned to head down the hall to the kitchen and saw her roommates staring at her from the stairs.

"Hell."

Maddie squealed. "Oh my gosh. You and Cam did the nasty *in our house*! You have sex head."

Abby nodded.

"What's sex head?" Vanessa asked, even though she knew better.

"When you have that just-gripped look." Abby nodded to a section of Vanessa's hair sticking out.

"Yeah." Maddie nodded. "Oh man. Vanessa did Cam in our house. In her room! So are you two getting married or what?"

Vanessa scowled. "So we had sex. You two do it all the time."

"I wouldn't say all the time…" Abby flushed.

"Please." Maddie rolled her eyes. "You're worse than me and Flynn." She turned back to Vanessa. "Vanessa, let's be honest. You never date a guy this long. I mean, you and Cam went to Beth's *as a couple*. You spend your time exercising and eating disgustingly nutritious food…*together*."

Abby smiled. "I think it's great."

"Yeah. Okay." Vanessa headed to the kitchen, in need of some peppermint tea. Unfortunately, the chatty twins followed.

They watched her put the kettle on for tea.

"Vanessa?" Abby asked. "Why don't you seem glad about being with Cam?"

She felt tense and deliberately relaxed before turning to face them. "Our relationship is great, but we're no big deal. Cameron and I are new. So of course it's all fluttery feelings and fun. I give it another few weeks before we cool down."

Abby shook her head. "Brody told me he's never seen Cam so happy before. I mean, really happy. That's even while living with his father underfoot."

Maddie nodded. "Flynn said the same thing. So are you going to let this relationship happen, or will you sabotage it like all the others?"

Vanessa frowned. "That was your MO before Flynn. Not mine."

"You're more subtle, but you're flawed, just like me. You find fault with everyone you date. I'm shocked Cam's lasted this long. But then, with a guy like him, it's got to be hard to find things you don't like. He's nice but not too nice. Sexy, handsome, smart. Your kind of smart. And he's rich."

"He doesn't have to be rich to be interesting."

"No, but that doesn't hurt. The man is just like you." Maddie glanced at Abby. "Am I right?"

"So I hit a bunch of duds before," Vanessa cut in. "Not my fault they couldn't keep up." She recalled John "Small Dick" Willington. She hadn't seen him since that dinner and actually liked dealing with Henry on business.

"Well, this thing you have going with Cam." Maddie pointed a finger at her. "Don't screw it up."

"What the hell does that mean?" Vanessa took the kettle off the burner when it whistled and turned off the stove. After pouring herself and her roommates some hot water, she girded herself for a verbal battle. "Why do you automatically assume *I'll* be the one to screw up?"

"Because that's what you do. Your parents did a number on you as a kid, and you always get weird when you find a guy you might like. I think you really like Cam. Don't search for problems where there are none. That's all I'm saying."

It grated that Maddie might have a point. Hadn't Vanessa been trying not to ruin her evening by suppressing thoughts of the future with Cameron? "You know, just because you happen to be getting lucky on a regular basis with Flynn does not make you an expert on relationships."

"Sure it does."

Abby cut in. "I think Maddie just means we like seeing you so happy. You seem lighter, not so tense."

"Why does everyone keep calling me tense?"

"Does controlling, dictatorial, or uptight work better for you?" Maddie asked with overdone innocence.

Vanessa slipped her the finger, to which Maddie chuckled.

"I'm just saying we like this new you." Maddie took her mug and tossed a tea bag into it. "Don't let your wacky parents ruin your love life. You're the fun Campbell, and that's saying something."

"Vanessa's not like them," Abby defended her.

"Not really," Maddie hedged. "But she's got a defense mechanism where she pulls back when she feels threatened."

"Well, Cameron is the sensitive McCauley," Abby said. "But he's still a man. So it's a given *he'll* mess up. That's what people do. The question becomes, will you be able to forgive him? I might not know your family dynamics like Maddie does, but I do know you like to be right."

"About everything," Maddie groused, then smiled. "It doesn't help that you often *are* right. That you're so self-reliant, and that you rarely mess up."

Abby nodded. "The problem is that when others around you do, you're not as forgiving."

"Hey, I put up with you two."

Maddie crossed her eyes.

Abby laughed. "But we're family. Can you be so forgiving with the man in your life? A guy you might come to love?"

Vanessa pondered that as they drank their tea and turned the conversation to Beth and James. She told her roommates what she'd said to Beth, and they gave her kudos for being bold enough to speak the truth. But all the while, she wondered about Abby's questions. Could she forgive Cameron when he eventually made a monumental mistake? His Y chromosome practically confirmed that at some point in their "relationship" he'd step on his own dick.

And then what?

Chapter 12

BETH MCCAULEY STARED AT HER REFLECTION IN AWE.

"Beth, I'm so happy you decided to go for a change. I mean, don't get me wrong. I've loved doing your hair the past five years. But man, I was dying to experiment with you. You look gorgeous."

"I look ten years younger." Beth gaped at herself in the mirror. Wearing the clothes Maddie had picked out with her a few days ago, she felt practically indecent in the form-fitting jeans and soft blue sweater. But Maddie had insisted she stop hiding herself in "old lady clothes." As if prints in paisley and stripes to hide her saggy breasts and tummy made her automatically old.

"I'd say fifteen years younger, not ten," Maureen, her hairdresser, said with a large smile. "That cut really frames your face and highlights your cheekbones. The last cut was nice, but not as interesting. And I love this color." Maureen ran a brush over the sleek layered cut that showed off the new black and silver strands mixed with a hint of dark mahogany. "It's beautiful."

A few other stylists came over to *ooh* and *ah*, and Beth felt like a million bucks. On her walk home, she gave in to impulse and stopped in a cosmetics salon. An hour later and several dollars poorer, she took her makeup and freshly done nails back home.

Feeling amazing and wanting to share her recent success, she called Abby, who had mentioned the other night at dinner that she'd planned to take Friday off. Abby answered on the first ring.

Beth walked a few blocks to the house she rented to Abby and the girls.

When Abby opened the door, she stared with wide eyes. "Oh my gosh. You look amazing." She laughed and hugged Beth with such enthusiasm that Beth laughed as well. "I'm so glad you called. I actually have to take my car in to get looked at and was going to see if Brody would follow me over. Would you mind, and then we could go to lunch after?"

"Sounds perfect."

Abby grabbed her keys and purse and continued to pester Beth about details of her salon visit. They drove to Beth's house to pick up her car, and Beth followed Abby to a small garage on the other side of town. She parked and followed Abby inside.

To her bemusement, they had to walk through a rough-looking establishment. Inside the garage, Beth noted several men who looked more like prison escapees than mechanics, and one particularly large older man who straightened and stared at her with an odd look that made her hurry her step to join Abby.

They entered the small office, where a young man, sporting tattoos and multiple piercings, greeted them as he typed at his computer.

"Hey. You here for an appointment or just need us to check out your car?"

Abby smiled. "I'm here to see Del and to drop off my car. Tell her it's Abby."

He nodded. "Sure thing." He dialed a number, asked for Del, then cringed at whatever she said back to him.

He managed to get Abby's name into the conversation then hung up quickly. "Ah, go on into her office. She'll be right in."

Beth realized where they were and wanted to meet this Del person. Her grandson had taken a real liking to the woman who sounded like Beth's worst personal nightmare.

"So I get to meet the infamous Del, hmm?" she asked Abby as they sat in a surprisingly clean, organized office.

They took the seats across from a large scarred desk covered in stacks of papers. A computer sat along the wall, and on the table behind the desk, bunches of tools, some covered in grease, some not, stacked like mini sacrifices to the gods of the garage.

The door to the right opened, one that led presumably to the work area. Instead of a woman, the large man who'd given her the shivers entered.

"Well, *hello*." He barely glanced at Abby and smiled widely at Beth. Good-looking in a rough, scary kind of way. "What can I do for you ladies?"

Beth blushed. She hadn't been looked at like she was an attractive, available woman in ages. To her astonishment, it felt…good.

"We're here to see Del," Abby said with a touch of amusement.

Beth glanced at the girl and tried to maintain her dignity. "Yes." She turned back to the giant. He wore stained coveralls, his silver hair in a military-short buzz cut. But my, what a body. Beth might be older. She sure the hell wasn't dead. This man could give James a run for his money in the build department.

"Ah, my lovely daughter." The man wiped his hand with a rag and stepped closer to Beth. Then he held out a hand. "Name's Liam Webster. Welcome to my garage."

She took his hand and gave it a firm shake just as another person entered the room—a woman with tattoos on her arms, wearing ash-blond hair held back in a ponytail, and sporting a ring on her eyebrow and a stud in her nose.

"Man. What did I do to deserve you?" she said in a husky voice with a grin at Abby.

"Hey, Del. We've just met your dad." Abby looked pointedly at his hand that still held Beth's.

Beth tugged and he gave it back.

He cleared his throat. "Sorry. But damn. You are just the prettiest thing."

"Dad." Del glared. "Sorry. This is my dad, Liam. I'm Del." She ignored Abby and cocked her head as she studied Beth. "You… You're Beth McCauley, I bet."

"I am." So this was the woman her grandson adored.

"Yeah, your sons look just like you. We went bowling once." Del shrugged. Then she smiled. "Your grandson sure is a charmer."

Beth smiled back, liking the woman a bit, if only for that comment. "He is. He's a handful."

"No shit. I—er, mean, no kidding." Del sighed and sat behind her desk. When her father continued to stand there staring at Beth—*how embarrassing*—she cleared her throat. "Dad?"

"Huh? Oh." He took a step back. "Just wanted to see who your visitors were. I'll be in the garage. Nice meeting you Beth, Abby."

Abby nodded. "You too, Mr. Webster."

He frowned. "Nah. Just Liam." He winked at Beth.

"You can call me anything you want to." He glanced at her bare ring finger, smiled wider, then left.

"Sorry for my dad." Del sounded as if strangling on her tongue. "He's a handful too. Jesus." She tugged her ponytail, and Beth noted the woman's dirty fingers. "I was in the garage working when Dale called."

"Dale?" Abby asked.

"The kid at the front desk. He's a new intern. Got skills with paint."

Beth watched the woman interact with Abby, seeing her confidence, a kind of kiss-my-butt attitude.

"So my car is out back. It's making a *chug chug* noise," Abby was saying.

"What?"

"Well, it's more like a *chug-clink-chug*. And sometimes it coughs."

Del stood and held up a hand. "Stop with the sounds. Just tell me what the car is doing."

As Abby explained, Beth glanced around. The automotive garage was old. But it seemed to have no shortage of work. She'd seen a lot of cars parked in the lot. They weren't junky cars at all. The doorway behind Del opened again, and through it Beth saw a few classic cars being worked on. Again, by a bunch of thugs who looked like they'd be at home behind bars. But then, she'd thought the same thing of James over thirty years ago.

Yeah, and look at how that turned out. You can't judge someone by appearances, Beth.

"…outside. Come on," Del said and walked with Abby into the garage.

Beth followed, more than curious about the manly area where so many mysterious things happened with cars. She'd never been particularly handy with tools and had never wanted to be. Beth knew her strengths. Organization—why she'd been so good at her job—motherhood, cleanliness.

She watched a few of the men leaning into the engines and listened as they swore at each other, rather creatively. In a way, they reminded her of her own sons when they didn't think she listened.

"So how do you know my girl?" Liam asked from behind her.

He startled her into a shriek, and all action in the garage ceased.

"Shit. Damn it. I'm sorry." He yelled at the mechanics, "Get back to work!"

Liam gently pulled her back into the office and shut the door behind him. "Sorry. Not safe out there. You're too pretty to get all dirty."

Again he'd called her pretty.

"Thank you." She gave him a shy grin, one he returned.

"Hope I wasn't out of line. We don't get many fine women in here. Mostly car guys, motorheads, the occasional collector. We do a lot of work on older cars. Bodywork, paint, remodeling. But Del's been working on bringing in new blood, people needing a good mechanic." He shrugged. "I'm told to shut up and mind her. Funny how the young always seem to think they know best."

She laughed. "I have four sons. Trust me when I say I feel your pain."

They started up a conversation about their children, and before she knew it, Liam had charmed her into a date for coffee. Coffee. Innocent, in broad daylight around other people. To her surprise, he seemed as tentative about seeing her as she felt about him. That hesitancy made her like him all the better for it.

As she drove Abby back to Queen Anne for lunch, she considered that she felt a bit guilty about seeing another man while still married to that lunkhead James. But coffee was only coffee.

"So Liam seemed to like you," Abby said.

"Yes. He was very nice."

In her periphery, Beth saw Abby's eyes narrow.

"So. Liam. You."

Beth swallowed. "He asked me to coffee next week."

"And?"

"I said yes."

Abby was silent a moment, then she started clapping. "Bravo. So you have a date with a hot guy. Nicely done."

"Oh, well. I don't know that I'd call it a date."

"Really? Because Liam sure liked you. He had a lot of muscle and a twinkle in his eye when he was checking out your butt."

"Abby." Beth blushed.

Abby laughed. "Good for you. Call it a date or not. I'm just wondering what James will think when he finds out."

"I'm not planning to tell him." Beth didn't want to resort to those kinds of tactics with her husband. Hell. She hadn't seen the man in a week. For all she knew, he'd been dating his little barista all this time. The knowledge shouldn't have hurt. They'd agreed to go their separate ways, after all. But it did.

"Well, I have no problem spreading rumors about your date with a sexy man." Abby paused. "Beth, do you want to get back with James?"

"He's the father of my children."

"So? Do you love him?"

Beth had thought about that question for a very long time. "I love the man he used to be. If I could have that James back, I'd never let him go."

Abby nodded. "Then let me know when and where your coffee is next week. Because if James is as over you as he acts like he is, then he won't care what you do, will he?"

"I guess not. No harm in telling him, I suppose." Beth's belly fluttered. Would he care? Would he put in an appearance? Who knew? The old James wouldn't have stood by while another man flirted with his wife. Then again, the old James would never have tolerated months without sex. Or years without really talking, holding hands, or being together in the ways that mattered.

Would he be there next week? Or would he be as absent as he'd been through the last years of their marriage?

―――

Cam waited until his last client of the day left and let out a happy sigh.

Hope leaned into his office with a thumbs-up. "I heard her mention her plans to share your name with her friends. Nice work, Cam."

He grinned. "Yeah. Noelle has contacts in some pretty impressive places. See? I told you you wouldn't starve working for me."

She entered and sat across from him. "That's what Alex said." His associate, who'd been diligently working in the back room before Cam had told him to go home. He'd more than earned his time off. "Well, this income is helping me pursue my dream job, for sure."

"I'm hurt. I'm not your dream job?"

"You're too easy." She snorted. "But then, that's what they all say about you."

"Ha ha. Remember, Hope. You're the *nice* Donnigan. Don't turn into your brothers."

"God help me." She gagged, and he laughed. "Don't get me wrong, Cam. I love this. But I really want to make a go of my other job."

"The one where you cater to personal fantasies? Sounds kinky."

"Shut up." Her cheeks grew pink. "It's not like that. More like we give our clients a fantasy—that's not *sexual*, you perv—but like a dream date or dream vacation. It's more a logistical job than anything. It's so fun putting the pieces together."

"The idea sounds exciting. I wonder what Vanessa would consider her dream date?" he mused.

"Anything with you, I'm sure." Hope sighed. "Ah, to be young and in love."

"Shut up."

"She looks at you with stars in her eyes. Really."

Vanessa had stopped by his office a few times and talked to Hope while waiting on him. He liked that she'd taken the time to see where he worked.

"Vanessa? Stars? Are you sure you aren't seeing daggers or knives?"

She laughed. "I like your girlfriend. She's no-nonsense. She doesn't let you get away with stuff. You need that."

Cam liked the idea he needed Vanessa as much as

she needed him. With him, she let herself have fun and laugh. With her, he didn't have to pretend to be more like his brothers or tone down his intelligence. She understood his caustic wit, even shared in it.

"I see you mooning again. That's my cue to leave." She stood and left, just as Brody and Flynn entered.

"Hey, Hope. Still not sure why you're working for this loser," Flynn remarked.

"Yeah. We can pay you double what he is. Come to the dark side," Brody added.

Flynn punched him in the arm.

"Ow. What the hell?"

"We don't know what he's paying her. You don't double a mystery number, dickhead."

Hope laughed and said something Cam couldn't hear. Then the outer door closed, signaling her departure.

"So are you two here to talk investment strategies?" Cam paged through his calendar, preferring to have one not linked to his computer or phone. "Because I could have sworn I had you penciled in for next week. I'd have seen you with Mike, but it's all I can do not to throttle his giant neck after an hour of talking numbers."

Brody and Flynn looked at each other before sitting down. "You haven't heard?" Brody asked.

"About what?" He'd been focused on growing his clientele and spending as much time with Vanessa as was humanly possible. He'd spent an entire night with her at her place two days ago. A victory of epic proportions. And the woman no longer flinched when he called her his girlfriend. He was on top of the world.

"About Mom and her date tomorrow afternoon."

Cam froze. "Date?"

Flynn frowned. "Yeah. And not with Dad."

"What the hell are you talking about?" He had the uneasy sensation he should have followed up with Vanessa about her discussion with his mother a week and a half ago.

"Abby told me not to mention it," Brody said slowly. "It's been killing me. I told Flynn, but we decided to keep it quiet. But now, this date's actually happening… I don't like it."

"Me neither," Flynn fumed. "Mike told Dad yesterday, and he said nothing."

"Wait. Slow down. What's going on?"

Before Flynn could answer and confuse him even more, Cam pointed at Brody. "You. Speak."

Brody glared even as he explained the situation.

"Mom is dating a mechanic?" Cam's voice rose. "What did Dad say?"

"Nothing." Flynn swore. "Fucking nothing. He just looked at Mike and shrugged, then went back to work. Mike's beyond pissed, I have to tell you." He paused, and he and Brody exchanged a look.

"What?"

"Well, apparently Mom got the idea in her head from something Vanessa said." Flynn shook his head. "Vanessa told her to stop being a 'whipped puppy' and do something about her single status. To get a new hairdo and some new stuff to wear." He scowled. "I had a talk with Maddie about that. My fiancée has apparently been taking Mom shopping for sexy clothes."

"Yeah, and how did that conversation go over?" Brody asked with a grin.

"Maddie told me to go fuck myself," Flynn muttered.

"But I got my point across. My mother is not sexy. She's...Mom."

"She's also a woman," Brody said flatly, surprising Cam that he'd stick up for her in a war between "Pop" and "Bitsy." "She hasn't been happy for a long time. If Pop thinks it's okay to hang with some stupid coffee chick, then Bitsy should show him what he's missing."

Flynn blinked and relaxed. "Oh. You mean, get Dad jealous."

Brody sighed. "Dude, seriously. You're not that stupid. I'm the blond, not you."

"Shut up, asswipe." Flynn laughed. "So she's out to make the old man jealous. Good for you, Mom."

Cam contained his urge to drive straight home and shake some sense into Vanessa. Evidently, her lame explanation that she'd advised his mother to get a makeover wasn't *half* of what her conversation had been.

"Hey, guys. Think about it," Cam suggested. "Maybe Mom isn't out to make Dad jealous. Maybe she's out to be with a guy who appreciates her for who she is, and not who she isn't."

Flynn frowned. "What?"

"You think she likes this guy?" Brody asked.

"What did Mike say?" Cam wanted to know.

"Not much. He's annoyed with the world in general, lately," Flynn answered

Brody cleared his throat. "Yeah, he is. The other day when Colin pulled one of his usual funny stunts, Mike went ballistic. The little bugger tried to talk Mike into taking him to Del's to say hi and Mike snapped. He's on serious edge."

"We all are." Cam seethed with the need to talk to

Vanessa. They were going to have their first big fight. He had no idea how she'd take it. But damn it. She'd been wrong for involving herself in something not her business without at least talking to him first. "Look. It's late, I'm beat, and I need to talk to Vanessa."

"I'll bet." Flynn shook his head. "Good luck with that one."

"Maybe you can get her to interfere again and call off this date with Bitsy and her 'sexy' man," Brody said. "I'm all for Bitsy being happy, but I think she and Pop can work it out. They just need to stop being so damn stubborn."

"Fuck yeah. But try telling that to either of them. They won't listen," Flynn said to Cam. "We've tried."

"I haven't. Yet."

"Good luck." Flynn stood.

Brody did as well, then whistled as he took a hard look around him. "You know, we will sit down with you next week. Just think, Flynn. Maybe if we listen to Einstein, we can have an office this nice. Did you see Hope's leather chair? It's quality, man."

Flynn snorted. "I know. Maddie told me how much he paid for all this." He turned to Cam. "So you know, she did give you a discount."

"Yeah, yeah. Whatever. Get out." Cam ushered them from the office and decided to leave as well. If he talked to Vanessa now, while thoroughly annoyed, he might say something he'd later regret. He locked up and walked home, pleased to find the evening clear. At home, he found his father in the media room sitting on the couch watching a sitcom. For the past several nights, his father had been in a black mood, so they'd steered clear of each other. But not tonight.

Cam jumped right in. "So you're good with Mom dating some hot guy with muscles?"

His father started. "Jesus. Give a guy some warning," he snapped.

"So you and Mom. You're done then?" he asked calmly, hoping to spark his father into doing anything but nothing.

"Not your business." James refused to turn and face him.

Cam rounded the couch and crossed his arms. "So are you and *Amelia* dating? Is she going to give me the little brother I always wanted?"

His father blinked and stared at him. "Are you drunk?"

"Are you? Do you even care that Mom's moving on?"

"Of course I do." His father stood and ran a hand through his hair. "What the fuck do you want me to do?"

"Talk to her." God. Was his father this obtuse on purpose? "Have you ever asked her why she preferred all those college men to you?"

His father flinched. "I didn't have to ask."

"Oh my God. You don't even know if she had an affair."

"I never said she did."

"You implied it." Cam wanted to choke his father into showing some sense. "You aren't a stupid man. Not all the time."

"Watch it, boy."

"Jesus, have some pride. Your wife is going out with another man tomorrow, and you don't care?"

"I fucking care! But what do you want me to do? She made her choice."

"After you made yours with Amelia! A woman younger than Mom, one who seems pretty and attentive any time you go for coffee. Yeah, she told me about your little girlfriend."

James flushed. "She's not my girlfriend. Okay, she flirted a little. Maybe I flirted back," he said, sounding defensive. "But Christ, Cam. Do you have any idea how long it's been since I've..."

"Had sex? Told Mom you loved her? Gone out on a date? No. I don't know. But I do know that burying your feelings like an ostrich with his head in the sand is fucking dumb. Hell. Maybe she is better off with her new boyfriend." Cam felt absolute disgust that his father wouldn't fight for the woman he loved.

Aggravated with the world and his family in general, he stalked off as his father threw a hissy, not in the mood to deal with more excuses. Vanessa might be a pain in his ass, but she wasn't afraid to tell the truth. When he confronted her, he'd see what she had to say for herself. In the mood he was in, she'd have to do a hell of a lot of groveling to apologize. *If* she'd apologize. Or would they be over before they'd even started?

Chapter 13

VANESSA STARED AT HER INFURIATED BOYFRIEND AND
realized her roommates had scattered the moment he'd
slammed into their house.

She stared at him still dressed in his work clothes.
They'd planned on a late run, but when he hadn't called
by six, she'd realized they might have to postpone their
jog. Then Abby had let it slip that Beth would be seeing Liam Webster—Del's father—tomorrow, and she'd
known the worst was yet to come.

"What do you have to say for yourself?" Cameron
asked, his voice oddly calm.

She felt defensive when she had nothing to apologize
for. "Excuse me?"

"Tell me exactly what you said to my mother at dinner that night. You know what I'm talking about."

He wore his suit without a tie, his shirt parted to reveal his strong, corded neck. He clenched his fists by
his side. She'd never seen him so angry. She swallowed
around a dry throat, determined not to let him see her
anxiety. She didn't worry that he'd ever hurt her, but she
did fret that he'd leave.

"I told her she should get a makeover and stop acting
like a wuss any time she had anything to do with James.
I might have mentioned that looking nice would make
her feel better about herself."

"And?"

"And that if he saw her looking that good and was jealous, more power to her."

He stared at her, his gaze disapproving, and sparked her ire.

"You can't be blaming *me* for this?"

He just watched her.

"Bullshit." She scowled. "Your mother is finally living her life, not the one your father thinks she should. Her decisions, her idea to be her own woman. I applaud her for her choices."

"Yes, but did you have to instigate them?"

"I was trying to help. Why should your father get to screw around when she's stuck in soapy water still taking care of her grown-ass boys?"

He paused. "What's that?"

On a roll and sure of herself, Vanessa continued, "Beth has always been about her family and putting herself last. Hell, she's been upset with James for a long time, but she kept quiet to maintain the peace for all of you. Now she wants to live life, and I say go for it. Why shouldn't she date? Your dad isn't begging her to come home. Oh no. He's off with some bimbo at the coffee shop getting free muffins and God knows what else." God forbid Vanessa say the truth. She was suddenly at fault for a rocky marriage?

"Did it never occur to you to talk to *me* about this?" Cameron asked, still quiet. "She's *my* mother. He's *my* father. Not yours. You're my girlfriend. But instead of *us* talking about them—together—of *us* trying to decide what to do to help my parents, you took it upon yourself to solve everyone's problems. Instead, you made more."

Expecting more of an argument, she frowned. "That's it? That's all you have to say?"

"What more is there?" He sighed, and his disappointment hurt her more than harsh words or an argument. "Once again, you're right and everyone else is wrong. I don't have the patience to deal with this right now." He shook his head, turned, and left.

Not sure how to handle this situation—a first for Vanessa—she followed him outside and rushed in front of him before he could enter his car and leave. "You have some nerve."

"Move, Vanessa."

Panicked because he seemed ready to leave and she had no idea how to stop him, she shoved him.

His eyes narrowed. God, but he was so sexy when angry. "Don't do that again."

"Why? You going to talk me to death?" She wanted to instigate him to anger, to feeling. Not that cold detachment she'd gotten all too often while growing up.

"I'm too angry with you to talk. When you realize what you did and how you hurt me, give me a call." He lifted her up and out of the way as if she weighed nothing, then got in his car and drove away.

No fuss. No scene or emotional mess. He was just gone.

She stared after his taillights until she started to shiver. When she went back inside, she saw Maddie waiting in the hallway.

"You okay?" Maddie asked softly.

"No, I'm not. But I'll live." Vanessa swallowed irrational tears and headed upstairs.

"I'm here if you want to talk."

That constant support from her cousin meant more than she could say. Emotion bottled up inside Vanessa, crippling her ability to process and making it impossible to accept Maddie's compassion for fear the fissure cracking inside her might shatter. "Thanks for that. But I'm going to bed. I have a long day ahead of me tomorrow."

Inside her room, she ignored the clock's glaring notice that it hadn't even reached eight and slid under her covers. She'd deal with Cameron and his issues tomorrow. Their breakup could wait. It wasn't as if she hadn't known it was coming, after all. As she'd done her entire life, Vanessa disassociated herself from the pending drama. Numbness settled in, and she closed her eyes.

Yet as she tossed and turned, she realized the others might also consider her the bad guy. In this new extended family of McCauleys, now including Abby and Maddie, Vanessa might find herself ass-out of her friends if it all went to hell. Maybe she'd do better to try to fix things in the morning.

With that in mind, she went to sleep.

The next day, Vanessa took an extended lunch and sat in a far corner of the coffee shop where Beth was supposed to meet Del's dad. She'd arrived early enough to get a table, and in the mad lunch rush, knew she'd made a wise decision.

Beth arrived, as Abby had said she would, exactly at noon. She glanced around, and Vanessa made sure to keep herself hidden behind the taller guys at the table in front of her, as well as behind a large magazine she'd brought along. She saw Beth light up and join an attractive guy across the room.

Hell. Abby had been right. This man might give James some serious competition. Tall, muscular, handsome, and he looked at Beth like she hung the stars and the moon. Then too, Beth looked gorgeous. The haircut and flattering clothing did make her look younger. Beth looked happier, more confident. And confidence was sexy.

She couldn't hear them talking, but she could see the behemoth of a man trying to sneak into the shop without drawing attention to himself. He'd entered through a side door, but his attention remained fixed on Beth and her new beau.

Vanessa threw up a hand and signaled his attention. When James McCauley saw her, he narrowed his eyes but joined her in the back. His leather jacket, dress slacks, and fancy tweed driving cap effectively shielded him from discovery. No way would she have ever thought James could look dapper. Not a bad disguise.

"What the hell are you doing here?" he growled in a low voice and sat with his side to Beth, most likely so he could keep an eye on her.

"Don't move. Pretend you're here to see me," Vanessa said back. "I'm keeping an eye on them, and let's face it, you're conspicuous."

He grunted. "I'd have stayed outside, but I couldn't see anything. Too many fucking people in here."

For James to swear in front of her meant he'd either found out she'd driven his wife to a date, or he was so frustrated he'd forgotten himself.

Then he flushed. "Sorry. I just… I don't know up from

down right now. And what the hell did she do to herself?" He glanced over his shoulder. "She's...*amazing*."

Vanessa saw Beth laugh, and the woman looked so happy and carefree. Vanessa had half a mind to leave the growly idiot next to her to his unhappy fate. "She is. She's smart, pretty, funny, and raised a terrific group of men. Yet her husband cheated on her. Go figure."

"I did not."

"Oh? She thinks you did. You have 'feelings' for Amelia, I've heard."

He sunk into himself and faced her once more. "You don't know anything about anything."

"No, and neither does your wife. Unlike you, I've talked to her. She isn't sure why you two went south. She thought you didn't like her job, so she quit. But you were still unhappy. Anytime she tried to talk to you, you clammed up."

"She was too busy clinging to her college buddies."

"Since her husband ignored her," Vanessa continued quickly before James cut her off, "she took solace in her college buddies. As many times as she invited you to be a part of her world, you ignored her. She grew unhappy, dejected, feeling ugly. Especially when you paid attention to the younger, prettier—her words, not mine—barista."

He was quiet for a moment. "Does she really think I cheated on her?"

"I don't know. She loves you. I mean, I get the impression she still does. But she's tired of being beneath your notice. Other men find her attractive."

"I find her attractive." He stared down at his hands on the table.

"But you never told her that. You made her feel like shit. How would you feel if she'd ignored you for years then told you she had feelings for one of her *younger*, attractive male college buddies?"

He glared up at her. "She did. She just never said anything. Woman was always trying to make me into her smart friends. Like everything I do is so beneath her. Do you have any idea how hard it is to always come up short?"

"Yes, I do."

He apparently hadn't expected that. "You do?"

"My parents have never considered me anything but a biological burden. I carry on their genetics, and that's about all I do of worth. So yeah, I get that sometimes you can't please everyone. That's not the situation with Beth. If you had ever talked to her, told her about your problems, all this might have been avoided. Because if you think you're the only one bothered that you two never have sex, think again."

He gaped at her.

"Yeah, she told me it's been awhile. It hurt her feelings. She's lonely, James. Looking as pretty and happy as she is now, do you really think she'll have to wait long to find someone who truly appreciates her?"

"Fu—hell if I know."

"Your son Cameron is thoroughly annoyed with me for telling your wife the truth. You can be as mad as you like as well. But the fact of the matter is you only have yourself to blame. If you'd actually gone to the counseling she asked you for or confided your problems to your wife, you two might be sitting at home laughing together—or something better. But hey. What do I know? You have Amelia, she has Mr. Hottie. Maybe it's all good?"

Beth laughed at something her companion said. Then the two stood and left the shop together, smiling.

"What are you going to do about it? Let your wife find happiness on her own, or convince her to stay and give you a second chance?"

———— ∾ ————

James ignored Vanessa's questions. He gave Beth and that dick with her a few minutes' head start before leaving the shop to follow them. The big guy gave his wife *a fucking hug* before leaving in a cherry Mustang. Beth continued to walk down the sidewalk, window shopping.

That or dwelling on what a fine time she'd had with the giant who'd left.

He hurriedly caught up with her, having dressed in his better clothes to not look like his usual self. He'd even gotten a haircut, shaved, and worn some cologne. He still couldn't believe Beth had gone on an actual date.

But Jesus, she looked good. He stepped next to her and saw her start when she noticed him.

"James."

"Beth." She seemed taller, her figure fuller. Damn, she sure filled out her jeans well. When was the last time he'd seen her looking so…beautiful? So different from Colin's grandma or Mike's mom? But as Beth McCauley, a woman, his wife?

"Something you wanted?" Her frosty tone warmed him. Why, he couldn't say.

"Saw you with that guy inside." They walked in silence. "New friend?"

"What of it?" She sniffed. "You're moving on. It's time I did too."

But he wasn't. He'd mooned over Amelia, flattered by her attention and wishing she'd been his wife. The one he'd fallen in love with so many years ago.

"Amelia and I aren't dating. Flirting maybe. But hell, woman. I haven't touched anyone but you in thirty-six years."

She turned on him and poked him in the chest with a finger his kids had always claimed was made of iron. "Well the same goes for me, you egotistical ass. For thirty-six years I ignored advances from other men and was true to you. I gave you *everything*," she whispered in a harsh voice as people walked around them. "I tried to help you. Tried to talk to you, to love you. And you did nothing but push me away. Well fuck you."

"*Beth*." He stared, not sure how to deal with this fire-cracker. Where had his mild-mannered wife gone?

"I'm done being your doormat, James McCauley. Now go away. I'm having a fine day and you're ruining it."

She turned and actually walked away. *From him.*

He ran to catch up and dragged her to a stop, then pulled her to the side of the foot traffic. "I never did anything with Amelia. But I can tell you this. She never made me feel like a loser."

"Neither did I." She yanked her arm away. "What nonsense. I never—"

"Yeah, Amelia never treated me like trash because I don't have a college degree."

She blinked at him. "What are you talking about?"

"She never told me to go back to school, to work

harder, to try something other than the job I came to fucking love. What's so wrong with construction, Beth? It put food on the table and a roof over our heads for over thirty years."

"I never said anything of the kind. I'm proud of what you do."

He huffed. "You've been trying to make me into Cameron since the day we met. I gave up the Corps for—"

"Now hold on. I didn't get pregnant all by myself, mister." She blushed, and even in his anger he found her a sight to behold. "Raising Mike and then Flynn all by myself was hard. You left the Marine Corps because you knew it was the right thing to do. I'm sorry if you regretted it."

"Not the boys or you," he said to clarify. "But yeah, I loved the Corps."

"Well, I loved my job. But I gave it up early for you."

He didn't believe that. "No way. You were tired of the hours."

"I was tired of you constantly harping that I didn't do enough at home," she said with more than a hint of steel. "I loved that job. But for you, I retired early."

"Figures you'd love work more than me," he muttered.

"You are so deluded." She poked him again, and he was so glad to have her hand on any part of him that he said nothing. "You always were a selfish man. This is just ridiculous. I let you and your little tramp enjoy yourselves without interference. But the moment I find a nice man who likes me for me, you have to interrupt my life all over again." He liked the fire in her dark green eyes, but not the tears that followed.

"Beth, honey…"

"Don't 'Beth, honey' me. I begged you for years to talk or go to counseling. You refused. Well, I'm done talking *to you*. Go away. Far, far away." She brushed the tears from her eyes and stormed down the sidewalk, leaving him behind.

But as she left, for the first time in a long time, James didn't want her to go.

Vanessa had no idea if she'd done the right thing or not by witnessing Beth's innocent date with Liam. But after three days of Cameron's silence, she'd had enough. After calling his cell phone and again getting no answer, she called James.

"Yeah?"

"It's Vanessa. Are you not talking to me too?"

She heard him sigh. "No. But I'm like you. In the doghouse with no way out. You want the boy, I take it?"

"Yes. Cameron," she said to clarify in case he had some confusion on which of his progeny she was after.

"Hard head, like his stubborn mother," James growled. "The know-it-all is working out in the gym downstairs, but he'll be back in a bit. I'm going out tonight, so feel free to come on over. I'll leave my key for you with the desk downstairs."

"Thanks." She hadn't expected him to be so generous. "Wait. Working out downstairs?"

"Why do you think he bought this place? When he's not working, he's always in there exercising. It's a sickness, but at least it beats those art clubs he used to hang out at."

"Thanks. I'll be over in half an hour."

"Sure." He paused. "Thanks for what you said at the coffee shop."

"No problem."

They disconnected the call, and Vanessa hurried to join the big fat liar—her *boyfriend*—before he could avoid her again. So he worked out at Jameson's Gym because his own was too busy? *Right*. She allowed herself the grin she hadn't been feeling since their fight. Cameron, that faker. Any man who bought membership to another gym just to be near her wouldn't break up over a stupid thing like a simple omission. She hadn't lied to him about her conversation with his mother. Not exactly.

Hope returned, crushing in its intensity. He might be mad at her, but he couldn't be too mad. Could he?

Resolved to end this passive-aggressive foolishness, she drove to his condo, parked, and retrieved the key to his unit without a problem. At his door, she used the key, not deigning to knock in case he decided not to answer. She entered but found no one home.

Wondering how best to deal with him, she went over some options and decided to start with basics. They had chemistry, and sex worked wonders to cure most men's foul moods. With that in mind, she went to his bedroom and stripped down, then dressed herself in his robe.

Twenty minutes later, the front door opened and closed. She waited in the bedroom on the off chance his father had returned. No need for forced awkwardness.

She recognized the tread as Cameron's and couldn't contain the race in her pulse. He'd simply have to get over his stubborn idiocy in thinking her wrong. Plain and simple.

She heard him puttering around the condo and waited with patience, which was soon rewarded. He entered his room in the midst of taking off his shirt. He'd tossed it to the floor when he saw her lying across his bed, and he froze.

"Hello."

He frowned. "Hi."

She toyed with the belt on his oversized robe. "Have a good workout?"

"Yeah." He sounded hoarse, and she realized the robe had parted to reveal a breast.

"I thought I'd come over and help you in the shower."

"Shower?"

"You were heading to clean up, I assume?" A glance down his front showed her how happy he was to see her, but she kept her joy contained behind a polite smile.

He stared at her, looking her over from her head to her toes. "Shower. Yes." He untied his sneakers and removed his shoes and socks, then stripped out of his shorts and underwear as well. Standing in nothing more than gleaming muscles with an enormous erection, he made her mouth water.

She rose and preceded him into the bathroom, not bothering to disrobe yet. She started the shower, then stepped back after the temperature reached an adequate heat and waited for him to enter. He did, then she dropped the robe and followed him.

Before she could blink, he had her back pressed to the tile, his mouth over hers, and a delicious melting of her senses overtook her. His tongue and lips trailed over her mouth to her neck, then her breasts. He took her nipples and bit and sucked, reducing her to a writhing mass of need. Not to be deterred, her wonderful Cameron continued down to that aching spot between her legs.

No words passed between them as he stimulated her into a rushing orgasm with just his mouth while his hands trailed up and down her thighs.

As she crested into ecstasy, he rose and turned her to face the wall, then thrust into her with force. He pounded into her with a fierceness that had her crying his name before he groaned and came, clutching her hips like a lifeline. Moments after his release, he continued to kiss her shoulders and neck, still not speaking.

They parted and cleaned each other. She watched him with an intense affection bordering on…something more.

After washing themselves thoroughly, Cameron leaned against the shower wall and cupped her breast. His eyes were heavy-lidded, dark with exhaustion and a lazy respite from his orgasm. "So you're sorry?"

"Not exactly."

The smile ghosting his lips disappeared. "Oh?"

"I came here to stop this stupid fight. I…care about you."

He seemed to relax, if a fraction. "Care, hmm?"

She frowned. "Yes. It took a lot of nerve to come up here when you've gone out of your way to ignore me."

He raised a brow in that way she often did to annoy Maddie. Now she could see why it worked so well. "Oh? Because I distinctly remember telling you that I would be waiting for your call when you realized why you were wrong."

Like waving a red flag at a bull, the word *wrong* had her back up. "I wasn't wrong for being honest with Beth."

"I never said you were." He continued to hold her, caressing her even while he damned her with his eyes.

Confused, she pulled back, letting the water rush over her once more. "Then what is your problem? Spit it out, Cameron."

He shook his head. "That you can't understand why I'm upset is just as much the problem as what pissed me off."

She scowled. "You know, if you'd stop all this sensitive, emotional bullshit and just tell me the problem, I'm sure I could fix it." It didn't escape her that once again, she acted the role of the one in the wrong, while her lover insisted his partner play guessing games. She swallowed her disappointment. She'd thought Cameron better than that.

"Vanessa, while I appreciate your honesty, I'm also annoyed enough to tell you that I expected better of you."

"My thoughts exactly."

"You're so concerned with being right you don't care about *us*."

"Wait. What's that?" Surrounded by hot water, she nevertheless felt cold. How had he come to that conclusion?

"Instead of coming to me and trying to share a discussion about my parents—two people with whom I'm directly involved—you took it upon yourself to solve their problems. In doing so, you might have made them worse. Honestly, I'm hurt you didn't come to me or be honest when I asked about my mother in the first place."

He had a point about his mother, but not about the rest.

"So that's your stance on things?" She felt naked all

of a sudden, when before she'd been wrapped around him like a vine and hadn't cared.

"It is. Don't get me wrong. I liked the sex. Very much." He smiled, but she saw anger, not affection, in his eyes.

"So we'll just keep fucking then. How does that suit you?" The hypocrite. He said he appreciated her honesty, then held it against her when it suited him.

"Fine. You want this to be just about sex? I'll try it your way."

Angry and strangely turned on, determined to show Cameron the error of his ways, she took the initiative and shoved him back against the wall. Then she rubbed her slick body over his, aware when his cock jumped against her belly.

"Terrific. So we're in agreement. This is just about sex. Like it always was," she tried to tell herself, wishing she wasn't so dismayed at how the evening had turned out.

"You can make yourself feel better by thinking that if you want, but we both know the truth," Cam murmured.

She didn't want to hear any more, so she muted him with another kiss before slowly going to her knees. He could say what he wanted, but his body didn't lie. Too bad the rest of him didn't follow suit.

Chapter 14

CAM WANTED TO BREAK SOMETHING. NAMELY Vanessa's stubborn hold on being right. If the blasted woman would simply acknowledge that she'd been in the wrong, they might get past their carnal détente. Instead, they continued to have rip-roaring sex in near silence.

That she continued to come to him gave him hope. She could have said to hell with him and his family. But she hadn't. Instead, they had angry, mind-melting sex that usually ended in at least two orgasms for him and two or three for her. After two long weeks of the stubborn woman's silence on the matter, though, he'd come to the end of his rope.

"Hey, boss, phone call," Hope called from the outer office. With no clients around, she often yelled out for him instead of using the intercom.

He smiled despite his bad mood and accepted the call she transferred. "Cameron McCauley."

"Hey, Cameron. It's me." Vanessa.

As usual, just hearing her voice got him half hard. He blew out a breath and tried to will away his erection, lest his cousin come in and put testament to the notion he really was a perv. "Vanessa. Nice to hear from you."

"Yeah, well. This stupid argument we're having is asinine."

"I agree."

Silence met his answer.

"Well, I just figured…" She paused. "Fine. We're through. Bye."

He stared in shock at the phone. "*What the hell?*"

"Cam?" His cousin appeared at the doorway. Seeing his expression, she walked in. "You okay?"

"No. Look, can you cancel my appointment for tomorrow morning?"

"I can try to reschedule for the afternoon. I remember Mrs. Foxxe asking for a later time if the morning wouldn't work."

"Perfect. Thanks. I'm taking off. You okay to lock up?"

Her eyes widened. "Sure. No problem."

He nodded and left, done with letting Vanessa take control of their relationship. The infuriating woman didn't know when to back down. If she couldn't figure out how to deal with him on an equal level, then maybe they *would* have to call it quits. But not over the phone, and not without talking things out, face-to-face. He wasn't his father, for fuck's sake.

A call to Vanessa's workplace told him she'd already left for the day. Four-thirty. Early for Vanessa to be gone from work. A good sign. She wasn't taking this supposed breakup lightly. He would have been more upset about things if he'd considered their relationship over. But that ridiculous breakup over the phone? No way in hell.

He called Abby after a glance at his phone.

"Hello?" Abby answered.

"Hey, Abby. Are you at home? It's Cam."

"Hi, Cam. Yeah, I'm home. Why?"

"Is Vanessa there?"

"She should be at work."

"She's not. I'm betting she's going to hit the gym before coming home. Would you mind if I came over and waited for her?"

"No problem." Abby paused. "Did something happen between you guys? She's been weird for days. I mean, more weird than normal."

"Nothing I can't handle. Thanks, Abby." He disconnected, not wanting to share his girlfriend's problems with her roommate.

He arrived at her house and parked down the street, not wanting her to see his car and avoid him. Like he'd avoided her before. Okay, in retrospect, he'd behaved childishly. But damn it, the woman aggravated and turned him on in the same breath. How the hell could he hold on to his mad when she had him coming while he tried to teach her a lesson? Instead, *he'd* been the one schooled.

Two rational adults would have talked things through by now. That Vanessa hadn't was telling. What did that mean, exactly? He tried to puzzle her out while he waited upstairs in her bedroom. Abby had agreed to keep his presence a secret. Now he just had to wait for her to come home.

While he waited for her, he totally took advantage of her privacy. He didn't stoop to looking through her drawers or at her computer, but he studied her artwork, the things on her bookshelves, and the few pictures she had of her family. Of the six photos on her shelves, four were of her, Maddie, and Abby. Another looked to be of Vanessa as a teenager with Maddie and what appeared to be their relatives. The last featured her as a solemn young girl, wearing a banner declaring her math champion, sandwiched between two attractive and un-smiling adults. Her parents.

She had her mother's eyes and her father's mouth. They really were a good-looking family. Too bad they'd treated their daughter with unfeeling regard.

He didn't see any stuffed animals, knickknacks, or objects indicating her personality. But in the corner, tucked away behind a ledger on probability and statistics, he saw a dried red rose. He recognized the small lace band around the stem as belonging to the bunch he'd bought for her on Valentine's Day and smiled.

"Sentimental after all," he whispered and gently stroked a petal. The brittle bud retained its beauty, as well as a lingering fragrance.

Yet this flower, this presence of feeling, told him more about Vanessa than words could. She felt. Deeply. But she didn't know how to show it, or handle it. He'd have to be patient, to show her just what he could offer. More than money or security, Vanessa needed love.

The downstairs door opened and shut, and he heard Vanessa call out to Abby that she'd returned home. Then her heavy footsteps pounded up the stairs. He waited, prepared to wear her down until he had the answers he wanted. He wasn't leaving without them. Or her.

Vanessa wanted to cry. Well, to shower, cry, then sleep. And maybe eat, though her appetite had deserted her after breaking up with Cameron. She'd been a mess at work, so much that even *Josh* had noticed and mentioned she might want to knock off early. She hadn't liked the empathy in his gaze, no more than she liked being an emotional basket case over something as stupid as a breakup. She'd known this was coming from the beginning. Yet she still had to fight back tears. Calling Cameron while at work, apparently, had been a stupid idea.

Who knew I'd cry over him? she asked herself. *He's just another man. Like all the rest.* She kept saying it in hopes she'd believe it.

She pushed through the door and threw her gym bag on the bed at the same time she saw him. Dressed in his business clothes, looking utterly masculine, graceful, and perfect. He stood by her bed and crossed his arms over his chest.

"Hello, Vanessa."

She swallowed the tears that wanted to return and called on the cold numbness that should have kept her company throughout their parting. "Cameron. To what do I owe the pleasure?"

He frowned. "You look terrible."

"Thanks." So nice for him to point that out. He, on the other hand, looked like he'd just stepped off the cover of *GQ*. "Why are you here?"

"We're through?" He snorted. "Try again."

"I'm sorry. Did I not speak slowly enough for you?"

Instead of growing angry, he had the nerve to grin. "You're cute when you're snotty."

She swore. "Damn it. I'm breaking up with you."

"Nope."

She blinked. "What do you mean *nope*? Did you not understand me?"

"Why are we breaking up?" He let his hands fall from his chest and stuffed them into his pockets. So casual, as if the notion of no longer seeing her meant nothing to him, while it broke her apart.

"Why are you being such a dick?"

"Why are you being such a bitch? Answer the question."

His insult took her aback. She gasped. "Did you just call me a bitch?" Cameron never swore at her, unless they were making love, which was sexy dirty talk, not verbal abuse.

"Did I stutter?" He sighed. "Look, Vanessa. I can play twenty questions all night long. Tell me why we broke up. Then, if your answer makes sense, I'll leave you alone. No harm, no foul."

"You arrogant asshole." She glared at him. "No harm?" He'd made her fucking *cry*, and Vanessa loathed tears with every fiber of her being.

"Still waiting." He blew out a breath.

"Fine. We broke up because… Because…"

"Because you won't admit to being wrong," he said quietly, no longer amused.

"No."

"Yes. Being right is everything to you. I was upset with you, not because you spoke to my mother. Okay, maybe a little. I got over that quickly. The fact that you didn't seem to trust me hurt. Why didn't you just tell me you'd talked to my mom? Why keep it a secret?"

"You make no sense."

"I make a lot of sense, and that has you scared. You're afraid to be wrong, afraid to share all of yourself." He shook his head. "I feel sorry for you."

"Fuck you." She scowled. "I don't need your pity or your platitudes. I just…" To her horror, her eyes filled. Uncontrollable tears coursed down her cheeks. "You're such an a-asshole."

"Oh, baby." He scooped her into his arms for a big hug before she could shove him away. His arms felt *so* good around her. She needed his warmth, his care. Vanessa Campbell, a woman who'd grown to know she could count on no one but herself, wanted Cameron to hold her up. He scared and unnerved her, and her heart bled like a sieve without him.

"I don't need you." She sounded pitiful, even to herself.

"Shh. It's okay." He hugged her tighter, rocking her against him.

And she let him, loving his comfort. "I don't," she whispered, wondering what the hell was wrong with her.

After a few moments, Cameron pulled back and wiped the tears from her cheeks. "Vanessa, answer me one question. Okay?"

"Fine." She felt like a fool. *Tears? Really, girl?* She could almost see her parents frowning at her, shaking their heads at her needless—useless—display of emotion.

"Would you rather be right, or would you rather have me in your life?"

An odd question. But put that way… "Couldn't I have both?"

He smiled and kissed her softly on the lips. "Pick one."

She knew he'd made a huge concession coming here. That he could have taken her immature parting and never looked back.

"You. I'd rather have you," she whispered, half ashamed to admit the truth.

"Oh, Vanessa. You're so stubborn. It's no wonder…" She didn't catch the trail end of what he said, because his lips found hers again.

Instead of a carnal kiss, the tender caress soothed

her. She'd been on pins and needles for days, unsure about herself, angry that she couldn't cut the ties she needed to. Then to just succumb because he was hugging her right now… She'd put off their inevitable separation yet again, confirming to herself she was as weak as she'd suspected.

"I won't get better, you know. I'll always be like this." He had no idea what she was really like.

"I know." He sounded more than satisfied. "Vanessa, you get me. And I get you. We're alike yet different just enough to complement each other. That's a rare thing, don't you think?"

"I guess." She cupped his cheek, taken with the stubble she could feel but couldn't yet see. "I don't want you to go."

"Was that so hard to admit?"

She blew out a breath. "God, yes."

He laughed.

"Cameron, I'm not used to you. I like being alone. But I also enjoy spending time with you—us, together."

"So do I, honey. But can you understand why I was upset?"

She thought about it and nodded. "I guess. You wanted me to share my thoughts and feelings, not just ignore everything in my mission to fix what your parents broke. Which I might have done anyway, thank you very much."

He frowned. "What's that?"

"I felt bad, I admit. So I kind of spied on your mom's coffee date. Your dad sat with me while we watched."

"He did?"

"Yeah. I also kind of let him have it with both barrels.

Told him what an ass he was for not appreciating your mom, and that maybe if he'd told her about his issues and problems a long time ago, none of this mess would have had to happen."

Cameron just stared at her.

"What?"

"Seems like maybe you should take your own advice, hmm?"

She flushed. "Maybe."

"Vanessa, I like our discussions and the fact that we argue about things. But sometimes we'll really fight, like we have been. Breaking up at every turn isn't the answer."

"Okay already. You're right."

He stepped back and put a hand over his heart. Then he flopped back on the bed. "My…heart…can't take… the shock."

"Idiot." She joined him on her bed, rested her head on his chest, and closed her eyes.

He stroked her hair. "*Your* idiot. So you'd better keep a close eye on me."

God, he was warm. And so strong. His heart beat steadily under her ear, and before she knew it, the rhythm lulled her into sleep.

She woke to a dark room, fully dressed and under her covers. She still wore her sweaty workout clothes, now dried and nasty. Cam wore his suit trousers and undershirt and cuddled up with her under her comforter.

For the first time in two weeks they had talked and hadn't made love. *Had sex*, she automatically corrected, feeling wary. Yet she'd had the best night's sleep she could remember, feeling utterly secure as he held her.

Man, I'm falling for you, Cameron McCauley. And just this once, I don't want to be right about being so wrong for you.

She turned over and leaned up to look down at him. Sliding his hair out of his eyes, she stared into his relaxed features, her heart warm, her thoughts fuzzy as she let herself just feel. The light from her alarm clock bathed his face in a soft blue, and the shadows over his cheeks encouraged her to stroke and memorize him by touch.

He blinked his eyes open, his focus sharpening as he stared up at her and smiled. "Hey, blondie. You're looking good, even with that hair from hell."

"Back at ya, morning breath." They sneered at each other, and she laughed, feeling amazingly refreshed and…happy.

After a pause, Cameron said, "No more phone breakups."

"No. Next time I'll do it to your ugly face."

"Thank you so much, Miss Charming." He sighed. "Good thing I canceled my eight o'clock."

The clock had just turned to seven-thirty. Dear God, she'd slept the night away.

"Shit." She tried to scramble out of bed, but he wouldn't let her.

"Vanessa, relax. If you left early yesterday, chances are they think you went home sick. You never leave early."

"True."

"So take the morning off. Be with me."

She stared at him, looking into his eyes and feeling as if she saw so much more than his features. "Play hookey?"

He gave a fake cough. "No, take care of me. I'm sick."

"Bull."

He pulled her hand over his chest. "My heart hurt at the thought of losing you."

She flushed. "Don't be melodramatic."

"I'm not," he said quietly. "I don't want us to be over."

She wanted to ask, "Ever?" but didn't want to hear his answer, scared he might mean forever. Dating was one thing. Permanence? Marriage? Kids? She could just see herself turning into a carbon copy of her mother and froze.

"Come on, Vanessa. Soothe me." He ran a hand over her back. "I'm male and I'm needy. But I'm not stupid. You should nurture me, in hopes that someday my good sense will pass on to future generations and spawn a gender of males who aren't complete fuckheads twenty-four-seven."

Her lips twitched at his fake earnestness. "Well, when you put it that way…" She squealed with laughter when he tickled her. Then his caresses moved lower, and her laughs became moans. And sighs, and pleas for more.

—◦◦◦—

By noon, Cam sat dressed in his wrinkled suit at her kitchen table while she prepared them an organic tofu lunch.

He couldn't hold it in any longer. "I told you so."

According to Vanessa, Josh had spread the word she was feeling sick yesterday, so when Peterman took her call earlier, he'd ordered her to stay home until tomorrow. Panicked at the thought of losing her during tax season, the man wanted to take no chances.

She frowned at him over her shoulder. "So you were right. Do you have to keep rubbing that in my face?"

"When's the last time you took a sick day?" The look she gave him said volumes. "And there's your answer. Slow down, eager beaver. You'll make partner. Just don't burn yourself out in the process."

"Yes, Dad."

"Shut up." He grinned at her. "Now admit something else. You like missionary. Sometimes being on the bottom is damn good."

"He who feels the need to brag hath something to prove." At his raised brow, she continued with a waspish, "Yeah, yeah. You're a stud in bed too. Happy now?"

She brought two plates to the table, and they ate in companionable silence.

"Are you going to ask me or what?" Cameron said as he finished his sandwich. "You're a wizard with tofu, you know that?"

"I know. Ask what?"

"I saw that note from your parents. The one you spent a good half an hour frowning over this morning."

She sighed. "My parents just received two major grants to continue their research at the university. I'm supposed to come home to celebrate the accomplishment. Put in the dutiful appearance as the proud and moderately successful progeny to make them look good."

"And?"

"And I need a date." She batted her lashes. "Pretty please, Cam? Won't you come with me?" she begged in a breathy voice.

"Yes, I'll go with you." He was more than curious to meet her stick-in-the-mud parents. The timing of the invitation and Vanessa's attempt to break up with him felt like too much coincidence. It would do him well to see the people who'd so influenced their daughter. "Is this going to stress you out? Me going along?"

"Oh no. Just the opposite. You might give me the buffer I need to stay somewhat human during my trip." She groaned. "I tried to tell you what I'm really like, but maybe if you meet my parents, you'll understand. If you just want to be fuck-buddies after that, I'm game."

He sighed, long and loud. "I thought we'd discussed this. I prefer the term fuck-*friends*. Not fuck-buddies. That's so…crass."

She smirked. "You're not crass, are you, Mr. Walk of Shame?" She snickered. "You're lucky your brothers aren't here to make fun of you."

"Nope. Just my leering girlfriend. My fuck-*friend*."

They continued to tease each other until he left to make a quick stop home. Except after darting upstairs to hurry and change for his appointment, he found his father and Mike arguing inside.

"Damn it, Dad. Enough is enough. Either shit or get off the pot."

"Nice way to talk about your mother." His father snorted.

"You know what I'm talking about."

"How many times do I have to tell you? This isn't your fight."

"Yeah? Well someone has to stick up for Mom. You're too busy playing footsie with the coffee chick."

"Whoa." Cam walked between his brother and father, shocked to see the pair truly angry. "What the hell's this about?"

Mike pointed at their father. "*James* has been harassing Mom."

"Harassing?" Cam frowned at his father. "Dad?"

"It's not like that." James's cheeks were flushed, his eyes dark with anger. "Your mother and I need to talk, but she's not letting me anywhere near her. Do you know she changed the locks at home?"

Cam bit back a smile. *Go, Mom.* Whatever had happened between the pair, Cam was all for it. Once disinterested in fixing things with their mother, his dad now seemed to be frothing at the mouth to see her again. "Dad, I thought it was over. Why not just move on? Let her go."

"Are you fucking insane?" Mike asked him, breathing fire. "We want them back together. We just don't want him making her cry every five seconds." Mike glared at James again. "Meet with a moderator, like she asked. A therapist can settle your differences down at the—"

"I'm not seeing a fucking shrink to talk to your mother."

"Yeah, because all that other great communicating you guys do has helped you so much 'til now," Cam said drily.

Next to him, Mike nodded.

"Jesus. You two are a real pair, you know? Why the hell am I suddenly the bad guy?"

"Maybe because you're dating the coffee chick?" Cam offered.

"Your mother is seeing some guy with no neck! A greasy mechanic who had his hands all over her," his father yelled.

"Greasy mechanic?" Cam frowned. "Isn't it a little hypocritical to call a brother in trade by demeaning names?"

His father's scowl turned ugly, and Cam took a step back.

"Dad." Mike stepped between them. "If you're serious about making things right with Mom, why not meet her halfway? She loses the mechanic, you lose the coffee lady, and you two focus on each other."

"For the last fucking time, there is no coffee lady! We flirted a few times. I got a free muffin or two. End of fucking story. Your mother's the one going out on *dates*."

"Dates?" Cam frowned. "Has there been more than one?"

"No, but that doesn't mean Liam Webster won't—"

"Webster? Liam *Webster*?" Mike frowned.

"What? You know the guy?" Cam asked.

"Dad said he's a mechanic. Del's a mechanic. Her last name is Webster."

Cam had a bad feeling. "I never did get the name of the guy, or how exactly he and Mom met."

Mike clenched and unclenched his fists. "Yeah? Well, I think it's time I asked Mom how she met her new boyfriend."

"See? Now you're thinking like a McCauley." His father slapped Mike on the back.

Mike turned on him. "*You* stay away from her. I'll find out what's up. Just… Cam, talk to him. Because acting like he's forgotten how to think will push her away even more."

Mike left and slammed the door behind him. Cam cringed. Then he looked at his dad and saw not a failure as a husband, but a man torn by pain and past mistakes. A future he might one day have if he forgot what was important and focused too much on the day-to-day.

With a sigh, he moved to the refrigerator and pulled out one of his father's generic beers. He handed it to his dad and nodded at the couch. Then he called Hope. "Tell Mrs. Foxxe I'll be there by two. I promise. And that we're not charging her for the consult."

"Good plan, because she was fine changing her schedule once. Twice? Now you're pushing it."

"Thanks for telling me something I already know." Cam disconnected and turned to his father, who sat holding his beer, staring out the window. "Okay, Dad. You want Mom back? This is how you need to play it…"

Chapter 15

VANESSA FELT QUEASY. SHE HATED FLYING, ALMOST more than she hated crying. But it was her own fault. She never should have tried that new goat cheese the night before her cross-country flight.

After a third trip to the lavatory, which thankfully had only produced dry heaves, she took the Dramamine tablets Cameron handed her.

"If you say 'I told you so,' I will forcibly stick my fingers down my throat and vomit all over you," she told him.

In the aisle next to them, an older man looked up at her in alarm.

Cameron chuckled and patted the seat. "Yes, dear."

She groaned, sat, and swallowed the pills. "I hate medication of any kind."

"Me too, but I took the pills. Notice I'm not having any issues."

"Oh, shut up. Are we there yet?"

"Just another three hours and we'll change over in Philadelphia." Cameron sounded way too cheerful. "I haven't been north of Philly before. Not in Pennsylvania, at least, so this will be fun."

"If you say so." She returned to her story. She managed to hold down the airplane peanuts and hot tea and dozed for a bit, enjoying that she could lean on Cameron's solid shoulder.

She also appreciated that he'd upgraded their seats from economy to business class. He'd been so cute when he scoffed at the notion of sitting in the "sardine seats."

Loretta and Scott Campbell hadn't met them at the tiny airport, but they had arranged for a taxi. Cameron and she rode for a while in silence. He had his arm around her shoulder, and she snuggled beside him, confident things had mostly returned to normal between them. She didn't know if this trip would push him away, or if he'd last a few months longer until he became angry over something else that wasn't her fault. That, or he'd simply grow bored with her. Either way, she refused to stress about it. She was pragmatic enough to realize she could do nothing to postpone the inevitable. Why not enjoy this time with him while she had it?

She let him hold her hand and gripped it tighter.

"You okay?" he asked and kissed the top of her head.

Those affectionate gestures that were unnecessary yet so fulfilling always amazed her. "Fine. Gotta love the snow."

The cabbie nodded and glanced in her rearview mirror. "Can you believe it? I know it's still March and all, but damn, we just hit spring! And then a snowfall. I think that groundhog was full of crap."

Cameron snorted. "Never trust a rodent. And especially not one named Phil."

They passed the rest of the short ride in a comfortable banter, and before she knew it, they'd arrived at her parents' home.

"Nice digs." Cameron eyed the palatial home on four acres of land. Her parents had done phenomenally well investing their earned income, as well as the money they'd inherited when Vanessa's grandfather, on her father's side, had died.

The four-thousand-square-foot home ensured her parents had enough room to spread out without feeling cramped and too close. Because God forbid they had to interact with each other more than twice a day—once at breakfast, and again at dinner. She doubted their routines had changed all that much.

After letting herself into the house with her spare key, Vanessa took Cameron with her into the kitchen, where her mother had informed her she'd find further instructions.

"This place is massive," he said as he studied their surroundings. Hardwood floors, neutral shades of tan and beige on the walls, accented with calming blues and greens around the living room, meshed well with the understated elegance of the antique-white kitchen, stainless-steel appliances, and granite countertops.

"My parents often have social functions here, catered, of course. So the house needed to reflect their wealth without being overly grandiose."

He gave her an odd look, and she realized she'd automatically reverted to the voice she used when back with her parents. Instructional, informative, and bland.

She infused herself with a sprinkle of enthusiasm. "They moved into this place right before I graduated from college—the same college they work in, mind you. The same one I had to pay my own way through because apparently an education means more if you pay for it. I'm almost done with my loans, thank God."

"Really?"

For what Vanessa made at her job, she could have afforded to live in a much bigger house than the one she shared with her roommates. But her student loan, in addition to the many varied investments she continued to make, took the brunt of her income. That and she liked living with Maddie and Abby, though she refused to admit it to her cousin.

She cleared her throat. "Really. Anyway, I still have a room here, which is where we'll be staying."

"You still have a room? I got the impression you don't visit often."

"I don't. They turned it into a guest room the day I graduated. But it's got the best sunlight and the bed is quality." She shrugged. After reading the note left for her on the counter, she handed it to Cameron and took a look in the refrigerator.

"Well. This is…"

"Perfunctory?" Her mother had welcomed her home, told her about different food choices, their meal for the evening—to dress for it—and the schedule, in detail, for the following day. Vanessa took out some carrot sticks and helped herself. "Want some?"

"Sure." He chewed and studied the house. "Don't take this the wrong way, but are you sure people live here? It's so clean and, well, the place looks like a show house."

"I know." She snorted. "It was like that when I lived here too. I used to have to hide my stuff in my closet, because even my room had to be organized." More like sterile. Was it any wonder she'd left State College as soon as she'd been able? "Come on. I'll give you the tour."

She hadn't been home in three years, and then only for the obligatory holiday visit, so that the family could continue their pretense of normality. After taking him through the open downstairs and into the spotless pantry and laundry room, she took him upstairs. "On that side my parents share a bedroom and have two separate studies." They turned in the hallway that bridged the sections of the upper floor. "You can see downstairs from here. Nice, hmm?"

"Beautiful. They certainly keep the place nice."

"Maids and gardeners. Makes you wonder why my parents have so much space if they never do anything with it." She shrugged. She'd been wondering about that for years. "My room—excuse me, the *guest room*—is this way." She walked to the large room in which sunlight patterned over the carpeted floor and pale blue walls.

"Pretty. Very soft."

"Unlike me?" She dragged her bag with her and pushed it to the side. "You can take that armoire and I'll use the dresser over there. Bathroom is through that door."

He left his bag on the floor by hers and moved into the bathroom. "Yep," he called from inside. "Like the rest of the house. Spotless."

"Uh-huh." She took off her shoes and sank back onto the bed, feeling exhausted. Between the flight and the tension creeping over her from being back home, she wanted nothing more than to take a nap, so she closed her eyes and tried to relax.

She heard the faucet go on and off. Then Cameron returned. "So when do you expect them back?"

"You read the note. Not before seven." She opened her eyes.

He glanced at his watch, one of the few men she

knew who still wore one, and said, "We have three hours to kill. What should we do?"

Recognizing that tone, she studied him. "I don't know. What do you want to do?"

He grinned and removed his jacket, shoes, and sweater. "I was thinking... You ever have sex in the 'guest room'?"

Her heart raced and her entire body lit up at the thought. "No."

"Well, I think you're due, don't you?"

"Cameron."

"No, honey. This is where you call me Cam, and then you get all breathless." He removed the rest of his clothing, taking his time. And he was hard.

"Close the door." Exhaustion had left her the moment he stripped down to his bare chest.

"Why?" He stalked her, then tugged her to the edge of the bed, her legs on either side of him. "This is a good height."

She flushed when his gaze settled between her legs. He took off her clothes slowly, but the door remained open.

"Cam."

"Ah, there it is. That turns me on, you know. When you say my name like that."

"The...ah, the door."

"Let's leave it open. Just imagine your parents coming home to see us fucking on your bed."

She gaped at him, not sure who the hell had taken over Cameron's brain. He hadn't given any indication he wanted to be watched. By her parents? The idea grossed her out, mostly. Except the notion of freaking them out, of playing the rebellious daughter, had more than its share of appeal.

"Now spread yourself for me," he ordered in a husky groan. "Yeah, let me see that clit."

"God." She was wet, and it was all his fault. When he talked like that, lost his veneer of civility, she liked him even more. Because it wasn't a front or a pose, but another part of Cam she brought out in him.

"I'm going to lick you up. You need it."

"Hmm?"

"Yeah. You need to be mussed a bit. You're too pretty, too controlled. How about we see what it takes to get you to scream my name?"

"Yes." She desired him like crazy, her arousal skyrocketing as he stared at her while he lowered his mouth to her core.

Then he kissed her, and she closed her eyes, lost in sensation.

His lips tugged, his tongue penetrated, and he rubbed her with abandon, his groans and grunts of pleasure stirring breathy cries she hadn't realized she could make.

"Yeah, that's it. More, baby." He gripped her thighs hard while he sucked her, and she rose to meet his demands, on fire to have him.

Before she could come, he kissed his way to her breasts. His warm lips encouraged pinpricks of desire that caused her to writhe beneath him, especially when he closed his mouth around her left breast.

As he teased her, he slid his thick cock over her clit, rocking against her arousal and pushing her past reason.

"Please, Cam. In me. Come inside me. Now."

She gripped his shoulders, but he wouldn't be

moved. Instead he tormented her other breast, gliding close but still leaving her empty. She knew he wanted her, could hear it in his harsh breaths, in the furious tugging at her nipple. He was rock-hard and hot, so close. But not close enough.

"Damn it, Cam." She moaned when he left her breast and kissed her. He rocked over her, not quite penetrating but leaving the tip of himself at her entrance. With short jerks he mimicked taking her, and she lost her mind as he continued to plunge in and out of her mouth with his tongue.

"Fuck me. *Cam, now*," she demanded, wishing she didn't sound so damn weak.

"Yeah. Oh baby. I have to have you." He kissed her again, but this time he angled himself differently and nudged her thighs wider. In one hard thrust, he shoved the whole of himself inside her.

She came like a rocket, crying out as he rode her orgasm into an impossibly long burst of pleasure.

He continued to hit the bundle of nerves inside her while his groin grazed her clit, and she couldn't stop the rush of ecstasy from obliterating all else.

"Yes, Vanessa. Oh yeah. I'm coming. So hard. So fucking hard," he groaned as he shoved one last time and shuddered. "Vanessa. *Yes*." He thrust in and out a few times, milking himself in her tight sheath.

She felt completely blown away, as limp as a noodle. Sweat plastered her hair to her forehead, and she felt dizzy.

"You totally destroyed me," he murmured, making no move to withdraw. He leaned up, so as not to crush her with his weight. "Damn, Vanessa. I think this might just be hotter than Valentine's Day. Doing it in your parents' house. You're such a bad girl."

She smiled. "I'd say something sarcastic, but I can't think at the moment. I don't even think I can move."

He kissed her cheeks, her mouth, her nose. "Why don't you take a nap? You look beat, and I'll just rest here with you. Don't worry. I'll keep an eye on the clock." He chuckled. "Wouldn't want your parents to meet me bare-assed naked."

She muttered something back, but she couldn't have said what it was. Instead, she closed her eyes and sighed into his embrace, still joined, still a part of him. Where she always wanted to be.

Cam had softened, but he didn't withdraw. He pulled the blanket over them and stared down at Vanessa. He knew he could no longer even *try* to deny to himself how much she meant to him. He had to have her in his life. Permanently. She fit him in every way. Even her snit on the plane had entertained him, though he'd felt badly for her nerves.

Seeing the house in which she'd spent some of her youth, he better understood her anxiety about the visit. Though she'd played it off as typical frustration with her parents, he could see something more bothered her. She kept expecting him to end things after meeting her parents too. Her attitude after reading her mother's note had been odd, but he comprehended more than she probably thought.

He kissed her cheek and rolled them to their sides, trying his best to stay inside her. She was so warm, so perfect around him. Their frames meshed, not too big or small for each other, but just right, especially when they'd sixty-nined it the other day.

He'd never had such satisfying sex with one person before or experienced this kind of chemistry. Not that he'd been an orgy guy or anything; he'd had his share of girlfriends. But it was so much more than that with Vanessa. He was enchanted with her personality and quick wit. So smart and savvy, so competent. He found her incredibly sexy and wanted to know as much as he could about her.

He couldn't wait to meet her parents.

Downstairs, he'd seen one family picture—everyone wore their Sunday best and polite smiles. Sterile. A lot like the picture-perfect house. He liked to be neat, but even he would have a problem in a place this devoid of personality.

He rested with Vanessa for another hour, then removed himself to take a shower. After getting clean in the spotless glass shower stall, he shaved and splashed on some cologne, then dressed and moved to Vanessa again. In sleep, she looked beautiful. No lines marred her forehead or pinched her mouth. She seemed at ease, and though he hated to ruin her sleep, he knew she'd want to be prepared for her parents when they returned.

"Vanessa. Honey, time to wake up."

She frowned and tried to push his hand away from her cheek. He'd make sure to tell her how cute he found her later, because she hated to be called "cute." Her anger, like everything else about her, turned him on.

"Come on, sleeping beauty. Time to rise and get cleaned up before your parents get home."

She groaned but woke, blinking up at him. "I need a shower."

"Yes, you do."

She froze. "Quick, get me a towel. I can't mess the comforter."

He laughed at her panic and fetched her a towel from the bathroom. After helping her out, he ignored her scowl and watched her dart to the bathroom. "Love that ass," he called after her.

He missed the insult no doubt lobbed back at him, drowned out by the shower. Realizing she probably had stuff in her bag she needed, he opened it and grabbed what looked like a makeup kit just as she shouted, "I need my shampoo."

"Just use the stuff in there. I did." Several nice-smelling bottles of shampoo, conditioner, and shower gel sat on the side ledge. The place seemed stocked like a hotel.

"You're not supposed to *use* it."

He rolled his eyes and handed her the shampoo. Then he left her to clean up. While using his laptop to catch up on his emails and read Flynn's account about the latest mess embroiling Brody and his dog, he noted a message from his father as well. For his dad to use email... Cam had no words to describe his shock. He had hope, though. His father wanted their mother back, and he'd finally started trying to do something about it.

Cam glanced at the steamy bathroom. "You people refuse to talk about what bothers you."

He knew his cease-fire with Vanessa would end again. If not during this visit, where she was bound to be defensive and off balance, then when they returned and he started to demand more of her. Cam wanted her closer. But asking her to move in with him would probably scare her. Maybe.

With Vanessa, he was never quite sure what she could or couldn't handle. At least she wouldn't break up with him over the phone again.

He grinned.

Two hours later, he sat with her and Doctors Scott and Loretta Campbell at the dinner table. Not the relaxed kitchen island, but the *formal* dining table. A cook had delivered their food half an hour ago, and he had to admit it tasted amazing.

"Thank you both very much for including me in your celebration," he said with gracious appreciation. He knew how to handle their type—savvy intellectuals who appreciated finer things, when they could take themselves away from their passion. In Scott's case, theoretical computational physics, and in Loretta's, theoretical math.

"It's a pleasure to meet one of Vanessa's friends." Loretta smiled absently at him. She wasn't cool, just not completely present. As if the joy had been leeched from her some time ago, and now she went through the motions, she seemed to smile without meaning it.

He'd been studying Vanessa's folks, and he readily admitted he found them fascinating. "Vanessa told me what a big deal the CAR-S Grant is, Loretta. You must be pleased."

"I am. That funding will do wonders for me. With it, I plan to hire another two post docs."

Scott nodded. "Smart move. I'm going to use mine for more time on the supercomputer. That doesn't come cheap." He'd earned a government-funded grant, and his status within his community had gone up several notches. "You'll see at the party tomorrow night. You two are attending." A statement, not a question.

"Of course." Vanessa ate with a slow, graceful politeness. She dabbed the corner of her cheek with a cloth napkin before lowering it to her lap.

Cam remembered his mother's last raise and promotion and recalled the family having a big old barbecue in the yard. When his father and Mike scored a huge contract a year ago, the family had enjoyed greasy ribs, played football, and laughed it up with friends over brownies and homemade pie. Very different from the Lobster Thermidor, grilled asparagus, and steamed baby red potatoes on his plate. Oh, and not to be forgotten, the big, rich chardonnay accompaniment. He felt as if he and Vanessa were dining at a five-star restaurant, not her parents' home.

"And work, Vanessa?" Scott asked after a careful sip of wine to bring out the flavor in his lobster. "How is accounting life treating you?"

"Well enough." She continued to eat, cutting her food in small pieces. Eating slowly, one tiny bite at a time. She said nothing more though, and Cam frowned.

"She's on track to make partner," Cam bragged. "The best accountant in the place. Bellemy Tech recently requested her to work with them. By name."

Her mother raised a brow. "Nicely done, daughter."

Vanessa flushed and mumbled a thanks.

He didn't understand why she didn't make more of her accomplishments. She'd been quiet and unassuming all evening. So not like the woman who knew her own worth back in Seattle and wasn't afraid to tell everyone about it.

"I'm to assume you're going to continue on your course in the private sector? No desire to join the faculty here?" her mother asked.

Cam waited for her to shoot that down. But Vanessa shrugged. "I never say never. Keeping my options open. For the present, I enjoy my work. It's financially satisfying, and I've made friends."

"A social group reinforces success." Her father nodded. "Is Madison doing well? Her mother sent out notices that she's become engaged."

It took Cam a moment to reconcile *Madison* with *Maddie*. "She's engaged to my brother," Cam announced. "They make a striking pair."

Scott nodded. "You know, people complain that surface attraction is no basis for compatibility. To an extent, I agree. However, after forming an association with Vanessa's mother, we decided that not only would our combined intellect create amazing offspring, but that our physical coloring and biological framework would complement one another nicely." He and Loretta studied Vanessa. "You'll notice the girl has my build and her mother's softer features. She's quite beautiful."

"And intelligent." Loretta nodded.

Vanessa sat up straighter in her chair.

"It's too bad you decided not to pursue a broader education. But there's always time. You're only twenty-eight. Your mind is fertile enough, I should think."

Cam sat there, staring at them. Her mind was fertile? Who the hell talked like that?

"Yes, Mom. I'm still plenty fertile." She shot a sly

look at Cam, and he breathed a sigh of relief. She might act like a Stepford kid with her parents, but his Vanessa was still in there.

"Oh, ho. A play on words, dear." Scott lifted his glass in a toast. "I take it you're being careful not to conceive, however."

Cam sputtered on his drink.

"No offense, Cameron. Like Vanessa, you have strong bone structure. She tells me you're a runner, and it's obvious you're in shape." Scott nodded.

"And this business of yours," Loretta commented, "I looked you up online. Your intelligence and drive have been duly noted."

He had a feeling that was high praise, coming from Loretta.

Even Vanessa blinked.

"Do you think you're guessing, most of the time, or are you aware of the many factors that go into sound financial advice?"

Digging into a topic that thoroughly fascinated him, he engaged with the Campbells for the better part of the evening, more than pleased that Vanessa joined him as well.

"Well, this has been an enlightening evening," Scott said sometime later as he pushed back his chair.

"Truly." Loretta nodded, her expression serious. "I don't know when I've enjoyed company more. Thank you for bringing him, Vanessa. Cameron, I'd love your opinion on our current financial advisor. We'd be more than happy to pay you for your time."

Vanessa blew out a soft breath. "Mom, I don't think Cameron's here to talk—"

"No, no. I'd be happy to take a look. As a friend, not in a professional capacity, though."

"That would be fine." Scott stood with Loretta, and Cam and Vanessa stood as well.

Cam shook Scott's hand, then Loretta's. No kiss from Vanessa's mom, as she maintained a safe distance between them. Vanessa nodded to her parents. There were no hugs or kisses for their daughter either. Come to think of it, there'd been no physical affection among the group at all that he'd witnessed.

"We'll see you both tomorrow. At the dinner," Vanessa added. "We're probably going to sleep in and rest up. So we'll be fresh for the party."

"Good idea," her mother agreed. "Travel takes its toll. Feel free to have the run of the house. Lisa will be in at seven." The housekeeper. "If you need anything, ask her."

"We will. Thank you." Vanessa tugged him away with her.

"The dishes?" he asked, having been raised to clean up after himself.

"Lisa will get them in the morning. Trust me. Mom and Dad don't want you messing your precious hands in suds."

He frowned. She seemed upset with him. "Vanessa?"

She continued to march up the stairs and into their room. Once inside, she quietly shut the door, then turned to face him, her hands on her hips. "What the hell was that downstairs?"

He sighed. "What did I do now?"

"All that kissing ass. You don't have to, you know." She scowled. "I don't like you being all…"

He took off his shoes and sat on the bed with his

back propped against the headboard. "All what? Polite? Mannerly? Nice?"

"Yes, nice. Be yourself."

He chuckled. "I am nice. It was refreshing to talk to your parents. They're so smart."

She looked less offended. "You mean that?"

"Honey, anyone with half a brain can see how intelligent they are."

"No shit." She shook her head. "I meant, you liked talking with them? You weren't making fun?"

To his shock, she seemed almost embarrassed on their behalf.

"Of course not. Your parents were great. They liked me talking probability and investment models. Not once did they yawn."

"That wouldn't be polite."

She wasn't kidding. "Vanessa, I like your parents."

"Oh." She paused. "It's just that most 'normal people' find them off-putting. Hell, even I do. My parents are like functioning autistic savants. Geniuses in their fields, but really not good with people."

"I thought they were both intellectual and polite."

"But cold." Her eyes narrowed. "You don't have to treat me with kid gloves, Cameron. Tell me the truth."

He patted the bed and waited until she sat beside him. Then he pulled her onto his lap and made her straddle his waist, so he could look at her. "The truth is your parents are lovely. Yes, they're a little off. No hugs or kisses for their wonderful daughter they haven't seen in what?"

"Three years."

"Three years. But there's a cold kind of affection,

there. I saw it. They're proud of you. The fact they want you to work here, with them, is a sure sign they love you. Even if they don't know how to express it the way, and I quote, 'normal people' might."

She eased into his hold. "I love them. I mean, they annoy the crap out of me too. Always so literal and sometimes so mechanical." She slapped her hand over his mouth before he could comment. "I know. I can be a lot like them. But sometimes I just want a hug or a kiss. Something more human." She eased her hand from his mouth. "Like your parents are. Were."

"Still are, if my father has his way." Cam brought her face to his for a kiss. "Thanks for making him think about what Mom has gone through. He's done his pity party, I think. I gave him some advice about how to deal with her. I can only hope it sinks in."

"It will." She kissed him back. "I can't believe my mother liked you. I mean, she barely likes me."

"Honey, I'm Cameron McCauley. What's not to like?"

She made retching sounds. "That ego. Ack. I'm sick."

He laughed. "Sick? I have some Dramamine left."

"Jerk."

"Now, honey. I believe it would be more appropriate to call me a dick." So saying, he lifted her up to unbutton his jeans. He took himself out, letting her have a good look at his erection. "You know, we never did get to dessert."

"But I wanted something creamy." She backed away and stared at him, and the look she gave his cock had his temperature rising in a hurry.

"Oh, it's creamy. You just have to lick extra hard for the good stuff."

She snickered. "That was lame. Good stuff? But you are handsome. I'll give you that. I don't think I've ever thought of a penis as a work of art. Yours is."

"Jesus, Vanessa. Quit seducing me with pretty words and get your mouth on me. I'm hard as hell."

"Lightweight." She stripped out of her clothes. "*Nancy*."

"I never should have told you he called me that," Cam rasped as she crawled, naked, over the bed and leaned in to him.

"Hey, he can call you whatever he wants. But I bet you're a lot closer to getting laid than he is right now."

"Ew. Please." He covered his eyes with his hands but nearly shot off the bed when her mouth engulfed him. "You know I'm desperate when even a mention of my parents won't kill my hard-on. *Vanessa…*" He lost his tie to anything rational and let her have him. Every hard, creamy bit of him.

Chapter 16

BETH STARED AT HER HUSBAND OVER THE CONFER-
ence table in the therapist's office. She had a hard time
believing he'd decided to talk to her. But it was nearly a
month after her coffee with Liam, and James had finally
agreed to talk to her in a neutral zone.

"So you still seeing the no-neck?" The first words out
of his mouth. He completely ignored Dr. Rosenthal, as if
the woman wasn't present.

Young and sharp, Ava Rosenthal didn't miss a beat.
"James, why don't you tell Beth what's been on your
mind lately? How you're feeling?"

He sneered at the doctor but answered anyway.
"Jesus. *Feelings*. Okay. I'm tired, I'm lonely, and I miss
you," he barked.

Beth did her best to keep calm, but inside, her heart
raced and she had butterflies in her stomach. Ever since
her coffee date with Liam, James had been different. As
if he'd seen that she had value, was wanted by someone
else? Or because he genuinely missed her?

"Dr. Rosenthal, can I ask him a question?"

James growled, "I'm right here, Beth. You can ask
me whatever you want."

"Yes, Beth." Dr. Rosenthal smiled. "But refrain from
hurtful words. You remember what we talked about."
The woman was a godsend. Dr. Rosenthal had been a
true balm to Beth's wounded spirit. She'd helped Beth

realize that not everything that had gone wrong in her marriage had been James's fault. That maybe if Beth had stood up for herself, realized that she herself had value, she might have nipped a lot of their problems in the bud.

"James, do you miss me because Liam made you jealous? Because you don't want anyone else to have me? Or do you miss me for me?"

He scowled, his dark brows close. "What the hell difference does it make? And what does that mean, miss you for you? Who the hell else am I supposed to miss? *Liam?*"

Dr. Rosenthal cleared her throat. "James, it would help if you weren't so antagonistic. Beth has told me that she values what you once had, and she agreed to see you here because she wants that back." James seemed to ease at her words. "I'm simply a facilitator for discussion. Neither of you is right or wrong. You're entitled to your feelings. Your problem was and *is* in talking to each other. So please, talk *to* her. Not *at* her."

He frowned but didn't snap back. "Fine. Yes, Beth, I miss you. I didn't like you dating that loser. At all. And yeah, I get where you were coming from with Amelia. Also known as the 'hated coffee chick.' That's what the boys call her."

She didn't manage to stifle a grin, and he saw it. He chuckled. "Our sons are such a pain in my ass. You know, we did something right by them."

"Yes."

He blew out a breath. "Look. That whole thing with Amelia. I think most of it was in my head. I was flattered another woman saw me as a desirable man. She gave me free muffins."

Beth raised a brow.

He held up his hands in surrender. "That's all. I swear. I never dated her, never said more than thanks or talked about the weather. I haven't been by that shop in a good month."

Not since she'd been with Liam. "Oh?"

"Don't give me that," he said in a rumble. "You know I'm pissed as hell about you and that guy. So what's the deal?" He paused and swallowed. "You guys, ah, dating?"

"No. As a matter of fact, I consider him a good friend." An understanding man she could talk to about life and things she didn't want to confide to her children or their girlfriends. Her sisters understood, but Liam had given her a perspective on James no one else had.

"How good a friend?"

"James," Ava said quietly.

"I'm asking. Nicely," he bit out.

"He's just a friend. That's all. I've done far less with him than you and Amelia." She even hated the woman's name. "I have no feelings for him other than friendly ones. Though I won't lie. I find him a very attractive man." She really shouldn't have added that, but seeing his jealousy empowered her.

Noting Dr. Rosenthal's raised brow, she hurried on. "Anyway, I wanted to talk to you here, so we could clear the air about a lot of things. I'll start, if you don't mind."

"Go ahead." He sat back and crossed his arms over his chest. He'd worn jeans and a nice sweater for the meeting. Though he looked as if he'd lost weight, it didn't diminish the man's fine face. Or the spark in his blue eyes that had always intrigued her, and still did.

"I love my children. I think I still love you. But you hurt me for a long time." She saw him listening and continued. "I never knew why you started pulling away from me. It started years ago. I tried to be a better wife, a better cook, more attentive to the kids. Nothing seemed to help. Then you pulled away, sexually, and—"

James coughed and his cheeks heated. "Beth, do we have to talk about this here?" He nodded at Ava.

Beth continued, on a roll. "It hurt me badly. I felt neglected, not worthy. And that wasn't right. I loved my job, but I retired early for you. I've thought long and hard about what we said a few weeks ago. About how you thought I wanted to better you." She gave a hard laugh. "Better? You've always been so strong and sure about everything. A man I could lean on, and what was I? The pretty secretary catering to more important people my whole life."

He frowned. "That's not true."

"It is. While you made your way in the world and everyone respected you—my strong, handsome husband—I was merely a Mrs. for longer than I can remember."

"No."

"Yes." She leaned over the table. "Working for the university helped me have an identity. I could manage things for others pretty easily."

"Hell, you kept us in line. Flynn and Brody were a headache at the best of times." He snorted.

"I loved being important to all of you. Except then I didn't seem to be much of anything where you were concerned. It's like I lost my job and my purpose once I retired. All my boys are grown, and Colin is getting so independent. I only had you, but you weren't there."

"Shit." He rubbed his forehead. "That's not the way I remember it. Here's this beautiful woman surrounded by all these college types telling her how smart and wonderful she is, and she has to come home to some loser who nails boards together for a living. I thought you were unhappy, because you were always trying to get me back in school. To be one of *them*."

Shocked, she just stared at him. He didn't seem to be making anything up to earn her sympathy. If anything, he seemed embarrassed to admit as much. "James?"

"I know we fell in love early. And that Mike was an unexpected surprise." He grinned at her before his expression sobered. "But I loved you, Beth. I think you're a wonderful mother. You raised our boys to be fine men. Even Cameron," he teased. "I just wanted you to want me the way I was, not always trying to make me into some college boy."

"*You told me* you wanted to go to school."

"That was years ago." He shrugged. "I kind of gave up the dream after I worked with my dad. Then he passed, and I knew what I wanted to do. The business has been good. I mean, yeah, we had our rocky times. But we're solid now. Mike's involved. Hell, it got Flynn and Brody into respectable work. Without the plumbing biz, I think they'd both be in jail."

"Maybe not Brody. He's a bit slicker than Flynn." She smiled. Good Lord, had James been self-conscious about himself for so long and she hadn't noticed? "I never cared about a stupid degree. I just wanted you to be happy."

"Then why did you constantly harp on it all the time?" he asked, looking annoyed. "I'd come home after busting my ass to have you nagging me to study and 'better myself.'"

"Nag?" Dr. Rosenthal cut in.

"Yeah, nag," James repeated, angry again.

"If it was nagging, it's because you avoided me anytime I tried talking to you," Beth answered, getting a little annoyed herself. "If you would have just *told me* how you felt, I'd have explained I only wanted you to not have to work so hard. Even when we had family time, you were on edge, hoping we could afford our next outing. It took its toll on me too. I just thought a degree would help you feel more secure in the workplace."

"Don't you mean you wanted someone smarter, who dressed better? I went to all those fancy university parties with you. I heard the things they said."

"What are you talking about?" Genuinely distressed about his animosity, she just wanted to understand. "What did they say? Who said it?"

"Your friends, the other secretaries, the professors. Most of them thought you'd married beneath you. That I must be good in bed because what else would I be good for?" He smirked. "Of course, we both know the good-in-bed rep was well earned."

God. She hadn't known her friends had said anything like that. "Are you sure that's what you heard?"

"From Jane and Sheila. Yep. Then there was Mark Sheffield, Carson Allen, Dr. Gresham. You want more names?"

"I have lunches with Jane and Sheila!"

"And that ain't helpin'. I can only imagine what they say."

"But they don't. They've never said anything to me. Why, those bitches."

Dr. Rosenthal raised her brows.

James blinked. "You believe me?"

"Why wouldn't I?"

He stared. "I guess… I just thought I'd do best to keep quiet. That you'd think I was making it all up, jealous or some shit."

"I can't believe they'd say those things." But what bothered her more… "Why didn't you tell me? I understand letting it go a few times but, James, I worked with those people for over twenty years. They were my friends."

"That's why I never said anything." He shrugged. "I didn't want you to have a bad time at work. I knew you liked it."

Flabbergasted, she didn't know what to say.

"I, um, you okay?" he asked gruffly.

"Yes. I'm just stunned. I never knew." She shook her head. "I guess I'm still not sure why you couldn't have said something. Even if you never mentioned my bitchy friends, why not tell me straight out that you enjoyed work and didn't want to go back to school?"

"I don't know."

"Because if you had, maybe we wouldn't be in this predicament right now." She was angry. At her supposed friends, at him, at herself for not realizing what had been happening right under her nose. To think, she had a lunch with her girlfriends scheduled for this afternoon. She couldn't wait to have a serious talk with them.

"Beth, remember. We're not here to point fingers. We're here to discuss feelings," Dr. Rosenthal commented.

"Well, I can tell you I'm feeling pretty mad right now. I want to punch you right in the head," she growled at James, "for not trusting me to stand by you."

"That's not why I—"

"Isn't it? If someone had been bothering me, I'd have told you. In fact, I did. Remember when Kenny used to tease me? Our neighbor back when we lived in Tacoma? Before we moved? I told you, and you took care of him. I *knew* you'd believe me over him."

"Christ, Beth. That was over thirty years ago."

"But I never felt that I couldn't trust you. I put my faith in you to be there for me. Was I that much of a witch that you never felt you could do the same?"

"Hell no. That's not the same thing at all."

Dr. Rosenthal verbally stepped in to give them a break, but Beth had had enough. She had a few people to see, and no more patience for her idiot husband. Not now.

James watched her leave, helpless to know how to fix things. He'd come to this stupid meeting to get her back, not to piss her off even more. Cam and his dumb ideas about how to deal with his mother.

Dr. Rosenthal nodded. "That went well."

He frowned. "It did?"

"She's been carrying a lot of resentment around, as have you. Now you understand where the other is coming from." Dr. Rosenthal removed her glasses. "This is a great first step, James. It's not going to happen overnight. You two have a little work ahead of you, but the nice thing is that you both love each other. Anyone can see that."

He wanted to smile with giddy relief. Beth loved him still. He'd been afraid, especially with that dickhead mechanic in the picture. James didn't do tender emotions

and lovey-dovey bullshit. He loved his wife, and somewhere along the line, he'd forgotten how much. But no
longer. He wanted her back with a vengeance.

He decided to put away his stupid embarrassment and
make use of this paid professional. He could only imagine what these sessions were going to cost him.

"What do you think about sex, Doc?"

Ava blinked. "Excuse me?"

"Sex. Does it bring people together or make
things worse?"

She put on her glasses again and pursed her lips in
thought. "I think it all depends on the circumstances.
Physical intimacy can bridge problems, creating an
emotional intimacy where there is none. It can also often
be misused for that very reason, when people have sex
but don't talk about their problems."

"Hmm." He knew how to bridge one gap. And he was
tired of waiting. He stood.

"James?"

"I'll be back next week. With Beth." He nodded, then
added, "Thanks."

The doctor watched him go with narrowed eyes,
probably not trusting his sincerity. Not that he could
blame her. He hated shrinks. Always had. His sister-
in-law was one, and the only one he tolerated. Sophie,
Beth's younger sister, was a funny lady, but he always
had the sense she was measuring him and finding him
lacking. Of course, she'd probably say it was his own
self-doubt talking, not her. Kind of like he'd always felt
around Beth's friends.

He wondered if she'd still see them, knowing the
truth. Or why it should bother him if she did. After

driving himself to the jobsite, he changed into his grubby clothes and got back to work.

Mike just grunted at him and continued supervising the guys. Their new project in Queen Anne was a ballbuster, and just what he needed to get his mind off his worries. So when six o'clock rounded, Mike had to force him to leave.

"Get out, old man. You can come back tomorrow. Seriously, or the neighbors will have our asses for too much noise at night."

Turning off the tile saw, James nodded. He'd been thinking hard about how best to finish today.

"You okay?" Mike rubbed his cheek and left a streak of dirt behind. "You've been less of a pain in the ass than usual."

"A little respect?" James did his best not to laugh. God, Mike was such a prick. Just like him.

"Pain in the ass, Father?"

James punched his son in the arm. "Smart-ass. Lot of asses in our family, you realize that?"

"Every damn day." Mike grinned.

"I'm going home. Well, back to Cam's anyway. You notice how happy the boy is lately? I swear, he's gone for Vanessa. A mean one, but a keeper, I'm thinking."

Mike nodded. "Yeah. I like her though. She doesn't let Colin get away with shit."

"True."

He returned to Cam's, where he hurried to shower and dress in his nicer clothes. He was in the media room when Vanessa and the boy returned, both sweaty from the stupid gym.

He left the room and casually strolled into the living room. Cam was doing something with his hips that put

James in mind of dry humping, but with his back to his father, Cam couldn't see him.

Vanessa did, and her broad grin grew into unbridled laughter.

Cam turned around and turned three shades of red. "Oh, er, hey, Dad."

James arched a brow. "Want me to give you two some alone time?"

Vanessa continued to laugh.

Cam sighed. "Oh God. No. I was showing her this move that some aerobics instructor… Never mind. Just… forget you saw that." Cam walked away, muttering under his breath about a shower.

"Priceless. Thanks, James, I needed that." Vanessa wiped her eyes.

"Good. Then maybe you'll do me a favor."

"I'm listening."

She heard him out, argued with him a few times, but after listening to his idea, she nodded. "You didn't get the key from me. I was already in trouble for talking out of turn before."

"Swear. I see nothing."

She glanced over his shoulder. "Keep a look out."

He turned and looked for the boy while she fished Beth's new key off Cam's key ring.

"Now get this back tonight. I'll leave the key ring on the table," she whispered.

"He can't hear you. He's in the shower." Hell, James could hear the water coming down.

"Your son hears everything. You take off. And again, you didn't get that key from me."

He grinned and lifted her in a bear hug.

"*Oof*."

"God love you, girl. Now go distract my boy. I have my own woman to woo."

He left her behind and drove quickly to Beth's— *their*—home. He parked by the neighbor's and looked around for her car. Not home. He checked the garage to be sure, and not seeing her coupe, let himself into the house.

A walk through showed everything just the same except… "Where the fuck is my favorite chair?"

———

Beth returned at eight after dinner with Abby and Brody. She'd broken down and told them what she'd learned from James today. Brody had lovingly called his Pop an idiot. Abby had agreed that Beth's friends were assholes and people she was better off not talking to.

Talk about a rude awakening. At lunch today, Sheila and Jane had pretended it was all just a joke, yet she'd seen the malice in their stares, their petty jealousy. The nerve. She'd said her piece, tossed her water at Jane, and left them embarrassed and shocked in the restaurant. But what a high. Her day had only gotten better after thinking about all she'd learned. Then dinner with Brody and Abby, such a wonderful couple. They gave her hope for her own situation.

After letting herself in and feeling the need for a bubble bath, she neatly put her things away and moved to her bedroom. She lit a bunch of candles and prepared her bath. Once ready, she undressed, then stared at herself in the large bathroom mirror.

Her breasts had lost their perkiness twenty years ago. Her belly was still slender, her legs slim from her daily walks. But there was no getting around it. Beth was old.

Large hands wrapped around her middle, and she shrieked.

"Shh. It's just me."

She sagged into his arms before slapping him, what she could reach of him. "Damn it. You scared the hell out of me!"

James chuckled, and the warmth of his breath on her neck made her tingly.

"Sorry. I was hoping to see you do something naughty. But it looked like you only planned a bath."

She turned scarlet, realizing he'd been watching her study herself. "I need my robe," she mumbled.

"No, you don't." He stared at them in the mirror, his blue eyes bright next to hers. "You wanted honesty. Fine. I want you more now than I ever have. I'm an ass, I know. I made a lot of mistakes. But I'll do whatever it takes to get you back." He rubbed her belly. "I love you, Beth. I always have. And shit, but I miss making love to you. You're beautiful, and I want you. How's that for honesty?"

The smile on his face faded as his gaze grew more intense. She watched him watching her, and needs long denied rose to the surface. For the first time in a long time, the right man found her desirable.

"Can I interest you in a bubble bath?" She smiled.

His broad grin was her answer. "Now you know why I wanted it big enough for two when we built the place."

"Is this where you say *I told you so*?"

"Nope. Not tonight. Tonight is just for you."

"Then prepare to deal with rose-scented bubbles."

"Only for you. Always for you."

Chapter 17

VANESSA WAS STARTING TO WORRY. IT HAD BEEN A week since returning from her surprisingly not horrible trip to her parents, and she hadn't managed to shake this bug. She closed her eyes to stem her light-headedness and resolved not to skip lunch tomorrow.

Josh entered holding a folder. "Vanessa? You don't look so good."

She didn't feel that well either. "Would you do me a favor?"

"Sure." He quivered like an overeager puppy. "What do you need?"

She dug in her wallet and found a few bills. "Could you grab me a yogurt from the cafeteria downstairs?"

"How about a turkey club?"

Her favorite. "Oh, sure. That would work. I skipped lunch today."

"Sure thing. Be right back." He left, and she sipped some water and concentrated on work.

When Josh returned a few minutes later, she felt much better. "Thanks."

"No problem." He handed her a sandwich, yogurt, and a banana. "Potassium helps."

"Good point." Suddenly ravenous, she started eating, then stopped and swallowed a mouthful of turkey. "Josh?"

He was staring at her. "Can I talk to you, Vanessa?"

She nodded. He didn't bother closing the door. They

and the partners were the last ones left on this early Tuesday—and by early, she meant six o'clock. With the corporate tax crunch, they'd taken to working late nights and weekends as well.

"What's up, Josh?" She didn't think she'd ever had a better turkey sandwich in her life.

"It's… I really appreciate that you got Gina and the others off my back."

"No sweat. They shouldn't have been bothering you in the first place."

"Right." He sat and then stood and started to pace. "Jeff has been a real help, but I think it's your tutoring that's made me so much better at work lately."

"I had some time, and you can learn a lot through the Bellemy figures." She'd brought him on her team and given him enough to instruct him while still keeping a firm grip on the company's account. To her surprise, Josh had proven to have a real grasp for the job.

"I like working here. A lot." He looked nervous. So cute, a tiny mouse scurrying around the hungry cat.

She smiled at her analogy, especially as she started on her yogurt. She'd definitely make sure to eat tomorrow. God, she felt *so* much better.

"I'm glad you like it. Have you noticed that the others are treating you with more respect?"

"Yeah. Even 'Mr. Peterman.'" He smiled. Then the smile faded.

"Josh?" She finished her yogurt and licked her spoon. Hmm. Maybe she'd go get another. After the banana.

He didn't answer, fixated on her mouth. She licked, hoping she hadn't been sitting there with a gob of yogurt on her lips. Josh turned around and groaned.

She stood, worried. "You okay?" She rounded her desk and touched him on the shoulder.

To her shock, he whirled around and kissed her.

She froze under his mouth, wondering what she'd obviously missed.

When he tried to pull her closer and deepen the kiss, she shoved him away. "What the hell?"

"Vanessa, I really like you."

She stared at him, nonplussed.

"You're all I can think about. You're so smart and funny."

"Josh, I—"

"You're so good at your job. Everyone respects you. I broke up with Angela. Not for you, I mean, we weren't good together. She's too clingy, like you said about some of your exes. It's just, I can't think about anything or anyone but you."

He looked so earnest. She couldn't crush him heartlessly. Could she? "We work together."

"I know, but I'm not your direct subordinate. Besides, you'd never play favorites. You're not like that."

"I know I'm not like that." Uncomfortable and wondering how to get out of the situation, she gauged his sincerity. "You're twenty-one."

"Two. Twenty-two."

"I'm almost twenty-nine." He stared at her mouth again, and now that she knew he wasn't looking at stray food, she grimaced.

"Josh, I *like* you. As a coworker. I have a boyfriend." *Do I.*

"But he can't know you. Not like I do. I love everything about you."

Oh, wow. How the hell did she get herself into this situation? "Josh, I'm flattered, but—"

He stepped back. "I know I sprung this on you. You need some time to think about us. I know this is sudden."

"It's not that, it's—"

"I don't want you to think I'm harassing you or anything." He gripped his hair. "I shouldn't have kissed you, but I've been dreaming about it for months. God, Vanessa. You're so hot. If you'd just give me a chance… Think about it." He turned and left her open-mouthed, gaping at the empty doorway.

Had that really happened? Not sure what to think, she powered down her computer and grabbed her purse. On the way home, she stopped at the grocery store. She didn't need to buy much, especially since she'd been spending more time with Cameron at his place.

As if on cue, he called. "Where are you?"

"Um, at the Met."

"Hey, get me some tomatoes and I'll pay you back."

"Don't worry about it. I can buy a few tomatoes without going into hock." He paid for most of their food, so she made sure to do her fair share.

"Fine, big spender," he teased. "I'm making a salad with our steak tonight. We'll have wine too. A nice merlot to tease your palate."

She heard his father growl in the background, "Go get a room if you want to tease your girlfriend."

Vanessa grinned. "So he's still not getting any, eh?"

"Stop." Cameron groaned. "Don't talk about my parents that way. Major taboo."

She chuckled, tossing groceries in a basket while she shopped. Ever since James had borrowed Cam's key, he'd been on cloud nine. Cameron had noticed his good mood, as well as his father spending time with his mother. But Beth must have called a halt on their truce, because it sounded as if James had returned to being a real bear.

"So is your dad joining us?"

"Nope. He's got plans tonight." Cameron's grin came through his words. "Mom invited Dad for dinner…along with Maddie and Flynn."

"Woman's cock-blocking me," James said.

"Dad, shut up," Cameron yelled away from the phone before returning to her. "Oh, sorry. Hope you didn't hear that. Hell, I wish *I* hadn't heard it."

She laughed, enjoying his embarrassment. "No problem. So maybe if your dad is gone, you and I can have our own party."

"Now you're talking."

She wanted him in the worst way. All the time. She continued to talk with him on her phone and had almost checked out when she realized she hadn't found her almond milk. After hanging up, she finished her shopping and nearly ran into John Willington. Talk about the perfect ending to her less-than-stellar day.

"Vanessa, you're looking lovely, as usual."

With him stood another man dressed in casual but pricey clothes. She recognized the label.

"John." She nodded and gave him the courtesy he didn't deserve. Mr. Small Dick. She bit back a grin.

"This is my cousin Ryan. Ryan, meet Vanessa. She's a whiz with numbers and currently heading our accounts with McNulty, Peterman."

"Oh, nice." Ryan shook her head. "I've heard a lot about you, Vanessa."

"I'm sure none of it's good." She gave John a look.

Not affected in the slightest—*the ass*—he grinned.

Ryan shook his head. "Oh no. Trust me. It's all good. The only woman to deny my cousin. That you're so beautiful must make the loss that much worse, eh, dickhead?" he said pleasantly to John as he winked at Vanessa.

That killed John's smile. "Don't be an ass. I'll meet you at the bread aisle."

Ryan chuckled at his cousin's abrupt departure. "I love him, but I don't actually like him."

"He is…unusual."

"A nice word to describe him. I'd have gone with narcissistic, but okay."

She laughed. Then a spell of dizziness hit her again, and she found herself in Ryan's arms as he held her from falling on her face.

"Whoa. You okay?"

"I don't know. That's twice today that's happened. Not sure why."

"Used to happen all the time to my sister when she was pregnant. Not that I'm saying you are, because you're thin and all."

She blushed. "No. I'm not…pregnant."

"Well, you should definitely get your blood sugar checked." He released her. "You sure you'll be okay? I can walk you out if you want."

"No, I'm fine. Thanks. And um, don't mention this to John. I don't want him to think I'm sick and can't handle his business. I skipped lunch today. I won't do that again."

"No worries. Yeah, not eating will do that to you.

Good luck working with my cousin, Vanessa. It was nice to meet you."

He left her, and she grabbed her groceries, feeling numb. She paid for them and took them to her car, feeling as if she'd entered a *Twilight Zone* episode. *I can't be pregnant. I'm on the Pill. Hell, I haven't missed a day in five years.* Yet she'd been sick lately, hungry at odd times, and God, horny.

No. Not possible. She refused to consider the prospect and drove to Cameron's. As she rode the elevator to his floor, she gauged every breath and beat of her heart, listening for anything different. She rang the bell and let herself in at his shout.

"Put the stuff on the counter," he called from inside the unit.

She shook off her worries, dismissing them as silly, and put the cold things away. Then she joined him in the bedroom.

She caught him buttoning up his shirt, his hair damp from a recent shower. The sight of his bare chest reminded her of what she'd been hungry for the better part of the day. It hadn't been a turkey club.

Without pausing to say hello, she walked up and kissed him. Not a *hi, how was your day* kind of kiss, but an *I want your body now* meeting of the mouths. She tugged the back of his neck, drawing him in closer as she unbuttoned his shirt and pushed it off him. Then she deepened the kiss, rewarded by his moan, and unbuttoned his jeans. She reached between them and dug into his underwear to grip his swelling cock.

Cameron groaned and rocked into her hand before turning them around and backing her against the wall.

He tugged at her jacket, and she had to let go of him to lose it and her blouse. In seconds he had her bra undone. Then his mouth was there, around her nipple. He bit down as he plumped her other breast, and she was perilously close to coming. The sudden arousal hit her hard, especially when he shoved his hand up her skirt and into her panties.

"You're so wet," he whispered as he slid a finger inside her. "So hot." He licked her ear and whispered more naughty things he planned on doing to her.

Before she could take action, Cameron moved with purpose. He impatiently peeled off the rest of her clothing, then pushed his pants down to his thighs. When he rose, he lifted her up over his erection and eased into her body with a sigh and a plea.

Vanessa wanted it hard and fast, but Cameron, damn him, was taking his time as he thrust into her.

"Faster. Make me come," she demanded and tried to ride him.

"My show. Slow down," he rasped and gripped her hips hard as he continued to pump inside her.

Not having it, especially after the day she'd been cursed with, she pinched his nipples and kissed him soundly. She *owned* him, using her tongue to show him exactly what she wanted.

Lord love him, Cameron caught on quick. He growled into her mouth and pushed himself deeper. He fucked her harder, slamming into her with force while she continued to rake her fingers over his chest and nipples, sucking his tongue, teasing his lips, and squeezing her inner walls to stimulate him into doing what she wanted.

He ground against her, and she was nearly there…

"God, Cam. Fuck me. *So good*," she moaned.

He thrust again and slapped against her clit, and she shattered while he rode her furiously to his own orgasm.

They stayed locked while they recovered.

"So how was your day?" Cameron asked with a chuckle. "'Cause mine just got a hell of a lot better."

"Mine too," she said on a breath and moaned when he withdrew. She wanted him to stay inside her, filling her up and surrounding her with himself. His body, his come, his scent. Instead, the practical part of her found a towel and cleaned herself up. She accepted the sweats he handed her to wear, a pair she'd accidentally left behind a few days ago.

"Not that I mind, but what brought that on?" he asked as he donned his shirt and buttoned it up, righting his clothing.

Though he and Vanessa had a healthy sex life, they normally instigated it together. Their kisses went from tender to combustible in seconds. But tonight she'd been frustrated and scared and needy. So unlike her normal self.

"I was thinking about you in the elevator. You know, it *has* been two days since we last had sex."

"I think we can call it making love now. We're dating, after all."

"So good of you to classify it for me."

He took a bow. "You're most welcome. Now, as soon as the blood comes back to my big head, I'll finish the dinner I was going to make you."

She laughed at him, feeling better, and followed him into the kitchen.

Until he asked her again about her day. "Oh God.

It was a nightmare. I worked my ass off, got hit on by my twenty-two-year-old coworker, then ran into Mr. Small Dick at the grocery store." She deliberately made no mention of her illness, sure she could handle her symptoms herself. She didn't want to worry him simply because she had forgotten to eat once or twice.

Cameron froze. He shut the oven door and leaned over the kitchen sink to stare into her eyes across the countertop. "Say that again?"

She'd expected a burst of jealousy, but Cameron regarded her with curiosity. Nothing more. "You remember Josh? Peterman's nephew and the kid I was kind of mentoring? Apparently he has a crush. It was so weird, because usually I'm attuned to that kind of thing."

"Thing?"

She shrugged. "I'm pretty good at reading people. I know when a guy is hitting on me. Usually." She frowned. "He said he loves me."

"Oh boy. Did you rip him a new one?"

She frowned. "I'm not that much of an ogre."

He just looked at her.

"I'm not," she snapped.

"You also don't mix business with your personal life. I take it you let him down easy?" Cameron sounded way too calm as he asked, "He does know you're not available, doesn't he?"

"Yes. I told him I had a boyfriend. I don't think he cares."

"You need me to talk to him, just let me know."

She stared at him, somewhat annoyed he didn't sound more aggrieved that another man had hit on her. Okay, it was just Josh. But still.

"I can handle Josh, thanks." She met his stare with a narrowed one of her own.

After a moment, he shrugged. "Your call. So you saw Willington too, eh? Did he ask you out again?"

"No. Nor did he ask for, and I quote, 'a fuck.'"

Cameron's lips twitched. "What a dick."

"Anyway, it lasted maybe thirty seconds, and it wasn't awkward at all." *Until I practically fainted.* "I did meet his cousin. And surprise, surprise, that guy doesn't seem to like John either."

"Good." Cameron fiddled with the oven timer, then drew out a bottle of wine. "How about some merlot?"

She paused. She knew for a fact she couldn't be pregnant, but her stomach had been acting up lately. "You know, I think I'll pass."

"You sure?" He frowned. "You okay?"

"I'm fine. I think there's something going around though, so I'm trying to eat healthy and stay away from bad stuff. I like wine, but it doesn't always like me."

"Huh." He put the wine away.

"You can have some."

"Nah. I'm good. Water then?"

She nodded, oddly touched he'd accommodate her so easily. But then, he was always doing things like that. Remembering small details about her. Helping without overwhelming her when she asked for his opinion and, in rare cases, his assistance. Cameron had to be one of the few men who had no problem with his masculinity, because he never gave her grief when she wanted to be in charge…so long as she didn't monopolize the control.

"You know, I like you, Cameron McCauley."

He turned from the refrigerator with two glasses filled with ice. "Um, thanks?"

She laughed. "You're pretty comfortable in your own skin. You always listen to me, and you don't try to take over all the time." She made a face. "Sometimes I see Flynn taking over with Maddie. And it's annoying."

"Flynn bosses her around? I hadn't seen that."

"No, no. He's great with Maddie. But she acts so helpless sometimes, and she's not." Vanessa frowned.

Cameron shrugged. "So he gets a kick out of being useful, and she feels good because he cares enough to help. I like the dynamic."

"I just meant... Oh, forget it."

"No, explain it to me." The timer beeped and he withdrew their steak. She came around the counter to help him set the plates.

"See? We work well together," she said. "I don't need you to cook for me."

He raised a brow.

"Well, yes, I'm not as proficient at cooking as I could be. But I won't starve if you don't make me something. I *like* you cooking for me."

"I like to do it." He gave her a quick kiss. "What's wrong with that?"

"Nothing. I was just trying to say that I don't *need* you to do things for me. I *like* when you do them. See the difference?"

"I guess." He joined her at the counter to eat. She enjoyed being closer to him, physically as well as emotionally.

The domestic scenes were starting to get to her. She found she took pleasure from eating meals with him, being with him, or just arguing for the sake of arguing

with an intelligent man. Cameron could talk about anything with a degree of intelligence she'd often found
lacking in most boyfriends.

"Why are you looking at me like that?" he asked
softly. "Your eyes seem really, really blue."

"I'm in love with this dinner," she said with enthusiasm. "I'm intense because I'm so hungry, and
you're doing your best to fill me up." Before he could
pounce on her unintended entendre, she held up a hand.
"Please don't."

The great thing with Cameron—she rarely needed to explain herself. It was like they lived on the same wavelength.

He grinned. "Oh, come on. A line like that and I have
to let it go? No references to filling you before? You
know, when you seduced me against the wall?"

She groaned. "Happy now?"

"I'm okay, but if I could be happy later, like I was
happy earlier? Then you'll have made my night perfect."

She laughed. "You think about sex a lot, don't you?"

"I'm a guy. It's genetic."

She snorted. "Speaking of guys and sex, how is your
dad doing with your mom?"

He cringed. "That was just cruel."

"I know."

As she ate, he filled her in. "So I got most of this from
Mike, because Dad is being closemouthed about Mom.
More than usual. Anyway, Dad is going to counseling
with Mom now, and they're finally talking."

"That's great." She felt genuinely happy for the pair.

"That's how we all feel, but we're keeping quiet.
No sense in screwing them up by butting in. Or so I
told the others when Flynn had some stupid notion

to involve himself. Honestly. He needs to remember his place."

"Oh?"

"Yeah. He's the charmer. Brody's the crook. Mike's the muscle. And I'm the calm, reasonable, intelligent, handsome son. The *best* one."

"Of course." She smiled. "I'm proof of that."

"You are?"

"I only date the best. You, by far, are the best McCauley."

"By far." He held up his glass of water and she clinked it. "Now would you like to hear about the rest of my week, since we've missed a few days?"

"You have more to add? Bring it."

"This past Wednesday, my cousin had a huge blowup with a rival at another job, and the woman decided to come to the office to bitch her out. Mind you, I was with a client at the time, so Alex did his best to step in and talk her down." Alex was Cam's other associate.

"Oh boy."

"Yeah. Hope was flabbergasted."

Trust Cameron to use a word like *flabbergasted* in casual conversation. Was it any wonder she loved— *liked*—him so much?

"The client thought it pretty funny," he was saying. "A good thing he's an old friend of mine. Anyway, when even Alex had no luck, I had to threaten to throw the woman out. Then, get this, she started coming on to *me*. I mean, really. Like I'm going to take her and her double Ds seriously while she's bug-eyed bitching out my cousin?"

A haze of rage came over her at the thought of another woman hitting on her boyfriend. *See? This is what* you *should have been feeling when I told you about Josh, Cameron*.

"She hit on you?"

"It was no big deal. I'm with you."

No big deal? Annoyed because she was annoyed, Vanessa forced herself to detach. Hell, if Cameron couldn't bring himself to care that another man had confessed himself in love with her, she wouldn't make a big deal about some bimbo with double Ds—*nice of him to notice*—flirting.

They spent the remainder of the evening talking and laughing, but for Vanessa, some of the joy had disappeared. The slight retreat she sensed in Cameron didn't help any.

Chapter 18

CAMERON COULDN'T PUT HIS FINGER ON IT, BUT something in his relationship with Vanessa had changed. Due to the heavy tax season, she'd been busier than usual, so they hadn't seen each other as much the past week. But now, a week and a half since that last dinner at his place, and he knew he had to bridge the strange gap settling between them.

He'd prepared a meal he planned to take to her at work, but a call from Mike had him detouring. He stopped at his brother's.

Mike opened the door before Cam had left his car. "Oh man. Thanks."

"Sure thing. What are brothers for?"

Mike wore his work clothes and had his tool belt in one hand, his keys in the other. "I wouldn't have asked you but we're shorthanded at the jobsite and we have the owners swinging by tomorrow for a look-see. There are a few items Rod and I need to hit before that happens."

"Can't use Dad?"

"Nope. He and Mom are at one of their counseling things, Flynn and Brody are on a job, and I couldn't reach Maddie or Abby."

"Did you try Vanessa?"

"Are you nuts?" Before Cam could chide his brother for being mean to a woman who'd never been anything but good to his kid, Mike ended with, "It's tax season. I may not be a genius with numbers, but even I know better than to bug an accountant until *after* April fifteenth."

"Most of her work is corporate, and they have different deadlines."

"Uh-huh. So where is your blond dictator?"

"At work." He flushed. "But that's mostly because she's a perfectionist."

"And you love that about her. I know. Gah. You kids make me sick." Mike winked. "Anyway, Colin's been fed, but he's going through some weird rebellious phase. I'm just warning you."

"Terrific. Hurry home."

"Two hours at most. Maybe three. This job's in Queen Anne."

"Take your time, Mike. I can handle Colin."

Mike waved and hurried to his truck parked in front of the house.

Cam entered and found Colin sitting on the couch, his arms crossed over his chest, a mutinous expression on his face. God, he looked so much like Mike had as a kid.

"Hey, little man. I'm going to hang out for a few hours while your dad's at work, okay?"

"I guess."

"Don't get all flowery with praise or anything," Cam said drily. "You're just like Vanessa." *Lately*. The woman made excuses not to talk to him, and when they did manage to connect, she wore sarcasm like a shield. And okay, no sex after having his world tilted on its axis by the sexual blond dynamo was killing him.

"I like her."

"Yeah? I thought she was too mean."

"She is, but I like her anyway."

"Me too." Cam sighed. "So why are you so angry with your dad?"

Colin's scowl grew blacker. "He won't let me see her."

"Vanessa?"

Colin gave him the McCauley *What are you, a dumbass?* expression.

"Ah, her who?" As far as Cam knew, Colin hadn't finished his anti-girl phase yet. Did the little stinker have a girlfriend?

"Del."

Cam blinked. "Del, as in, blond lady with tattoos?"

"Yeah." Colin sniffed. "She was so nice when she came over. We played and she talked to me. She's so funny." He smiled, then frowned. "But I heard Daddy yelling at her. Then she yelled back. And she left." His eyes filled. "She won't come over, because I can't ask her to, because Dad won't let me call her." He started crying. "I want to play with Del."

Astonished that Colin had taken to Del so deeply, Cam weaseled what details he could out of his nephew. When Colin finished filling him in, Cam sat there a moment. Since when had big brother ever yelled at a woman before? One who had done nothing worse than share candy with his kid? Cam recalled how Mike had watched every move Del had made at the bowling alley weeks ago. Clearly his brother had some unresolved feelings about the lady mechanic.

"I just want to talk to her, Uncle Cam. I don't want her to think I don't like her too." Colin had been known to cry on command, but these tears were genuine.

With a sigh, Cam told Colin to fetch her number. The boy bolted off the couch and returned seconds later, breathless. He handed a scrawled phone number to Cam, and Cam reached for his cell phone.

After a few rings, Del picked up. "Yeah? Who's this? How did you get my personal number?"

She didn't sound pleased. Terrific. "Hey, Del. It's Cameron McCauley." A pregnant pause. "You know, Colin's uncle? Mike's brother? You met Abby when you fixed her tire?"

"I know who you are."

He had the sense she readied to hang up on him, so he spoke quickly. "I'm sorry for whatever my idiot brother said. I just wanted to thank you again for watching Colin—"

"That was two months ago."

"—and to tell you how much he misses you." He glanced at Colin to see the boy staring at him with big blue eyes, as if pleading for Cam not to screw up his chances. "I think he overheard you guys arguing. He's really upset he hasn't been able to talk to you himself."

"Well, hell. Is the kid there?"

"Staring at me and waiting for his turn to talk to you. Yeah."

She chuckled. A good sign. "Put him on."

Cam handed the phone to Colin, and the kid lit up. He chattered happily to Del for a few minutes. His end of the conversation steered toward his butthead dad until Cam gave him "the look." Then he talked about school, his buddy Brian, his grandparents kissing, and the possibility that he might get a dog.

Knowing his brother had no intention of adopting a dog until Colin aged a few years to take care of said canine, Cam thought it funny the boy was already plotting to outmaneuver Mike. In many ways, Colin had a lot in common with Brody and Flynn. His intelligence, of course, he got from Cam.

"Okay, dude. Time to let Del get back to her life."

Colin nodded, a wide grin on his face. "Thanks, Del. I miss you. Bye." He handed the phone back to Cam, but before Cam could thank the woman, she'd disconnected.

"We good?"

Colin nodded happily. "Thanks, Uncle Cam. Do you want to watch TV?"

With nothing better to do now that he'd been roped into babysitting his nephew, he nodded. "Sure. I can bring my girlfriend dinner tomorrow night, I guess."

"Vanessa's your girlfriend, isn't she?"

For now. He had high hopes she'd be more in the coming future. "She sure is."

Colin frowned, and a moment later asked, "Do you kiss her?"

"I do."

"Gross. You like it?"

"Yep. It's an acquired taste. Most boys hate kissing until they turn thirteen. Then you mutate from a normal person into a freakish alien and all you can think about are girls."

"Ew. I think I'll just be an alien. The kind that eats girls."

Cam deliberately avoided the rejoinder inappropriate for his nephew. "Ah, right. So how about a snack? I bet you want something to eat before bed."

Colin nodded, then slanted a cagey look his way. "I have a new bedtime, so we could probably open the new bag of cookies Dad bought."

"Good try. Eight o'clock, teeth brushed, face washed. Snow your other uncles. I'm on to you, kid."

Colin sighed. "Fine. But if I can't have cookies, then I should get two scoops of ice cream because I was nice to Del."

"Sure thing."

They sat together watching television, and Cam had to admit he enjoyed the time he spent with Colin. He'd enriched all their lives, not just Mike's. Looking at Colin, Cam imagined having a little boy he could teach and love. A small child with Vanessa's blond hair and his blue eyes. And their brain. God, their kid would be so smart. And fast.

He grinned.

Colin smiled at him and moved to sit in his lap.

All in all, though he hadn't gotten to see Vanessa, Cam thought his day had ended pretty damn well. He snuggled with Colin and watched mindless TV, planning to visit the neighbors before he went home.

But once again, his plans were for naught. He knocked and met Abby.

"Hey, Cam. Brody's here. Want to come in?"

"Sure. I'm here to see Vanessa."

"She's in bed."

"She's asleep?" He looked with disbelief at his watch. "It's barely nine."

Abby shrugged. "She's been under the weather lately. I think she's sick, but she refuses to go to a doctor. She's phobic like that." She stepped back and Cam entered. In the living room, he saw Brody lounging.

"Hey." Brody waved.

Cam nodded back. "Hey." He turned to Abby. "I'm just going to peek in on her."

"We'll be here."

He heard thumping and saw Hyde poke his head up over the couch.

"Vanessa must really be sick if the dog is here."

Brody nodded. "She looks fine, but I think she was throwing up earlier."

Cam frowned. She hadn't mentioned she was feeling ill to him. At least, not lately. He walked upstairs to her room and knocked softly. She didn't answer, so he went inside. She laid on her side, her hair obscuring her face, her covers up to her chin.

He crouched next to her and drew her hair from her face.

She looked tired, even in sleep. He frowned. On her nightstand, he saw antacids and cold medication. All natural, of course.

"Wearing yourself out." He stroked her hair, and it seemed to him that she eased into a more restful sleep.

She sighed and tucked into his hand on her cheek. The trusting reaction hit him right in the heart. He wanted her to come to him. To trust him with all of her. She talked about want versus need, but to him, they both mattered. He wanted to love her. He needed to be with her. Without Vanessa, life felt stale and much less interesting. He loved everything about her. He loved...*her*.

Cam pulled up a chair and sat with her awhile, wondering how long it would take to convince her that he meant to be in her life for the long haul if she'd let him stick around, and how to get her to admit she just might be falling in love with him too. Because the probability that her odd behavior in dating him for so long, of them finding joy with each other, and that her intense study when she didn't think he was looking pointed to the notion she might be falling in love with him.

———

"You're pregnant, Vanessa. The test is conclusive."

It was a good thing she'd been sitting down, because Vanessa's vision blurred when the doctor delivered such devastating news.

"You're sure?" she croaked.

"Yes. Your hCG levels make it certain. Urine tests are about ninety-seven percent accurate. But we can do a blood test as well to be positive."

"Yes. Let's."

Half an hour later, Vanessa returned from the lab to her doctor.

"You'll have the results in two days. Maybe sooner," Dr. Johnson advised. The older woman smiled, as if Vanessa should be thrilled to find herself knocked up. "But from all your described symptoms and the hCG results, I'm pretty certain you're pregnant."

"But I can't be. I take the Pill."

"Which is ninety-eight percent effective, yes. But that still doesn't account for that two percent, especially if you don't use other means of birth control."

"I didn't miss my last period."

"Was it normal?"

"Well, lighter than normal. Mostly spotty. But still. I had a period. I'm on the Pill." She figured if she kept repeating that enough, she might undo the pregnancy. It simply couldn't be possible. Vanessa had a five-year and ten-year plan. She made lists, organized, and plotted her future carefully. Having a baby wasn't supposed to be part of her plan until she'd found a man worthy of donating his sperm.

Of course, Cameron was more than worthy. But they hadn't discussed conception, hadn't even mentioned the possibility.

"Because I'm on the Pill," she said again.

"Vanessa, it will be okay. I take it the father doesn't know?" Dr. Johnson asked kindly.

"No." *Oh my God. I have to tell Cameron.*

"Easy, Vanessa. Just relax." The doctor patted her shoulder. "You're in excellent health. You're one of the most capable women I know, and you have choices."

"Choices?"

The doctor nodded. "You have to know there are several choices available to you. Having the baby and keeping it. Giving the child up for adoption. Or terminating the pregnancy."

The word "terminate" made her inwardly cringe. Despite the chaos a baby would bring to her life, she'd conceived it with a man she respected, a man she'd amazingly come to believe she might love, were she capable of such an emotion. At the very least, she held him in great esteem. And like. And lust. *A lot.*

"In any case, we need to book a follow-up appointment for you. I'll personally call you with news of the blood test as soon as I get it. In the meantime, why don't you see Barb in reception, and she'll get you back in here in another week. Time for you to settle into this news, and we'll see how you're doing and where to go from there. Okay?"

Vanessa nodded.

"In the meantime, cut back on the caffeine and alcohol.

No smoking, but then, I don't need to tell you that. Your best bet is no more than one or two cups of coffee a day. And it's okay to engage in sexual intercourse."

"Because there's no guarantee I'm pregnant."

"Vanessa, you'll get your results in two days. My dear, you have to accept the possibility you might in fact be pregnant. Get plenty of rest and fluids, and I'll see you at your next appointment, okay?"

Vanessa waited until the doctor left before straightening her clothing. She felt shaky, unsure, and for the first time in her life, panicky about her future. She couldn't have a baby! She'd make a horrible mother. She hadn't planned for this.

Before she could suffer a meltdown in the doctor's office, she got herself together and left. Detaching herself from the situation, she made her appointment and engaged in small talk with the receptionist. She drove herself home and said hello to Maddie and Abby before going upstairs to her room, where she undressed and put on her robe, then walked to the bathroom for a shower.

She turned on the water and after the temperature warmed, got in. The water coursed over her body, but Vanessa could do nothing but stroke her stomach and stare at the drops cascading down the wall.

Pregnant.

As in, eighteen-plus years of commitment. An emotional, physical, and financial obligation. She'd have to totally change her lifestyle. No more freedom to jog at night. Who would watch the baby? And her savings. Babies cost a lot. Diapers, medical bills, food, and clothing. She'd have to readjust her finances. In her mind, she started working the numbers and realized she had more to work with than she'd thought, especially with those student loans near completion.

But even that joy didn't sustain her, because money meant little next to the reality of a child.

And Cameron. Their relationship had been okay. Great, mostly. But with her workload and his, they'd started drifting. He didn't seem to care that Josh had hit on her. And he didn't think it a big deal that some bimbo had hit on him. How many other women had flirted that he ignored? Did he ever mention to any of them that he had a girlfriend? *He told his family, and they matter*.

She ignored her rational consciousness and focused instead on the negative, dwelling on worry and uncertainty until the water turned cold.

"Vanessa, are you okay?" Maddie asked from outside the door.

Vanessa realized the noise she'd tried to ignore had been Maddie knocking on the door.

"Fine." She sounded hoarse.

"Well, okay. We're downstairs if you want some late dinner." A pause. "Oh, and Cam called again. Are you avoiding him?"

"I'll be down in a few minutes."

"Fine."

Cameron. What the hell should she do about him? He deserved to be told. But how did one go about informing a man he was about to become a father? Would he be glad? Mad? Disappointed?

She'd find out in another few days, as soon as she received her blood test results. Until then, she'd step gently around him and avoid mentioning the baby. Cowardly, yes. But she needed time to absorb this possible game-changer.

She still didn't know how her pregnancy would affect her candidacy as a partner at her firm. Once again, the lid on her emotions shifted as anxiety poured off her in waves. She shivered in the now lukewarm water and turned it off, then sank to her knees in the tub, trembling.

"What am I going to do?" She allowed herself a few tears and hugged her legs tight. Then she wiped her eyes and reached for a towel. She dried herself off and put her robe back on. Back in her room, she closed and locked the door behind her. She'd eaten a hearty lunch, but she couldn't make herself eat anything else tonight. Nor did she relish facing her nosy, though well-intentioned, roommates.

She loved them to death, but she wasn't ready to talk about the situation. Because if she admitted the truth out loud, to witnesses, that made it all real.

With a few choice words at fate, she decided to take a nap, completely forgetting she'd had a date with Cameron until he woke her from a nap, pounding outside her door.

"Vanessa, open up."

She opened the door in mussed hair wearing a robe, only to see him looking like a cover model in his suit pants and crisp blue shirt and tie.

He studied her face and softened. "Honey, are you okay? Vanessa, talk to me."

She sighed and tried not to look so pathetic, but she didn't think she'd succeeded because he cupped her cheek and gave her a sweet smile. "I don't feel good."

He took the step to bring them together and enfolded her in his arms. "You feel smaller."

"I'm just as tall as I was the last time we met," she mumbled against his chest. But she didn't fight his hold.

"No, smart-ass. You seem frailer. Like, you lost weight." He pulled back to look at her. "You went to the doctor today? Abby told me."

"Yeah."

"So did she give you anything? Is it the flu?"

A nine-month flu. "Ah, she said it needs to run its course." *Technically.* "Not the flu."

"Good. But you need someone to take care of you. No, strike that." He interrupted before she could speak. "I *want* to take care of you. You're perfectly capable on your own. But I want to help."

Oh man. Why did he have to be like that? So nice and helpful? Confused and on edge, she wanted to lash out and fight. But one, she didn't have the energy. And two, Cameron was just too darned nice to argue with.

"Okay."

"Okay? Good." He drew her back to bed. "You hungry?"

"I could eat." A seven-course meal. Suddenly, her missed dinner made itself known in the loud rumble of her stomach.

"Sounds like." He nodded. "You know, I made you dinner a few nights ago. I was planning to bring it to you but Mike needed me to watch Colin. So I had left-over lemon chicken for two days, and you got bupkiss because you've been avoiding me."

She smiled, the first time she'd done that in days. "Lemon chicken, huh? That's your signature dish."

"I'm trying to impress you."

"So whip out your cock."

He blinked, then grinned. "Good to see your sense of humor hasn't deserted you."

Nor had her hormones, apparently. Because as miserable as she felt, she meant that part about his cock. She hadn't had sex in nearly two weeks, and being so close to him gave her...urges.

"Let me get you something. I'll be right back." He settled her into the bed and kissed her. On the mouth. Good thing for him pregnancy wasn't contagious.

He returned in a few minutes bearing a tray of fruits and veggies and two nice big glasses of water. He'd brought enough to feed them both, because he sat next to her on the bed and ate as much as she did.

"Feeling better?" he asked.

She nodded, though exhaustion still pulled at her. The trauma of shocking news, tax season, and worry over an uncertain future bombarded her nerves.

"Good. Now why don't you tell me why the hell you've been avoiding me?"

Crap.

"Vanessa."

She swallowed. "Look. It's not like we're tied at the hip. Sometimes I need space."

"So tell me that. I know you've been ass-deep in work lately. It's not a problem. But not returning my calls or texts? Just blowing me off? What gives?"

She shrugged.

"No. I want the truth."

A burst of anger filled her, that resentment she thought she'd cured herself of. "You don't care about me. About *us*."

He opened his mouth and said…nothing.

"Women come on to you, and you don't even mention me? What am I supposed to think about that?"

"First of all, it's woman, singular. I don't feel a need to defend myself from someone I'm clearly not interested in."

God, she felt like an emotional twit, but she couldn't stop herself. "What about Josh? My running into John? You couldn't have cared less."

"Now hold on. You don't want a clingy, restrictive boyfriend. We've talked about this. First of all, I know you made Josh cry not too long ago, and you hate Small Dick. So what's the problem? That I didn't throw a fit and demand to beat their faces in? That I didn't go all boyfriend jealous and get crazy on you? That I didn't make some pretentious and totally irrational statement of possession by becoming macho stupid?"

"*Yes.*"

"I…oh."

"No. I mean, I just think it would be nice if you cared about my feelings." *Feelings*. Vanessa didn't do deep emotion, yet she found herself tangled in a knot of misery, jealousy, and affection for the intelligent but clueless man sitting next to her. The small smile on his lips irked her. "Oh, forget I said anything."

"No, no. Vanessa, you want me to be jealous. Admit it."

"No."

He laughed. The asshole. "Honey, I've been working hard not to crowd you. You don't think I wanted to pound Josh's face in? Or that I still want to stomp Small

Dick? Because I do. I'm trying hard to be enlightened and not clingy. For you."

"I...oh." The exact words he'd used a minute ago. But they fit. "So you didn't like the junior hottie in love with me?"

He just looked at her.

"Or Small Dick talking to me?"

"About as much as you apparently disliked Hope's frenemy trying to entice me with her cleavage. No, I didn't mention you to her, because I didn't find her a threat to our relationship. And yes, Vanessa. We have a *relationship*. Just you and me. Dating. Monogamous. I brought you a key." He reached into his pocket and pulled it out. "To my place. You don't have to knock anymore. Hell, you could move in tomorrow. But I don't want to freak you out. I've been treading lightly."

"*What?*" Move in? That implied permanence. A big step. Almost as big *as a friggin' baby*.

"I do not want to become my father. So I was going to force a confrontation tonight if I had to. Look, you know how I feel about phone breakups."

"Bad."

"Yep. Same goes for avoidance. Just tell me straight out. If you have a problem, let me know and I'll fix it."

"Oh?"

"Yeah. Go ahead. Lay it on me."

Her opening. But she couldn't stand to watch his hopeful smile falter, to see his hopes and dreams for his future fade under a yoke of responsibility she wasn't yet sure she'd have to undertake. *Just a few more days, and then we'll talk, Cameron. I promise.*

"I like being your girlfriend," she said slowly. "Calling you my boyfriend. I don't care who knows."

His bright grin reflected in his blue eyes. "Good. Because I sure as hell want everyone you know to see us as a couple. Why don't I come in Tuesday to bring you lunch? I'd do it Monday, but I have clients all day. That's if you're going to work."

"Of course I am. Just because I was sick doesn't mean…" *Can't bring a baby to work though, can you? Can't breast-feed during the nine-thirty meeting. Working overtime and holidays with a baby isn't right. Remember when Mom and Dad did that to you? Nannies aren't the same as loving adults.* As if Vanessa knew how to love.

"You drifted. You okay?"

"Yeah. Just tired," she added, her voice thick. The need to cry again was overwhelming. She blamed her faulty hormones on her pregnancy. Then she erased the thought, not wanting the baby prediction to come true. Not really.

But either way, she'd know for sure in a few days. And then so would Cameron.

Chapter 19

CAM HATED TO SEE VANESSA WORKING LIKE A DEMON in her glass office from hell. All around him, people scurried to copy, send faxes, memos, and worked like dogs. Ah, the stresses of the IRS. Had to love 'em.

He walked past a young man who kept an eye on him as he headed into Vanessa's office. A glance showed his pinched frown, and Cam figured he'd just walked by Josh.

Vanessa had talked to the guy yesterday, forcing him to hear her out. Like her, Josh had been avoiding a confrontation. But good old Vanessa had shown some spine and set the kid straight.

He didn't consider the good-looking younger man as a threat. Barely out of college and too new. He was well out of Vanessa's league.

Cam knocked and entered when she waved at him. "Hey, beautiful." He noted her strain and shook his head. "Honey, you need to learn how to relax. Why so stressed?" He rounded the desk to rub her shoulders and noted several stares from her coworkers outside. "Why do I feel like a goldfish in a big glass bowl?"

She sighed under his hands. "Welcome to my world."

"I saw Josh."

She tensed, then eased under his ministrations. "Yeah. Poor guy. He didn't take it well when I told him I had a boyfriend, and I never mix business and pleasure."

"Oh?"

"*Now* you sound jealous?" She turned to glance up at him, her eyes wide. "Seriously?"

"Since I know that's acceptable to you, I can go kick his ass if you like. Or I could do it big and invite all the McCauleys to take down your 'junior hottie.'"

She gaped, then started laughing. "Thanks. I needed that. Yeah, I can just see the brood tromping down here to pick on our newbie college grad."

"Hey, whatever makes you happy." At that, her grin faded. "So what's up?"

She ran a hand over her hair, smoothing down some imagined imperfection. She looked like a million bucks, even frazzled. She wore her hair in a French twist, paired with a discreet and tasteful skirt suit. One he wanted hiked around her waist while he took her from behind. After Saturday, when he'd visited the sleeping beauty, they'd spent a good portion of their Sunday making up for lost time.

Vanessa sighed. "I've been waiting for an important phone call I should have had yesterday. Unfortunately, I've left several messages and had no response. It's driving me crazy."

"I feel for you. I can't stand the big brush-off." He made a point of looking at her extra long before taking their lunch out of the bag.

"Seriously? Are you going to bring this up all the time now? I apologized for the phone breakup."

He just watched her.

"And for avoiding you. What do you want? My promise written in blood?"

Or an "I do" in front of over a hundred witnesses. He

had a feeling she wouldn't be ready for that. "I suppose I'll have to take you at your word."

"Thanks, so much."

He grinned. They ate their salads and sandwiches together, discussing work and her roommates possibly moving out.

"Brody bought the place, so it's only a matter of time before Abby moves in with him." Cam chewed slowly, wondering if he should bring it up again. What the hell. He'd take a chance. "You know, you could always move in with me."

She paused in the act of chewing, then finished and swallowed. After a large sip of water, she answered, "Why?"

Not the yes he'd been hoping for, but at least she hadn't outright rejected him. "Why not? We're totally compatible in about everything we do. I have an incredible fitness center—did I mention the spa?—as well as a restaurant in the lobby. Residents get ten percent off."

"The restaurant is expensive and the gym too crowded. Remember?" She smirked.

He swallowed a laugh. "For your information, the restaurant is quite reasonable. The bar is the perfect place to hang out. You can drink and don't have to drive. If you were so inclined."

"I see. And the gym?"

"I may have misled you about the fitness center."

"Uh-huh."

"It's got state-of-the-art equipment, it's always clean, and it's rarely crowded."

"Oh?"

"Hey, I had to have some way of hanging out with you. I was tempting you with my manly thighs and calves." He pulled back in his hair and reached down to tug his pant leg up. "See these legs? I'm amazing."

She grinned at him, then her cell phone rang and she picked it up on a laugh. "Hello?"

Her face lost all expression, and she turned white. "Yes, this is she."

That phone call she'd been dreading.

She watched him while she listened, and with blood-less lips, she thanked the caller and disconnected.

"You okay?"

"I'm not sure." She took a long drink of water, not breaking eye contact.

Her stare made him uneasy, because she seemed very focused on him after that distressing phone call. "Vanessa?"

"Cameron, you're going to have to trust me on this. I'm going to be honest with you."

Dread sat like a ball of lead in his stomach. "Okay."

"I had some unexpected news. I can't tell you any more right now, but I promise to share with you when I can. I need some time to myself. A few days at least."

He wondered what the hell had happened. "Is it something I did?"

The bark of hysterical laughter mystified him. "Just give me time. You wanted me to tell you when I needed space and, Cameron, this is one of those times when I need space." She licked her lips, a sure sign of her nerves. "Just…give me a little time, okay?"

"Sure. Vanessa, I…" Not the best time to spill his guts and tell her he loved her. She was going through something. But she'd been considerate enough to ask for space. As he'd told her to. "I'm here for you. You have to know that."

She squeezed his hand. He wasn't sure, but her eyes looked glassy. As if she meant to cry?

"Thank you." Sincere in their tone, her words gave him hope she would explain to him what had happened.

"I guess I'll let you go then. I mean it. You can tell me anything, and it won't change how I feel about you."

She nodded. "Thank you again."

He left, unsure, off center, and sick to his stomach in love with a woman who held so much of herself back. Was he bound to get burned by her? Or would she eventually put him out of his misery and accept his love?

Thursday night, Beth sat with Abby and Maddie at their home, invited for an evening of snacks and fun. And to be pumped for information about her relationship with James. She laughingly accepted their curiosity as their due. Her future daughters-in-law had big hearts, and they loved her boys to distraction. To hear James tell it, all three of them could barely function without their female counterparts. It tickled her to think that Cam might have found true love with Vanessa.

Beth asked, "Where's Vanessa? I owe that girl. She certainly put James in his place. He credits her with some straight talking that made him wake up and stop being such a jerk."

"She's like that. She made me see how stupid I was being when dealing with Flynn." Maddie blushed. "I'm sorry, but your son is too charming for his own good sometimes. He made me nervous."

"Gets that from his father." Beth nodded.

"She helped Brody decorate the house for me.

Remember how romantic it was? Rose petals,
Christmas decorations. He even put a ribbon around
Hyde." Abby sighed.

"True. She let the dog in the house. Which for
Vanessa is huge," Maddie agreed.

The girls looked at each other, then at Beth, and
leaned in closer. "But something's not right with her
lately." Maddie frowned. "She's too quiet, too withdrawn. Even for her. It's not work. Not Cam either, I
don't think."

"I'm worried about her." Abby bit her lower lip.
"She's been sick a lot too. The stress of deadlines. What
if she's getting an ulcer?"

Beth wondered.

Maddie nodded. "She came home at seven and went
straight to her room. Told us she's going through some
stuff but can't talk about it yet. That's typical Vanessa.
She's super capable to help everyone else, but God forbid she need a helping hand."

"Too much pride." Abby gave Maddie a long look.
"Must be a Gardner thing."

"Oh shut up." Maddie nudged her.

"You think I could talk to her?" Beth asked, concerned for the girl.

"You know, that's a great idea. I think she'll come to
us eventually, but I hate waiting, especially since I know
she's upset about something." Abby nodded with enthusiasm. "Not that you heard any of that from us. But don't
use the bathroom down here. Use the one upstairs." She
nodded at the hallway. "I heard her go in a while ago
but never heard her leave. She might still be in there."

Beth left them and walked upstairs.

In an effort to help Cameron's new girlfriend and, according to James, their next daughter-in-law, she walked softly to Vanessa's room and saw the door open, no one inside. Like the rest of the house, Vanessa's bedroom was neat as a pin and clear of disorder. Beth liked the girl's sense of organization, as well as her attachment to Cameron. In that, they both had a few things in common.

She approached the bathroom door and knocked. "Hello?"

"I'll be right out." Vanessa sounded so lost.

Beth had no right to push, but she heard the water running in the sink and opened the door, surprised to find it unlocked.

Inside, she saw Vanessa sitting on the lid of the closed toilet. On the sink counter, three pregnancy tests lay flat. Beth walked closer and saw all of them with positive results.

"Oh my God."

"Hi, Beth." Vanessa had circles under her eyes and looked as if she'd lost weight. The glow she normally wore had been replaced by worry and dismay. "Well, I guess the cat's out of the bag now."

Beth blinked at her. "You're pregnant?"

She hiccupped on a sob and turned off the sink. "Yeah."

Beth wanted to congratulate her, ecstatic at the thought of being a grandmother once more. But Vanessa didn't encourage joy. She looked miserable. "I take it this wasn't planned."

Vanessa shook her head, her eyes shining with tears.

"Oh honey." Beth pulled her up into her arms and hugged her, letting the girl's head rest on her shoulder. Like trying to console her boys, who all towered over her. Vanessa hugged her tight, and Beth knew she must have been terrified. "How long?"

"I'm not sure. I go in for an appointment next week. I just found out two days ago. Cameron doesn't know."

Beth didn't know how to feel about that, but right now she wanted to help Vanessa.

"I'm going to tell him. I just don't know how yet."

"And you're sure it's positive?" Beth glanced at the three tests.

Vanessa backed away and sat on the closed commode once more. "Yes. I went to the doctor last week because I felt sick and it wouldn't go away. She did the pee test there. It was positive. So I had her do a blood test. She called Tuesday and told me it was positive."

"But you had to be sure." Beth nodded to the tests.

"I kept thinking she had to be mistaken. I'm on the Pill. Cameron and I never talked about children. I don't understand how this happened. I mean, I understand the mechanics, obviously. But the probability of conception is so low with the combination pill..."

It was meant to be. She didn't think Vanessa wanted to hear that, though. "Honey, this has to be hard. You don't have to go it alone. Have you talked to your parents?"

Vanessa snorted. "Guess Cameron didn't tell you about our trip out East."

"He mentioned it, but he was vague about your parents. He told me how proud they are of you."

"Well, they aren't warm and fuzzy folks."

"How about Maddie and Abby? They love you."

Vanessa wiped her eyes. "I can't. They're so happy right now with the guys, and they have so much to do with work and stuff. Besides, I don't make mistakes."

She paused. "I mean, no offense, but this baby wasn't planned. I'd always intended to have children, but I wanted to be more secure. Married, or at least in a relationship in which I'd chosen to procreate. But..."

"Life happened. Oh honey, I've been there." Beth sat on the lip of the tub across from her. "I married James when I was just twenty. He was in the Marine Corps and gone when I found out I was pregnant with Mike. I had one boy, and while James came back from deployment on leave, we had a grand time, and I ended up pregnant with Flynn. It wasn't easy, raising two babies by myself. But I had family close, and James left the Corps for us."

"But Cameron and I aren't married. He has no ties to me except that we're currently dating."

"You're the mother of his unborn child." Beth paused. "It is Cameron's, isn't it?"

"What?" Vanessa blinked, as if the notion hadn't occurred to her it could be anyone else's. "Of course."

Beth breathed a sigh of relief on that score. "Are you going to have it?"

"I...I know all the reasons I shouldn't. But inconvenience isn't a reason to kill this baby." She cradled her belly, and Beth could see the confusion and love lingering in the poor girl's gaze. "I just... I don't want to screw the kid up. I'm a lot like my parents." She cried and put her face in her hands. "I'm sorry. I can't do this."

Beth stroked her hair. "It's okay, Vanessa. This is a big deal. The biggest you've probably ever faced. You're so smart and good at everything you do. It's no wonder my boy has fallen in love with you."

She jerked her head up. "He has?"

Cameron. Not you too. Why did the men in her family tend to keep the most important words so close to their chests? "Of course he has. I know he gave you a key to his condo. And that he's asked you to move in. No, Cam didn't tell me." She chuckled. "His father is demanding he move back into the house because you and Cam will soon be shacking up. James's words, not mine."

Vanessa managed a laugh. "God. So everyone assumes I'm moving in with Cameron?"

"No. Not everyone. Cam seems nervous to me. He's seriously in love with you, Vanessa. If he hasn't told you yet, he's even more an idiot than I thought he'd ever be."

Vanessa shook her head. "You can't know that. You just want your next grandchild to grow up in a stable environment."

"What?"

"You know. Marriage as stability. I'll move in with Cameron, we'll marry, provide you with a grandchild. But that's all logistics and finances. We should have feeling between us. Trust me. I grew up in a cold household brimming with *things*. There's more to life than money."

"Vanessa, I'm not sure where you're coming up with the impression I want nothing more than a package deal without the love. Of course marriage would be nice, but are you telling me you and Cameron feel nothing for each other but basic lust?" *Great. Now she's got me calling him by his full name.*

Vanessa blushed. "I'm not saying that at all. Cameron is the least mercenary, selfish person I know. It's not him. It's me," she ended softly, staring at her hands. "I'm not good with people. I'm too aggressive. Too blunt." She paused. "I don't think I can love the way you McCauleys do, the way Abby and Maddie do. They're full of laughter and fun. I'm me."

Beth wanted to smile, but Vanessa would take that the wrong way. "I think you're wrong. I think you love my son, and though you're scared to death, you're going to be an incredible mother. You're smart and funny. Yes, you make me laugh. And you're loyal. Your baby won't get anything but the best."

"Well, that's true."

"You'll educate him or her, make sure the child is hugged and kissed. Won't you?"

"I'd never let my baby grow up to feel unloved. But, Beth, what if I can't give it what it needs?" The real root of Vanessa's fear.

"Why would you think that?"

"I don't know."

But Beth thought she did. From what Cam had actually told her about Vanessa's parents, the pair were brilliant but cold.

"I know two people who can help you in more ways than you might think." Beth took Vanessa by the arm and led her down stairs. "When I had my hands full with Mike and Flynn, my sisters helped tremendously. And what do you know, you have two sisters waiting for you in the kitchen. Concerned and more than willing to do whatever they can to make you feel better. I'd remind you, also, that we McCauleys love children. You have me and James, two perfect grandparents."

She drew Vanessa into the kitchen, where Maddie and Abby had gone silent.

"And you have Cam, who knows what it means to

take responsibility. Not to mention his brothers, who just love spoiling their nephew to bits. A family to lean on, Vanessa. That's worth its weight in gold."

Abby's eyes grew wide with shock, as did Maddie's when they realized what Beth had been saying.

Vanessa didn't leave anyone in doubt for long. "Okay, you two. I'm pregnant." Her eyes welled again. "I didn't want to tell you until I was certain, and I know you're busy with stuff. The engagement, your deadlines—"

Maddie squealed. "I'm going to be an aunt! Wow!"

Abby jumped up and hugged Vanessa. "Me too! I'm so excited. When are you due? Is it a boy or girl? Oh wait, you can't know that. Can I help with names?"

Vanessa looked over Abby's shoulder to Beth and gave her a watery smile. "Thank you."

Then Maddie grabbed Vanessa out of Abby's arms. "I'm so going to help you design your nursery. I'm thinking blue."

Abby frowned. "I like yellow."

Beth sighed. "No, no. You have to wait until you find out what she's having. Then you pick your colors." Kids these days. "Now let's sit down and talk about this like real women." Planning was her forte. She knew just how to help Vanessa—by being organized. "We need to make some lists."

Vanessa brightened. "I'll get some paper."

Chapter 20

CAM COULDN'T CONCENTRATE ON HIS CARDS. THOUGH it seemed like forever since he'd last played Friday night poker with his brothers, he wanted to be with Vanessa, figuring out why she'd closed off from him. Was this his fate? To be so in love with a woman who seemed to have forgotten he existed? *I mean, shit. Why can't she share with me? Why can't I help her get over whatever's eating at her?*

"Would you wake up, Nancy?" Mike sneered and elbowed him to pay attention. "Jesus, it's like playing with Flynn."

"Suck it, asswipe." Cam glared. "Nancy this." He shot Mike the finger.

Mike grinned. "Oh good. He's back."

Their father had Colin at the house, where he and their mother now cohabitated once more. The pair was taking it slowly, keeping separate rooms. Cam knew it was only a matter of time before they were back to being embarrassingly in love. He'd seen them holding hands and mooning at each other a few nights ago. The only thing to perk up his sour mood.

They played a round while he did his best to focus.

"This is just embarrassing." Brody shook his head as he put down four of a kind and took the pot. "I get beating Flynn."

"Hey." Flynn scowled.

"And Mike's a no-brainer."

"Keep it up, blondie." Mike pounded his fist into his hand.

"But, Cam, come on, dude. I thought you were the smart one."

"Vanessa's still not talking to him," Flynn had to say.

The table grew quiet.

"What did you do?" Mike asked.

Cam blew up. "Why the fuck do you assume it's my fault? She's the one needing 'space.'" He put air quotes around the hated word.

"Oh boy." Mike left the table and came back with a bottle of JD. "Drink."

"I don't need alcohol to relax."

"Well, I do. Because if you keep moping, I'm liable to put your face through my table." Mike poured himself a shot and downed it. "Ah, that's better."

Brody shuffled and reshuffled, fanning cards one way then the other. Like a professional, he manipulated the deck with amazing skill. "What's up, bro? Come on, Cam. Tell us. We can help. We have ins with her girlfriends."

Cam frowned. "Something happened to her. I have no idea what, but she's been sick lately. And then she got a call. I'm afraid she's dying or something."

Mike shook his head. "No. No way. If Abby or Maddie knew, they'd have said something."

"If they knew." Flynn shrugged. "She's been keeping quiet because Maddie can't get anything out of her. Even Abby told her she's worried. Because when Maddie and Vanessa clash, Abby's usually the one to calm everyone down."

"True." Brody nodded. "My woman hears nothing from the blond dictator."

"I'm worried," Cam admitted, and for the first time since everything with her had gone down, he felt better for sharing his concern.

"Talk to her," Mike advised. "You're good at that."

"I would but I promised to give her space." Cam sighed. "I can't imagine life without her."

"Oh boy. I knew this was coming." Brody rubbed his hands together with glee. "Today's the twenty-third, right?"

"Shit." Flynn dug in his pocket and handed Brody a few bills.

Then Mike swore and handed Brody a twenty.

"What the hell?" Cam stared.

"We bet on when you'd admit you loved her. It was obvious from the day she moved in." Mike shook his head. "Only took you fourteen months."

"Slacker." Flynn grinned. Then he lifted his beer in a toast. "To Cam. He may be small, mouthy, and kind of a dork, but he's joined the brotherhood of the damned."

"The engaged. The married. The living dead," Brody intoned.

Mike grinned. "Before you know it, you'll be having mini-dictators. Little Vanessas with robotic movements and harsh words for any boy who dares wear shoes in the house. Hell, your kid'll probably freeze the neighbors with her mom's mini-death glare."

The guys laughed.

Cam smiled, envisioning his eventual kids. "My kids will be so cute. And smart. Cameron Junior will be kicking your kids' asses." He heard something from behind

Mike, and through the window in the back door saw Vanessa disappearing. "What the hell?"

"What?" Brody asked.

"I think I just saw Vanessa at the door."

Mike groaned. "Great. More pissed-off neighbors. Think she overheard us teasing?"

"Maybe." Brody shook his head. "Good thing I don't have to explain myself to *my* girlfriend."

"Amen." Flynn cringed. "Good luck, Cam."

Cam sighed. As if he needed more to come between him and Vanessa. Would she be offended they'd been talking about her? With his luck, probably.

He left the guys' good-natured ribbing and condolences and pounded on the back door to the kitchen. Vanessa appeared at the window, the icy glare directed his way telling him he would have no easy time apologizing.

"Let me in," he said through the glass.

She finally unlocked the door and stepped back, and he entered. "Hey."

"Cameron." She walked away and sat in the living room, then turned on the television. "You wanted something?"

"Yeah. How about you finally sac up and talk to me?" He'd try a page from the Vanessa playbook. Frank talk, borrowing from some of Mike's more graphic phrasing.

"Excuse me?"

"Vanessa, I've been waiting for you to come to me for days. Then I see the back of your head through Mike's window?"

"Oh, I'm sorry," she apologized with saccharine insincerity. "Should I have waited until the four of you were done insulting me, my mothering skills, my body, my brain, and my ineptitude at all things human?"

"What are you *talking* about?" Sometimes she gave him a huge headache.

"I heard what you said."

"You can't be upset about that teasing." But the sheen in her eyes said otherwise. "Hell, Vanessa. The guys were playing."

"They called me bossy and robotic."

He'd hoped she'd missed that one insult. Robotic would surely put her in mind of her parents. "They were joking. And if you'd stuck around, you'd have heard me tell them how our kid would kick their kid's ass. Even Colin, and I'm partial to him."

She opened her mouth to retort, then closed it. "Oh?"

He shook his head and moved around the couch to sit next to her, face-to-face. "Tell me what's wrong. I've been trying to be patient, but it's hard. I want to help you."

She clenched her hands together, and the anxiety was killing him.

"God. Are you okay? Is something wrong with you?" He paled. "Is that why you've been so sick lately?" He took her hands in his and kissed the backs of them. "Tell me. What can I do?"

She gave him a tentative smile, then wiped a stray tear. "God, I can't seem to stop crying."

"Talk to me. *Please*."

"Cameron, I'm pregnant."

He froze, not sure he'd heard her correctly. "What?"

"I'm pregnant. I don't know how, because I really am—*was*—on the Pill. But somehow you got me pregnant."

Her recent bout of weirdness—even for Vanessa— had started some time ago.

"Cameron?"

She still didn't trust him. He loved her, and she couldn't tell him the most important thing in his life without being forced to? *Damn it.* "How long have you known?" he asked around a ball of shock and anger, trying to keep calm.

"I've been sick since that trip to Pennsylvania. I thought it was the flight, but I think I was pregnant back then."

In a careful voice, he asked, "You never thought to talk to me about it?"

She watched him warily. "I didn't know myself until a few days ago."

"The phone call." He nodded, remembering her pale face in her office. Her anxiety. "Was there some reason you didn't tell me about any of this before now?"

"I wasn't sure about the pregnancy. I mean, it never occurred to me."

Her genuine bafflement erased any notion she might have deliberately gotten pregnant—not that he'd believed that in the first place. He knew her well enough to know she'd never do that. But he recalled how upset she'd been learning the news.

She doesn't want the baby. The knowledge scarred him deep inside.

"I didn't want to worry you until I knew for sure."

"The doctor called and told you."

She nodded.

"But you couldn't tell me."

She shifted, seeming uncomfortable. "I could barely

wrap my mind around it. I wanted to tell you, but I had to handle it first. It's so bizarre, and so new. I mean, me—a mother." She shook her head. "I'm scared, Cameron."

He wanted to tell her it would all be okay, but suddenly, he just didn't know. For so long he'd assumed they could get around her insecurities. But time and time again he felt like he had to prove something to her. He fucking loved her, and she could barely bring herself to discuss his own child with him. If he could believe she wanted to keep it. What if she insisted on an abortion?

He stood before he said something he'd regret. The joy about his child was mired with pain, anger, and soul-deep weariness.

"Cameron?"

"I—I need a minute." He started for the door, needing to get away.

"Cameron, wait." She hurried ahead of him and stopped him from leaving, her hand on his wrist. "I'm sorry."

He pulled his hand away, in love and aching, not wanting to touch her right now. "Sorry you're pregnant?"

"Yes."

The truth really hurt. "I loved you, Vanessa. Through all your bossiness, your issues, your everything. Again and again, I've tried to be there for you. But you just keep throwing it all back in my face. Now you're pregnant, and I'm sure I'm somehow an ogre for getting you that way."

"What? That's not true."

"You know what? *I* need space. A lot of it. I can't talk to you. I… I guess I need time to process too. Before you go assigning blame that I'm a shithead about the baby, though, I'm *thrilled* to know I'm going to be a father. It's the mother of my child I'm not too sure of anymore." He walked around her and left before he said anything else.

Then he pulled out of Mike's driveway and drove home. His mind kept circling around the fact he'd soon be a father. In another eight months. Lightheaded at the thought and still needing to pound something, so frustrated by a woman who wouldn't know love if it bit her on the ass, he hastened to his place and changed. Then he went down to the fitness center, grabbed an open treadmill in the nearly empty gym, and started running.

Monday evening, Vanessa sat in her kitchen after another long day at work. She hadn't heard from Cameron all weekend. Surrounded by well-wishes from his entire family, from Maddie and Abby, her aunt Michelle, and even her own parents—who shockingly liked the idea of her having Cameron's child, marriage or no marriage—she still felt like the loneliest woman alive.

Cameron refused to talk to her. He'd answered her first phone call with a terse reply, asking if she felt all right. When she'd assured him her health wasn't in question, he'd toned down his aggression and quietly asked her to give him space. What could she say but yes to that simple, polite request, considering it echoed the one she'd given him?

She didn't feel any different, physically. She still had bouts of morning sickness, but knowing when to eat and when not to eat helped stay the nausea. But nothing could cure her sick heart. God, she missed Cameron *so much*.

Behind her, the door opened.

"So. You pissed off the youngest. Not good."

"Please. Do come in," she drawled, not in the mood for James's unasked-for comments.

He closed the back door behind him and joined her at the table. "Got any coffee?"

She nodded to the pot Abby had made.

He poured himself a cup and sat across from her. Unlike her, he looked great. Had a huge smile, big blue eyes that unfortunately reminded her of Cameron, and seemed happy.

"Abby's in the study if you want her. Problem with your website?" Her roommate had a side web design business when she wasn't writing her books.

"Nope. Came by to harass you."

"Get in line. Your wife left an hour ago. Flynn and Brody are tag-teaming with baby names. None of which are even remotely acceptable. Mike keeps offering Colin like some kind of human sacrifice, as if I need to be tormented to know having children will not be easy." He guffawed at that. "My roommates have been walking around on eggshells and spending *way too much time in the house*," she said in a raised voice for Abby's benefit, who was supposedly typing in her office down the hall. "You'd think I'm on my deathbed with all the attention. Not that your son has gotten me pregnant and ditched my ass or anything."

James winced. "Ouch. Still got that wicked tongue, I see."

"Contrary to what Cameron thinks, it's not forked." It felt good to feel angry, not sad.

He grinned and sipped from his mug. "You gave

me some sound advice not long ago. Figured I'd return the favor."

She lowered her forehead to the table. "God. Why me?"

"As I see it," James boomed, "you hurt his feelings. Cam's always been more sensitive than the rest of us. But you know, I think this time he has cause to be pissed at you."

She raised her head and glared at him. "Do tell."

"You don't trust him. He's not sure you even like him."

"*Of course* I do. That's stupid to think I don't. Hello? I'm pregnant?" Not counting her first lover, Cameron McCauley was the only man she'd had sex with sans a condom. *And look where that got me.*

"Right. You found out you were pregnant but didn't tell him."

"I knew for all of four days." She did the math in her head. "Well, maybe I suspected a little longer than that, but I didn't know for sure."

James shook his head. "Come on, girl. You know Cam. He's got that white knight complex. Likes to be needed. Problem is, you don't need anybody."

"That's not true."

"Not to hear him tell it. Boy had to beg you not to break up with him *over the phone*, tracked you down when you stopped taking his calls, then he finds out you're pregnant and disgusted by the thought of carrying his kid."

"Now that's a downright lie," she fumed. "Did he say that?"

James shrugged. "It's what I heard. Didn't say he told me that."

"Who told you?"

"Beth, but Cam told her. Said you were sorry you were carrying his baby. Now any way you look at that, that ain't right."

"Damn it. I didn't mean it that way. I just meant I was sorry about how all this turned out. I'm growing to love the idea of a little McCauley. One that won't cheat at cards and cry on command like your *other* grandchild," she said pointedly.

James grinned. "Love that kid. Little Colin keeps Mike on his toes. Trust me, you'll have your hands full with that one." He nodded at her flat belly. "Cam is no saint. Don't believe half of what he tells you. Boy was a major pain in my ass growing up. The *why* years about killed me."

She smirked before her smile faded. "Cameron is no longer talking to me."

"Vanessa, Jesus. It's been what? Two days since your last spat?"

"Three, technically," she snapped. *Counting today*.

"When you weren't talking to him, it didn't stop him from finding you and settling your nonsense."

"I don't have 'nonsense.'"

"Of course you do. You're pregnant and all emotional. Yes, you." He pointed at her, and she fought the urge not to lean over the table and bite his finger off. "See? All that anger. More so than usual. Normally I'd blame one of my sons for that. But there's just you and me here, and I'm at my most charming. Beth has been working with me." He smiled, and she totally understood what Beth McCauley saw in the guy. Under the bluster and the looks lurked a man with a big heart and the need to do right by those he loved.

She sighed. "Go ahead. Say what you came to say."

"I'll be blunt."

"Please."

"As I see it, you did nothing wrong."

She blinked. "Really? You're on my side?"

"Yeah. You needed time to adjust. But you know what? So does he. So I'm thinkin', in Cam's squirrelly head, you screwed up. Question is, are you woman enough to make it right? I know what it's like to have made a mistake. Because I messed up big. You helped me get right. Now it's your turn."

"My turn?"

He drained his mug and put it in the sink. Then he left with a wave and a warning, "I think Beth's coming over tomorrow evening to talk to you about a baby shower. But you didn't hear that from me. So if you want to avoid baby talk, stay late at work." He left her alone, and she sat and thought about what he'd said.

She still didn't know how to patch things up with Cameron. Every time she thought she'd been doing better, really connecting, trying to take a chance, she screwed up. She'd tried to do right by him and end their relationship. He hadn't let her. She'd avoided him so she wouldn't regret saying something mean or acting out of jealousy. Yet he'd forced her to face her emotions and own them.

Seeing a trend yet, moron? She groaned as she realized she kept running away, and he kept doing the chasing. Nothing mature or stable about that. So why did Cameron continue to come after her?

"I loved you, Vanessa," he'd said. *Loved.* Past tense. She still got chills thinking about that confession. And she still cried into her pillow at night when she thought she might have destroyed that love.

But hadn't he also said that nothing she told him could make him change his feelings about her? Didn't he owe it to her to at least hear her out? Maybe he did need space. She'd taken a good two weeks to adjust to the truth. He'd had two days. But so what?

She'd force him to listen. She still had his key, and he couldn't avoid her forever. The problem wasn't making him listen, it was in knowing what to say. How to convince him that she wouldn't always be running away during the difficult times in their relationship, and that if she could love anyone, it would be him? Would that be enough for him?

Determined, she retrieved her laptop from her room and returned to the table. Then she started to write. After ten minutes of more of the same, she swore and yelled for her roommate—the writer. She'd damn well nail Cameron with eloquence. He was hers.

It was about time he realized it.

—⁓—

Mike stared at Cam sitting like a lump on his couch and did his best not to groan. Everyone wondered why he had no interest in dating again. Losing Lea had been bad enough, but all the bullshit drama he'd once gone through, jumping through hoops because of a woman... In truth, he had a hard time remembering why he'd thought it was worth it. Of course, if Lea was still alive, he'd do it all over again. A hundred times.

With a sigh, he joined his little brother on the couch.

"Dad, I'm going to be an uncle!" Colin danced around the room holding alien figurines he used to pretend-shoot each other. "Uncle Colin. Just like Uncle Cam and Ubie and Uncle Flynn."

"Ah, not exactly. More like a cousin, son." Mike glanced at Cam, not surprised to see his brother unsmiling. Friggin' Vanessa and her control issues. Yeah, he'd heard an earful from his mother. The woman loved the idea of Cam and Vanessa together, but she knew they had shit to get over.

"So."

Cam ignored him and stared harder at the news.

"So," he said again. His mother had demanded he intervene, and though he hated to succumb to maternal pressure, anything was better than watching Cam sulk. Two days was two days too many.

"What?" Cam snapped.

I'll bend you like a pretzel if you give me shit, boy. Mike forced himself to go easy on his lovelorn brother and relaxed his fists. "You're going to be a dad. Congrats."

"Yeah."

"You don't sound too happy about it."

From behind him, Colin made shooting noises. Mike tuned him out.

"I'm happy about the child."

Pause. Mike waited.

Cam didn't say anything more.

Mike swore to himself. "Hey, Colin?" Colin rushed over. "Get me my phone, would you?"

Colin rushed off to grab Mike's cell and returned quickly. "Can I play a game, Dad?"

"No." He took the phone and dialed Abby. "Can Colin come over to play for a minute? I need to talk to Cam about something."

"God yes. They need help." She hung up.

Pleased, he disconnected and ordered Colin to scram. "She has cookies." Knowing Abby, she really did.

"Woo hoo!" Colin took off, and Mike turned to watch through the window as his little guy darted into the girls' front yard. He knocked and disappeared inside.

"Just say what you need to say." Cam groaned and leaned his head back.

He looked exhausted, but the sadness in his eyes was worse than annoying. It hurt Mike to see it. Time to pull off the gloves. Man, Cam so owed him for this. And so did their mother.

Mike took a deep breath and exhaled hard. "Okay. Bottom line. Your girl is high maintenance. Not Maddie-high maintenance." They both knew Flynn's fiancée was beautiful but high strung. "Vanessa likes control."

"Can't admit when she's fucking wrong, either." Cam snorted.

"So wait 'til she has the kid, then petition for joint custody. Stay friendly because you want to see—"

"What are you talking about?" Cam lifted his head off the couch and scowled "Custody? That's my son or daughter. *Mine*."

Mike shrugged. "You could always just do visitation. Let Vanessa raise the kid. You keep on track with your ten-year plan, because yeah, I've seen that list, and it's gonna be time-intensive. So you go on with life and we all get to be uncles while you do the distant dad thing."

Cam blinked at him. "Are you drunk?"

"Look, you obviously want nothing to do with her. She's bitchy, cold, and robotic. Like a statue until she opens her mouth." He forced a chuckle, ready for it.

Cam took a while to get angry, but when he did, he was worse than their father. "What did you say?"

Mike grinned. *Don't knock out my teeth, Cam. Please.* "But hell. She's sexy. Long legs, a nice rack. You could always keep her around for a fuck now and—"

Cam exploded. He hit Mike's cheek hard and took him off the couch to the floor. They crashed into the coffee table, but before Mike could roll Cam over, the fucker had gotten in two blows. One that truly rang his bell and a knee that would have unmanned him if he hadn't shifted and taken a strike to the inner thigh instead.

"That's *it*." He knew his brother needed a fight. So he gave him one. Careful not to bruise him too badly, Mike fought back.

They grappled, broke two lamps, and cracked the already scarred table before Mike wrestled Cam to his belly and locked him into a full nelson.

"Damn it. Fuck off." Cam rasped and struggled but couldn't break the hold.

Mike panted, "You done now?"

"Done? Hey, at least I'm trying. You're so damn afraid of a woman you won't let your kid talk to her. Yeah, I saw you looking at Del's ass. Please. Like I can't see you're scared."

Mike tightened his hold but refused to take the bait. "Like I said, you done?"

"You're such an asshole," Cam yelled and tried to break free. After a few seconds spent tiring himself out, he stopped.

"Yep. I can do this all damn night. Look, fuckhead— that I'm actually calling *you* a fuckhead hurts me deeply. Vanessa loves you, but like you, she's a moron. You smart people never do things the easy way. Yeah, she didn't tell you she had a bun in the oven. Can you blame her? Her parents are distant. She's a control freak. She fucking took birth control, and somehow she still managed to lose control of her own body. Think, Cam. She's scared. She needs you. So she tells you. And then you're pissed off?"

Cam remained silent, so Mike shook him.

"Ow. Cut it out!"

"Are you hearing me, *little brother*? Your girlfriend is scared and going it alone cause you're too busy blathering about hurt feelings. Suck it the fuck up. She needs you, and you can deal with your shit later. Do you love her or not?"

"Of course I do. But it's not me. She doesn't care."

"Oh? Then why is she always crying for you? Why is she so mad and sad and royally pissed at the world? The two times I was brave enough to go next door, she slipped in a few questions about you. The woman loves you. And for a chick like Vanessa, that's saying something. Oh, simmer down. You know what I'm saying. She's different. Your kind of different. Now get over there and fix what you broke. Or I'll start thinking you're more like Flynn and Brody than I thought."

Cam muttered, "Now that's just mean."

They remained locked, Cam's body unmoving in Mike's grip.

Then Cam sighed. "You'd think I was avoiding her forever. It's been two damn days, but fine. I'll go talk to her…if *you* apologize to Del. Whatever you said really pissed her off. And you hurt Colin's feelings. He likes her, Mike. She's a nice woman. Different, yeah."

But not my kind of different. Mike cleared his throat and slowly let Cam go. "Yeah, okay. I'll apologize." He'd been meaning to talk to her father ever since his mother had confided what Liam had really done. Maybe he could kill two birds with one stone. *Not literally, Mike. You can't do life, not with a kid at home*. Ignoring his off sense of humor, he watched his brother dust himself off, looking only slightly worse for wear with a bruised cheek and fat lip.

"You look like hell," Cam said and shot him the finger. "Nice face."

"Please. You hit like a girl."

"Well, this girl gave you a shiner. Now make sure you explain to Colin why fighting isn't right."

"Hell."

Cam whistled as he neared the door. But at the doorway, he stopped, his hand on the knob. "Thanks, Mike. Even if you are an asshole. It's nice to know you're here when I need you."

"Sure thing, Nancy." He snickered at the look Cam shot him before his brother left.

Then, thinking about what he'd promised Cam, he jumped on his computer and Googled Del's garage. Time to balance some scales. He cracked his knuckles and smiled, wincing when the motion pulled his right cheek.

"Friggin' Cam and that sissy right hook." The little bastard packed a punch. A pain, but a pain Mike could be proud of.

Chapter 21

Vanessa had just finished editing her first argument when someone knocked at the door. Colin raced to get it. When she heard Cameron's voice, she froze. *Not yet. I'm not ready.*

He walked down the hallway, and she deliberately hunched over the table, not looking over her shoulder to see him in the hall. She heard him stop and talk to Abby. Then Abby and Colin were leaving and she had Cameron all to herself. Oh joy.

She glanced up when he sat down across from her. Confrontational. Not next to her, but across from her. The challenging gleam in his gaze put her on alert.

"Cameron."

"Vanessa." He stared at her, looking for what, she had no idea. His gaze traveled down her breasts to her stomach—what he could see not blocked by the table—paused, then moved up to her face again.

"Are you here to apologize?" She held her breath, thinking things might not be so difficult after all.

He just glared at her.

"Fine." She stared at her monitor and started to read. "Dear Cameron. I'm sorry to have to write this, but—"

"What the hell are you doing?"

"I wrote something for you. I don't want to get it wrong."

"Jesus, Vanessa. Can't we just talk to each other like

two grown-ass adults?" He didn't curse like that unless he was seriously annoyed.

She hurried to read what she had written with Abby's help. Maybe it would be enough to sway him to hear her out fully. "I'm so sorry to have to write this, but we need to talk. I know you think I'm hard to deal with. I am. I tried telling you many times that I'm not like most people." She swallowed hard and didn't dare look over at him. "I try, but I can't be that nice quiet girl next door. I'm assertive and take-charge by nature. So when we finally connected, I wanted to take charge with you.

"I like you a lot. More than I should. I'm almost certain that if I could love anyone, it would be you. I'm just afraid I don't have that quality in me. It's so hard to know if I'm emotionally stunted or just a woman who hasn't found the courage to stand up and say what she thinks to be true.

"I like to be a hundred percent right. I admit it. I don't like maybes or half-truths. Mostly for that reason, I kept the possibility of my pregnancy to myself. But I was also scared, because I don't think I'll be a good mother. And I really want to be."

She stopped speaking and looked at him.

He was staring at her, his eyes narrowed. But she couldn't read him.

"I stopped there. I was going to write more, but you surprised me."

Cameron tapped the table, his gaze fixed to hers. "Is what you said true?"

"Have you ever known me to lie?"

He paused. "No. I haven't. You avoid me when you don't want to talk, but you don't lie to me. I suppose if

I'd asked if you were pregnant, you would have admitted you were."

"If I'd known. I honestly only recently found out. I had my suspicions, but I didn't want it to be true. *Not* because I don't care about you or like the thought of carrying your child," she said quickly to forestall his protest. "I just never wanted to get pregnant like this. So messy, unstructured. I had a plan."

"Five-year or ten-year?"

"Both."

He crossed his ankle over his knee. "I work off a ten-year plan."

She nodded. "So you know. I wanted to have children someday. I think. It was easier not to be afraid of failing when there was never a possibility of kids. I always used condoms with other men. Not that there were all that many. But I was careful."

"You weren't with me."

"You're…different."

"How?" he asked quietly.

"You're smart and funny. You make me laugh. You never make me feel like I'm an outcast or I'm odd because I'm direct. You accept that about me. Or you used to."

"Vanessa, I told you I love you."

She grew all tingly hearing it again. Then she scowled. "No. You said you *loved* me. Past tense. Right before you stormed away after I bared my soul to you."

"Your soul?" He blinked. "You told me you were scared. You never once told me you loved or even liked me. Vanessa, I'm supposed to be your boyfriend. I'm going to be the father of your baby. Don't you think you could share how you really feel about me? It's enough to give a guy a complex."

He sounded upset, but the slight smile on his lips eased her worry. Maybe, if she was very careful, she could salvage this. "In all honesty, I don't know how I feel about you. I've never felt like this before for anyone. I don't like when we fight. I, a woman known for reveling in confrontation, would rather turn away than hurt you. I don't like that you scare me."

"How do I scare you?" He remained seated, his gaze mesmerizing.

"You make me want things I probably can't have. I tried breaking up with you, Cameron. I knew eventually we'd split up."

"Why?"

She huffed and forced herself not to cry. *Tears of rage, not sadness.* "Haven't you been listening? Because I'm me."

He stood and walked right into her personal space, looming over her.

"You're crowding me."

He smiled, a slow curl of his lips that made her entire world right. "Honey, I'm going to be crowding you for the rest of your life. I love you. Present tense. Just like you love me. You're just too scared to admit it."

"I'm not scared, I'm..." A flash of his past words struck her, deeply. *Would you rather be right, or would you rather have me in your life?*

For the first time, she understood what he'd really been asking. More than winning an argument. It wasn't about right and wrong, but about living with mistakes and learning from them. Being the better person and understanding that he'd often be wrong. And she'd forgive him. But more, that she'd make mistakes too. He'd love her enough to ignore them, to take her as she was. Dysfunctional, super smart, pretty, and pregnant.

"I'd rather have you in my life than be right, Cameron."

He kissed her, and the touch of him went straight to her head. "I'm sorry I got so angry. You took me by surprise. Maybe I do get oversensitive sometimes. But, Vanessa, I love you like crazy. I have for a while now. I just… I don't want you to stay with me because of the baby. I'll always support you, no matter what. Be there for you and the child. But I want so much more from you."

She cupped his cheek. "From me, and for me. That's why you're the only man I could ever love. You care. About me. The real me. The competitive, intelligent, highly efficient woman who doesn't need anyone." She swallowed hard and forced herself to bare it all. "But I need you, Cameron. I need you to love me."

He kissed her again, and then his hand rubbed her belly, over the spot where their child would grow. A warmth unfurled, a deepening sense of intimacy she'd only ever felt with him.

"Vanessa." He sighed. "I think you're the biggest pain in the ass I've ever met. Too bossy, too blond, too beautiful. You're the only woman I can think of that I want to spend forever with."

She blinked away stupid tears. "Jesus, you're good."

He laughed. "If I tell you that last line came from one of Abby's books, will you hit me?"

She chuckled with him. "No. Because she helped me with my speech." She kissed him. "I'm so sorry. I should have told you when I first suspected."

"You were scared. I assumed too much and should have realized how hard this has been for you. But, honey, you knocked me for a loop too."

"I swear I'll do my best by our baby."

He hugged her. "*Our* baby. We made a miracle, Vanessa."

No, *he'd* made a miracle. He'd seen the real her, and he loved her anyway.

He wasn't pressing for the words, though she wanted to give them to him anyway.

"Cameron, I—"

"Let's figure out where this is going, okay? Because I'm not falling out of love anytime soon. McCauleys fall, and we fall hard. You're it for me, Vanessa. Baby or no baby, I'm keeping you."

"This from the savvy McCauley? 'I'm keeping you'?" She couldn't contain her joy. Or her desire.

She pulled him closer and felt his erection against her belly.

"Damn. You got me. I want you, and I'm suckering you into my clutches with sweet words."

She blinked rapidly. He wiped away a tear and kissed it.

"Oh my God. That is so sappy."

He laughed. "But I got you to cry. I win. Now kiss me."

She kissed him.

"Tell me I'm right."

"About what?"

"Everything."

She decided to humor him. "You're right about everything."

"I am so incredibly hard right now."

"Cameron." She flushed.

"Now tell me the other thing. What you wanted to say before, but didn't. Are you still not sure about me, Vanessa?"

They stared at one another, blue eyes to blue eyes. Heart to heart…and all that gooey crap that Abby typically put in her love books. But man, Vanessa really felt it for this man. "I…love you, Cameron."

"There. Now was that so hard to say?"

"Yes," she whispered, still scared, but no longer unsure about being able to love.

"Now let's go upstairs and make a memory. So when little Vanessa Junior is born, we can tell her how you begged me to marry you and I said yes."

She blinked as he tugged her with him toward the stairs. "Marriage?"

"Oh, God. Vanessa. Yes, yes, I accept," he said with shrill enthusiasm.

"Wait. What?"

He was laughing hysterically by the time they got to the top of the steps. Before she could ask him to repeat himself, he drew her inside her bedroom and locked the door behind them.

"Get undressed, baby. Right now."

"Baby, is it?"

"I'm practicing for the little one. Don't worry, I'll be gentle."

"Screw that. It's been a week. I have needs. This kid is going to be as strong as a Campbell and a McCauley combined."

"Now I'm really, *really* hard." He tore off his clothes while she did the same, and they came together on her bed, kissing each other senseless.

He moved down her body and concentrated on her breasts.

Vanessa surrendered to him. To sensation. To love.

He continued to kiss his way down her body, until he came to her wet core. He moaned against her, his hands gripping her thighs hard enough to bruise. Not unaffected, Cameron was far from gentle as he licked and sucked her to a crushing orgasm.

She screamed as she came, and then he was over her and in her, riding her to another unbelievable climax.

He whispered her name as he poured into her, kissing her cheeks and neck while he trembled above her. "Vanessa, oh sweetheart." He kissed her, sweaty and sexy and hers.

When she could breathe again, she murmured, "We should have make-up sex more often."

"Hell, yeah." He moaned when she squeezed him with her inner walls.

"Hey. What happened? I meant to ask." She grazed his bruised cheekbone.

"Mike. I owe him."

"A fat lip?"

"No. I already gave him one of those." He smiled. "He gave me some tough love. About kicked my ass over here."

"Yeah well, your father gave me a visit as well. Got me writing my apology. Yes, I said apology. Think we should thank them for interfering?"

They stared at each other, then said together, "No."

"Mike will be impossible to live with." Cameron shook his head.

"James already is."

"Not according to Mom." He sighed. "I'm so glad they're back together."

"I'm glad we're back together."

"We weren't really apart." He paused. "Well, maybe we were. You scared me. Had me thinking you'd never be able to love me like I love you. But then I realized, with the help of Mike's large fists, that maybe you were entitled to be a little more kooky than usual."

"Gee, thanks, Cameron."

"Well, it's not every day you find out you're pregnant when you're taking birth control." He puffed up like a peacock. "I'm potent. Don't you forget it."

"You're going to be impossible to live with, aren't you?"

"Marry me and find out."

She smiled, then sobered quickly. "What? Really?"

"Really." He kissed her gently. "Vanessa, I'm so in love with you it's not funny. I want our baby. I want you. I'll take you any way I can get you. But think about this. I have a media room. Twenty-four-seven access to a state-of-the-art fitness center. A pool. A great location. My condo kicks ass."

"True." She felt her world changing again, slipping out of her control.

"Think how successful we'd be if we combined our portfolios. My financial genius combined with yours? We'd be unstoppable."

Vanessa remained quiet, trying to process everything. "You know I'll always support you," Cam said. "After the baby, you'll keep working for your company, and I'll deal with mine. We've got family to help us if we need it, and we're flush enough we can get the best child care we need. We can make this work. I know we can."

"I know too." His support meant the world to her.

He withdrew and quickly used his shirt to clean them up. "Anyway," he said, returning to lie next to her in bed. "My point is that as long as you're with me, I'm golden. Marriage or no marriage, Vanessa, you're my girl."

She stared into his eyes, at the face of the man she loved. *I really am a girl after all,* she thought with amusement. "Will I have to change my name?"

He broke into a wide smile. "No. But I'm not changing mine." He kissed her and hugged her. "Now that we've made up, can I go to your office and kick Josh's ass?"

She tickled him until he cried uncle. "No. That boy was torn up over losing me when he never had me to begin with. He's been sulking all over the place."

"You have no idea how hard it was to pretend I didn't care about him and that fucker Small Dick."

She snickered. "Now whenever I see him, I think of him as that. You really have no worries on that score. Cameron, you have to know I won't lie to you."

"Me neither. But omission counts."

"Yes, it does. I love you. I want to marry you and have this baby together. But part of me still worries that maybe you don't get what I'm about. That you might reconsider what you're getting yourself into."

"As long as I'm diving into a pool of one cool, hot blond who's sexy when she's mean, sign me up."

She smiled. "You know, we could always take our honeymoon before we get married. A trip to the Rockies would be terrific. We could run in the mountains."

"And maybe mountain bike?"

She nodded, excited.

"Well, no. The baby. No biking." He frowned. "When do you need to see your doctor again? Because I'd like to go with you."

She leaned close to kiss him. "Have I told you how glad I am to be wrong?"

"About what, exactly? You're wrong so often, you have to be more specific."

She pinched him.

"Ow."

"Wrong about not knowing how to love you. I am good for you."

"Duh. Please, Vanessa. Anything but that."

"What?"

"Don't turn into a typical blond. Only someone phenomenally stupid might think we weren't right for each other."

"Don't go there." She narrowed her eyes, seeing his teasing glint but resolving herself against it.

He'd made a blond dig. He had to pay.

She exploited his vulnerability and had him pleading with her for forgiveness.

"I mean it. I'll invite your father, not only to give me away at our wedding, but to stay with us in the condo until I feel comfortable with his son—the same man who got me pregnant and left me."

"For two whole days. Jesus, would you let that go? I was emotionally wounded."

"Nancy."

"Okay, okay. No more blond jokes. Ever."

"Hmmph."

"Not even a number joke. Like why couldn't the blond dial 911?"

"Cameron…"

"She couldn't find the eleven."

She laughed and made him pay all over again. First with slow kisses, then a massage that centered at his groin and grew more intense as her kisses deepened. She teased him until he begged for mercy. And then she teased him some more.

———

Cam spent the next afternoon floating in a sea of happiness. Vanessa had forgiven him. He'd forgiven her. And *hot damn*, she said she'd marry him. They planned to go ring shopping this weekend.

"Cam, no offense. But are you on something?" Hope asked from the doorway to his office, staring at him with a frown.

He laughed. "Hope. I have hope." He chuckled to himself. "Vanessa and I are getting married."

She raced to hug him. "That's so great! So she finally put you out of your misery, huh?"

"In another eight months, I'll be a dad too."

She gaped. "Married and a father. Boy, you McCauleys sure do grow up fast."

He laughed. "I'm feeling like I can do anything today."

As if on cue, his father walked into his office.

"Well, I'd say somebody got lucky." James gave Hope a kiss on the cheek, then sat across from Cam.

Hope laughed at him as she left and closed the office door behind her.

"Dad. Even you can't bring me down. Vanessa and I are getting married." Cam had planned on telling his parents this coming weekend, together with Vanessa.

But he figured to cut his dad off before the old man ruined his mood.

James laughed. "Congratulations, son. That's terrific."

"Vanessa said we have you to thank."

"And Mike. Boy looks like crap. You did a halfway decent job on his face."

"I live to make you proud." Cam snorted.

His father didn't laugh.

"Dad?"

"Cam, you always make me proud. Hell, you always have. You're a chip off the old block, and I don't mean your mother. It never sat right with me that we argued so much."

"Ah, okay." Would wonders never cease?

"I just thought you should know I respect you and what you do. Even if you are sometimes a Nancy," he teased. "So we'll see you Saturday at five. Barbecue."

"First one this spring." Cam smiled. "We'll be seeing you at home. Your home."

"Damn straight." His father rose and left.

Cam whistled as he got back to work. At the end of the day, he went home to the love of his life. Vanessa.

Epilogue

MIKE TOOK IN THE OLD GARAGE, IMPRESSED WITH the vintage muscle cars in the barricaded lot. He walked inside and found a small waiting space beyond the noise of the mechanics. Behind him, he could see a bunch of heavily muscled guys working on cars. Half of them sported earrings, gang symbols, and a few had prison tats. Nice place.

But the tools and the cars were cherry.

"Can I help you?" a bored kid with earrings asked from behind what might have passed for a reception desk.

"Yeah. I'm here to see Liam Webster," Mike growled. *Not Del. I didn't come to see her. I came for the old man.*

The kid's interest sharpened and he pointed to a door on the far wall. "Go through there."

"Thanks." Mike had come straight from work. He wanted to get this over with so he could tell his mother he'd thanked her hero in person. That and he wanted a look at the guy his mother thought could do no wrong.

He stepped inside a neat but cramped office. A scarred wooden desk sat between two chairs, and a long bench covered in tools and instruction manuals took up space along the back wall.

An open door sat next to the bench, and it was through that entrance that a guy as large as Mike entered. He had a silver buzz cut, dark brown eyes, and a square jaw.

"Liam Webster?"

"Yeah?" the guy growled back.

"Mike McCauley. Beth's son. Well, one of four."

At the mention of her name, the man's wary gaze softened into a warm smile. "Hell. It's great to meet you, Mike. Can I get you something to drink?"

"Nah. I just came by to thank you for being so good to my mom. She's had a hard time with my dad. Truth is the guy's heart is always in the right place, but sometimes his mouth and instincts are off."

"Sounds like a man for sure." Liam grinned.

Mike grinned with him. "Anyway. My mom thinks the world of you. She was in a pretty vulnerable spot, and you could have taken advantage but you didn't. I appreciate it."

"Plus you came down here to get a look at me and warn me to stay far away. Message received."

Mike laughed. "Nah. My dad can handle the 'she's my woman' warnings. I just wanted to say thanks. From my mom, and from me."

"No problem, Mike. Hey, you ever need any body work done, keep us in mind. I'll cut you a good deal."

"Will do. If you think about remodeling this place, let me know. Same goes."

"That's right. You guys are contractors, aren't you?" Liam frowned. "Though if you work with your dad, I doubt he'd want to help."

"He'll do it. Hell, right now he'll walk on hot coals to make Mom happy."

"Good man." Liam shook his head. "Lucky man. Your mother is one fine woman. She deserves to be happy. I know she loves your father." He studied Mike. "She said you're his spitting image. Must be a big guy then."

"He tries. It's getting harder for him to keep up with me since I sic my kid on him."

Liam chuckled. "You know, speaking of remodels, I wouldn't mind—"

"You," Del spat from behind her dad in the doorway. "Get your ass out of my office. You're not—"

Liam turned. "*Delilah Webster*. What the fuck? Can't you see I'm having a conversation here?"

"He—He's not here to screw with me?"

"*What?*" Liam's previously welcoming smile turned dark in a hurry.

Mike swallowed a groan. "Uh, not sure what you mean by screw with you. I came by to see your father." Not to be intimidated, Mike scowled at her. "Unless you've been flirting with my kid again."

"Flirting?" She gaped at him, looking so damn sexy he had a hard time not staring. For some reason, her tattoos and piercings turned him on, when Mike had never been into women who didn't look soft or petite. Lea had been on the small side with curves in all the right places. No piercings anywhere, and definitely no ink.

"Del?" Her father stared from her to Mike and back again.

"Dad, please. The kid is six."

"Robbing the damn cradle." Mike shook his head, enjoying her father's disbelief.

"I babysat him once. That's it. We had fun, until killjoy here returned and jumped my ass."

Not the way I'd like to. He cleared his throat. "I don't think so. I merely pointed out that I didn't want my son eating so much sugar. But your daughter tried shoving candy Kisses and chocolate down his throat."

"Don't forget the Coke." She sneered.

"*What?*" Liam stared.

"Not that kind of coke. Jesus, Dad. I'm talking about soda."

"What the hell's going on?" Another mammoth-sized man, this one wearing a sleeveless tank and a huge tribal tattoo over his left shoulder, glared at Mike. He didn't have hair, looked like he ate small children for breakfast, and glowered.

"Mike, meet my son, J.T. J.T., meet Mike. Apparently your sister is crushing on his son."

"What?" J.T. stared from Mike to Del. "I know you're hard up for a date lately, but how old can this kid be?"

"You two are a laugh riot."

While she argued with her brother, Mike tried to see the family resemblance but couldn't. Del had ash-blond hair and gray eyes. Her brother had light brown skin, no hair, and deep brown eyes. He looked a lot like that wrestler turned actor in all the racing movies. One of Colin's favorite wrestlers, as a matter of fact. *Definitely have to keep the boy away from Del's garage or he'll never want to leave her side.*

"Anyway, Liam. Thanks again," Mike said loudly to be heard over the siblings now arguing like cats and dogs.

"Anytime, Mike. We'll have to get a beer sometime."

"That would be great." He leaned over the desk and shook Liam's hand.

When he turned to move, he found J.T. in his face.

"You fucking with my sister?"

Mike didn't exorcise his inner demons often. He worked out on his heavy bag at home and occasionally hit the gym for rough boxing matches to rid himself of stress. But it had been a while since he'd had a decent opponent in the ring. Even his brothers didn't know how often he needed to vent his aggressions.

"Buddy, you might want to back up a pace."

"And if I don't?" J.T. raised a brow.

"Then I'll feed your head to your ass one bite at a time." Mike leaned forward, more than ready to turn his lust for Del into an emotion he understood. Anger.

Apparently J.T. saw his threat as genuine, for he backed up and held up his hands in surrender. "Easy, guy. Just looking out for my little sister."

"Your sister ain't little. And she sure as hell doesn't need saving from me." He took a step forward and found it blocked by Del.

She didn't back down as she poked him in the chest. "What does that mean?"

Tired of dealing with too many Websters, he leveled a threat of his own at the most dangerous of the bunch. He leaned closer to whisper, "It means, princess, that if you touch me again, I'll give you the kiss you've been begging for since day one."

Her gray eyes widened, and she took a hesitant step back.

Mike walked past her quickly, before he gave in to temptation and planted one on her. Then had his ass handed to him by her brother, father, and the now silent mechanics glaring at him through the doorway.

He'd made it outside, halfway to his truck, when she tracked him down.

"Hey. I'm not through with you."

He swore to himself. "Fine. Where do you want it?"

"It? What it?"

"The kiss. In front of everyone, in my truck, your office. Where?"

She planted her hands on her trim hips. Damn, he liked the muscle tone in her arms. The woman had strength. And that funky way of keeping her hair back in braids, in a kind of retro goth look. Or punk. Hell, something different and sexy and wild. She made him want to toss her against a wall and fuck her silly. Nothing gentle or caring about it.

And that scared him.

"I don't want anything from you," she spat.

"Yeah? Then why are you following me?"

"I... I... You're an ass, you know that?"

"Yep. Yet you still want a piece of me."

"Fuck off, McCauley. And leave my dad alone."

"Or what? You'll sic your brother on me?" He got into his truck, started it, and rolled down the window. "Now leave my kid alone. He's attached to you, and he doesn't need to be."

"Why? Afraid he might like me?"

"Yes," he answered truthfully.

She frowned. "What?"

"Look. I'm sorry we got off on the wrong foot before. Colin likes you a little too much. He's attached and has no right to be. You did Abby a favor, and she likes you. Fine. But I don't want Colin getting hurt when you decide to cut ties. So just keep your distance."

She frowned as he pulled away.

That went well. So why do I feel like I only made things worse?

—〰—

"You don't want Colin getting hurt? What the hell does that mean?" Del watched him leave with a frown.

"Yo, D. You good?"

She turned to see her brother and father standing outside the garage, watching her. Oh boy. She sure hoped they weren't taking that kiss nonsense to heart. Not that she was. Guys like Mike McCauley weren't her type, for one. The build, the face, yeah. But the baggage... A dead wife, a kid, too many brothers, and a connection to her new friends, Abby and Maddie. And hell, Vanessa too.

Del didn't do baggage. She had enough of her own to last a lifetime.

"I'm fine," she informed her brother. "Now tell me again why you're here badgering me when I have a job to do? And why you feel it necessary to bring up my dating life in front of complete strangers?"

"Strangers, huh? Seemed to me like you knew the guy." J.T. crossed his arms over his chest.

So much sheer strength in her brother, yet Mike hadn't blinked when he'd issued his threat.

Her heart raced and she clenched her fists. Nope. Mike McCauley definitely wasn't her type. Mr. Wonder Bread and his cute kid belonged to a nice house and family in the suburbs. Not her scene. At all.

Even if she did wonder what a kiss from him might have been like. If he'd been her type. Which he so clearly wasn't.

Enjoy a sneak peek at book 4 in the McCauley Brothers series,

What to Do with a Bad Boy

FINALLY. ALL WAS AS IT SHOULD BE. MICHAEL McCauley nodded to himself as he glanced around his parents' dining room table.

James and Beth McCauley—his parents—were back together again. Happy, smiling, and doting on Colin, Mike's pride and joy. Or, as his brothers called the boy, Mike's little clone.

Colin grinned and exposed a missing front tooth. One that had cost Mike five friggin' bucks. The tooth fairy had definitely succumbed to inflation. Then again, it was a first tooth. With any luck, he could get away with leaving quarters under his six-year-old's pillow in the near future. That bottom tooth looked suspiciously loose.

"Thank you, Grandma." Colin took the extra roll from Mike's mother and smothered it in butter and jelly, ignoring his vegetables in favor of bad carbs and sugar.

Terrific. "Mom, no more. Okay? Colin needs to finish his broccoli."

She frowned at him. So of course, his father frowned at him as well. In an attempt to suck up to his wife, James would do anything and everything to stay out of the doghouse.

"Jesus, boy. It's just a roll. Ease up."

"Yeah, Dad. Ease up." Colin smirked.

James winked at his grandson.

"*Colin*. Dad," Mike growled. When his mother turned to help Colin cut his steak, Mike leaned closer to his dad and whispered, "Laying it on a bit thick, aren't you, old man?"

James shrugged. "Hey, I learned my lesson. When your mother's happy, I'm happy."

Nice that his father had learned that after thirty-six years of marriage. Mike considered himself a fast learner. After three dates with Lea, he'd known how to please his girl.

Pressure balled in his chest at the thought of her name.

He coughed to hide the pain building inside him and drank his water. *Shit*. He hated being like this, an emotional basket case. But he turned a little nutty this time of year, no matter how much he tried not to. Thank God he'd learned to hide his feelings, or his mother would be all over his ass to share.

"Del said hi," Colin said around a mouthful of dough. "Her daddy's really big. Just like Grandpa."

Mike started. "Del?"

His mother talked over him. "Isn't he, though? Liam is just a big sweetie." Beth smiled, prompting James to scowl. "Oh, stop, James. So we had coffee a few times. Liam is a very nice man. He said encouraging things about you, you know."

His father's scowl faded. "Oh?"

"Yep. Said you were so in love with me, you couldn't help acting like a fool."

Back when his father had been separated from his mother, Mike had worried they might never get their acts together. He breathed a sigh of relief when his mother's sly grin soon appeared on his father's face. Mike didn't have the energy to go to work day after day and watch his father turn back into a shell of a man. And having seen his mother cry… He never wanted to witness that again either.

"Well, Liam was smart about one thing. He knew better than to lay his hands on my woman." James pulled her close for a kiss.

"Ew, Grandpa. Gross." Colin made a face.

"Yeah, Dad. Really? I'm trying to eat here." Secretly, Mike reveled in his parents acting lovesick. It had been too long since they'd engaged in playful banter. Yet the clear affection showed him how much he was missing as a single dad. It didn't help that his brothers had all recently found love, either, making Mike the odd man out. Everything was changing, and he didn't like it. At all.

He pushed around his mashed potatoes and focused on what mattered—the here and now. Turning to Colin, he asked, "Since when are you and Del hanging out?"

Delilah Webster. His sexy nemesis and constant headache, though she'd captured Colin's admiration easily enough. Mike didn't like the woman. Not her sexy tattoos, her brow ring, the stud in her nose, the funky way she wore her ash-blond hair, or those wolf-gray eyes that seemed to stare through him. *So not my type.* The woman and her mouthy attitude totally put his back up.

Colin frowned. "When Uncle Cam watched me, we went bowling. And Vanessa and Del were there."

He could see Vanessa ignoring his wishes to keep the woman away from Colin. Now pregnant and engaged to his youngest brother, she had a way about her that didn't invite question. But Cam knew better.

"Vanessa shouldn't have—"

"Ahem." His father frowned at Mike and shook his head. Then he turned to Colin. "Did you have fun?"

Colin grinned. "Yeah. Del has big muscles and her arms are so cool. I want arms like that."

Sleeves of tattoos. *On a woman*. Mike did his best to convince himself she turned him off.

"J.T. came too, and he's huge." Colin had stars in his eyes. *Damn Del*. "As big as Daddy."

"J.T.?" Beth asked.

"Her brother," Mike muttered, not pleased at all. He'd known as soon as he'd met the guy that Colin would idolize him. The resemblance to a certain celebrity, one of Colin's favorite people, didn't help matters.

"I'll bet he might be as big as your dad, but he's not as strong," Beth said gently. For his sake or Colin's?

"He's a wrestler, Grandma."

Mike sighed. "No, son. That's the Rock you're thinking of. Del's brother is someone else." J.T.—the big bastard—had tried screwing with Mike not long ago. Unfortunately, Mike hadn't gotten the fight he was still itching to finish. With J.T. *or* Del.

"He's fuckin' awesome." Colin beamed.

The table fell silent.

Mike met his mother's stunned gaze, but his father continued to eat and question the boy, so he figured he hadn't heard what he thought he had. She shrugged and returned to her dinner as well.

After a few moments, he chimed in. "Colin, tell us about your field trip coming up. You're not going to the zoo, are you?" Seattle's Woodland Park Zoo had always been one of Colin's favorite places to go.

"Nope. We're visiting the Reptile Pit." Colin waxed on about his upcoming visit to the Pit, a popular place that taught kids about reptiles.

Enthused that his son liked school and showed signs of being as gifted with academia as his grandma, Mike encouraged him with questions.

"Yeah, Dad. I'm going to sit next to Brian when they bring the snakes out. He likes them too. Maybe you can come. They need chaperones."

"I'll try." But the timing would be tough. He was right in the middle of a massive remodel that was behind schedule due to some screwups courtesy of the home-owners. He hated being behind.

"Do you get to handle the snakes?" James asked.

"Ew. How about lizards instead? Maybe some cute little frogs," Beth suggested.

Colin smirked. "Grandma, don't be such a girl."

For all that Colin loved his grandmother and crushed on Del, he still had a bias against girls. Not that Mike could blame him. His mother's recent matchmaking efforts had nearly driven him insane with the opposite sex. Now that she had her hands full dealing with his father, he could ease back into—

"Pass the fucking potatoes, Dad." Colin waited.

"*What?*"

His mother dropped her fork. His father choked on his drink.

Colin blinked innocently. "Pass the potatoes?" The mischief in his blue-eyed gaze was straight-up Brody—another troublesome brother too busy playing house with his girlfriend to come to Sunday night dinner. "Did I say something wrong, Dad?"

"Oh hell no. We're not playing Ubie's game." Ubie—Colin's nickname for his Uncle Brody.

"Mike," Beth warned.

"Where did you hear that word? The F-word." Mike had said his share of choice phrases. He worked in construction with his father, for God's sake. Swearing was a McCauley way of life. But the F-bomb… From his six-year-old?

"Um, well…"

"It was Del. Wasn't it?" The woman plagued him, even on a Sunday with his family.

"No."

Mike knew that tone. "Tell the truth."

A mulish frown settled over his son's face. "J.T. said he wanted some fucking nachos. So Del told him to get his own. Then she told him to 'mind his damn mouth because of the kid.' She nodded at me. I'm the kid, Dad." Colin glowed.

"I get that."

"So it wasn't Del. I *told* you."

The little smart-ass. "Watch your tone, boy. And your mouth."

"Well, if that ain't familiar," James said in a low voice. "Déjà vu, eh, son?"

His mother coughed to hide a laugh.

Mike narrowed his eyes at his old man. "You know, I remember getting my butt handed to me the first time I said 'damn' at this very table." Trust his folks to turn on him when they'd been the ones hammering him with manners for the first eighteen years of his life.

"Pass the damn potatoes, please." Colin held out his plate.

"Colin." Mike glared. "We don't curse, and we don't use bad words at the table. Especially when you don't even know half of what you're saying. One more smart remark and you're going to bed early tonight. Understand?"

Colin heeded the warning. Finally. "Yes, Dad."

"Try again. How do you ask for the potatoes?"

In an exceedingly polite voice, Colin asked, "Dad, would you *please* pass the mashed potatoes?"

"Sure thing." Mike pushed them next to the boy and knew he couldn't avoid it any longer. Time to talk to Del again. He squelched any sense of anticipation, knowing the time had come to put a stop to his son's growing attraction to the female mechanic draped in piercings and tattoos.

And this time, Mike wasn't going to play nice.

Acknowledgments

I can't thank Hilary Craig, of HWC (Tax and Business Consulting), enough. Your vast knowledge of accounting and your help in defining several areas of Seattle were priceless. Thank you!

To Bonnie, for letting me stay in the nicest place in Seattle during my research trip and any other time I'm in town. You're wonderful! Bill P., you are a wealth of information and one of the nicest guys I've ever met. You answer all my questions and have limitless patience. Thank you!

To Cat C., you really make the work stand out. I'm so glad you're my editor.

About the Author

Caffeine addict, boy referee, and romance aficionado, *USA Today* bestselling author Marie Harte is a confessed bibliophile and devotee of action movies. Whether hiking in Central Oregon, biking around town, or hanging at the local tea shop, she's constantly plotting to give everyone a happily ever after. Visit marieharte.com and fall in love.

The Troublemaker Next Door

The McCauley Brothers—Book 1

by Marie Harte

USA Today Bestselling Author

—◊◊◊—

She's sworn off men

It's been the day from hell for Maddie. Instead of offering a promotion, her boss made a pass. She quit, then got dumped by her lukewarm boyfriend. As the fiery redhead has a foulmouthed meltdown, her green-eyed neighbor Flynn McCauley stands in her kitchen...completely captivated.

Until he throws a wrench into her plans

He was just there to fix the sink as a favor. He's not into relationships. She's done with idiots. But where there are friends... sometimes there are benefits. And sometimes the boy next door might be just what you need at the end of every day.

Introducing...the McCauley brothers

Welcome to the rough-and-tumble McCauley family, a tight-knit band of four bachelor brothers who work hard, drink beer, and relentlessly tease each other. When three independent women move in next door, all hell breaks loose.

For more Marie Harte, visit:

www.sourcebooks.com

How to Handle a Heartbreaker

The McCauley Brothers
by Marie Harte
USA Today Bestselling Author

He can't get her out of his head

It's lust at first sight when Brody Singer first lays eyes on Abby Dunn. The dark-haired beauty looks a lot like a woman he once knew, who died years ago. At first Brody fears his attraction is a holdover from that secret crush, but Abby's definitely different. She's a lot shyer, a lot sexier and, despite her attempts to dissuade his interest, absolutely mesmerizing.

She can't get him out of her books

Abby isn't having it. She's still trying to put her last disastrous relationship behind her and overcome the flaws her ex wouldn't let her forget. But somehow Brody isn't getting the hint. It doesn't help that when writing her steamy novels, she keeps casting Brody as the hero.

Brody is more than happy to serve as her muse and eager to help make sure her "research" is authentic. But when their research turns into something real…will she choose her own happily ever after?

Praise for Marie Harte:

"Harte has a gift for writing hot sex scenes that are emotional and specific to her characters." —*RT Book Reviews*

For more Marie Harte, visit:

www.sourcebooks.com

What to Do with a Bad Boy

The McCauley Brothers
by Marie Harte
USA Today Bestselling Author

—∿—

She can fix anything...

It's great that all his brothers are finding love, but Mike has been there, done that. He had his soul mate for a precious time before she died giving birth to their son. She left him with the best boy a guy could want, so why is everyone playing matchmaker? He's sick of it...until he meets Delilah Webster. For some reason, the foul-mouthed, tattooed mechanic sets his motor running.

But can she fix his heart?

When Del first met Colin, Mike's young son, she fell in love with the little scam artist. But his father's like an overprotective pit bull. Too bad they rub each other the wrong way, because Mike is seriously sexy. But when a simple kiss turns hot and heavy, she can't get him out of her head.

Mike can't forget that kiss either. He sees the loving woman buried under the rough exterior. But the closer they get, the more the pain of past wounds throws a monkey wrench into a future he's not sure he can handle...

—∿—

Praise for Marie Harte:

"Charismatic characters and sexual tension that is hot enough to scorch your fingers." —*Romance Junkies*

For more Marie Harte, visit:
www.sourcebooks.com

Find My Way Home

Harmony Homecomings
by Michele Summers

—⁓—

She's just the kind of drama

Interior designer Bertie Anderson has big dreams for her career, and they don't include being stuck in her hometown of Harmony, North Carolina. After one last client, Bertie is packing up her high heels and heading for her dream job in Atlanta. But her plans are derailed by the gorgeous new owner of that big old Victorian she's always wanted to renovate…

He's vowed to avoid

For retired tennis pro Keith Morgan, Harmony is a far cry from fast-paced Miami—which is exactly the point. Keith is starting a new life for himself and his daughter Maddie, and he's left the bright lights and hot women far behind. Bertie's exactly the kind of curvaceous temptation he doesn't need, and Keith refuses to let their sizzling attraction distract him from his goals. Keith and Bertie both have to learn that there's more than one kind of escape, and it takes more than wallpaper to turn a house into a home.

—⁓—

For more Michele Summers, visit:

www.sourcebooks.com

Frisky Business

by Tawna Fenske

There he is again

No more rich men for Marley Cartman. Absolutely not. Thanks to her dad, her ex-fiancé, and the overbearing donors she schmoozes for a living, she's had more than her fill. From now on, she wants blue-collar men with dirt under their fingernails. But when Marley makes a break to handle donor relations for a wildlife sanctuary, she finds herself drawn to the annoyingly charming—and disturbingly wealthy—chairman of the board.

The kind of man she doesn't want

Judging by his hipster T-shirts, motley assortment of canine companions, and penchant for shaking up stuffy board meetings, you'd never guess that William Barclay the Fifth is a brilliantly successful businessman. Will has good reason to be leery of scheming women, and as he and Marley butt heads over the wisdom of bringing grumpy badgers to charity events, he can't help but wonder if his new donor relations coordinator is hiding something other than a perfect figure beneath that designer suit…

"Sparkling romantic comedy—wickedly clever humor and crazy sexy chemistry." —Lauren Blakely, *New York Times & USA Today* bestselling author

"Fenske's fluffy, frothy novel is a confection made of colorful characters, compromising situations, and cute dogs." —*RT Book Reviews*, 4 Stars

For more Tawna Fenske, visit:

www.sourcebooks.com

The Longest Night
by Kara Braden

Two fiery personalities living together in a remote cabin…

When a car accident leaves gorgeous but prickly genius Ian Fairchild with a debilitating injury and an addiction to painkillers, this city boy has to find a safe place to recover. He escapes to the remote Canadian wilderness, as far from the lights of Manhattan as he can get—and in the company of a woman he has no reason to trust.

Will they make it through the winter?

Former Marine Captain Cecily Knight prides herself on being self-sufficient. Her nearest neighbor is miles away, she has to fly to town for basic necessities, and she can go weeks without seeing another soul…and that's the way she likes it. But when she's called on to repay a debt, she agrees to allow Ian to stay with her in her isolated cabin, on one condition: just because he's invading her privacy doesn't mean she's willing to open herself up to him, even if he is as tempting as sin.

But as they spend day after day in in the wilderness together, Cecily and Ian's wary friendship turns into a love these two lost souls needed more than they ever knew.

For more Kara Braden, visit:

www.sourcebooks.com